*In GOING ALL IN, a good ol' Georgia boy teaches a Myrtle Beach princess how to get down and dirty…*

*It's been two years since Callie Holden helped put her father in prison, and since then, she's learned a lot about life and herself. To Callie's surprise, she actually likes working and has discovered money is a tool to be used for good… or evil. She also realizes even though she's traveled the globe, she's never truly lived. She longs for adventure and to experience a wildly passionate romance. The last place she expects to realize her dreams is in the arms of the ever-surly man she's dubbed "The Beast." But when Callie and Wade Neumann are forced to work together, unexpected chemistry changes everything. In Wade's arms, Callie finds the excitement and passion she's been looking for, as well as a few other surprises.*

*Wade Neumann has spent the last year burying the pain and humiliation of being left at the altar by a woman who used him as a novelty toy before settling down with someone more like herself—someone rich. He's lost himself in a stream of nameless females since then, but instead of the trysts helping him heal, he's only grown colder and more jaded. He hasn't moved on with his life. He's merely stuck going through the motions… until he meets Callie Holden, a woman who looks like his ex but is actually the opposite—sweet, compassionate, loyal, and most importantly, not wealthy. Or so he thinks. Because just as he starts to believe things with Callie are real and true, she gives him thirty million reasons to doubt all over again.*

# Going All In

## Book #4 in the Heat Wave Series

## Alannah Lynne

*Dedicated to Janelle Denison*

*To say I owe you everything isn't an exaggeration, and thank you will never be enough!*

# Acknowledgements

It's kind of funny that writing is often called a "solitary" career, yet there are so many wonderful people who help create a book and a whole slew who help an author promote their work.

I'm not sure this book would've ever come together without the help of my critique partner, Janelle Denison. The do-over was painful, but It made the story so much better. Thank you! As always, thanks to Cassie McCown from Gathering Leaves Editing for taking the words and polishing them up, and to ProofreaderLouise for buffing off any left-over wax Cassie and I missed.

A huge thanks to my cover models, Brittani and Hayes Askew! You guys were awesome, and I had a great time at the beach with you. And while you guys totally rocked, an equally huge thank you to Robert Weston, who captured the sweet moments and gave me the daunting task of picking one image from over seven hundred! Thanks, Violet Duke, for putting it all together to create a an amazing cover!

Writing scenes for things I've never done, and will never do, like SCUBA diving, is a bit of a challenge. Special thanks to Jamie and Shannon Farrell as well as John Whichard for sharing your experiences and expertise. Any mistakes or misrepresentations are my fault and not theirs.

Thanks to Paul Salvette at BB eBooks for taking all the pieces and putting them together in one file for the readers' enjoyment.

But most of all, thank YOU, the reader!! Without you, there wouldn't be a need for me.

# Chapter One

$\mathcal{A}$ sudden burst of cold air rushed through Wade Neumann's construction trailer office, tossing the papers on his desk into the air like confetti on Times Square Rockin' New Year's Eve. As they floated to the floor, his boss, Kevin Mazze, stomped his boots on the concrete block steps to knock off the mud, then stepped into the trailer and let the door slam shut behind him. The framed site plans hanging on the walls rattled from the force, as did Wade's teeth.

"Jesus Christ." Wade propped his elbows on top of his gray-metal desk and cradled his head in his hands. The viselike grip helped steady the sloshing brain cells and slightly reduced the throb in his temples but did nothing to lessen the rising tide in the pit of his stomach.

"Sorry, the wind caught the door before I could stop it from slamming."

Kevin Mazze, owner of Mazze Builders, wasn't just Wade's boss. He was also a close, personal friend. However, given Wade's current condition after having spent the past twenty-four hours with *friends,* he was considering the need for new, less rambunctious... kinder friends. Especially given the extra little twinkle emanating from Kevin's dark eyes and the shit-eating grin splitting his face. Bastard wasn't sorry. Hell, he wasn't even in the same time zone as sorry.

"I can tell. Your face shows how deeply pained and remorseful you truly are."

Kevin's booming laughter filled the air, and the chair across from Wade's desk squeaked with Kevin's weight as he took a seat.

Wade leaned over to pick up the papers but found keeping his head higher than his thumping heart to lessen the bass in his head was an impossible task. In an effort to minimize the impact as much as possible, he dove to the floor, scooped up the mess, and dumped it all in a pile on his desk. His own chair *thwumped* from the impact as he dropped back into it, then took a couple of deep breaths to fight off the pain and nausea brought on by the sudden movement.

"You must've had one hell of a night."

Without moving his head, Wade met Kevin's curious stare but didn't answer. Not because he didn't want his boss to know where he'd been or what he'd been doing, but the old heave-ho in his stomach made him fear more than words would fly out if he opened his mouth.

It didn't matter if he answered or not, though. Kevin was perfectly content to carry on the conversation by himself. "Let me guess"—he dropped his head back and stared at the ceiling—"Bernice the bartender?"

Wade let his heavy eyelids slam shut over his burning eyes, like shutters being drawn over storefront windows. He imagined hanging a *CLOSED* sign to the front of them with the hopes Mazze would get the subliminal message and go away or, at the very least, shut the hell up. However, in all the years he'd known Mazze, subtlety had never worked, so he didn't know why he thought it would now.

"Cathy at the Citgo?" After another no-comment from Wade, Mazze continued. "Sandy at the Strip?"

*Sandy?*

Wade cracked an eye and scrunched up his face. "Who the hell is—"

Kevin threw his head back with laughter. "Gotcha."

Unwilling to acknowledge Kevin *did* have two of the names right, or that his life had been reduced to a revolving door of women with names that sounded like they belonged in tongue-twisters, Wade sighed and grabbed his cup of strong-enough-to-double-as-a-heavy-duty-degreaser coffee and took a hefty gulp. Now he needed a plate of greasy eggs, potatoes, and a pound of bacon. All wouldn't be right with the world, but it'd sure look a hell of a lot better.

"It wasn't that kind of night." He took another hefty sip of the coffee and set it back on his desk. Probably best not to overindulge with anything this morning after last night's binge. "Tyler, Alex, and a few other guys from home are here for vacation. I spent the night at Huntington Beach State Park with them. Tyler brought some of his famous apple pie moonshine—"

The words caused a resurgence of flavor on his tongue and he swallowed deeply, forcing back the gurgle in his gut. After the wave of nausea passed, he said, "I don't think I'll ever be able to eat Grandma's apple pie again."

Kevin shook his head and chuckled.

If Wade's mom shook her head like that, he'd assume her thoughts were something like, *Where did I go wrong? What makes my reasonably intelligent son do such stupid things?* However, he imagined Kevin's thoughts were more like, *Damn, I miss the good old days.*

Wade had known Kevin for eight years and had lived with him for the first six months of their friendship. He'd been around long enough, seen enough, and heard enough stories to know Kevin wasn't a saint, and there wasn't anything Wade or his friends did that Kevin hadn't also done. Probably in multiple. But since marrying Sam and settling down, the guy had grown wings and sprouted a freaking halo. Against all odds, Wildman had been tamed.

"Erik and Steve are crazy," Kevin said, referring to his two best friends, "and we've done some ridiculous things over the years. But your boys are balls-to-the-wall crazy."

Wade shrugged. "That's mostly Tyler. The rest of us just like having a good time."

Right, 'cause feeling like he'd been put through a blender the next morning was soooo much fun.

Kevin's eyes narrowed. "Are you still drunk?"

"I'd give my left nut to still be drunk. Unfortunately, I'm not. I switched to water early"—early being two—"so I could make it to work this morning."

He might be an idiot, but at least he was responsible.

"I'm more tired than anything." Well, except for the pounding headache and the possible regurgitation issues. "I poured myself into my sleeping bag around four, but they were still going strong, so I didn't get much sleep."

"They didn't bring a camper this year?"

Wade rubbed the back of his neck and grinned. He knew where this line of questioning would lead, but there wasn't any stopping it now. "No, and I wasn't about to spoon with Tyler in his tent, so I slept in my sleeping bag under the stars."

Mazze cranked his head around and watched the rain blow sideways against the window. "You must've been doing more than moonshine to see stars." This time when he shook his head, Wade figured his thoughts were more closely aligned with disappointed parent than jealous friend. "Not only has it been raining most of the night, but the temperature got down to thirty, *and* we have gale warnings." Another shake of the head. "And you say you're not bat-shit crazy."

Wade scrubbed a hand over his face. "Okay, I wasn't under the stars. I was under the tailgate of my truck. And I'm not crazy, just country."

"Country folks everywhere should be insulted." Mazze studied him from the corner of his eye. "Seriously, are you okay to drive? Legally?"

"Yeah, I'm fine."

To prove a point, or maybe just to prove he was an ass, Kevin crossed his foot over his knee and, in the process, kicked the shit out of the front of Wade's metal desk with his heavy work boot. The sound reverberated off the paneled walls and collided with a resounding clang in the middle of Wade's head, forcing him to grab his skull and hold on for dear life.

"Shit, what did Sam do to put you in such an evil mood? You're not normally this big of a dick; it must've been extreme." Kevin didn't answer the rhetorical question, so with the gong still echoing in his ears, Wade amended his previous answer. "I'm fine to drive. Where do you need me to go?"

Sighing, Kevin watched the rain fill the concrete forms where the circular driveway and sidewalk were supposed to be poured today. As foreman, Wade oversaw the day-to-day operations of specific Mazze Builders' projects, while Kevin took care of the big-picture items on all Mazze Builders' jobs. Because of his busy schedule, Kevin didn't get many opportunities to play in the dirt. He'd been looking forward to helping Wade finish up the last few items on their punch list so they could get The Chesapeake—Mazze Builders' latest golf course community—open.

Mother Nature, however, had other plans. Regardless of their time crunch and the need to finish the concrete work so Wade could get their Certificate of Occupancy, they weren't finishing today. The only thing currently on Wade's agenda was finishing up last week's paperwork so Marianne, Kevin's sister and Mazze Builders' office manager, could do payroll. After that, he was headed home for a much-needed nap.

"Since we're obviously not moving forward here today, I need you to go over to The Bellamy and help Callie finish the staging in the clubhouse. The open house is next week. At least we can get one property up and running and generating revenue."

Hearing Callie's name caused Wade to stiffen as if he'd been hit by an all-over body cramp. The last thing he wanted to do, today or any other day, was work with the uptight princess again. The first time they worked together, she made it clear he was far beneath her station in life. She successfully managed to make one of the worst periods of Wade's life—the week following his broken engagement—nearly unbearable.

God, it had been over a year, but he still remembered it like it was yesterday. Salt in open wounds tended to leave a long-lasting impression. They'd been in the final stages of the Vanguard development—Wade's first job as foreman—and as a favor to a client, Kevin brought Callie in for an interview. She suggested ways to stage the clubhouse and sales office for their grand opening, and, just his shitty luck, Kevin and Marianne loved her ideas.

They hired her on the spot and the next thing he knew, he was working with a clone of his ex. Not only did she physically resemble Miranda, but she had an identical attitude—that of a spoiled-rotten, self-absorbed daddy's girl. She treated him like a set of hands, arms, and legs that were great for moving furniture, but he had nothing above the neck worth paying attention to. As far as she was concerned, he was the puppet, there to serve her every need, and she was the master. The craziest part was she didn't even seem to enjoy pulling the damned strings. She was one of the most uptight individuals he'd ever met, and if he never had to work with her again, it would be too soon.

His throat clogged with a million arguments as to why he couldn't go, but he pressed his lips together and held them in check. His and Kevin's personal relationship often entailed a lot of joking, much like this morning, and Kevin was the brother he never had. But Kevin was also his boss, and Wade had a ton of respect for the guy. For that reason, he kept his bitter comments locked behind sealed lips.

He considered calling one of his crewmen to go do Callie's bidding, but they'd all worked a ton of overtime and weekends lately and were enjoying a rare day off. He couldn't bring himself to shit on their parade, just to save himself a little discomfort. He looked at his watch. *Eight thirty.* She probably hadn't even rolled out of her pedestal bed yet, so hopefully he'd have time for another pot of coffee and a greasy meal before dancing with the devil. "What time do I need to be there?"

Kevin grinned and shoved to his feet. "As soon as you can. Callie's on her way now."

The coffee—or maybe the dregs of the moonshine—bubbled up. He glanced at the papers on his desk, then curled his lip in what he hoped projected a relaxed smile and positive attitude. "Okay. I'll get these timecards signed and over to Marianne, then head that way."

"Good." Kevin paused with his hand on the door handle and glanced over his shoulder. His normal laidback, happy-go-lucky demeanor melted into an uncharacteristically serious glare. "Be nice to Callie."

*Huh?*

Kevin's tone was flat and sharp as a knife's edge. "I know she favors her, but she's not Miranda. She's actually a sweet girl, and you need to stop being an ass." As an exclamation point to the directive, he stomped down the steps and let the door slam shut behind him like a warning shot.

Wade wanted to yell out the window that there wasn't anything sweet about Callie Holden, but rather than act like a toddler trying to get in the last word against a scolding parent, he took off his favorite Georgia Bulldogs cap and ran his free hand over the top of his head.

After their last dance, rather than being a little bitch and running off to tell Kevin Callie should be named Cruella, he kept his head down, did his job, and focused on their mutual goal of getting the property ready to open. And after they finished the project, he made sure he never had to deal with her again.

Until today.

"Fine," he growled to the empty space around him.

He'd been through worse and survived. At least this time, he wasn't trying to keep the pieces of his obliterated heart from falling out of his chest while working, so he could go in, get shit done, and get out. He didn't know how much she'd already finished, but he thought she'd been working there for a couple of days. With any luck, he'd be done by lunch and headed home for his much-needed nap.

# Chapter Two

Callie Holden chewed on a sliver of fingernail and watched the rain slide down the oval clubhouse window in a solid sheet. It reminded her of her favorite wall fountain at the country club, the one she loved to stare at while the water carried her imagination to far off places and into endless dreams.

Except the torrential rain beating against the window wasn't nearly as peaceful as the tranquil fountain.

And neither was the scene beyond it.

Wade Neumann sat in his truck, cell phone gripped in one hand while the other cut violent slashes through the air. He'd been sitting there for ten minutes, and the longer he talked, the more agitated and animated he became. Which in turn caused her to become exponentially more nervous and unsettled.

Kevin's offer to send someone over to help her unpack the shipping crates and place the new furniture had brightened her gloomy mood. But when she looked out the window and saw the Beast, panic clawed at her insides, urging her to run for her life. She'd actually considered turning off the lights, locking the door, and hiding in a closet so he'd think no one was home and go away.

A little fog circle appeared on the glass as she blew out a puff of breath. While taking evasive action held a lot of appeal, that was the old Callie's way of doing things. The new Callie, or at least the woman she wanted to become, didn't run. She met difficulties head-on and dealt with them in a mature, responsible way.

A small part of her brain suggested she ditch the new plan for today and start again tomorrow, especially when he climbed from the cab of the truck and slammed the door with enough force to rock the entire vehicle. She could swear the concrete sidewalk buckled under the weight of his boots as he stormed toward the sales office front door.

Sweat broke out under her arms and across the back of her neck as she shrank back from the glass. This had the potential to be bad—very, very bad—but she refused to show her fear. Swallowing the lump in her throat, she squared her shoulders, grabbed a pen, and began making unintelligible notes on one of the packing slips attached to the furniture crate. A burst of cold air rushed into the lobby ahead of him, sending a shiver down her spine and splintering her resolve to appear unperturbed by his presence.

His imposing size and rugged alpha vibe always reminded her of a wild animal. Since their first meeting, she had the sense their boss, Kevin, was one of the few people who could keep Wade in check. However, she also believed were they a pack of wolves, Kevin only remained in charge because Wade never challenged him.

He blinked a couple of times against the bright overhead lighting, then squeezed his eyes shut and retrieved a pair of sunglasses from his coat pocket. After slipping them on, he lowered his forehead in what might have been construed as a nod. "Morning."

Based on the way his eyes and mouth remained pinched at the corners, she assumed he had a severe headache and the sunglasses weren't blocking enough light to make him comfortable. She dashed across the expansive lobby, zigzagging through wooden crates and random pieces of furniture and flipped off the light switch, plunging them into semi-darkness.

Working with the Beast was scary, especially given the way things had gone their first time working together. Working with a wounded beast was unacceptable. She'd rather quit her job than get eaten, so if knocking out the lights didn't help, she was outta here.

"Is that better?" she asked in a calm, soothing voice, like one would use when trying to approach a snarling stray.

The darkness seemed to ease some of his pain, but as she spoke, his brows dipped into a sharp, scowling V. Okay, that wasn't the reaction she'd been going for.

His answer was slow in coming, like he had to think about it, but eventually he said, "Yeah." After a brief pause, he added a terse, "Thanks."

She couldn't see through his dark glasses in the dim light, but she had the feeling he was closely watching her—*like a lion stalking a gazelle before the kill*—and without conscious thought, she found herself sidestepping to her left and positioning one of the larger crates between them.

She hated the deep resentment and dislike Wade harbored for her, but she understood his reasoning. The first and only time they worked together hadn't been pleasant for either of them.

It had been her first job with Mazze Builders—her first job, ever—and Kevin had given her specific instructions: *Work Wade like a dog. Keep him busy. Don't give him so much as a second to think or get all up in his head.* He hadn't given her an explanation as to why he wanted Wade worked so hard, but one look at Wade's hollow, nearly dead eyes told her all she needed to know.

Someone had not just broken his heart, but left him shattered.

In retrospective, she wished she'd taken a different approach and tried talking to Wade as someone who'd also suffered devastating losses. But she hadn't.

Since then, whenever they passed in the office, she'd had to endure his sidelong glares filled with contempt and a snarling lip. God only knows what he said about her when she wasn't around. It had been over a year since that time, and she'd often contemplated approaching him to try and clear the air. But she always chickened out, and rather than address the issue head-on, she maintained a safe distance and avoided eye contact.

His current state of health indicated this definitely wasn't the time to try and explain herself, so the old Callie stepped forward and took the reins. "If you don't feel well, why don't you go home? I can take care of this by myself."

He took a deep breath, then sighed. "I'd love nothing more, but no can do. Kevin gave me specific orders, and besides"—he tossed a large paw, errr... hand in the air and waved off her concern—"it's self-induced. I deserve to feel like hell."

"Ohhh..." A wave of compassionate understanding propelled her to leave the safety of the crate and head for her purse. "I can help with that."

She gave him a sidelong glance and smiled, then reached into her bag for her emergency bottle of Dramamine. Since it had been recently used—as in the past hour—it was right on top. She also snatched up her half-full forty-eight ounce strawberry Gatorade sitting next to her bag, then crossed back to where he stood, flat-footed, a look of bewilderment on his face.

"This will help rehydrate you. I don't have an unopened bottle, but I don't have cooties, so you're safe drinking after me."

His eyebrow lifted and his lip twitched as he took the Gatorade from her. When he didn't reach for the Dramamine tablets, she grabbed his thick wrist and twisted so his hand went palm up.

She was completely unprepared for the effect of the touch and their close proximity. Standing inches away, staring at his chest, she was shocked to realize how big he really was. And he smelled incredible. Nothing like a wild animal... very much like a virile male.

Despite her better judgment and the awkwardness created, she leaned forward and drew in a breath, pulling more of his woodsy scent deep into her lungs. His body heat pushing against her, the weight of his hand in hers, and his intoxicating scent mingled together to make her a little lightheaded and a lot overwhelmed.

A primal pulse rose from her core, urging her to step forward and slide her free hand along the solid wall of his chest. But before she embarrassed herself further with her unwanted advances, she dumped the tablets into his palm and took one... two... three steps back. She wasn't far enough away to escape his heady scent or to cool the tropical heat building around her neck, but at least the distance kept her from sniffing him up like an exotic leather bag. Again.

Clearing her throat, she said, "Those will help with the nausea. I assume you already took Tylenol?"

Along with learning animals could sense fear, she'd also been told to never look them directly in the eye. However, standing this close and able to see through his sunglasses, the risk seemed worth the reward.

He blinked a couple of times, like she'd spoken a foreign language he didn't understand. After several heartbeats, he gave another of those barely perceptible nods and said, "Yeah, I took some as soon as I got home this morning."

*As soon as I got home this morning.*

Meaning he'd spent the night away from home.

A flush of unease, more commonly known as jealousy, settled in the pit of her stomach. She'd once overheard Marianne, Kevin's sister and Mazze Builders' office manager, and Kevin's wife, Sam, talking about Wade. Callie had been right in her assumption about Wade being badly hurt, and according to Marianne and Sam, he handled the pain by "burying himself"—their words, not hers—in an endless string of willing women.

*So who was last night's lucky woman?* she wondered while chewing on a hangnail.

Good grief, what was wrong with her? She'd gone from being afraid of working with him to wondering about intimate details of his personal life? All because he smelled good—okay, great—and his warmth drew her in like a blanket straight out of the dryer, tempting her to curl up on this cold, rainy day and get comfy?

No, she needed to be honest, at least with herself, and admit there was more at work than just his cologne. She often found herself watching him prowl around his job sites, drawn to and completely captivated by his dangerous, bad-boy vibe.

And darn if that magnetic pull didn't strengthen ten-fold as he twisted off the bottle cap and started drinking. She parted her lips and drew in slow, even breaths as Wade tossed the tablets into his mouth, closed his eyes, and tilted his head back, swallowing in long, healthy gulps. The way his throat muscles worked up and down, flexing and relaxing, mesmerized her.

*Sex.*

That's the way he'd look in the throes of sex... wild and unbridled. Carnal longing, unlike anything she'd ever felt, unfurled in her lower belly and pulsed between her thighs.

As the last of the red liquid drained into his mouth, she shook off the trance she'd fallen into and busied herself with an already-buttoned button on the sleeve of her blouse.

"Thanks, I appreciate that."

The sharp edge of his tone had been replaced by soft gratitude, and she looked up, encouraged this might be the opening she needed to approach him about their last time together. But as he took off his sunglasses and rubbed at his eyes, she chickened out again.

His eyelashes were a shade darker than his dirty-blond hair, and his brown eyes, which were much prettier when not surrounded by bloodshot whites, reminded her of soft, rich suede.

"Did Kevin call and forewarn you, or are you always armed with a hangover care pack?"

She briefly considered lying but decided the truth might be a tiny thread of commonality she could work with toward making amends. She grinned and shook her head. "Kevin didn't call me."

His eyebrow kicked up a notch and he chewed on the inside of his cheek while studying her like she was a puzzle he couldn't quite piece together. "Interesting."

She wished her hangover was the result of a wild and crazy night, but unlike him, she hadn't used a bevy of men to deal with her humiliating and devastating loss of a man who'd never been hers to begin with. Fighting the urge to squirm under Wade's close scrutiny, she tossed the Dramamine back into her purse and said, "No, not interesting at all." Feeling awkward and somehow less-than because of her boring and chaste existence, she crossed her arms before turning back to face him. "Movie night with my friends Jen and Tiffany usually includes popcorn, margaritas, and sometimes a movie. If we can find something we all agree on." Which lately hadn't been much.

"I see."

The situation had been unusual and awkward, to say the least, the first time they worked together, and since then, she hadn't had a lot of up-close-and-personal time with him. Watching his broad chest move side to side as he worked his coat sleeves down his long arms might become her new favorite pastime. Standing in front of her in a white T-shirt, a blue-and-black flannel shirt, relaxed-fit jeans, and work boots, rugged virility rolled off him, and she practically bit her tongue in half, holding back her appreciative sigh.

And that was before he tossed his coat off to the side, then rolled up the sleeves of his flannel shirt, exposing thick forearms roped with veins and the bottom edge of a tattoo.

Lord have mercy, try as she might—and there was tremendous effort going into the task—she couldn't locate an ounce of fat anywhere.

"Okay," he said, finishing the final roll of his sleeves, "where do you want me to start?"

She unglued her tongue from the roof of her mouth and worked it around, trying to gather enough moisture to speak. If she were Jen, an incorrigible flirt, she'd say something like, *We can start anywhere you want, just as long as we finish.* But she wasn't Jen, and even though Wade had her mind traversing all kinds of unfamiliar terrain, she wasn't brave enough to venture into the dark forest with the Beast.

She also wanted to make sure this working arrangement went better than the last, so she cleared her throat and said, "Those go into the back corner office. Let's start there and work our way out."

Wade stared at Callie's slender, delicate fingers with mangled nails as she pushed against the top of a crate to tilt it away from her, then slid the metal hand truck under the front edge. They'd spent the past three hours repeating this routine over and over—she'd load the crates onto the truck, then reluctantly step aside and allow him to move it into position.

Even after three hours, he was having a hard time adapting to the drastic differences between Callie of a year ago and the Callie of today. Everything, from the way she acted and treated him to the way he responded to her, was different.

Last year, she'd been cold and aloof and behaved like a self-serving brat. She hadn't made small talk, which was fine with him, but she'd barely even looked at him—not even when ordering him to move this or place that. Today, she was friendly and polite, and he was struggling to keep up with her ever-changing facets.

As soon as he walked in the door, she picked up on his headache— not the actions of a self-centered individual—and sprang into action to help. Cutting off the lights had been kind but hadn't really cost her anything. Sacrificing her drink, one he suspected she needed herself, had been a strong right hook that caused him to drop his guard and stumble, and he had yet to regain his balance.

When she handed him the drink and said she didn't have cooties, she revealed a rare, endearing innocence he never saw in the women with which he associated. But then she took hold of his hand, and thoughts of innocence evaporated. When she leaned forward and drew in a deep breath, his body turned traitor. Heat swept through his system and cognitive reasoning dissipated. His anger and contempt for her was replaced by something basal, a primal need and instinct that has been controlling men since the beginning of time.

He'd been around the block enough times to recognize an aroused woman, and she'd been as affected as him. She'd also seemed equally shocked and confused.

Unfortunately for him, things had continued to go downhill.

The only explanation he could come up with for his strong reaction to her was the moonshine. There must've been one hell of a powerful aphrodisiac added to that shit, because nothing else made sense.

This was the woman who treated him like a work horse the last time they were together. She'd been rude and uptight, and the way she'd held her chin up while looking down her nose made it clear he was below her station in life. She drove a Mercedes SUV, a woman he assumed was her mom picked her up in a Jag, and friends driving a Beamer dropped her off one morning.

In addition to her obvious wealth—which meant he had nothing to offer her but a good time—she so closely resembled his lying, cheating ex, her effect on him should've been similar to a snakebite.

So why did he keep finding himself tongue-tied and flat-footed with his body simmering with the slow burn of arousal?

Her long hair was a thick profusion of curls that lay around her head in a just-out-of-bed sexy mess. Her bangs were long enough to pull to one side and tuck behind her ears, but trying to get it to stay that way was futile. Every time the thick chunks fell back into her face, his fingers twitched with the compulsion to re-tuck it, just to find out for himself how silky soft the corkscrew locks really were.

She wore a black button-down and a pink pull-on sweater, nothing-fancy black slacks, and plain flat shoes. Her fingernails weren't polished and filed to the point they could be considered deadly weapons—she hardly had any nails left—and she didn't wear a ton of makeup.

She reminded him of the girl next door… Except none of the girls in his neighborhood drove fancy cars.

Most shocking, however, was how hard she worked and how freely she smiled while doing it, like she truly enjoyed her job. Last time, she'd pointed and directed and did very little of the heavy lifting herself. This time, he couldn't slow her down and had to keep fussing at her to not overdo and hurt herself.

Like now.

"Dammit, Callie. Stop."

As he wrapped his hand over the top of her shoulder to stop her forward progress, he took particular notice of her petite frame—something that was easy to do since his palm was curved over the hard ridge of her shoulder, but his fingers fell dangerously low on her chest. He hardened and tightened as his fingers brushed the curving swell of her breast, and an electrical charge shot up his arm, down his chest, straight to his cock.

"I thought we had a deal." The raw rasp in his voice had him clearing his throat before starting again. "You could load the furniture, but you'd let me move it."

A cute little dimple popped out in her cheek as she flashed him a broad grin. "I waited for you to come and get it"—his body burned and his brain sizzled at all the ways he'd love to come and get—"but you'd zoned out and didn't notice. I can get it by myself. It's no big deal."

She shrugged nonchalantly, which brought his attention back to her shoulder... and breast. *Christ.* "Wrong."

And wasn't that a friggin' understatement? It was wrong for him to think anything about her was cute, let alone a dimple. It was wrong for him to lose focus. And it was all kinds of wrong for him to lose focus because he was thinking about her like a man thinks about a woman he's interested in getting to know better.

A whole hell of a lot better.

"Give me that," he said gruffly, letting go of her shoulder to grab the cold, hard handle.

Her eyes widened, the grin slipped from her face, and she let go of the handle like it was on fire. He hadn't meant to sound so harsh, but this bizarre, out-of-control attraction had him pissed off and edgy.

She inched away and watched him from the corner of her eye while angling her body toward the door, ready to run for her life. But then she stopped, straightened her spine, and lifted her chin.

Seeing her fight against the fear flickering in her eyes to stand her ground sent a wave of pride through him and puffed out his chest, nudging out the guilt he felt for alarming her in the first place.

What the fuck was wrong with him?

He shook his head and rubbed his eyes in frustration. Pickled. His brain was pickled. That was the only explanation that made sense as his lips parted and he said, "I need food. Let's grab some lunch, then come back and finish this up."

What about his plan to finish *before* lunch?

What about his nap?

His vision swirled as his mind conjured an image of Callie curled into his side, her head propped up on his shoulder as they slept—

With a hard shake of his head, he cut the bullshit thought, quick, and forced his gaze to stay on her face, not her killer body. "So... lunch?"

She cut her eyes to a brown bag—the kind he used to carry his lunch to school in. "I brought mine with me." She licked her lips and smiled nervously, like she feared setting him off again by declining. "I appreciate the offer, but you go ahead." As an afterthought, she added, "If you want to take the rest of the day off, I can finish by myself. Really. There's not that much left."

The first time she made that offer, he declined because Kevin would've kicked his ass for not following orders. This time, he declined because his conscience wouldn't let him bail on Callie and because he wasn't ready to call it a day yet. Which was also what prompted him to check out her lunch bag, in the hopes of persuading her she was better off with him than on her own.

His lip curled and a fresh wave of nausea hit as he pulled out an apple, a banana, and a package of ramen noodles. "What the hell is this? Some kind of weird new diet?"

When he glanced over his shoulder, he was surprised to find a dark, defensive gaze meeting his. "Hardly. Have you read the nutritional label on those noodles?"

He dropped the contents back in the bag and leaned against the desk. "Then why are you eating them?"

She averted her gaze and shifted from one foot to the other. "They're cheap."

*Cheap?* Why would Callie be concerned about the cost of a meal? He stared at her, figuring she'd eventually grow uncomfortable enough with the scrutiny to be a little more forthcoming. It took longer than expected, but she finally caved.

"I'm saving for a pair of boots." Her eyes brightened as if she were seeing them in her mind and her lips curved into a smile. "They're the softest leather I've ever felt and they come up to here."

His gaze drifted to her leg as she swiped her hand across the middle of her thigh. He gulped, envisioning her in thigh-high boots with a short skirt, flashy belt, and low-cut top. Every guy in the room would froth at the mouth like a buck during rut. Tempers would flare, horns would lock, and it would be a fight to death to be the one to take her home.

She laughed self-consciously. "Sorry, you don't care about my boots."

Unfortunately, he did care. With tremendous effort, he dragged his gaze away from her legs and up to her brown doe eyes, shimmering with excitement over the new boots. If he had a chair handy, he'd pull it up beside her, plant his ass, and have her tell him every last detail about those boots, right down to the stitching and how they were made.

He drew in a deep breath, then slowly exhaled. He really wanted to see her wearing them. And, heaven help him, he couldn't deny he also wanted to be the lucky bastard who got to take them off.

As he grew increasingly uncomfortable in not only his tightening jeans, but also his skin, he took off his cap, rubbed the top of his head, then worked the cap back in place. He was sure she'd already made this connection for him, but somewhere between the soft leather of the boots and her thighs, he'd gotten lost. "So what do the ramen noodles have to do with these new boots?"

"Rather than eating out all the time, I bring my lunch to save money. That way I can get them out of layaway sooner. And you can't get much cheaper than ramen."

"That's the truth." He'd singlehandedly kept the company in business for years. But why did she need to save up to buy new boots? She drove a Mercedes. Why didn't she have access to Daddy's fat bank account or credit card?

What about a rich boyfriend?

Until now, he hadn't considered the possibility of her having a boyfriend, rich or otherwise. Hell, until today, he couldn't have cared less. But now... yeah, now he wondered.

"You're doing that zoned-out trance thing again," she said, breaking into his thoughts. "What's on your mind?"

There wasn't any way to ask what was on his mind without being rude, but she'd opened the door so he decided to step through it. "Why do you need to save up for new... anything? Why not let your rich daddy or boyfriend buy them for you?"

*Way to go, Slick. She'll never catch on to your fishing expedition with that question.*

She crossed her arms tightly over her stomach and her spine snapped arrow straight. Her face, however, turned into a blank mask, showing no emotion. "I don't have a boyfriend," she said flatly. "And my father is in prison, so it's a little difficult for him to buy me anything."

His breath caught in his throat and he blinked a few times, trying to make sense of her words. He thought she'd said her father was in prison, but that couldn't have possibly been right. Could it?

When she swallowed roughly and looked away, he realized she'd been expending a tremendous amount of energy to keep her blank face in place, so he must've heard right.

But... prison? If she'd said, *My father is an alien who doesn't believe in worldly possessions,* he wouldn't have been more shocked. He thought of all the news reports on white collar crimes over the past few years and decided her father must've fallen into something of that nature.

"Was he like Bernie Madoff or something?"

Her mouth smiled, but her eyes remained cold and detached. "No, nothing as innocuous as insider trading. He tried to kill his right-hand man and would-be successor." Her breath hitched and her mask slipped.

"Shit, Callie, I had no idea." He wanted to wrap her up in his arms to comfort her... and then carry her off and spend the rest of the rainy afternoon making her forget the pain he'd just caused.

*Jesus, get a grip.*

He couldn't do a damned thing about the other circumstances in her life, and he sure as hell wasn't going to follow through on his ridiculous urges, but he could save her from a horrible, gassy fate that was sure to follow her brownbag lunch. "C'mon, go with me instead of eating"—he pointed to the bag—"that."

She turned, prepared to strike—probably because she thought his offer stemmed from pity and she was too proud for charity, another point in her favor—but he put his hand up to cut off her rejection.

"You saved me this morning." She rolled her eyes. "Seriously, I haven't been that hung-over in a long time. Your quirky remedy worked wonders, so I owe you."

She pressed her lips together, clearly not buying his bullshit, but when she cut her eyes to the brown bag, he knew he had her. "Okay, you win." Her grin was quick as she ducked her head, seemingly embarrassed by her quick capitulation. "Where are we going?"

"Didn't they just open a Five Guys Burgers and Fries about a mile down the road?"

Her face lit up and her brown eyes widened with excitement. "Yes. I've never been to one but always wanted to."

He was surprised by her excitement to try out the burger joint and terrified by the pleasure he took from making her happy.

Food… food was good. It would clear out the residual effects of the alcohol causing him to act in such a weird, reckless, unpredictable way. He should also call Mercy, or one of his other friends-with-benefits, to see about a late-night hookup to work off some of his pent-up sexual heat, because this line of thinking where Callie was concerned was completely out of hand and unacceptable.

# Chapter Three

*A*s they made the short ride from The Bellamy to Five Guys, Callie forced herself to ignore how much space Wade took up in the seat, the way the interior of the work truck carried his unique scent, or the condensation forming on the windows. The patches of fog reminded her of the scalding hot car scene from *Titanic,* and the urge to recreate the scene, here and now, had her shifting uncomfortably in the seat.

Lord, her head was a hot mess, and not just because the rain and humidity had turned her natural curls into a tangled rat's nest. Her cranial scrambled eggs had nothing to do with the weather and everything to do with the perplexing man beside her. The morning started off as she expected, with Wade being surly and gruff. But as the day wore on, his hostility lessened and gradually slid down the scale to… something else.

However, because of her limited experience with men and her inability to see situations clearly, she couldn't figure out what the *something else* was. In direct proportion to his lessening wildebeest impression, she caught rare glimpses of his true nature, things she'd never been privileged to see before. Like the soul-deep kindness that radiated from his eyes when he was concerned about her hurting herself by trying to lift too much. Or the way his soft, sensual lips pulled higher on one side when he smiled, giving him the appearance of a mischievous little boy.

An impression that was quickly dispelled when the eye wandered lower than his mouth. One look at his large, hard body proved there was absolutely *nothing* boyish about Wade Neumann.

He also seemed to be noticing her in a way he never had before, and based on the scowl that usually followed one of his heated glances, he wasn't pleased about the newfound interest.

Callie had a reputation for being a prude, and she'd never been more dismayed about the validity of that reputation than now. If she were like Jen—whose moral compass had been zapped by the same unknown forces that caused planes and ships to disappear in the Bermuda Triangle—she'd know exactly what to do to capture and hold his attention.

But she wasn't like Jen, and she was clueless.

She'd had a few casual boyfriends over the years, but never anything serious. They'd all been nothing more than slot-fillers for Gavin, her father's protégé and the only man she'd ever loved. Or what she thought had been love. After realizing her parents' marriage was nothing more than one of her father's orchestrations and recognizing Gavin wasn't actually the man she thought him to be, she doubted she knew anything about love.

Or herself, for that matter.

Her last kind-of-sort-of-not-really boyfriend, Jason, came into her life as her world crumbled. He was an incredible friend who constantly reassured her there wasn't anything wrong with her, that some things just weren't meant to be. He'd repeated it often enough she'd started to believe him, and then he helped her restore her faith in herself and rebuild her self-esteem. She was still a work in progress, but she was light-years ahead of where she'd been two years ago.

While Jason had been, and remained, a great friend, they didn't have the chemistry necessary for sustaining a romantic relationship. Part of that stemmed from her belief he was just plain too nice. As ridiculous as that sounded, even to herself, she wanted someone with more layers, not someone who always wore a million-watt smile because they never had a bad day. She wanted someone like Gavin, who was mostly content but wasn't afraid to show emotion when pissed off or frustrated… Because face it, life wasn't always perfect.

It took her a while to figure out exactly what she wanted, but she'd recently realized the elusive quality she sought was passion. Someone who displayed a passion for life, but more importantly, a passion for her. A man whose look could sear her… or heal her, whichever she needed at the time.

"Hey, you okay?"

Wade's voice, softer than usual and laced with concern, startled her and broke her dashboard stare. He had his keys in his hand, ready to exit the truck, and she hadn't even noticed they'd stopped. Jeez, now who was zoning out?

"Yeah, I'm fine." Pleased to hear the lie sounded believable, she added a quick-flash smile for emphasis.

Ready to escape her thoughts and the painful emotions they dredged up, she grabbed her purse, shoved the door open, and bolted for the safety of the restaurant. However, as Wade quietly followed her inside and paid for lunch, her uneasiness grew. Her mind began processing this as a date, which wasn't only ridiculous, but dangerous.

Wade was dangerous.

From all she knew of him and had seen, not just today, but since their first meeting, he had wide and deep layers like she'd been searching for. He wasn't afraid to express his opinion; over the past year, he'd made his extreme dislike for her crystal clear. His alpha nature reeked of sexual prowess and confidence that drew her to him like a curious kitten creeping up on the elusive and ever-changing light of a laser pointer. And she didn't doubt for a second his intensity carried through in everything he did, from his job to his play to his personal relationships.

Which made him completely out of her league.

Besides, they'd just barely started being civil toward each other, and she still wasn't sure exactly what his sidelong glances—the ones that started at her toes and ended at her mouth—meant.

However, if he didn't eat like an animal and continued to be kind, she knew she'd find herself lying in bed, tossing and turning and conjuring all sorts of wild fantasies about him, because that's what she did when she was attracted to someone.

And, unfortunately, no man had ever lived up to the hype.

It had been nearly twenty-four hours since Wade last ate, and it took every ounce of willpower not to go face down on the butcher block table and scarf up his bacon cheeseburger and Cajun fries like the starving Georgia Bulldog he was at heart. But rather than give in to his gluttonous urge, he forced himself to slow down, keep his face off the table, and use his hands like the well-mannered man his mama raised.

However, even on his best behavior, he still finished his meal in half the time of Callie.

*Damn, that was a great burger.*

He wiped his mouth with his napkin, balled it up, and dropped it on the grease-laden burger wrapper, then stretched his legs out so his feet slid under her side of the booth.

Fifteen minutes… just fifteen minutes of shuteye would knock off the lingering effects of the tequila and beer. And oh yeah, don't forget the friggin' apple pie moonshine. He rubbed his hands over his face and yawned as he rested his head on the back of the booth.

"Looks like you didn't get much sleep last night and could use a nap."

He cracked his eyes open and watched as Callie sucked in a breath and pressed her lips together. With a huff, she dropped her gaze to the table and fiddled with a fry, then dragged it through a mound of ketchup before tossing it into her mouth. She seemed to be working hard to keep her focus on her food and not him, and his super-sized ego wondered if she was fishing for personal information.

*Interesting.*

Damn, it felt good to be able to tell the truth, rather than a watered-down version of how he normally spent his evenings. "I desperately need a nap." He yawned and rubbed his face again and pulled himself out of his slouch. "Sorry. I have friends in town on vacation. They lay around and sleep all day, gearing up for another round, while I schlep my worn-out ass around and try to work. And usually fail miserably. It happens every year. You'd think I'd get better or smarter, but I never do."

She laughed and nodded. "I understand how that goes. My best friends, Jen and Tiffany, don't work, so they don't understand why I go home early on weeknights. Although, to be fair, I didn't used to get it either, so I can't get too upset with them."

Without allowing himself to put much thought into why it mattered, or why he was interested, he used the opportunity as an opening to learn more about her. "How do you normally spend your evenings?"

"I spend a lot of time with Jen and Tiffany, either going out to clubs or hanging out at mine or Tiffany's condo. If I'm not with them, I work on one of my projects. She grinned sheepishly. "Or I lie on the couch and watch TV."

He found it endearing she was embarrassed about being a couch potato, especially since he hadn't expected a whole lot more from her in the first place. At least not until this morning. Now that he'd gotten to know her better, he felt bad about his rush to judgment. "What kind of projects?"

She took another bite of her burger and a big gulp of her sweet tea. "I restore old furniture. Well, not exactly restore. I usually give the pieces a fresh coat of paint to liven them up but rarely restore them to their original look."

He stared, speechless. Something that didn't go unnoticed.

"Mountain lion got your tongue?" Her grin was sly and playful as she scooped up another glob of ketchup.

"Mountain lion?"

"Yeah." Her grin grew and that damned dimple that seemed to be mocking him made another appearance. "It would be silly to say 'cat got your tongue.' You're too big and tough for that. Although, it's probably silly to say anything got your tongue. What does that even mean?" She snapped her mouth shut and ran her tongue over her teeth, then grabbed her burger and shoved it into her mouth like a plug, stopping the flow of words.

He laughed at her quirkiness and switched his attention to her mouth, opened wide, and her pretty pink lips wrapped around the burger. The nasty thoughts that had started getting their groove on were cut short, though, as her white teeth sank into the burger and reality cut the fantasy off at the knees.

He cleared his throat and tugged on his jeans while shifting his position. "I admit you surprised me with the restoring furniture thing, but that's cool. Where do you get the pieces?"

"Here and there, mostly secondhand shops." She paused and diverted her gaze. "I haven't gotten up the nerve to go to yard sales yet, but I'm working on that. What about you? How do you spend your evenings?"

A chill slivered through him as he looked into her eyes, once again projecting an inner naivety and innocence that would be permanently sullied if he answered her honestly. Lying wasn't his thing, but he also found the-whole-truth-and-nothing-but incredibly unappealing in the face of her guilelessness. Searching for a truthful answer that wouldn't be brutally honest, he said, "I hang out at a couple different clubs." Details beyond that weren't necessary. "If I'm not doing that, I sit next to the campfire on the beach and watch the night sky change."

She froze with a fry halfway to her mouth. "Campfire?"

"Yeah, you know… a pile of wood, a match, a log to sit on, and a cold beer."

She shook her head and the ends of her hair swished back and forth over her shoulders. "I've seen them on TV and in the movies, but I've never been to a campfire." She paused and gave him that cute little grin again. "It's not that I have anything against them. I've just never had the opportunity to… sit around one?" She posed it as a question, like she wasn't sure of the proper terminology.

He wasn't surprised by her admission, but it was beyond his comprehension that someone could reach her age without ever having hung around a fire, either for pleasure and relaxation or for heat. Apparently he also found it unacceptable, because without thought he said, "We'll have to rectify that."

Her smile weakened, but she nodded anyway. "Uh, okay. That'd be great."

"Let me guess. You're not an outdoorsy girl."

"I don't know." She laughed self-consciously and studied her food again. "I like sitting around the pool, and I enjoy shopping at outdoor malls. I know this sounds crazy, but I've never had much of a reason to be outdoors. I don't like the beach." She shivered. "I don't like the feel of sand on my skin, and… well, I had a bad experience at the beach once."

*How could anyone have a bad experience at the beach? Unless sharks were involved…*

"I've never been in the woods or to a campfire. I've never gone golfing." She brightened. "I do like to play tennis."

The conversation was surreal because she'd never done any of the things that were a normal part of his life. Well, except the golf thing. He didn't play either, so at least they had that in common. But he grew up in the North Georgia mountains. He was more comfortable outside than inside, and he couldn't imagine not spending part of his day—a large part—outside, soaking up nature.

"You think I'm weird."

He started to tease her by agreeing, but when he looked at her sad face and the way she worried her bottom lip, he found himself reaching across the table for her hand. A gesture that surprised her as much as him. "No, not at all. I'm just surprised."

In a million ways over a million things.

"I spent more time outside than inside as a kid. Still do, actually. It's one of the reasons I love working construction. Except for the god-awful paperwork, everything I do is outside." The paperwork that accompanied the foreman's position had taken a lot of getting used to, but it was a small sacrifice for the additional pay, as well as the satisfaction of overseeing a project from start to finish. "Would you be interested in trying some outdoor activities?"

What the hell was wrong with him? Why was he asking her that? Why was he holding his breath, waiting for her answer?

And why, for the love of God, was he still holding her hand?

Her smile held more confidence this time as her head bobbed enthusiastically. "Absolutely. Stepping out of my comfort zone is something I've been working on. I can't guarantee I'll be any good at it, but I'm willing to try."

He laughed at her excitement and squeezed her hand... then let go like he'd been stung. He was enjoying the contact entirely too much, and he absolutely refused to give his mind permission to wander down the primal path illuminated by her desire to step out of her comfort zone and experience new things.

His mind, however, didn't need permission to carry on. As innocent and naive as she appeared, he couldn't help but wonder how experienced she was in love, specifically sex. He'd guess her to be at the beginner to intermediate level, and damn if he didn't like the idea of being the one to take her to expert.

Trouble with a capital T.

With a sharp shake of the head, he cleared out the thoughts and got back to the campfire, which had started him on this path in the first place. The guys wanted to go to a club tonight to hear a band Alex liked. Aside from that, they didn't have any plans other than their traditional Saturday night trip to the Sunset Strip... assuming they survived Tyler's dumbass plan to SCUBA dive Saturday morning.

"You're snarling again."

Wrenching his gaze away from the window and a raindrop making a lazy trail down the glass, he snapped his attention back to Callie. "Again?"

She lowered her lids and nodded. "You do that a lot around me."

He'd never thought about it, but he imagined he did. He considered broaching the subject of their previous work history, so they could get it out there and clear the air, but things were going so well he didn't see a need to dredge up the past, at least not right now.

"I was thinking about my friend Tyler's suicide mission."

"What?" Her shrill voice caused customers at nearby tables to glance at them as she surged forward in the booth, ready to bolt for the door.

He smiled and waved a hand in the air to diffuse her panic and also let the other now-alarmed patrons know all was well. "I don't mean literally, but…" It sure felt that sometimes. Wade sighed and shook his head, then slumped even lower in his seat. "He's a bit of a daredevil. An outdoor adventure enthusiast," he explained, using Tyler's sugarcoated title for what most people called adrenaline junkies. "He has the general location of a previously undiscovered ship and wants to go diving for it. The weather forecast isn't conducive any day this week, but he called me this morning to let me know he's setting things up for Saturday morning."

"Is that who you were talking to while sitting in your truck?"

"Yeah." He nodded as he replayed the frustrating conversation in his mind. "He's always been wild and more than a little crazy, but since his wife Laney left him, he's out of control. Personally, I think he's gotten too reckless and is on a self-destruction course. But he doesn't see it that way, and it really pisses me off that he's willing to take unnecessary risks."

This time she was the one reaching for his hand. "It sounds like you care a lot about him. He's lucky to have you as a friend."

"We've had each other's backs since middle school and have been through some crazy stuff together. But there's nothing I, or anyone else, can do to help him through this painful situation with Laney."

Just like Tyler had been forced to stand on the sidelines, helplessly watching Wade battle the demons that chased him after his breakup with Miranda. He knew from experience he couldn't take away Tyler's pain or beat back the monsters for him, but that didn't keep him from wishing like hell there was something he could do. "I feel like I'm somehow letting him down. Like there's something I should be doing, but I'm not."

Well, hell. When did he become a jibber-jabber, sharing his personal crap with a stranger?

The thing was Callie didn't seem like a stranger anymore. He was also having a hard time remembering she was the same person who'd treated him like shit the first time they worked together, and the more time they spent together, the more intrigued he became with this Callie. He was curious about her painted furniture pieces, and he wanted to share parts of his world with her. And he really wanted to spend some time fulfilling fantasies that involved expanding her boundaries and introducing her to lots of new things.

Okay, case closed. While out tonight, he needed to find someone to take the edge off his libido and get these crazy thoughts under control.

But even as the thought crossed his mind, a large piece of his soul balked at the plan. He'd gotten into these troubled waters because the nameless-faceless-mindless-fucking lifestyle wasn't doing anything for him anymore, and he'd recently taken on the role of a celibate. Truth was that lifestyle hadn't ever done much, except keep his mind and body occupied so he didn't spend too much time dwelling on the past.

Recently, his soul had started sending out distress signals, demanding he find a new plan. Something that involved less sloppy sex and more emotional, personal connections. The whole prospect scared the hell out of him, and he'd been fighting the idea for months. And as he looked at Callie and imagined sloppy sex *with* an emotional, personal connection, panic flooded his system.

Any involvement would only lead to heartache—hers, not his because he refused to get *that* involved—and Kevin would fillet him alive if he screwed Callie over. Surprisingly enough, though, it wasn't the dread of disappointing Kevin that strengthened his resolve to get himself under control and keep things platonic. It was his concern for Callie and this newfound whacked-out image of her as a rare gem that needed protection from his tarnished reputation and less-than-stellar past.

A friendship with Callie was fine. A friends-with-benefits friendship was not.

# Chapter Four

Callie zipped her silver-and-black ankle boots, then stood and examined her reflection in the antique floor mirror. Another tug on the hem of her skirt didn't garner more inches, so with a resigned sigh, she twisted at the waist and looked over her shoulder, making sure her butt was mostly covered. Jen and Tiffany constantly harassed her to dress less conservatively, so as a concession to their nagging, she got a shorter skirt to wear to the club. As a concession to her angst, she got thick, black tights to wear underneath.

"Are you ready?" Tiffany called impatiently.

*Ready or not...* "Just about." Even though the rain had stopped, her silk blouse wouldn't provide any protection against the cold, so she grabbed her wool coat from the back of the chair, picked up her black-and-white polka-dot Kate Spade handbag from the dresser, and gave another futile tug on her skirt.

"Tell me again. Why am I doing this?" she asked Tiffany as she slipped on her coat and walked down the short hallway leading from her bedroom to the living room.

"Because you haven't been out with us all week, and you're going to turn into a crazy cat lady if you keep sitting at home by yourself."

Callie flipped her hair out from under her collar and turned to stare at Tiffany. "Do you really think I'm going to turn into a crazy cat lady? Especially since I don't have a cat. Or are you being a parrot and repeating something Jen said?"

Pink crawled up Tiffany's neck to her cheeks and she cut her eyes to the side. She cleared her throat, preparing to speak, but before she answered, the door burst open and Jen stepped inside. "What's taking so long? If we don't hurry, we won't get a decent seat."

Callie rolled her eyes. "Oh, c'mon. We all know you already called Mario and had him reserve your favorite table."

"Okay, you got me." Jen's smile was smug and unapologetic. "But if we get there early enough, we'll get backstage before the bands go on."

The Blue Lagoon, a favorite Myrtle Beach hangout, had gained popularity with the locals by booking up-and-coming local bands, as well as regional bands gaining widespread acclaim. Jen's father was one of the original investors, so since inception—which was before Jen, Tiffany, or Callie reached the legal drinking age—they'd been able to sneak backstage to meet the bands, then park their prissy little butts at the front table and pretend to be college students. Jen thrived on the attention and the chance to be a groupie. Tiffany and Callie just tagged along, pretty much like they'd done all their lives.

How it came about, Callie didn't know, but Jen had always been the leader of their trio. She decided what they did, who they did it with, and how long they'd stay. For years, Callie had been content to follow along—wasn't that a constant theme in her life—but that wasn't working for her anymore. She didn't want to continue traipsing after Jen like a well-trained puppy, and her growing disobedience was becoming a source of conflict between them.

An unbidden image of Wade flashed through her mind. One day of working together didn't make her an expert on the man, but she'd bet every penny she had he didn't ever blindly follow anyone. He might do things he didn't want to, but there was a difference in not wanting to do something and *choosing* to do it anyway, and doing something because he was afraid to stand up for himself and say no.

She envied anyone strong and sure enough about themselves to live life on their terms, without consulting parents or friends or anyone else for that matter. She wasn't there yet, but she was getting closer and she liked the progress.

As they made their way down the steps to the sidewalk and the waiting car, she was forced to admit hanging out with Jen had some perks, Raul, the family driver, topping the list. Whenever they went out, he picked them up at home, dropped them off at the door of the club, then remained on call until they were ready to leave. They'd never been tempted to drive drunk, had never gotten in the car with someone who was drinking, and had never waited for a cab.

Fifteen minutes after Raul helped them into the back of the car, they were bypassing the line and walking in the front door of The Blue Lagoon like Hollywood celebrities. A large crowd comprised mostly of twenty and thirty-year-old working professionals had already gathered, and Callie sighed at the thought of spending the night crammed into a club with a thousand other people. She'd much rather be at home in comfortable clothes, working on her current project, daydreaming about Wade.

She checked the clock on her phone. She could probably survive the next three hours. And then she'd be back home, crawling into bed, having real dreams about the man she couldn't stop thinking about.

"Aw, shit in the fire and fuck me running."

Even though Callie hadn't told Wade which clubs she frequented, he should've known this one would top her list. The swanky club was too upscale for his personal tastes, but Alex saw an ad for the band that was playing, so the guys decided tonight was the perfect night to dress up and hit the town. Since they all lived in the boonies, they didn't get many opportunities like this, so Wade rummaged through his closet, found a decent button-down and a nice pair of jeans, cleaned up his cowboy boots, and attempted to put a little shine on himself as well.

Running into Callie wasn't part of the plan, and it certainly didn't help his efforts to get her off his mind. It also didn't make him feel any better about finding a nice, willing body to crawl into to help him scratch his mad itch.

Following his line of sight, Tyler looked at the VIP section in the center of the club, then coughed and sputtered around his drink. "Shit. Is that Miranda?"

Wade sighed, then drained half his beer. Prior to today, he would've said Callie might as well be Miranda. They had the same chestnut hair, same deep-brown eyes, same petite frame, and he thought they had the same attitude of entitlement. But after spending the day working with Callie, he barely saw the resemblance anymore. "No, it's not Miranda. Her name is Callie, and I work with her. She comes in after I'm finished with a project and pretties shit up."

From the corner of his eye, he saw Tyler studying him. "And."

"And what?" The fact he refused to meet Tyler's gaze head-on should've been a clear indicator there was something going on where Callie was concerned, but he was too damned stubborn to address the possibility, even privately to himself.

"You've got the hots for her."

"What?" He glanced at Tyler, then looked away. "No. I barely know her." He took a deep breath and forced himself to relax his defensive stance before continuing. "I normally do everything within my power to ignore her, but"—he shrugged—"after working with her today, I think I might've been wrong about her. She's actually pretty nice."

"Nice," Tyler repeated before cocking his head to the side and watching, along with Wade, as a preppy-looking dude sat down in the empty seat next to her.

Wade strong-armed back the inclination to get his back up as Callie's lips curved into a smile. Propping an elbow on the bar and leaning into it like he didn't have a care in the world, he reminded himself this was a good thing. She would find a nice guy, he'd find a stranger, and they'd all go home happy.

But the longer he watched, the more irritated he became. Especially when her smile faltered and her eyes grew wary. She either didn't know the guy or didn't like him, because when he leaned in to speak, she stiffened and shifted away.

Wade's eyes narrowed and his neck muscles tensed as the guy ignored her obvious signs of discomfort and scooted his chair a little closer.

"What a dick," Tyler muttered, echoing Wade's thoughts. "Are we gonna have to go over there and kick his ass?"

Wade swiveled his head around and laughed. "We? You think it'll take two of us to toss his scrawny ass out of here?"

"No, but your feet aren't moving yet, sooo…"

Callie's desperation grew as she turned to her friends for backup but found them talking and pointing to something he couldn't see, unaware of her distress. The last thing he needed was more face time with the woman he was determined to forget, but he couldn't sit back and let the asshole continue to encroach on her personal space and make her more uncomfortable. With a vision of bucks locking horns and fighting to the death flashing through his mind, he slammed his beer down on the bar, then put his feet into gear, muttering expletives to himself as he crossed the open bar area into the VIP section.

She didn't see him approaching, so when he reached her side and said, "Hey, baby," she jumped like she'd been shocked.

Her head whipped around and wide eyes stared at him before a big, breathtaking smile spread across her face. She seemed confused, but not unhappy about seeing him, and a fresh wave of carnal longing tightened his body and sent his inner caveman into kill-to-protect-what's-mine mode.

He leaned down to kiss her cheek and whispered, "You know this guy?" After a slight shake of her head, he said, "Want some help?"

He leaned back to see her face and was totally unprepared for the way her bright smile and eyes, shining with gratitude, punched him square in the gut.

"Where've you been?" she asked, playing along. "I was getting worried." Okay, scratch that. She wasn't playing. This guy, whoever he was, had her concerned, and that was absolutely not okay with Wade.

He pinched her chin between his thumb and forefinger and held her gaze, making sure she saw his sincerity and that he recognized her nervousness. "I can tell. I'm sorry I didn't get here sooner."

He wasn't the least bit worried about his ability to take out the scrawny asshole whose oily look had turned murderous, but for fun and added effect, he drew himself up to his full height of six-four and bowed up as he glared down at the guy. He might be dressed up—at least as dressed up as he ever got—but a spit shine didn't cover up a red neck or the proclivity for busting heads, especially when provoked. "Who the hell are you?"

The guy's eyes narrowed and his jaw locked, like he was considering his options, which made Wade laugh. Dude only had two choices: leave on his own, or get tossed on his ass. Fortunately for him, he came to the same conclusion. Common sense had him pushing the chair back, nodding good night to Callie, then beating feet toward the bar like his ass was on fire and he needed a drink to douse the flames.

But that left Wade with a problem. If he retreated back to his place at the bar, the guy would know it had all been an act and he would undoubtedly come slinking back, probably pissed off and carrying an oversized chip on his underwhelming shoulders. So taking one for the team—he was such a friggin' hero—Wade spun the recently vacated chair around and sat facing Callie.

Starting the conversation over on a more pleasant note, he smiled. "Hey."

"Hey, yourself." Her smile and dimples carried a one-two wallop, and just that fast, the other guy was forgotten and no one else existed but her and him. Re-tucking her hair, she said, "Thanks for the save."

"No problem." Feeling a lot like the predator he just sent packing, he couldn't stop his eyes from taking a leisurely stroll over her tightly buttoned silk blouse, awesome short skirt, hideous tights, and cute ankle boots. "I like the boots." He grinned and leaned in closer. "Although, I'd really like to see you in those boots that come up to here."

He ran his finger across the middle of her thigh and smiled when she drew in a sharp intake of breath in response. After a harsh swallow, she licked her lips, then parted them to draw in a slow breath, which caused her chest to expand and push against the blouse, which caused his already primed cock to start a little expansion project of its own.

Nothing had changed since the afternoon when he'd lectured himself about the dangers of messing with Callie. He still believed she was a good girl who wouldn't engage in one-night stands. He was still wavering between finding someone to satisfy his ravenous sexual appetite—so he could cease and desist the crazy thoughts about Callie—and trying a new way of doing things. A way that definitely didn't including indulging the Callie fantasy. And, last but not least, Kevin would still castrate him if he fucked with Callie, literally or figuratively.

Given all that, he should push his chair back about four feet and give them both plenty of breathing room. But the primal drum that had beat within men since the beginning of time drowned out the warning cries of his mind and drove him forward.

When she turned sideways in her chair to face him, he also shifted so his legs framed the outside of hers. Leaning closer, he wrapped his arm around the back of her chair and said, "I've thought a lot about those boots."

If his admission surprised her, she didn't let it show. She also didn't blink or look away as he moved his finger to the side of her neck and swept it along the top edge of her cool, silk blouse. When he bumped into the delicate silver chain of her necklace, he followed the links like a trail of water would, down to the chunky pendant hanging in the center of her deep cleavage.

He paused and gauged her reaction as his finger lingered on her top button. Had she appeared nervous or apprehensive or, worse yet, repulsed by his touch, he would've dropped his finger and breathed a sigh of relief. But rather than shunning his behavior, her eyes dilated, her breathing grew choppy, and the pulse in her neck pounded in rhythm with his.

His thumb joined his finger and slowly slipped the button free. "In my fantasy, you're wearing those high boots, a short skirt—minus the tights—and a low-cut blouse that comes down to here." His finger slipped down the center of her breasts until he met with the resistance of another button.

Her mouth parted farther, showing him her perfect white teeth and a tiny glimpse of her pink tongue. His mouth watered and his lips actually tingled as he stared at her mouth and imagined kissing the ever-loving shit out of her. As if reading his mind, she drew her lower lip in between her teeth and chewed nervously. Christ, it required every ounce of self-control he possessed to not take over the job for her.

However, his focus became diluted when she dropped her hand to his thigh and wrapped her fingers around the excess fabric of his relaxed-fit jeans and twisted. A moan pressed against the back of his throat, making it difficult to breathe as she twisted a little more and pulled the coarse fabric tight against his rapidly expanding cock.

*Warning. Warning. Warning.*

He needed to heed the screams of his mind and get the hell away from Callie as fast as possible. But with her holding his jeans captive, he was locked into place and incapable of breaking free.

From the corner of his eye, he saw her friends—the same ones who hadn't paid her any attention when she felt threatened by Slimeball—watching her now with great interest. He had no idea how long he'd been sitting there or if the slug was still watching, but the truth was none of that mattered. Despite his internal warning system, he wasn't ready to leave her yet.

She had a great seat in the front and probably wouldn't want to go back to the bar to hang out with him and the boys, but he didn't want to bail on the guys—

His randy side cut to the chase. He and Callie could get the hell out of here altogether and go back to his house… which circled him right back around to her being a good girl and Kevin ripping off his nuts. He twisted his head to work out the uncomfortable kink the image created and tried to come to grips with leaving her and going back to his seat at the bar. Alone.

"Um, Cal… you going to introduce us to your *friend?*" The blonde's nasally tone and emphasis on *friend* made Wade's skin crawl.

Callie didn't break eye contact with him right away, but the burning desire in her eyes dissipated into regret and something that looked a lot like despair. He'd seen this look before. It was similar to the expression Miranda wore at the beginning of their relationship when she was forced to introduce Wade to her friends.

All of his old resentments toward Miranda and every one of her ilk burst to the surface. As his demons reared their ugly heads to point out he was a fool for thinking she wouldn't be embarrassed about mixing it up with a blue-collar laborer, he leaned back in his chair and gave her room to negotiate away from him. But thank all the saints in heaven above, she didn't let go of his leg and she didn't move away. Instead, she scooted a little closer to the edge of her chair—and him—as she turned her head to look at her friends.

"This is Wade. We work together."

The friend closest to her smiled politely and gave a little wave. The one on the end, the one who asked to be introduced, stiffened like someone had poked her in the ass with a cattle prod. Damn if he didn't wish he could do it for real.

At least part of his dilemma was settled. Sitting here with Callie and her friends was out of the question. Leaning forward and settling his elbows onto his knees to keep the conversation private, he said, "Our seats aren't all that great, but you're welcome to join us in the bar." He smiled and notched his eyebrow playfully. "It'll make it easier for me to keep you safe. At least from that other guy. I can't make any promises about you being safe from me."

He kind of hoped the half-joke would scare her off, and when she dipped her head, bashfully reiterating she was as inexperienced as he suspected, he had a heart-dropping moment where he thought his non-wish would come true. But then, to his surprise, she grabbed her purse with one hand, his hand with the other, and said, "I'm going to sit with

Wade. I'll catch up with y'all later."

Callie knew there'd be hell to pay for leaving their exclusive, front-row table in favor of hanging out with the common folk in the back bar, but she didn't care. Normally one to avoid conflict at all costs, she found herself hoping for an argument with Jen, one that might be the impetus Callie needed to finally set some boundaries.

Her heart pounded in rhythm with her feet as Wade dragged her along behind him through the crowded club. Getting through a crowd this size normally required a thousand "excuse me's" and even more jostling, but not with Wade leading the way. A simple "'Scuse me" did the trick, and most of the time, he didn't even need to say that. He just moved in the direction he wanted to go and the crowd parted.

She put her free hand over her mouth to stifle a laugh. Apparently, the old saying was true… Size did matter.

He didn't slow his pace until he reached a group of four men, two seated, two leaning against the bar, all watching with more than mild curiosity. As they approached, Wade nodded to the one with dark hair and piercing blue eyes seated closest to them. The guy rolled his eyes, grabbed his beer, then shifted his weight to the side and rolled off the stool.

She assumed Wade asked him to move so she could have the seat but was unprepared for the sudden lift onto the newly vacated seat. "There ya go, princess."

She squeaked, then stiffened and sucked in a breath at his use of the moniker.

He released her so fast he practically dropped her, then took a long step back. He tilted his head to the side and studied her from the corner of his eye. His gaze dropped to the pounding pulse in her neck, then down to her heaving chest—neither of which were because she'd jogged across the club behind Wade, but because being this close to him had the same oxygen-starving, heart-racing effect on her.

He moved back in a half-step closer. "I didn't scare you." When she confirmed the observation with a nod, he said, "Then you must not like being called princess."

"No." She glanced away. "My dad used to call me that."

He blinked a couple of times, trying to connect the dots, then his eyes widened as the picture came into focus. "Shit, I'm sorry. I didn't know." A slow, easy smile crawled across his full lips as he brushed her hair off her shoulder. "That's a shame, because you remind me of that princess in England. You could be the Princess of Pawleys Island."

"That'll be tough since I've never been to Pawleys Island."

His mouth dropped open and his eyes narrowed. "Seriously?" When she did a what-can-I-say palms up, he shook his head with further disbelief. "It's like thirty miles down the road. How could you never go there?"

"I guess I've never had a need." She bit her lip and tried to hide her smile and said, "I have been to England, though."

He tossed his head back with laughter. "Of course you have. Okay, we'll add a trip to Pawleys to your new bucket list." Something shifted in his eyes as he held her gaze, and she wondered what was so special about Pawleys Island. Clearing his throat and his eyes, he said, "Whatcha drinking?"

She'd already had two margaritas and didn't need anything else, but she was nervous as all get out and needed something to settle her down. "A margarita."

After flagging down the bartender and placing her order, he shifted to the side so she could see his friends as he made introductions. Starting with the guy closest to him, the one who'd given up his seat for her, Wade said, "This is Tyler, a royal pain in my ass that I only keep around because the statute of limitations hasn't expired on a few things, and I can't afford to cut him loose."

She recalled their lunchtime conversation about Tyler as she smiled and shook his hand. The affection shining in Wade's eyes proved how much he cared for his friend, but Tyler, who was shorter and thinner than Wade, didn't have much of a light in his eyes. A smile rested on his mouth, but his blue orbs were dull and lifeless, revealing the deep-seated pain Wade had spoken of.

Tyler's brother, Alex, was next. He was shorter and stockier than Tyler, but the two looked so much alike she wondered if they were twins. Next came Matt and Garret, and given their barely contained laughter, she figured Wade was in for as much grief as her. His, however, would probably be good-natured ribbing, not condescending ripping.

After taking her drink from the bartender and nodding to have it added to his tab, Wade said, "We all grew up together and have been friends forever. Despite the horrendous hangovers I have to deal with, I love having them come to visit."

More verbal jabs were exchanged, making it obvious how close the guys were. She was about to ask him how he ended up in Myrtle Beach on his own, but the opening band took the stage and conversation became impossible. She made a mental note to ask him about it later, grabbed her drink, and settled in for the show.

Two and a half hours later, Callie's body was a humming, tingling, vibrating mess. The residual echoes from the electric guitars rang in her ears, but the pulsing beat thrumming through her central nervous system had nothing to do with the drums and everything to do with

Wade.

He'd dialed back on the earlier hammer-down flirtations, but several times she'd noticed him sliding the ends of her hair through his fingers or smiling at her more intimately than was usual for casual co-workers. His smell, smile, and eyes were dangerous. Throw in the killer body she'd been pressed against all evening, and she didn't stand a chance against his magnetic pull.

When Jen and Tiffany stood and grabbed their coats, indicating they were ready to leave, he brushed her hair away from her ear and leaned in close to be heard over the noise of the electrified crowd. "Are you riding with them, or do you want me to take you home?"

He didn't act like a guy trying to get into a girl's apartment and ultimately into her pants, but she still shivered as his warm breath caressed the side of her neck. Her hormones and imagination joined forces to create a host of enticing images, heartily encouraging her to accept his offer. But it was silly for him to make the trip when Raul had to go to her condo building anyway to drop off Tiffany.

When Tiffany held up Callie's coat, silently asking the same question, she sighed regretfully and held up a finger. Returning her attention to Wade, she said, "Thanks for the offer, but I need to ride with them. I've had a great time tonight. Much better than I expected thanks to you."

He smiled and muttered, "Yeah, funny thing about those expectations."

It wasn't unusual to run into him at the office or on one of the job sites, but it also wasn't a daily occurrence. Careful not to sound too desperate or clingy, she lightly asked, "Will I see you at work tomorrow?"

"I'm not sure. Hopefully I'll be at The Chesapeake tomorrow, finishing up so I can get ready to move on to Anticue."

Like Pavlov's dogs experiencing a conditioned response, her breath caught in her throat and she froze. "Anticue?"

"Yeah, I'm getting ready to start a bed and breakfast renovation up there."

She knew the property and clients well, but hearing that Wade would be working on the project, rather than Kevin, caught her off guard. She took a moment to run a quick mental and emotional scan to assess how she felt about that and was thrilled to realize she didn't have any feelings one way or the other.

It had taken her a long time to come to grips with the fact that Gavin wasn't ever going to see her as anything more than a surrogate sister, and she rejoiced in the knowledge that she had finally reached the point of full acceptance.

"Well, I guess I'll see you around." She slipped her purse over her shoulder and prepared to hop off the barstool, but Wade stepped in front of her and blocked her escape.

"I don't know what these guys have planned over the next couple of nights, but I promised you a campfire, and I haven't forgotten."

The gold-and-yellow flecks in his brown eyes were hypnotizing, and his scent wrapped around her like a comforting pair of arms, drawing her closer to him. But she refused to let him see how strongly he affected her. Again.

She'd done enough of that earlier in the evening when he reduced her to a quivering mess with a simple brush of his finger. And when he looked at her like she was the most enticing woman in the world and slipped the button of her blouse loose, she'd nearly begged him to strip her bare just to save her from a heat stroke.

But as Jen always pointed out, Callie was a prude.

And he was a playboy.

And that was a no-win proposition for her.

Before she could continue her internal debate on why all of that mattered, he wrapped his hand around the back of her neck, pressed his soft lips to hers, and kissed her so tenderly it knocked the breath out of her. When he drew back and put a few scant inches between them, she stared into his eyes, searching for a clue as to what the kiss meant.

He seemed equally confused by his actions but recovered quicker than her. Flashing her a wolfish, egotistical smile, he said, "Sweet dreams, sweetheart."

Oh, he was an arrogant man.

Despite her attempt to play it cool, she was as transparent as glass. He was teasing her, daring her to go to sleep and not have naughty dreams featuring him.

Fortunately, he'd never know she planned to take her blouse to bed with her because it smelled like him. Unfortunately, not only was he arrogant, but he was probably also a fortuneteller.

# Chapter Five

$B$etween finalizing everything at The Chesapeake, packing up his construction trailer, and getting ready to start Gavin and Sunny's renovation on Anticue Island, Wade stayed busier than expected over the next couple of days. The evenings remained unseasonably cold and, at times, had even been too harsh for him to enjoy being outside. Hanging out around a campfire for pleasure was different than being wrapped in layers of clothes and still unable to get close enough to the flames to stay warm. For that reason, he hadn't invited Callie to go with him to the state park, and he hadn't run into her at work.

The lack of visual, however, didn't keep him from thinking about her, or texting, or calling to ask about her day. He also hadn't been able to stop thinking about *the kiss*. Even though he'd replayed the whole incident a million times, he still couldn't figure out what prompted him to go lip-locked-and-lovin'-it.

One minute they'd been engaged in innocent conversation about work, and the next he was moving in. The sigh that escaped her pretty pink lips as he closed the gap unraveled logical thinking and made it impossible to stop. Her lips were as soft as he imagined, and he wanted nothing more than to coax her into opening for him so he could explore further.

But Tyler and Alex's voices cut through the roar of blood pumping in his ears and brought him back to reality. His friends… Her friends…

A thousand strangers in a club… Callie, not the stranger he'd set out to find when the night began, and he refused to treat her like one, especially with an audience.

As he packed up his construction trailer and prepared to pull out of the job, he was keenly aware of preparing the project for her hands. She'd come in and pretty up the clubhouse and sales office so they could launch the grand opening, and everywhere he looked, everything he touched, reminded him of her.

*Shit.* He scrubbed a hand over his face and growled in frustration. Something had to give, and soon. He was sporting all the signs of a man in over his head, not to mention a fairly consistent erection whenever he thought of her, and they weren't even dating.

As he finished putting the final strap on the filing cabinet, ensuring it stayed put while the trailer was moved to Anticue, the door opened and Kevin stepped inside.

He looked around, saw Wade had everything wrapped, packed, strapped, and ready to roll, and burst into laughter. "You're ready to get the hell out of here, aren't you?"

"Yes, sir." Wade loved his job, but some projects were more enjoyable and fulfilling than others. The Chesapeake had been an *other.* "This project has been a pain in the ass from start to finish, but I guess some are just that way." He grinned as he thought about his first job as foreman. "Compared to The Vanguard, though, this has been a piece of cake."

Kevin rolled his eyes and dropped his head back. "You're not kidding. I'll never jump the gun on a project like that again." His annoyance melted into a mushy-gushy look as his thoughts flipped to his wife, Sam. "But if the water issue hadn't come up, I wouldn't have gotten to know Sam, so it was all worth it."

Wade muttered, "Speak for yourself," as he secured his chair so it wouldn't roll during transport.

Even though Wade had been acting foreman, Kevin made the decision to move the project forward before the county completed construction of the water tower necessary to operate the sprinkler systems in the buildings. Wade had no control over the situation, but when shit hit the fan, he'd been convinced his first job as foreman would also be his last.

Fortunately, Sam wasn't just the building inspector who shut them down, but she was also the brilliant woman who figured out the solution to their problem. Wade had been grateful. Kevin took his gratitude to stratospheric levels and married her. But they were a perfect match, and Wade was glad Kevin had gotten lucky enough to find her.

After a final check of the break room, Wade returned to the main office where Kevin stood, flipping through the box holding the project paperwork. "This ready to go to Marianne?"

"Yes, sir. It's pretty well organized, but I'm sure she'll find something to bitch about."

"She usually does. She doesn't feel like she's being thorough and doing her job well enough if she doesn't find something out of place." He replaced the lid and turned to Wade. "Speaking of bitching… How'd things go with Callie the other day?"

Wade snapped the bottom of the blind next to his desk into place and carefully considered his answer. Fearing Kevin would see through him if he said too much, he decided to downplay the day and say as little as possible. "Things went fine. She's nice." He grinned. "I wouldn't go so far as to say she's sweet, but…" He shrugged and checked another blind. "She's all right."

He didn't have a clue where he expected things to go, but he supposed he didn't have to have all the answers right now. She wasn't anything like he thought, nothing like Miranda, and he enjoyed spending time with her. Because of that, and because he'd promised her a campfire, he would see her again. Tonight if possible.

End of story. Simple as that.

Except even as he had the thought, he called bullshit on himself. The topic had never come up—because, yeah, why would it—but he knew with all his being Callie didn't do casual sex. The thing was, he didn't think she did anything casually. She approached everything in life with gusto and one hundred percent commitment.

Not only had she proved it Monday at work, but he also saw the same intensity at the club. When the band started playing, she became completely involved in their performance. When he talked, she gave him her undivided attention. And while he'd love to think he was just that interesting, her captivation hadn't been reserved for him. She'd been the same with his friends when they started a conversation with her.

She didn't half-ass anything, and that would certainly be the case with her relationships. She was an all-or-nothing kind of girl, and to a guy like him—who was terrified of *all* and had spent the past year swimming in *nothing*—those were treacherous waters.

Miranda left his heart so shredded he'd doubted he would ever piece enough of it together again to be of value to anyone. However, regardless of the fear jetting through his system, he felt the stirrings of something for Callie, and the compulsion to follow through and see where it led wouldn't leave him alone.

"Then I don't need to worry about you being an ass to her anymore?"

Wade cut his eyes to the side and glanced at Kevin but didn't meet him head-on. "No, you don't have to worry about me being an ass."

He hoped. Depending on how things went between Callie and him, she might end up considering him a first-rate asshole, which would land him back on Kevin's shit list. But hey, he'd just remind Kevin he was the one who insisted Wade be nice.

And then he'd duck before Kevin connected with a solid right hook.

"Why are you so interested in Callie anyway?"

Kevin shoved his hands into his pockets and rocked back on his heels. "You and Callie are going to work together on the Anticue project."

That had Wade snapping to attention. Kevin was deadpan and matter-of-fact, while Wade's mind splintered into a million directions and his nerves sizzled like he'd been blasted with a bolt of lightning. "Say what?"

"It's a renovation rather than a new build, so she'll need to make a lot of decisions along the way. She'll be there as much as you, and since you'll be riding back and forth together and sharing the office, I want to make sure you guys are copacetic. Gavin will pick up on any tension between you guys right away, and I don't want any calls."

Wade blew out a long, slow breath. Well, hell, that added another layer of complication to an already complicated mess. He needed to be nice, but not too nice, because he couldn't afford to let a romantic relationship develop—at least not until after they'd finished the project.

He wasn't planning on problems. He'd gotten the message loud and clear, but he felt the need to remind Kevin he knew how to keep his personal shit from affecting his job. "I didn't let personal get in the way of business last year. I'm not going to start now."

Kevin drew in a deep breath and slowly nodded. "No, you didn't, and I have a shit ton of respect for you because of it. But I have to cover my bases. Gavin is a good customer, and I don't think he and Sunny are finished expanding their operations. I want to make sure nothing messes up our working relationship with them."

He opened the door a notch and grabbed the box off the desk. "I'm headed to the office. I'll take this with me. Anything else I can do to help you here?"

Wade flipped off the light and followed Kevin out. "Nope. It's all ready to go first thing in the morning."

"Great. You have plans tonight? Let me rephrase that. You have any plans that will prevent you from hitting the road to Anticue first thing in the morning?"

"Nope. I'm going to the state park, but I'm taking an insurance policy with me to ensure I leave early."

At least he hoped Callie would go. He tried calling her earlier in the day, but her phone went straight to voicemail. He started to send a text, but the building inspector showed up to do the final walk-through, and he'd forgotten to finish sending it.

"Your stripper friend have to be at work at midnight?"

The question caught him off guard, especially since he was thinking about Callie, and his hackles rose. He turned to face off with Kevin but realized he wasn't being an ass. He was simply asking a question. And sadly enough, given Wade's recent past, the question was reasonable.

"No." Wade kicked the ground with the toe of his boot and mentally chastised himself for the way he'd been living lately. "I'm not taking Mercy tonight. Just a friend."

A friend he'd kissed.

A friend who dominated his thoughts.

A friend who invaded his dreams, causing him to wake up every morning primed for action.

Shit, taking Callie with him tonight—even as a friend—was a bad idea on so many levels, one of which was standing in front of him, eying him suspiciously. But Wade had never been the cautious type, and he supposed not even the threat of death or castration would change him. He just needed to make damned sure he didn't fuck up.

"Are you ever going to finish that thing?" Jen asked, settling into Callie's sofa, a margarita in her hand, a sour expression on her face.

For the past month and a half, Callie had been working on an old dressing table she picked up at a consignment shop. The ornate corner carvings called her like a siren's song, and she'd immediately envisioned painting the piece in bright colors to showcase the details. For her, it had been love at first sight. She was still waiting for the dressing table to share its feelings, but she was pretty sure, once finished, it would be thrilled with its new paint and thankful to have been rescued from its previous boring existence.

Holding back her huff of annoyance with Jen, she concentrated on her paintbrush. She swirled the sable bristles in the well of blue paint, dipped the tips in the white pot, then swiped most of the paint off on the towel lying across her knee. "Finishing is my plan." Leaning in close and focusing on the edge of the carved flower, she touched the end of the bristles to the top of the petal, then pulled a downward stroke so light she barely left any paint.

*Perfect.*

"You've been working on it for weeks. Why not go buy something new and be done?"

This time she wasn't nearly as successful at hiding her irritation. They'd had this conversation three, possibly four times, but Jen never listened. Mostly because she didn't bother to try and understand.

She changed her bedroom furniture nearly as often as she switched boyfriends. Once she got bored looking at the same pieces, she'd shop for a new suit, charge it all to her father's account, then call the movers. They'd show up, box up her personal items, move out the old, move in the new, then replace her things. It happened so often, Callie couldn't begin to guess how many bedroom suits—or boyfriends—Jen had been through.

By comparison, Callie had changed bedroom suits twice. The first when she graduated kindergarten, the second when she started high school. And she hadn't had *that* many more boyfriends. She wasn't a big fan of change, so once she got comfortable with something, be it a bedroom suit or favorite pair of pants, she tended to hold on.

Admittedly, that thinking caused her problems sometimes, like when she latched on to her infatuation for Gavin and refused to let go But overall, she'd rather be a keeper than someone like Jen, who tossed things away when they were no longer new and shiny.

"I don't want something new. This table has a lot of character and reminds me of the summer I spent in the south of France." She sat back on her heels and admired the detail. Someone put a lot of time and effort into making this table, and she took pride in adding her personal touch.

Gavin always referred to her parents' home as a mausoleum, and at the time, she didn't understand why he disliked the marble floors or heavy, highly polished pieces filling her father's office, or the cool, crisp whites in her mother's sitting room. But as she traveled Europe, especially the various regions of France, she noticed not only the differences in decorating styles, but also a difference in the way the homes felt. They were warm and inviting, perfect for relaxation.

As soon as she moved into her own condo, her personal decorating tastes revealed themselves, and they were nothing like her mother's. She painted the walls soft, muted colors and started collecting painted, not polished, furniture. Her condo felt like a home, not a house, and she finally understood why Gavin always seemed so uncomfortable at her parents'.

"Okay," Jen said, refusing to give up the battle. "Go buy something new that's similar and hire someone to paint it for you. Between the sale of the fishing pier"—her lip curled in an involuntary reaction to speaking the words she found distasteful—"and your trust fund, you can buy whatever you like."

Callie repeated the dip-dip-wipe with the paintbrush and made another barely visible stroke down the opposite side of the flower petal. Callie would never be able to find a new piece of furniture with this kind of character, and she enjoyed painting. On most days, it relaxed her. Tonight, however, Jen's yammering was zapping her Zen.

"We've been over this a million times." Callie set down the brush and picked up her water bottle. "I'm not using any of that money."

"Why? Why are you so stubborn about this?" Frustrated, Jen shook her head. "It pains me to see you going to work every day, then coming home to"—she flipped her hand over and waved it in the general direction of the dressing table—"this. You were born into a life of luxury. You're not made for manual labor." She pursed her lips. "Some women have to marry for money, but you don't. With your trust fund, you can do whatever you want, whenever you want, with whomever you want, for as long as you want."

Callie sighed and traded in the bottle for the brush. She might not achieve Zen, but keeping her hands busy would keep her from slapping Jen. A part of her recognized this as the chance she'd been waiting for to release her pent-up frustrations and resentments, but she was tired and not mentally prepared for battle tonight.

At the club, she'd been itching for a confrontation, and she questioned if her courage stemmed from being with Wade. He made her feel more carefree—some would say less uptight—and a whole lot braver than she really was. He made her want to expand her horizons and experience life from a different angle.

But he wasn't here now, so she settled on a more docile approach. "I like painting. It's calming." *Usually.*

"Painting is fine. There are lots of famous painters, and lots of celebrities paint. But... well... they paint on canvas, not used furniture." She shuddered. "You don't know where that thing has been. I can't believe you actually brought it into your condo."

"That's why I scrubbed it really well." Callie couldn't hide the mischievous smile pressing against her lips. "It's also why I painted the whole thing with Kilz. That way, any remaining nastiness is sealed in, and I don't have to worry about it getting on me." There was a grain of truth to the statement, but she'd scrubbed the entire piece with bleach a couple of times. She wasn't the least bit worried about crud. She mainly wanted to get under Jen's skin, and from the look on her face, it worked.

"That's disgusting."

The front door opened and the smell of fresh-baked goodies poured in, punching up Callie's hunger and causing her stomach to growl in response. Water pooled in her mouth and she stood, as if in trance, following the scent.

"I made fresh-baked brownies," Tiffany said. "Who wants one?"

Jen rolled her eyes. "You two are turning into a couple of Martha Stewarts." She leaned forward and peered into the pan as Tiffany set it on the coffee table in front of the sofa. "But I have to admit those look tempting."

Tiffany, who had the uncanny ability to ignore the negatives and focus on the positives, beamed. "They're white and dark chocolate marble. Try one."

"Just one?" Callie said with a laugh. "I'm counting on that being dinner."

"We made something similar last week in cooking class. I tweaked the recipe a little, so…" Hesitation and uncertainty crept in. "If they're no good, I can whip us up something else."

"I'm sure they're great," Callie called over her shoulder as she went to the kitchen to wash her hands and grab some plates and napkins. "So far, everything you've made has been incredible."

Since Tiffany bought the condo next door and started taking cooking lessons, Callie had become her culinary guinea pig. The arrangement worked perfectly. Callie didn't have to cook—something she'd discovered after moving out on her own she wasn't very good at—and Tiffany had someone to try her new dishes. They'd also agreed on a bartering system of sorts. Tiffany kept Callie fed, and Callie helped Tiffany decorate her condo.

Tiffany had spent the past two years watching Callie pave the way, and she'd been taking notes. Six months ago, she decided to leave the comfort of the heated pool in favor of life's more turbulent waters. She had yet to break free of her parents' checkbook, but she was working hard to figure out her place in life, and total freedom was just around the corner.

Jen, however, was content to remain entrenched in the world of maids and Daddy's credit card and didn't understand why they wanted to make their own marks on the world.

After drying her hands, Callie grabbed the plates and napkins and headed back to the living room. She stopped short as the scents of fresh paint and brownies hit her. She drew in a deep breath and enjoyed the rush of endorphins the unlikely combination caused. Who knew those smells could be so comforting?

Tiffany scooped a brownie from the pan and placed it on one of the plates. "The dressing table looks great."

"Thanks, I'm happy with it." She took a bite of brownie, then moaned with pleasure as the warm, gooey treat melted on her tongue.

"God, these are good. I don't know how they tasted before, but you nailed this recipe."

Tiffany's smile grew and she bounced on her toes. "You really think so?" She looked to Jen for confirmation, then back to Callie.

"Absolutely. They're incredible." Callie took another big bite. Then another. And another, then finally gave up the fight to be polite and crammed the rest in her mouth.

Jen's reaction was more subdued, but after a dainty bite, she agreed. "Yeah, they're good."

"You know..." Tiffany started, then stopped and cranked her mouth around as she worked up the nerve to finish her thought. She sat down in a chair and tucked her leg beneath her. "I've been thinking a lot about the idea of starting a catering business." As soon as the words spilled from her mouth, she sucked in a breath and held it, waiting for their response.

Jen blinked a couple of times and fiddled with her earring, like she was adjusting the dial on her hearing.

But Callie knew she'd heard right, and excitement for her friend bubbled up. "Seriously?" She dropped into the chair next to Tiffany's. "You think you're finally ready?"

Callie didn't doubt Tiffany's abilities. She'd been eating her food for months and had no complaints. Ever. But Tiffany wasn't as sure of her culinary talent, and Callie worried Tiff's self-doubts would get in the way.

Tiffany's eyes misted with fear and trepidation, but the fog quickly burned away as underlying determination shone through. "Yeah, I am. I've done a lot of thinking since our last conversation—"

*Oh crap.*

"—and I think it's time."

Callie held her breath as Jen's gaze narrowed and swung between

Callie and Tiffany. "I don't remember talking about this before."

"You weren't there."

Callie's retort was harsher and more defensive than intended, but she loved the conversations she and Tiffany had without Jen, and she was protective of them. Their private sessions were real and genuine, about important things that mattered. They talked about their futures and made plans—plans some would say were nothing more than pipe dreams—but they were quickly learning there wasn't much of a difference between plans and dreams, and they were excited about the possibilities life held for them.

She'd rather continue this conversation without Jen, the pessimistic voice of doom and gloom booming loud and strong from the sidelines like James Earl Jones narrating a film: *The end is near... Prepare for destruction.* But Tiffany had started the discussion and was excited, so Callie encouraged her to continue. "Tell me more. What are you thinking?"

As Tiffany began to talk—more or less thinking out loud and brainstorming—Jen rolled her eyes, swirled her drink around in her glass, tapped her foot, and checked the polish on her perfectly painted nails. Of course, Jen's increasing boredom intensified Tiffany's anxiety and uncertainty.

Jen's insensitive, selfish, immature attitude was to be expected, but it still pissed Callie off. Stepping in to diffuse the situation before Jen stole Tiffany's dreams before they had a chance to fully develop, Callie said, "You're off to a great start." She grabbed Tiffany's fingers and squeezed while locking gazes with her. "Let's go to lunch one day this weekend to celebrate. We'll make a day of it."

Her blatant dismissal of Jen caught all of them off guard, but Callie didn't care. She refused to let Jen's negativity poison Tiffany's hopes and dreams.

After Tiffany's quietly spoken, "Okay," everyone fell silent and tension filled the room, making it difficult to breathe. Callie searched for a safe subject to get them back into neutral territory, something they could all talk about and enjoy, but her mind was a blank.

Okay, not completely blank, because Wade seemed to be taking up a lot of space there recently. But given the awkward atmosphere of her living room, she decided to keep thoughts of Wade to herself. Seeking an escape from the expanding tension, she grabbed another brownie and opened her mouth to take a large bite.

Before the chocolate morsel hit her lips, her phone pinged with a text message. She'd given Wade a special ringtone, so without even looking, she knew it was him.

Her heart took a few beats to get back into rhythm, as did her breathing, so she did her best to hide her reaction as she picked up the phone and read the message. *Campfire tonight. U interested?*

She felt Jen and Tiffany's curious stares on her but refused to meet their gazes. Nervous excitement made her mouth too dry to speak, and she didn't know what to say anyway. She pressed her lips together and slid them back forth, thinking things through.

Oh heck, who was she kidding? She didn't have to think this through. She was so excited by the invitation she could jump out of her skin. So without conferring with Jen or Tiffany or seeking confirmation she was making the right choice, she replied, *I'd love to. What do I need to wear? Pick me up or meet somewhere?*

# Chapter Six

*C*allie battled her trembling fingers, trying to steady them enough to attach the back of her earring while Tiffany and Jen stood guard at the window, watching over the parking lot like a couple of sentries guarding the fort.

"What does he drive?" Jen called from the living room.

"No idea. I've only seen him in company trucks."

She sighed with relief as the back finally slipped onto the post. Then she fixed the collar of her turtleneck and adjusted her necklace. Wade told her to dress casually, jeans and a sweatshirt if she had one, then nonchalantly offered to bring something of his if she didn't.

She'd been tempted to take him up on it for the silly, girly pleasure of wearing his clothes, but she finally admitted she'd be able to find something on her own. After twenty minutes of rummaging through her closet for something casual-not-drab, she settled on a black turtleneck and red sweater.

As she grabbed her ankle boots from the closet floor, the memory of Wade at the club flashed through her mind. The searing heat pouring from his eyes as his hand sliced the middle of her thigh made her even more determined to get her thigh-high boots out of layaway as soon as possible.

"Tell me again why you're going out with this guy," Jen said, throwing off a ton of barely contained revulsion, much like she had at the club when Callie introduced them to Wade.

Callie wanted to believe Jen's reaction was subconscious, that she wasn't intentionally being snobby, but Callie knew better. Wade was a construction worker, and a couple years ago, Callie shared the same unfounded, erroneous opinion of blue-collar workers. For the first several months after meeting Kevin, she could hardly stand to look at herself in the mirror for the way she'd previously thought and spoken of men and women like her amazing co-workers. She'd eventually learned to forgive herself for her ignorance but doubted Jen would ever come around to sharing Callie's newfound way of thinking.

Callie sat on the edge of the sofa and zipped her boots. "He's a nice guy." She shoved her hair out of her face and made eye contact with Jen. "He's different than the other men I've dated, and I like that."

She ignored the glance exchanged between Jen and Tiffany and poured herself a glass of wine. Besides the obvious off-the-charts sex appeal, there were so many things about him that attracted her. He wasn't a huge talker, but his self-confidence and quiet sense of humor carried a punch. She liked the way she felt with him: free-spirited, adventurous, brave.

He made her want to drink the Kool-aid of life, to get out there and live rather than sit back and watch time go by. He was obviously a loyal and true friend, or "his boys," as he called them, wouldn't visit every year, and she appreciated that quality more than most.

Her gaze slid across the room to Jen and Tiffany. She'd known them since middle school, like Wade and his friends, so she knew the value of long-term friendships. Jen often made hurtful comments, but Callie doubted she even realized how badly her words cut. And when things blew up with Callie's dad, Jen stood by her side as a fierce protector every step of the way.

On more than one occasion, like at the country club when Callie came under fire, Jen put her razor-sharp tongue to use, fending off the attacks on Callie's behalf. When the newspaper started reporting the story, Jen made every newspaper in the neighborhood disappear. Of course, she denied any involvement, but Callie found the pile of papers in the trash, and no one else would've had the nerve to steal everyone's paper to save Callie and her mother further humiliation.

Tiffany took a less aggressive approach, but she'd been no less fearless in her protection. In the immediate aftermath, one of them accompanied Callie whenever she left home, making sure she didn't have to face the world alone. Some may wonder why she tolerated Jen's rude and often crass comments, but Callie understood no one was perfect, and sometimes the bad had to be abided along with the good.

"Where did you say you were going?" Tiffany asked, peering over her shoulder.

Callie smiled and took another sip of wine. "I didn't."

They hadn't given her too much grief about hanging out with Wade and his friends at the club, but if they knew she was going to a bonfire... campfire—was there a difference?—at the state park, a place they all agreed was highly overrated, she'd never hear the end of it.

A heavy rumble filled the air, causing Jen and Tiffany to press their cheeks to the glass and crane their necks toward the entrance, seeking a better view. She'd never seen Wade's personal vehicle, but based on what she knew about him, she was sure he drove a truck. And based on the game of hopscotch her heart was enjoying and the heavy warmth sinking low in her belly, she'd bet the approaching growl, growing louder by the second, was that truck.

"No way," Tiffany whispered as her eyes grew wide and a smile spread across her face. She whipped her head around to face Callie, burst into laughter, then resumed staring out the window.

Jen was less amused. "No fucking way. Friends do *not* let friends go out with rednecks." She slammed her margarita glass down onto the windowsill and turned on Callie. "Flirting with a construction worker is bad enough. Going out with a redneck construction worker is going too far." Her face reddened and she spit and sputtered, unable to find the necessary words to fully express her anger. "Have you lost your damned mind?"

Fighting back a laugh, Tiffany said, "I don't think we have to worry about her actually going anywhere, Jen. She'll never get up into that truck."

Curiosity pushed at Callie's back, trying to drive her across the living room to the window, but she forced herself to stay seated on the barstool and assumed a casual I-could-care-less-what-you-think attitude.

"I told you guys. I want something different. I've gone out with rich guys. I've gone out with foreign guys. They've all been boring." She lifted her shoulder and shifted her gaze away from their stares. "I want someone who excites me. Who makes me laugh and challenges me." She leaned forward on her barstool, beseeching them to understand. "I want someone who quietly encourages me to be brave and try new things. Dammit, I want passion."

Jen snorted and rolled her eyes. "Did you just say you want passion?"

Yeah, unfortunately, she had. She hadn't meant to speak that last part out loud, but so what? She'd answered honestly, and she was no longer willing to settle for less.

"Yes, I want passion. I know you think I'm a goody-two-shoes prude, but maybe I'm stuck in that place because I've never met someone capable of bringing out another side of me."

"Oh my," Tiffany said on a breathy sigh. "I thought he was good-looking the other night, and I kind of understood what drew you to him. But"—she gulped—"he could bring out *another side* of anyone."

Unable to stand the suspense any longer, Callie jumped off her barstool and raced to the window.

Wade had just jumped down from the cab of his big—massive—black truck and was in the process of slamming the door shut. He wore cowboy boots, faded jeans, and a red-and-green flannel shirt that hung loose, like a jacket, over a stretched tight, white T-shirt.

Even though she told him she would find something to wear, he brought a couple of extra shirts with him. He slung them over his shoulder, then dug into his pocket for his phone. He glanced at the screen, then at the numbers on the building, then at the doors. As his gaze swung up to the window where they stood and he caught sight of them staring, a broad smile broke across his face.

Without thought or verbal communication, the three of them shrieked and hit the floor with a collective thud.

"Oh my God. This is so embarrassing." Callie crawled away from the window, stood and brushed herself off with as much dignity as she could muster, then ran for her wine glass.

"Which part is most embarrassing to you?" Jen demanded as she stood and straightened her skirt. "Going out with a redneck? Or being caught staring by said redneck, which would indicate he's smarter than us?"

Tiffany ran her hand under her eyes and wiped away tears of laughter. "Oh, shut up, Jen. He might be a redneck, but he's really hot." She leaned forward on her knees and peeked out the bottom of the glass. "Shit, he's still down there looking up at us, laughing."

"No," Callie said. "He's looking and laughing at *you*. I'm all the way over here"—she rested her elbow on the counter and leaned into it—"waiting for my date to arrive."

She barely had time to regain her wits when a knock sounded at the door. She jumped and nearly dumped her drink, proving she hadn't actually gathered anything yet. She steadied the long-stemmed glass on the counter, wiped her hand on her jeans, and slowly made her way to the door. Glancing over her shoulder, she found Jen on the couch, looking suitably bored, and Tiffany running for the safety of the kitchen.

Barely contained laughter lit Wade's face when she opened the door. "They didn't seem to approve at the club. Am I faring any better tonight?"

She scrunched up her face and chewed on the side of her finger. "It's a split decision."

"Damn, that's disappointing. I thought for sure my truck would bring 'em in." The humor glinting in his brown eyes amplified his sarcasm. With a wink and a tug on her hair, he added, "Good thing I don't care what *they* think."

He held her gaze for several beats, and the realization he'd just opened himself up enough to reveal he *did* care what *she* thought sent a wash of heat cascading over her. She drew in a ragged breath and steadied her voice. "I like your truck, but the driver is spectacular."

Heat infused her face with the admission, and she turned away to lead him into the living room. She'd introduced Wade at the club the other night but hadn't introduced Tiffany or Jen. "Wade, this is Jen"— she pointed to the couch—"and Tiffany." She nodded to Tiff as she slunk out of the kitchen, wearing a sheepish smile.

"Ladies, good to see you again." He might be referring to the night they met at the club, but his mischievous smile led Callie to believe he was teasing them about the window incident.

Tiffany must've thought the same thing because she giggled, then ducked back into the kitchen.

"You said you were set on clothes, but I brought some anyway." He dragged a long-sleeved T-shirt and sweatshirt off his shoulder and held them out to her. "Just in case."

"Okay," Jen said with a punch of anger and frustration. "This is ridiculous. We need to know where you're going."

Startled by the severity of her tone, Tiffany gasped while Callie froze with shock and anger.

Tiffany recovered first. "Right," she said in a diplomatic tone, leaning casually against the end of the counter. "We wouldn't be good, responsible friends if we didn't make sure she was going somewhere safe."

"Oh, for the love of God, guys." Callie threw her hands in the air in frustration. "I work with Wade. He's good friends with Kevin. Stop with the overly protective parent routine. And stop being nosey."

He glanced from Callie to Tiffany and Jen, then back Callie. His face was mostly blank, except for the muscle popping in his jaw, but the tension in his shoulders and the white-knuckle grip on the shirts let her know he was feeling a lot of something, and none of it good.

She had her reasons for not wanting to share the details of their date—aside from not wanting to hear crap about their destination—but given the way he slowly and methodically drew in breaths, as if to calm himself, he was angry, or maybe hurt, that she'd kept their date a secret.

After another tense moment, he turned to the girls and said, "We're going mudding."

Tiffany's eyes widened, Jen gasped in horror, and Callie said, "What?"

Despite their reactions and her confusion, Wade continued without missing a beat or cracking a smile. "If we get stuck, she'll need to get out and push, so I brought some of my clothes for her to wear." His grin was pure evil. "I have overalls in the truck, too, so she won't get too muddy." He picked up her hand. "She doesn't have any nails, so you don't have to worry about her breaking one or messing up the manicure. I promise I'll get her home in one piece."

Despite the anguish she felt for the unintentional hurt she'd caused him, the shock and revulsion on their faces had her bursting into uncontrollable laughter.

She'd almost regained her composure when Wade shook the shirts at her. "C'mon, tighten up. We gotta get going."

When she collapsed into a fit of laughter again, he muttered, "Aw, hell," then picked her up and slung her over his shoulder in a fireman's carry. "Which way is the bedroom?"

Tiffany's gaze slid to the hallway and then, as if realizing she was giving away a great secret, she jerked it back to Wade.

Picking up on the tell, Wade nodded. "Thank ya, ma'am, I appreciate the help."

Wade carried Callie into her bedroom, kicked the door shut behind them, and set her on her feet.

She dabbed at her eyes to clean up the mascara streaking down her cheeks and blew out a deep breath. "If I live to be a hundred and ten, I'll never forget the looks on their faces. Thank you…" She rested her hands on his chest for balance and stood on tiptoes to kiss his cheek. "For making me laugh harder than I ever have before."

Her hands took a slow glide down his chest to his abs as she rested back on the flats of her feet. The sultry look in her eyes and the slow caress of her tongue across her bottom lip indicated she'd welcome another less-chaste kiss.

And even though his body read the cues and heartily responded, he didn't feel all that romantic at the moment. "You're welcome." He lifted his shoulder in a careless shrug. "They think I'm nothing but a dumb-ass country boy. I figured I might as well live up to the expectation and give them something to really lose their shit about."

The lusty haze filling her eyes evaporated as he stepped back from her. "You didn't tell your friends where we're going." *Hello, Captain Obvious.* "Did they know I was the one coming to pick you up, or did you think they'd be gone before I got here?" He tried to sound matter-of-fact without allowing his past hurt to harden his tone, but he failed miserably.

"Of course they knew." She chewed on her lip for a minute, then grabbed his hand and dragged him behind her to the bed. Tugging him down beside her, she said, "I'm not ashamed of going out with you, and I'm sure that's what you're thinking. It's just…"

She sighed and chomped down on the side of her pinky fingernail. "I've always shared everything with them. I mean everything. We have no secrets." She glanced away and worked her mouth around, agitated. "That's why they have… certain impressions about me. Over the past several months, though, I've found myself becoming more private. I want to keep some things for myself." She tucked a piece of hair behind her ear and glanced at him shyly. "You're something I definitely don't want to share."

He didn't know what to make of her answer since he rarely shared anything with anyone. Kevin was pretty nosy and sometimes put together bits and pieces of information. And because of his relationship with Lizbeth, Miranda's sister, he'd been privy to all the ugly details of his and Miranda's breakup. But for the most part, Wade kept to himself and preferred it that way.

He wanted to trust Callie was telling him the truth, but he found himself torn between his heart, which against all logic and sensibilities was falling deeper and deeper into her big brown eyes as she implored him to believe her, and his head, which screamed for him to remember the past and never allow history to repeat itself.

All arguments ceased, however, when she smiled sweetly and swept her fingers down the side of his temple, then cupped his jaw in her hand. The gears controlling head and heart seized, leaving the door wide open for his body to step in and take control.

"I'm sorry. I would never intentionally hurt you."

He might be an idiot, and she might be lying, but at the moment, none of that mattered. They were sitting on the edge of the bed, she was looking at him with soulful eyes that implored him to believe her, and, fuck him, he did. Before he did something stupid like drag her up on the mattress and spend the next four or five hours having their first round of make-up sex, he jumped to his feet and held the shirts out to her again.

"We're not going mudding, and you probably won't get dirty, but you will smell like smoke. Are you sure you don't want to wear these instead of your nice clothes?"

Something mischievous shifted in her eyes as she grinned and looked from the long-sleeve Guy Harvey shirt to his red-and-black Georgia Bulldogs sweatshirt. After a moment, she stood and pointed to the sweatshirt. "I don't need the T-shirt, but I'll trade in my sweater for that."

His body coiled like a too-tight spring as she stripped her sweater over her head. Beating back the urge to slide his fingers under the hem of her turtleneck to rid her of that too, then follow through on the make-up sex extravaganza, he turned away and took advantage of being in Callie's most personal space.

As he rotated in a slow circle, he was surprised to find it less frilly than he'd expected, barren of personal touches. Her bed didn't sit on a pedestal. It had a basic head and footboard and was free of ornamental carvings or anything else to give the impression a princess slept here.

There weren't any pictures anywhere. None of her family. None of her friends. Not even a family pet. No horse show ribbons. No tennis trophies or pom-poms from her high school days. No college memorabilia to give away her alma mater. By all indications, the younger version of Callie never existed.

He moved over to the open closet door and peeked inside. "Holy shit."

This space was the antithesis of bare. At least a hundred pairs of shoes and an equal number of handbags littered the floor, hung from hangers, and sat atop shelves covering yards and yards and yards of fabric. Tops, dresses, skirts, slacks, long formal dresses... The place resembled a mini department store packed into thirty-six square feet.

It was hard to imagine the woman who owned all of these clothes and matching accessories was the same woman eating ramen noodles to save up for a pair of boots.

"It's a hot mess, huh?" He turned to find her standing behind him in his sweatshirt, the sleeves flapping off the ends of her arms like six-inch flags. "I keep meaning to clean it out but never seem to find the time."

His gaze dipped from her pouty pink lips and white teeth doing a number on them to the badass bulldog snarling at him from the front of his extra-large sweatshirt. Few things ramped up a guy more than seeing a woman—*his woman*—wearing his clothes. But this closet, filled with more... *stuff* than he could afford to buy her in a lifetime, along with her refusal to tell her friends where they were going, served as harsh reminders she wasn't, nor would she ever be, *his woman*.

With a pang of longing for something he'd never have stabbing him in the chest, he stepped forward, took hold of her arm, and rolled the sleeve up to her wrist. After doing the same with the other one, he let go of her, took a step back, and winked. "Ready to go mudding?"

She grinned, that damned dimple winked, and everything that seemed wrong moments before righted themselves. "Absolutely."

As they crossed the parking lot toward his truck, Callie tilted her head in one direction, then the other, then scratched her head.

"Wanna run back upstairs for a stepstool?"

She cut her eyes to the side and grinned. "I assumed you'd have one in the back."

"Nope, you're out of luck." As he unlocked and opened the door, a memory from his ancient past had him laughing out loud. "My brother used to carry a stepstool around in his truck when his wife was pregnant." He shook his head, thinking about the day it became obvious Theresa wasn't going to be able to get into Cody's old Ford without it. "His truck was higher than mine, and he threw his back out on Christmas Eve, trying to lift her into it. After that, he always made sure he had a stepstool in the back."

"Why didn't they drive her car?"

"She didn't have one. They got married right out of high school, and she didn't have one then. A few months after they tied the knot, she found out she was pregnant. He didn't want her standing on her feet all day, waiting tables, so she quit work. They could barely make the rent, so getting a second car was out of the question."

"Oh." She dropped her gaze to the ground. "That's awful."

And here they were again. Another example of the extreme differences in their backgrounds and further proof he'd lost his mind to think, for even a second, anything could come of them—regardless of her cute dimple, the way she made him feel, or the boots that continued to fill his fantasies.

Her friend, Tiffany, lived in the condo next door, and when he and Callie left, she and Jen migrated east. When he glanced up to Tiffany's window, as expected, he found the pair watching Callie and him.

They judged him by his looks—much the way he'd done with Callie—and all they saw was a dumb hick with nothing but a big truck to offer their friend. He still didn't understand why she treated him the way she had their first day of working together, but he'd been wrong with his other assumptions about her. Her friends, however, were pretty close to the mark with theirs.

He was smarter than they probably gave him credit for, and he would take care of her to the best of his abilities, giving her everything he possibly could. But he'd never be able to give her a mansion or a new Mercedes or a closet full of the world's finest clothes. Eventually, she'd get tired of eating Hamburger Helper and would want a man who could keep her in fresh lobster and fillet mignon.

"They don't think I can do it." Callie was standing next to him, staring at her friends, her arms crossed tightly over her stomach.

"They don't think you can do what?"

"Get into that monster truck by myself." She turned and squared off with him, shoulders back, chin up, eyes hard. "Don't you dare help me. Understood?"

Damn... this fired-up Callie was smoking hot, and his internal temperature soared from the heat and intensity she put off.

"Yes, ma'am. I get it." And he did. The women staring down at them might be her best friends, but he'd picked up on a lot of static between the trio, especially with Jen. Callie had something to prove, and he was happy to support her in that effort. "I'm disappointed I don't get to grab your ass as I shove you in." He winked as she shifted her weight to the side and gave him a lot of attitude. "But yeah, I hear ya. Have at it, princess."

*Shit. She doesn't like that.*

She sucked in a breath and opened her mouth to blast him, but before she got the words out, he leaned over and planted a kiss on her pretty pink lips, stopping the rant before she started.

"I'm sorry, Callie. I forgot that was a hot button for you." He swept a lock of hair away from her eye and brushed his knuckles down her cheek. "It just comes out without me thinking, because…" *Well, won't this sound stupid and like I'm a total sap?* "That's how I see you." He scratched the back of his head. "Hell, I don't know how to say what I mean and not sound like a pus—pushover, but I mean it as a term of endearment, like baby or sweetheart."

She stared at him, barely breathing, hardly blinking, lost by his convoluted explanation. Which made perfect sense, since he hadn't actually said anything of value, and her confusion was for the best. One of them realizing she was getting under his skin was one too many.

The differences between them were like raging floodwaters, too deep, too wide, and too dangerous to attempt crossing. Staying on their respective sides and watching from a distance was definitely the safest choice.

Past time for a subject change, he nodded to the handle running down the bracing of the truck between the door and the windshield. "You'll have to use your leg strength to get started, but once you get high enough, grab hold of the shit grip and use it to pull yourself into the seat."

She stared at the truck, her confusion building. "Shit grip?"

"Yeah, this." He tugged at the handle. "You know, when someone goes around a corner too fast and you grab hold and say, 'Oh shit!'"

She chewed on the inside of her cheek, scrunched up her cute little button nose, and shook her head.

"Oh, c'mon. Seriously? You've never been riding with someone who went around a corner too fast or slammed on brakes at a light?"

"Well, yeah, but I just grab hold of the dash."

Of course she did, because she usually rode in little sports cars where the dash was at her knees.

"That won't work in my truck. The seat is pushed too far back. You'll never be able to reach the dash. So during those terrifying moments, you'll wanna use the shit grip." He paused, giving her a moment to catch up. When her mouth dropped open and her wide-open eyes snapped to him, he laughed. "I'm kidding. Mostly. Jesus, would you get in already?"

"Okay." She rolled her head around and twisted her back, like she was loosening up for gym class. "Wish me luck."

She put her left foot on the running board, braced her left hand against the seat, and readied her right hand to grab the handle. She might be a novice, but she had incredible leg strength and took to the task like a pro.

He might not be able to touch, but he sure as hell could watch, so while she hauled herself up, he stood back and enjoyed the sway of her ass swinging side to side.

"Ha!" She dropped into the seat and gave him the biggest, brightest smile he'd ever seen. "Please tell me they're still watching."

He glanced at the window in time to catch the back of Jen's head as she walked away, but Tiffany was still standing there, smiling and waving, clearly enjoying Callie's accomplishment. "Yep, they saw it all."

*Including the kiss.*

Callie leaned back in her seat, peacock proud, and reached for the seatbelt. "You didn't think I could do it either."

Pride for her pushed at his chest and had him vehemently shaking his head, denying the charge. "You're wrong. I knew you could."

She studied him from the side of her eye as she clicked the seatbelt into place. "Then what's wrong? Why are you staring at me like that?"

*Because you're the most beautiful woman on the planet and make me happier than I've been in a long time.* But logic slipped through the door, reminding him of the temporary nature of their relationship, stealing his happy and replacing it with a slow-burning sadness.

"Nothing's wrong." He swallowed the lump of emotion clogging his throat and squeezed her knee. "You're a lot of fun, and I'm looking forward to spending the evening with you."

# Chapter Seven

*I*t took a while for Callie to become acclimated to the bounce and sway of Wade's truck as they traveled south on Highway 17 headed toward Murrell's Inlet, towering above everyone else, but she gradually settled in and learned how to roll with the motion rather than fighting against it. She wasn't, however, comfortable enough to let go of the shit grip.

"Why do you drive a truck this big?"

Wade glanced at her from the corner of his eye and grinned. "Why do the guys you know drive little sports cars?"

"Because they're fast." She didn't know much about this truck, but she was pretty sure it wouldn't win any races. She giggled and added, "They're also popular with the girls."

Wade threw his head back, laughing… which reminded her of the way he'd looked drinking her Gatorade… which made her think, again, about the way he'd look in the throes of sex.

"There ya go. Where I'm from," Wade said, interrupting her daydream, "girls like trucks." He slid her a heated gaze and smirked. "And the bigger the better. Always."

A tropical heat wave erupted within her and she broke out in a pool of sweat.

Before meeting Wade, she rarely thought about sex and never during general conversation. Not even when a guy threw out subtle—or not-so-subtle—innuendoes. Most of the time, the remarks went right over her head. But Wade had flipped some kind of switch inside her head, making it impossible to think of much else. And that was without him tossing double-entendres around while sweeping a hot gaze down her body.

What kind of lover was he? Did he go slow, allowing things to build to an amazing crescendo, or did he get in and out with little to no thought for his partner's pleasure?

She thought about the way he held doors open for her, helped her with her coat, and brought a sweatshirt so she didn't get her clothes smelly. If he paid attention to the little things that made a girl feel special, he'd pay attention to the biggies.

*The bigger the better.*

Her gaze slid over to his lap as the words echoed in her brain. He was tall and heavily muscled… Did that mean he was big everywhere?

Could she handle him if he was?

Could she handle him even if he wasn't?

*God, stop it, stop it, stop it!*

She was Callie the Prude; she didn't think this way. But the truth was she didn't want to be a prude. That hadn't been her life's goal. She hadn't made a conscious decision to stick with the bland, boring items on life's sexual buffet. She'd just never met someone who made her want to be adventurous and try the spicier entrees. Until now.

"Are you okay?"

She snapped her gaze up to meet his. *Oh, God.* Had he caught her staring at his crotch? She squeezed her eyes shut and drew in a deep, calming breath. And then another. And another. "Yeah, I'm fine."

The light in front of them turned red, and after coming to a complete stop, he turned his head to fully face her. "Is my driving scaring you that bad?"

"What? No. Your driving is fine. Why?"

His eyebrow rose and he glanced to her hand. "You're gripping the handle like your life depends on it, and you're breathing like you just finished a marathon."

Okay, this was good. He thought his driving was responsible for her heavy breathing, not her runaway imagination sizing him up. Literally. After a hard swallow, she released the handle and eased back in her seat. "No, see, I'm fine. Everything's fine."

*Crap.* Maybe if she shut up and quit going on about everything being fine, he'd actually believe her.

He didn't seem convinced, but when the light turned green, he accelerated and returned his attention to the road while she massaged the cramp out of her fingers and tried to focus on something less dangerous... an impossible task with him sitting so close, tossing sideways glances her way.

At the next light, her fine-and-dandy crumbled. His gaze was the flame and she was the pot, and the longer he stared, the hotter she got. His nostrils flared—as if picking up on her cat-in-heat scent—and his rich-brown eyes darkened. Hiding her reaction became impossible, so rather than try, she gulped and turned to stare out the window.

"Care to tell me what's going on in that pretty head of yours?" His voice was low, his tone coarse.

"Nope." She shook her head emphatically, causing her curls to swing back and forth in front of her face. She not only didn't want to tell him what she'd been thinking; she couldn't. Never in a million years, not even under the threat of torture or death, would she be able to voice all the crazy thoughts she'd had about him over the past several days. "I'm good."

Hey, check her out... Progress. She'd improved from fine to good, and thank God, the light turned green.

Rather than accelerate immediately, though, he kept his laser-like focus trained on her and muttered, "I bet you are."

It took her frazzled brain several heartbeats to catch up, and when the words finally registered, instantaneous heat flashed over her and her lungs forgot their proper function.

God, what was she doing with him? She was so far out of her element and in over her head she doubted she'd make it out alive. And not just in a sexual context. She was riding in a truck, and to the best of her knowledge, this was a first. They were headed to the state park—nope, never been to one of those—to sit around a campfire, something she'd already admitted to knowing nothing about.

Jen was right. She had lost her mind. And crazier still, she didn't want to be saved from the insanity.

She was, however, anxious to turn the spotlight away from herself and onto him. "You said where you're from, girls like guys with big trucks."

Did she sound a little testy about other women liking him for his big truck? She screwed her mouth to the side and sighed. Probably, because she'd definitely noticed the attention he and his friends got at the Blue Lagoon, and she hadn't liked it. "Where is home?"

"North Georgia mountains, near the Tennessee and North Carolina borders. Tyler and Alex live in North Carolina now. Garrett's moved to Tennessee, but Matt's still in Georgia."

Okay, this was good. Switching the focus was helping her relax, so she took a slow, deep breath and kept the conversation going. "How did you end up in Myrtle Beach?"

He glanced over his left shoulder and changed lanes, then gassed it to pass a BMW not driving fast enough to suit him. "After I got out of high school, I floundered for a few years. School wasn't my thing, so college wasn't a viable option. There's not a lot of work in our area, but

I found a good construction job, at least through the summers. Winter months are tough, so I bounced at one of the local bars, did a lot of hanging out, and tried not to get into too much trouble."

A smile played on his mouth as he stared out the windshield, lost to a memory. After a moment, he continued. "I've always loved the beach, so one day I got the bright idea to move here." He glanced at her and the broad smile revealing a slash of white teeth sent a river of warmth cascading through her chest and into her belly. "I had enough money for the gas to get here and a week's worth of food." He chuckled and shook his head. "And balls. I was young and invincible, and failure wasn't an option, so…" He shrugged and laughed again.

Determined not to think about the last item on his list, she focused on the first two. "How in the world did you survive once you got here?"

"I lived in a tent in the campground for about six months"—he nodded toward the road ahead, so she assumed he meant at the state park—"and I worked whatever odd job I could find."

She stared in disbelief, waiting… silently hoping he'd break into laughter and say, *Kidding,* but he didn't. "You lived in a tent?"

"Yep."

He glanced at her again, waiting to see if she had more to say. Undoubtedly, she'd have a whole lot more to say later, but right now, she was still trying to grasp the concept of living in a tent. Not for a weekend, but for six months.

When she didn't say anything else, he continued. "Fortunately, I met Kevin. It was the beginning of November, and I really didn't want to live in the campground through the winter. I would've survived, but showering in the campground bathhouse was getting old. And not having a television to watch my Bulldogs play football sucked."

Her mind, for the most part, was blank. She had no frame of reference to comprehend what he'd said, except for one tiny part… him showering. She really wanted to know what he looked like standing beneath the hot spray, water and soapsuds cascading down his body.

He would be magnificent, more hypnotic than her beloved wall fountain at the country club, and an image she'd never forget.

"Kevin not only gave me a job, but also let me crash at his apartment until I saved up enough money to get my own place."

Shaking off the fog of the shower fantasy, she said, "Wow, I had the feeling you guys were friends, but I didn't realize you were that close."

"Yeah, since he saved my life, he's stuck with me forever." He laughed. "I tease him about that all the time, but there's some truth to it. I owe him everything."

She'd been proud of herself for moving out of her parents' home, getting her own condo, and finding a job to support herself. Compared to Wade, who'd moved to a different state and lived in a freaking tent for six months, her accomplishments didn't seem so amazing.

She frowned. No, that wasn't true. She might not have braved the elements, but she'd faced her father's tornadic fury and stayed on her feet in the aftermath. Going behind her father's back to sell Gavin the Anticue fishing pier—a piece of property her father had put in her name in an effort to hide his underhanded development scheme—had taken tremendous courage. Standing before her father to tell him what she did had required even more. She'd bent, but not broken, under the threat of being disowned and the threats of physical violence he'd made against Gavin.

However, had she realized he was serious about making an attempt on Gavin's life and not just blowing off steam, she'd have torn up the paperwork on the spot.

With a deep exhale, she released the renewed anxiety the memories brought on and the tension twisting her gut. Her approach had been different than Wade's, but she *was* brave and so much stronger than she'd ever believed herself to be. She needed to give herself credit for that.

"Kevin saved me too." Technically, Gavin saved her by making the recommendation to Kevin in the first place, and it had been up to her to capitalize on the opportunity, but Kevin gave her a chance, and she'd forever be grateful. "I wasn't living in a tent, but I was desperate for a job. I had a degree in interior design but no previous work history." She grimaced as she glanced at him and admitted, "None. Like ever. He gave me a chance, and I've been working hard to prove myself since."

"I'm glad."

He spoke so softly she wasn't sure she'd understood. "Pardon?"

He flipped on his left turn signal, veered into the turn lane, and rolled onto the long winding road leading into the state park. "I'm glad he gave you a chance."

They stopped at a security gate and an older gentleman she assumed was there more for show than actual security ambled over to the truck. "Evening, Wade. Back for more punishment, I see."

The corner of Wade's eyes crinkled as he grinned affectionately. "I've never claimed to be smart, Mr. Jimmy."

She shouldn't have been surprised he knew the older man's name, but the realization hit her square in the chest. Her parents had lived in the same gated community for fifteen years, and she'd never once thought of calling any of the guards by name, which would be difficult to do since she didn't know their names. Had she ever bothered to even wave at them or thank them when she drove through the entrance?

"The boys behaving?" Given Wade's smile and tone, the question seemed rhetorical.

The man pulled a toothpick out of his mouth and grinned. "What do you think?"

Wade laughed and nodded once. "That's one of the reasons they come this time of year, fewer people to annoy."

"I assume you'll be leaving late?"

Mr. Jimmy's eyes widened with surprise when Wade shook his head. "No, sir. I'm getting too old to make this a nightly thing." He leaned back so the older man could see Callie. "I brought an insurance policy with me tonight. This lovely lady won't think sleeping in the back of my truck is all that spectacular, so I'll be outta here early, getting her home to a nice, warm bed."

She gulped as he kept his eyes locked on hers, and the cab of the truck turned into a sauna. She tugged at the high collar of her turtle-neck, desperate for air and relief from the oppressive heat.

"All right, then," Mr. Jimmy said with a pat on the windowsill that snapped her and Wade out of their private moment. "I won't worry about fixing the gate."

Wade stuck his hand out and clasped the other man's in a solid shake. "I appreciate you looking out for me the way you do. Have a great night."

Jimmy waved at Callie and inclined his head. "Good luck, ma'am. You're gonna need it with this crowd."

As they pulled away from the security stop, Callie said, "What did he mean about fixing the gate?"

Wade's grin was mischievous—not a full-on smile or laugh, but a lopsided hint at the bad boy who lived deep inside. "The park closes at ten, but Mr. J knows I have a hard time getting out of here on time. He sets the lock to appear latched, but it's not. I lock up on my way out. He used to do that for me when I lived here, too. Only then, I had a hard time getting in before the witching hour."

As they crossed a bridge that had water on both sides, Callie sucked in a breath and leaned closer to the window. *Holy crap! Is that an alligator?*

Wade's chuckle cut through the air. "Don't worry, Callie. You're safe with me."

Oh, God. What had she gotten herself into?

As they turned into the campground, the sound of waves rolling onshore had her stiffening again. "Are we on the beach? Literally?"

"Not exactly. There are dunes between us and the water." He slowed the truck so they were barely moving forward. "Are you afraid of the water?"

"No." At least not the heavily chlorinated kind surrounded by concrete. "I've never been a fan of the beach. I don't like getting dirty."

The dim lights of the dashboard provided just enough light to reveal the heat radiating from his eyes as he said, "That's a damn shame. Getting dirty can be a hell of a lot of fun."

Wade parked next to a burgundy truck similar in size and height to his. In the open space in front of them, four tents were arranged in a large circle, the campfire centered between them. The word campfire instantly took on new meaning and understanding for her. This wasn't a movie, and in this scenario, the men were literally camping around a fire for warmth.

She shuddered as she thought of Wade living like this for six months. If Kevin were here, she'd throw her arms around his neck and hug him silly for not only giving Wade a job, but also a place to live.

Wade climbed down from the truck, circled around to her side, and opened the door.

"Where did you sleep the other night?" she asked. "The night before we worked together?"

He scratched the back of his head and grinned. "In a sleeping bag under the tailgate of my truck."

"What?" He laughed as her jaw came unhinged. "It was pouring down rain that night!"

He ran his finger and thumb across his forehead, then dropped his hand to his waist. He seemed to be working hard to hold back his laugh when he said, "That's why I slept *under* the tailgate. I still got wet, but not as much as if I'd been out in the open." When she continued to stare at him in utter disbelief, he shrugged. "My only other option was to crawl into a tent and spoon with one of them, so…" His grin broadened. "Thinking you bit off more than you can chew?"

"Absolutely." Realizing how that sounded, she grabbed his hand and squeezed. "But not the way you think." As he continued to stare, half bemused and half confused, she blew out a breath and went for the truth. "I've traveled the globe, but you're so much worldlier and experienced than me." She glanced away. "In everything, I'm sure. So yeah, I'm definitely in over my head, but so far, I've enjoyed the ride, and I'm looking forward to exploring more of your world."

She risked returning her gaze to him and found he'd stopped breathing and moving and didn't even blink for the longest time. It was hard to read his thoughts because his expression rarely gave anything away, but she hoped he hadn't missed the sexual reference she'd tossed in about him being more experienced. As well as looking forward to exploring more.

After a moment, he blinked a few times and said, "I'll do what I can to share my expertise with you."

The reply was more innuendo than blatant come-on, but she'd come to expect that from him. She'd noticed with the guys on his crew, he was direct and matter-of-fact, but with her, he always seemed to dance around the periphery of what he truly meant. Did he do it intentionally and with all women, she wondered, or just with her?

"Do you want help getting down, or have you got this?"

He didn't seem to be teasing or mocking her, and her heart warmed at having someone understand her motivation for doing small, seemingly inconsequential things for herself. When she felt the need.

"Nope," she said with a smile. "I've got nothing to prove here, so help would be great."

She turned sideways in her seat, making it easy for him to reach in and pick her up. His grip was strong and sure and her elevator ride down took only a second, but she took advantage of the opportunity to wrap her hands over his shoulders and enjoy the feel of hard man under the soft flannel.

Her feet touched the ground too soon, and she wasn't ready to break contact yet, so she pressed her palms into the solid wall of his chest, then ran them up to his neck and back down to the top of his jeans.

Using her eyes, she pleaded for him to kiss her. His nostrils flared and his throat bunched as he swallowed, but rather than following through on the kiss he obviously wanted as much as her, he took her hand, slammed the door shut, and headed toward the campfire at a brisk pace.

# Chapter Eight

$\mathcal{W}$ade's friend, Tyler, was rummaging through a cooler when he noticed Wade and Callie approaching. "Hey, Wadell, you finally made it." He dug down into the cooler, grabbed another beer, and tossed the can to Wade.

Wade snatched it out of the air like a baseball player catching a fly ball and leaned in close to Callie. "You repeat that to anyone, especially Kevin, I'll be forced to exact revenge."

Callie poured on a sugary-sweet smile and met his threat with one of her own. "I guess you better never do anything to make me mad."

His pained expression had her super-sweet smile melting into a happy laugh. "You do realize I'm a guy, right? We screw up. All the time." He shook his head and sighed. "I'm doomed."

Tyler, keeping the cooler open for business, said, "Hey, Callie. Want a beer?"

Even though she'd met Wade's friends at the Blue Lagoon, she'd been nervous about spending time with them. There was a big difference in being part of a crowd at a large club where conversation was next to impossible and being in a confined setting. But she should've known better than to be concerned, and the last vestiges of fear slipped away on an exhale. "I'm fine for now, but thanks for asking."

"Let me know if you change your mind." While Tyler dropped the

lid back into place and took a seat on a log by the fire, Wade watched
Matt and Garrett argue about the correct way to cook fish on the grill.

She had the feeling he'd watched them do this before, because his
lips lifted into a smile and his eyes shone affectionately, as if recalling a
fond memory. After a moment, he shifted his attention back to Tyler.
"Where's Alex?"

Tyler nodded to a block building off to their left. "Taking a quick
shower."

Her gaze slid to the building, and unbidden images of Wade shedding his clothes and stepping under the spray popped into her mind.
Heat spread across her neck and up her cheeks when he tugged at her
hand. Thank God he wasn't a mind reader, because she'd die of
embarrassment if he found out he'd become a permanent fixture in her
fantasies.

"The wind is blowing to our backs here," he said, leading her
around the right side of the fire, "which means the smoke will blow
away from us."

"Okay." She glanced at the low logs scattered around the fire and
thought about the shadow she'd seen from the bridge. An alligator
could sneak up from behind and eat them whole, and they'd never
know what happened. A shiver racked her body and had her scooting
closer to Wade for protection.

"You can sit in the chair with me," Wade said, grabbing a lawn
chair leaning against the stack of firewood. "I'll help keep you warm."

She wasn't concerned about the cold—just being in his presence
kept her internal temperature hovering at the scorching mark—but the
thought of being chomped in half by a nasty set of teeth terrified her.

She glanced around at the tents sitting on the ground and the logs
that seemed to have gotten their fair share of use. Obviously, these guys
weren't afraid of such trivial things—Wade slept on the ground under

his truck, for heaven's sake—so she kept her fears to herself and allowed him to continue to think she was cold. "Okay. Thanks."

Public displays of affection—heck, all displays of affection—had been noticeably absent in her parents' relationship, and she was self-conscious about sitting on his lap, a gesture that seemed too intimate for their current status. But a quick glance at his friends revealed none of them were paying Wade or her any attention.

Garrett and Matt had settled their dispute and were chatting in regular voices. She spotted Alex ambling across the parking lot, towel tossed over his shoulder, hands tucked into his pockets, appearing to not have a care in the world. And Tyler stared at the hypnotic flames, seemingly a million miles away, lost to his own thoughts.

Wade extended his hand as he took a seat, so she ignored her reservations and allowed him to pull her down with him. It took a few minutes and lots of adjustments, but she eventually found a comfortable position angled across his lap, her back cradled in the crook of his arm.

She'd never spent time with a group of men, and it also took a while to get accustomed to the way they interacted with each other—which was very different than the way Tiffany, Jen, and she spoke to each other. The men thrived on rattling each other's cages—all good-natured fun, nothing malicious—with Wade taking the most hits. The hottest topic: him sleeping under his tailgate and the lightweight he'd been since that night.

"You had to work with this sorry bastard on Monday, right?" Alex asked.

From the corner of her eyes, she saw Wade roll his eyes. "Yep."

"I bet that was fun," Tyler added sarcastically. "He can't hold his liquor for shit."

"I can handle *liquor* fine. The stuff you have isn't liquor." His eyes brightened and he glanced at Callie, then to the guys. "She has a home remedy that works like a charm. I don't think I would've survived the day without her Dramamine and Gatorade."

Tyler's head snapped up and a wide grin split his face. "Laney does the same thing..." His expression changed from joy to sorrow as the words fell off and gaping silence filled the air.

Wade and Alex exchanged glances. Then Wade said, "Five Guys helped too." He was more animated and enthusiastic than normal, and she suspected he was trying to pull his friend out of the black hole that swallowed him up before their eyes.

Going along with his plan, she laughed and said, "A heavy dose of grease normally does." She grimaced and ducked her head. "Believe it or not, Jen, Tiffany, and I have been known to hit Waffle House in the middle of the night."

"Oh, no, you didn't!" Wade's lousy impression of a Jersey girl had his friends—including Tyler—erupting into laughter.

Wade's chest expanded with relief as he took a deep breath, so she kept the conversation going. "I know, right?" She dipped her eyes, then batted her lashes. "If we had a good-looking cook to fix us bacon, eggs, and greasy hash browns, we wouldn't have to resort to such desperate measures."

Three hands shot up around the fire as Wade's friends, with the exception of Tyler, eagerly offered their services.

"I'll fix pancakes," Alex offered.

"I'll see your pancakes and add waffles," Matt interjected.

Garrett kicked his legs out in front of him and crossed them at the ankles. "Sweetheart, I'll fix whatever you want." His smile was slow and easy and tempting even before he added the wink. "Give me a call."

Sheesh, good thing Jen wasn't here. She'd be working out a schedule.

Wade didn't make any outrageous offers, but the arm wrapped

around her waist tightened, silently staking his claim on her, while his friends made their case as to why they'd be the better choice, at the same time disputing the others' unique talents and abilities.

After several moments, Tyler resurfaced from the ugly well of despair he'd fallen into and briefly joined the conversation before switching his attention to Wade. "I've got the boat and the magnetometer lined up for Saturday morning. We need to be at the dock by six."

Wade hardened like stone and a deep growl escaped his throat. "Bro, I'm telling you. Your mystery boat isn't out there." He huffed and shook his head. "Someone would've found it by now if it was."

Tyler was far less intimidated by Wade's glare than Callie would've been. With a confident smile and nonchalant shrug, he said, "They're not looking in the right spot."

She didn't know these men well, but she had the suspicion being best friends hadn't kept them from landing a few solid punches over the years. Based on the anger that continued to build and spill out of Wade, and the less than receptive response from Tyler, she imagined this could easily become one of those instances.

Hoping a slight change of subject would diffuse a quickly escalating situation, she said, "I can't imagine diving in this cold weather. Although, I'm not a good judge of these types of things, because I wouldn't dive on a balmy, summer day." She shivered. "That would require me getting on a boat, going out into the ocean, and getting into the water with creatures that would make a quick snack of me." She shuddered again and checked around her feet for alligators as she huddled in closer to Wade.

"The cold isn't a problem," Tyler explained. "We have dry suits, so we don't even get wet."

How could they not get wet while swimming in the ocean?

She turned to Wade, expecting him to smile at Tyler's joke, but instead, he nodded and said, "He's not kidding. The suits zip around the neck and ankles, they have hoodies to protect their heads, booties for their feet, and their masks cover most of their faces. They wear their clothes under their suits, and when they come out of the water, they're completely dry."

He narrowed his gaze and slanted a glare at Tyler. "Dry suits, however, don't protect against stupidity. And diving when you're trying to thread a damned needle between storm systems is downright ass-hat stupid."

Callie released a long-suffering sigh. Her plan had worked for a minute, but she should've known Wade wouldn't be easily distracted. Unwilling to give up without her own fight, she made another attempt. "None of that would be a problem for me because I'm a total land lover. I don't even like seafood."

Wade tensed again, then released a deep breath and relaxed beneath her. "So you don't like lobster?" He laughed a little and tried to make the question sound like a joke, but there was something serious going on behind his eyes.

Her lip curled reflexively at the question. "Yuck. I'll sometimes eat salmon or shrimp, but only if it's cleaned really well."

His eyes darkened and narrowed in focus. "What about filet mignon?"

"Ummm…" His line of questioning was strange, but he no longer appeared to be joking, so she worked hard to remember the last time she'd eaten any kind of steak at all, let alone filet. "I like it okay, but I don't eat much red meat. I mostly stick with chicken."

"How do you feel about Hamburger Helper?"

Confusion had her giggling nervously. "What?"

His gaze held hers for a little longer than the conversation seemed to warrant, but then he shook his head and muttered, "Never mind," before returning his attention to Tyler, who'd jumped back to the subject of diving.

"Don't knock it 'til you try it. Diving can be the most fun you've ever had."

Wade snorted and muttered, "Not even close, baby. Don't believe that bullshit for a second." He cut his gaze to the side and looked at her through hooded lids. "He's obviously doing something wrong."

Callie struggled to breathe as she latched onto Wade's deep, penetrating gaze, and her mind filled with images of all the things he would do right.

"Hey, you two listening?" Tyler's voice broke the magical spell spiraling around them, forcing them to break eye contact and return their attention to him. Mischief lit his face and his eyes brightened. "I'm trying to convince Callie to go diving with us."

She wanted to return to the previous moment and the intense connection drawing her and Wade closer together, but she did her best to stay focused on Tyler as he told her about the shipwrecks he'd been in, the sharks he'd seen, as well as other marine life, and something about a cool reef. It was all a lot of white noise humming in her brain, but she'd succeeded in thwarting the argument between him and Wade, so as he enthusiastically shared his stories, she nodded and smiled and drained the last of Wade's beer.

Matt tossed Wade another, which he handed off to her as Tyler handed him a mason jar filled a quarter of the way full with an amber liquid. Wade, working on autopilot, took the jar without much thought. A few minutes later, seemingly realizing for the first time what he held, he shook his head and handed the jar back to Tyler—who'd finally stopped talking long enough to take a breath.

When Tyler didn't take the jar from Wade's hand, Wade said, "No way. I'm not drinking that shit tonight. I have to drive, we have to be home early for work tomorrow, and my sleeping bag is still drying over the line at home."

"Oh, c'mon. It's barely a swallow."

Wade dropped his chin and looked at Tyler from the tops of his eyes. "A swallow is all it takes."

"What is it?"

Callie leaned forward for a better look, but before she got too close, Wade stretched his arm all the way out to the side, keeping the jar away from her like the liquid was a poison he feared. "Nothing good."

"What? It's great." Alex grinned at Callie. "It's apple pie wine."

Wade barked out a laugh. "And you're a liar. That is *not* wine."

Alex drank from an identical jar and licked his lips. "I'm not lying about it being good, though."

Giving up the argument, Wade continued to hold the jar but didn't take a drink, nor did he ask for his beer back.

As conversation between the friends resumed, she settled back down and became absorbed by the environment. The campfire flames performed a hypnotic dance, and the fire crackled and popped, sending bits and pieces of ash into the night sky, like confetti flying upward instead of falling.

She looked to the sky, expecting a similar view to the one she had at home, but she couldn't have been more wrong. She gasped in awe at the massive canopy twinkling over their heads. She wasn't often away from the city's orange glow and she'd never paid attention to the sky when she was. How could that view have been there all along and she never noticed?

A gust of cold air swept through the camp, sending her closer to Wade and his body heat.

"Are you cold, baby?" His mellow gaze was that of a man carrying a feel-good buzz, except he'd only had half a beer. The stress lines he often wore around his eyes were gone, and even though he showed concern for her, he appeared as relaxed as a person could be. He was as comfortable around this fire and took as much pleasure from being outside in nature as she did sitting at home with her blender and the television remote.

"I was, but I'm okay now." She wiggled and gave him what she hoped came off as an impish grin. "It's a good excuse to get closer to you."

The corner of his mouth lifted and his lids relaxed even more as his arm constricted and pulled her tightly against him. "Yo, Matt, throw me that blanket next to you."

The blanket was transferred from person to person, and when it reached them, Wade switched the mason jar to the hand wrapped around her so he could use the other to spread the blanket over them.

"No misbehaving under the covers," Alex said. "It's not fair to the rest of us lonely sons of bitches."

"Hey, I had you hooked up with our waitress last night. Not my fault you couldn't close the deal."

Alex muttered under his breath and the other guys added their opinions to the matter, while Callie snuggled in under the wool blanket.

Even though she didn't want to think about it, she wondered where they'd been and if Wade had closed the deal with anyone. Before jealousy devoured her, she shut off the flow of unproductive thoughts and refocused on the here and now. She was the one cradled in Wade's arms right now, and she'd be the one he took home.

But what did that mean?

She knew he was attracted to her—that was obvious, even to someone with limited experience—but something kept holding him back. He wasn't willing to move beyond spontaneous kisses and flirtatious banter, and she suspected if things were to progress, she'd have to be the one who got them there.

Not a good scenario for someone clueless in the art of seduction.

The weight of the heavy wool pressing down on her made her more consciously aware of the delicious heat and solid mass of Wade's compact body beneath her. After having been seated for so long, she'd grown accustomed to his hard ridges and was somewhat numb, so she wiggled around to wake up the nerve endings.

In response, he stiffened and shot her a dark look she assumed he intended as a warning to stop.

Funny thing about a warning like that. Rather than taking it as a sign to back off, her feminine instincts kicked and rejoiced in awareness of the power she held. Testing the theory and her newfound wiles, she wiggled again, slow and purposeful.

A spike in tension tightened his muscles and his breathing grew ragged as he cut his eyes to the side and gave her an even darker, more heated look. This one didn't seem to be saying she should stop but instead warned her of the trouble she'd be in if she didn't.

God, she wanted to suffer for the sin of pushing him too far.

Her gaze settled on the forgotten jar still dangling from his fingertips. In order to keep driving forward enough to break through his barriers, she'd need to be bolder and more aggressive than her nature would allow. She needed to lower her inhibitions, and the only way that would happen was with a few drinks.

Based on Wade's reaction, the contents of the jar must be stronger than beer or wine, so even though there was only a small amount, it might be enough to give her the courage she needed. He'd made it clear he didn't want her anywhere near the stuff, so without giving him the opportunity to deny her again, she slipped her arm free of the blanket and snatched the jar from his hand.

"Whoa," he said, making an unsuccessful attempt to take it back as she stole his move and held her hand to the side, out of his reach. "What are you doing?"

"I'm well beyond the legal drinking age," she said, sounding way too prim and proper for someone haranguing over a mason jar filled with what was probably moonshine.

He grinned and pressed a kiss to her temple. "Yeah, well, that stuff's not legal."

She hesitated, wondering if she should heed his warning, but dammit, the new Callie wanted spice and adventure. She wanted to be brave and seduce Wade, but years of conditioning wouldn't allow it without something to loosen her up. Without further thought, for fear of chickening out, she leaned to the side out of Wade's reach, put the jar to her lips, and took a healthy gulp.

Liquid fire ran down her throat, stripping away the protective lining in the process. Her eyes, throat, and stomach burned like a tree that had been struck by lightning. Her insides splintered and shredded and she expected flames to shoot out of her mouth or butt or both at any second. She coughed and sputtered, which sent the flames up the back of her mouth and out her nose like a fire-breathing dragon. An infection wouldn't dare touch her sinuses for six months—if she had any sinus cavities left—and the rest of her body would never be the same.

She gasped for air and handed the mostly empty jar to Wade as he patted her back like a parent trying to help a choking child. Her eyes watered so badly she struggled to see, but she thought one of guys grabbed a fire extinguisher while the other grabbed a bottle of water.

Once the coughing slowed, Wade gently asked, "You okay?" His lips twitched and she knew he wanted to laugh, but he held it at bay, saving her further humiliation. At least for the moment. Later, she'd be the butt of their uproarious laughter, probably for years to come.

She nodded but failed to maintain eye contact. "Yeah, I guess I should've listened." She tried to laugh it off, but on the inside, she wanted to run for the safety of his truck. Of course, by the time she got there, the full effects of the lethal cocktail would hit and she'd fall flat on her face, thereby doubling her trouble.

A bottle of water and a red Gatorade—that she'd mistaken for a fire extinguisher—appeared in her line of sight. Still unable to make eye contact with anyone, she smiled weakly and took both of the bottles. "Thanks." She downed the water first, then went to work on the Gatorade.

"It's an acquired taste," Wade said. "It helps to start off slow and easy."

She harrumphed. "I'll have to take you at your word."

The hand running slow circles over her back crawled up to her neck. He twisted his fingers around the hair at her nape, then gently tugged, encouraging her to tip her head back to look at him. Her lingering embarrassment faded as she watched him take a sip from the jar, then slowly lower his mouth to hers.

Without hesitation, she opened to him as his lips pressed against hers. His tongue made a slow, languorous sweep of the inside of her mouth, allowing the liquid to spill into her mouth and seep down her throat. She prepared herself for the hellfire and damnation, but the small amount didn't burn at all. This time, she actually tasted sweet apples rather than gasoline—or what she suspected gasoline would taste like—and she could understand a little better why they drank the stuff.

Wade, however, was far more potent and overwhelming than the moonshine, and as he continued to deepen the kiss and sweep his tongue across hers in a slow, leisurely fashion, she melted from the inside out. The moonshine created a flash fire, capable of destroying her. This was a slow, simmering heat that drew her in and left her desperate for more. She sighed and relaxed so deeply she would've slipped off his lap if he hadn't been holding on to her.

His kiss had been filled with more passion and care than any of her previous lovers had shown during the pinnacle of sex, and she was hooked.

"Better?" he asked, his voice deeper and huskier than normal.

"Infinitely." She imagined her eyes were glassy orbs as she tried to open her weighted lids to focus on him. She rolled her head to the side, wondering if his friends were staring at the show she and Wade were putting on, but all she found was the roaring fire. "Where'd everyone go?"

"They left a few minutes ago. I think they were afraid you'd throw up, and they wanted to give you privacy. If it'd been me, they'd have had their phones out, taking video for YouTube. They must really like you."

Warmth and pleasure at having been so easily accepted by his friends filled her, but she'd had enough of them for one night. She wanted to be alone with Wade for a while, and she prayed this relaxed feeling stuck with her long enough to get home so she could make her move. She pressed her hand to the side of his face, holding his gaze steady, and asked, "Will you take me home now?"

# Chapter Nine

*O*n the ride home, Callie grew more and more lethargic as the moonshine's dizzying buzz dissolved into a warm hum in her chest and belly, and her arms and legs turned into lead weights. Jen's car was still in the parking lot, and Callie was sure the throaty rumble of Wade's truck sounded like an alarm in Tiffany's condo, but she didn't care if they watched or not. It would require more energy than she could produce to climb down from the seat, and she didn't even pretend to want to get down by herself as Wade opened the door. She twisted in her seat, rested her hands his shoulders, and enjoyed being in his arms for the second it took her feet to hit the ground.

As they crossed the parking lot and began climbing the steps, her fatigue was crushed by a wave of sexual desire and nervous anticipation. By the time she reached the door, she was dizzy with excitement and her hand trembled so badly she couldn't get her key into the lock.

After several failed attempts, Wade took matters into his own hands. Literally. He stepped up behind her, pressed his front to her back, and wrapped his fingers over hers. The contact was so delicious she forgot all about the lock. Nothing mattered except leaning back against him to gain more contact, and a deep moan escaped her throat as Wade's heat and essence wrapped around her like a set of strong, steady arms. She still felt some lingering effects of the moonshine, but the alcohol was nothing compared to the intoxicating effects of Wade's body pressed against hers.

She must've swayed in place—*hallelujah*—because he wrapped his free arm around her waist and drew her solidly against him while twisting their wrists to victoriously open the door. She didn't want to break contact, but there was only so much they could do standing on the stoop—especially with nosey neighbors—and oh-so-many more possibilities awaiting them on the other side of the soon-to-be-closed-again door. She whimpered with regret as she took the necessary step forward into her condo, and he followed her lead and released her.

After dropping her purse and keys onto the coffee table, she was surprised to turn and find him still standing in the doorway, forearm braced on the casing above his head, forehead resting on his arm.

"Why are you standing there? Come in."

His breath was slow and deliberate, his smile sad. "I don't think that's a good idea."

"What? Why?" She had zero practice seducing men, but she'd watched Jen approximately two million times over the years. Hopefully, she'd picked up a little something along the way. Putting an extra swing in her step, she worked to infuse a sexy vibe to her walk and crossed the foyer to stop in front of him. "It's an excellent idea."

"You're awfully cute when you're drunk."

"I'm not drunk. I'm happy."

When his grin widened, she dropped back, thought over her options, then tried a more direct approach. Stepping close enough to run her hands down the middle of his chest, she said, "Seriously, I'm not drunk. The buzz faded on the way home and now I'm just relaxed. At least, I was."

Her gaze settled on the erratic pulse pounding in his neck, then slid down the center of his chest, over his stomach, to his belt. "Now that we're alone, I'm not quite as relaxed as I am nervous and excited." She tried to make eye contact but chickened out and ended up staring at his full and tempting lips. "Very excited."

He squeezed his eyes shut and pinched the bridge of his nose, then muttered something about being hot-blooded and coldhearted, but definitely not Superman, along with a few other garbled expletives. After a moment, he pressed his lips together, opened his eyes, and stepped into the foyer.

Her heart jumped and the nervous jitters spiked as the door shut behind him with a solid *clunk*. She wasn't sure what to do with him now that she had him inside, but before he changed his mind and reversed course, she grabbed his hand and dragged him into the living room.

It had been a long time since she'd been to the bathroom, and while she feared him running away while she took care of business, nature was screaming too loudly to ignore. "I have to run to the bathroom." She stepped in front of him and studied his face, trying to get a clear read on his thoughts. "You won't escape while I'm gone, will you?"

His eyebrow rose. "Escape?"

She nodded and gripped the front panels of his flannel shirt. "You don't seem entirely convinced this is where you want to be, so I'm afraid I'll come out and find you gone."

His expression softened and he worked his head around in a circle. "I don't think being here is a good idea, but there's nowhere else I *want* to be."

Gee, talk about a pile of mixed signals. It was like a back-handed compliment one was never sure how to take. They were both consenting adults, and even a novice like her detected the four-alarm fire raging between them. So why the reservations?

Rather than spend more time trying to figure out the problem, she was going to focus on the solution. He'd at least agreed to stick around, so she'd just have to convince him he was in the right place… as soon as she finished in the restroom.

"I have an assortment of drinks in the fridge. Help yourself to anything that looks good, and I'll be right back."

She hadn't been to church since she was a little girl, but she found herself saying a prayer of thanks when she returned to find him seated on the couch, arms stretched out along the back, legs kicked out in front and crossed at the ankles.

He was the sexiest man she'd ever encountered, the potency made even stronger and more dangerous by his easy confidence. He was totally at ease, while she felt like a cat that had been rolling around in a field of catnip all day. Her eyes and thoughts bounced here, there, and everywhere, trying to figure out the best place to sit.

The chairs across from the sofa were too far away and would knock out any chance for more of those spontaneous kisses or snuggling and cuddling. If she sat next to him, he'd have to turn sideways to look at her and that would quickly get awkward and uncomfortable for both of them. She bit down on the inside of her lip as her gaze settled on his lap. She'd grown comfortable sitting on him at the campground, so why not go with what worked?

She planted a knee on one side of him, straddled his legs, then settled onto his thighs.

His eyes danced with humor as he tilted his head to the side and grinned at her. "Comfy?"

"No. Not yet." She scooted around, trying to find a soft spot on a man who was all hard muscle. "I'm trying to find a soft spot."

The muscles in his jaw tightened as he clenched his teeth and gripped her waist, stilling her. "Sweetheart, there isn't going to be a soft spot if you keep wiggling your ass around like that."

She froze and a gust of heat swept through her. Without conscious thought, her gaze dropped to his lap, and she sucked in a breath as the proof of his words appeared beneath the thick denim fly of his jeans.

His raw masculinity and deeply primal nature melted her ultra-conservative shell, allowing her to be more aggressive than ever before. Her hands burned with the need to touch him, so she started with something relatively safe and familiar—his chest. As she made broad sweeping strokes across the soft cotton fabric of his T-shirt, the heat radiating from him seeped into her palms and turned to lava in her veins.

Even though he wasn't making any moves of his own, she quickly realized that didn't mean he was less involved. The rapid rise and fall of his chest and the way his nostrils occasionally flared showed his struggle to control his breathing and possibly even himself.

His reaction bolstered her confidence, so she continued her exploration, going up to his collarbone, then down to his pecs. When her fingers swept across the rigid peak of his nipple, he sucked in a sharp breath and stilled completely.

Unsure if the reaction was positive or negative, she ran a quick body scan, searching for clues. The fluttering heartbeat in his neck along with the rapid-fire rise and fall of his chest seemed encouraging, so she lifted her gaze to his face. The hot, searing hunger flowing from his eyes scorched her and stole her breath.

That look, right there, filled with blazing intensity and desire for her, was something she'd longed to see all of her adult life but had begun to fear she'd never experience.

The carnal longing pouring from him fed her hunger and drove her to continue her exploration. She'd never taken the time—or been given the opportunity—to study a man like this before, and she was fascinated by the breadth of his chest and the sharp ridges and hard lines of his shoulders. There wasn't enough space between them to allow her to move lower, so she braced a hand against him and slid back to the edge of his knees.

Her fingers bumped across the ridges of his ribs and abs until she ran into the cool edge of his belt buckle. His relaxed-fit jeans were no longer relaxed, and adrenaline zinged through her at seeing how strongly she affected him.

She wanted to continue, but this was well beyond her comfort zone, and fear and insecurity crept in, stealing her confidence and slowing her progress. She paused with her hand on his belt buckle and flipped her gaze to his, silently seeking permission to continue.

Her stomach lurched and nausea rose to her throat as she studied his expression. He had his head cocked to the side, looking at her through hooded lashes, but something in his expression told her to be prepared.

Rejection loomed on the horizon.

As Callie rested her hand on his belt and flipped her doe eyes up to meet his, Wade thought his head would split in half from the tug-of-war going on in his mind. He was so turned on the slightest touch would set him off. Which, of course, meant his body was eager to proceed and urged him to undo the buckle himself to save time.

But the tiny part of his mind that remained in control was screaming to stop the insanity. He'd been over this a hundred times. He knew all the reasons this was a bad idea, and none of them had changed since he walked through her door.

Yet as Callie ran her hands over him in careful, measured strokes, one by one, the reasons wilted and died a slow, meaningless death.

While yellow caution lights flashed in his head and he tried to decide if he should hit the brakes and come to a screeching halt or stomp on the gas and go, she apparently decided it was better to ask forgiveness than permission. She suddenly gave a swift tug on the end of his leather belt and the clasp popped free of the latch.

"Be careful, baby." He sounded like he'd gargled with nails, further proof of how juiced he was. After several unsuccessful attempts at clearing it, he started again. "Things are going to get messy, and soon, if you keep going."

Rather than discouraging her, the warning fueled her determination. "I want to watch you…" She licked her lips and swallowed, then dipped her head and tried again. "I've imagined how you would look… I want to get messy."

Her innocence, while a little disconcerting for someone who was used to women as free and easy about sex as him, was also one hell of a turn-on. The combination of holy-shit-she's-too-good-for-me and I've-gotta-have-her-now thrashed around in his head like an out-of-control blender and left him confused and angry and sweating profusely.

He wanted her so badly he couldn't see straight, but his conscience forced him to make sure she wasn't wasted and acting under the influence. "Callie, are you sure about this? You're not still drunk, are you?"

She locked gazes with him, and the staggering desire mixed with something deeper and more emotional than pure lust should've cooled him off like a blast of cold water. But rather than pull away, he allowed himself to be drawn into the warm depths of her soul. For the first time in over a year, the warmth of a strong, personal connection seeped into his bones and chest and the edges of his ice-cold heart began to melt.

"I'm not drunk. I'm lucid and know exactly what I'm doing." She cut off the words and twisted her mouth to the side. "Okay, that's an exaggeration. I'm way out of my league with you and know very little about"—she hesitated and her eyes bounced around—"this stuff. But I'm fully cognizant of my actions." She dipped her gaze and quietly added, "Please don't stop me."

*Boom.* Battle over; war lost. He would probably chew himself a new asshole in the morning for having been so weak, but he couldn't stop. He didn't know how far she intended to take things tonight, but it didn't matter to him. His throttle was stuck wide open and he was along for the ride with no safety measures in place—except for the condoms he always carried in his wallet.

He closed his eyes and breathed deeply as she took his non-answer as a yes, finished unhooking his belt, and went to work on the button of his jeans. He was too far gone to stop, but with his hand over hers, he gave her a final warning. "Be absolutely certain, because when you undo that button and zipper, you're going to get more than you bargained for."

A slow smile spread across her face. "My, aren't you humble?"

He choked on a laugh and shook his head. "That's not what I mean. I go commando, so once you undo that button and zipper... it's all yours."

She looked up and blinked. "Commando?"

Again, her innocence should've doused the flames, but knowing very few men had been privileged enough to be with Callie had him ready to melt the fuck down. Heaven help him, he loved being one of the honored few and would do everything in his power to make sure she didn't regret her decision to allow him in. "I don't wear underwear."

Her mouth slipped open and her head fell forward as she snapped her gaze to his lap. She drew in a ragged breath and whispered, "Ever?"

His lips twitched with amusement as he shook his head, something she failed to see since her eyes weren't looking anywhere near his face.

"Nope. Never."

She gulped and slowly lifted her gaze to his. "So... all those times I've watched you walk around a job site, or seen you in the office... or when you helped me move furniture on Monday... you've been..." She swallowed again. "Nothing under your jeans?"

Well, well, well. That little reveal had his chest swelling with all kinds of happy. "You watch me walk around jobs?"

"Uh..." Pink tinged her neck and crawled up to her cheeks as she shifted her gaze to the cushion next to him. After a moment, her embarrassment faded and resolution took over. Recapturing his gaze, she kicked her chin up a notch and said, "Yeah, actually, I have."

She might be sheltered and innocent, but she was also brave and determined. He loved how once she made her mind up about something, she went for it, whether it was stealing his moonshine or seducing him.

Her sweet honesty was perfect.

Slowly, feeling every bump and dip of her rib cage, he slid his palms up her sides, over her shoulders, and around to the back of her neck. Drawing her to him, he leaned forward to meet her halfway and nipped at her lip. "Yes, when you watch me walk around at work, I'm naked under my jeans." He captured her lip again with his teeth, then soothed the sting with a slow slide of his tongue before angling his head to take her mouth in a deep, deep kiss. Pulling back for a breath, he added, "And the next time you see me, you won't have to imagine what's underneath. You'll have firsthand knowledge."

She stared like a deer frozen by headlights, dazed and unblinking. He was a bastard for setting her up like that, but he couldn't help himself. He knew every time he passed her in the office or saw her working on a job, she'd think about him in a way that was totally inappropriate for co-workers... just as he would her.

She blew out a breath and blinked a few times, as if coming back from a trance. "Why don't you wear them?"

He returned his arms to the back of the couch and slumped lower. He could lie to himself and pretend to be getting more comfortable, but the truth was he wanted to make himself as open as possible. Waiting and ready whenever she was.

"I lived in a tent for six months, remember? I didn't have a washer and a dryer, so wearing flip-flops—I didn't have to worry about socks—and going without underwear became a matter of convenience. Less laundry to deal with." He shrugged. "I got used to going without and didn't see a need to go buy some just because I was suddenly able to wash them."

Her eyes narrowed and she studied him sharply while chewing on the side of her fingernail. "My friends, especially Jen, can *never* know that."

This spunky, spirited side of her was cute as hell and spread his face wide with a big, fat smile. The pleasure he took from her possessiveness was dangerous as hell and another clear indicator of just how much trouble he was in. He should be tossing her off his lap and bolting for the door. Instead, he sank lower into the couch and said, "They won't hear it from me. Guaranteed."

She nodded, almost thoughtlessly, and her eyes began a slow, leisurely stroll down his body. As the silence grew, he thought she might be having a moment of clarity and common sense would finally stop the madness, but then she grabbed hold of his T-shirt and tugged it free of his jeans.

He sucked in a breath as her palms flattened against his stomach and then slid upward, dragging the hem of his shirt to his chest. Watching her tongue flick across her lip was torture. Her sweet mouth, slowly easing closer until her lips were pressed against his chest, was like being hit with a defibrillator, and he nearly jumped off the couch at the contact.

He dropped his head back and groaned with pleasure and in defeat as she licked and kissed a slow, burning path down the center of his chest to the top of his jeans.

When her mouth couldn't go any farther because of his pants, she eased back and set to work on the zipper. Her fingers shook like an alcoholic's in the depths of withdrawals, which should've made him nervous as hell, but her concentration was so intense as she lowered the clasp and slowly worked the teeth apart that he didn't have any concerns. He was more worried about her gnawing her lip off than taking a hunk out of him.

He curved his stomach inward to make extra room for her to finish her task, then hissed when her tiny hand wrapped around him and tightened. Christ, if she exhaled sharply enough to send a gust of hot breath over him, he'd explode.

"Oh, wow." Awe filled her voice and eyes and stoked his fire even more. "I want these down more."

He damned near whimpered when she let go of him to use both hands to tug at the fabric of his jeans.

"All the way. I want them gone." Her words spilled out in an excited rush as she shifted her weight onto one knee and gave him room to lift his hips to slide off his pants. When he didn't move fast enough, because he was still trying to get enough blood flow circulating to his brain, arms, and legs, her eyes turned dark with hunger and she said, "I *need* to see all of you. I need to *touch* all of you."

He was ninety percent sure she wasn't a virgin, but he was also ninety-*nine* percent sure she wasn't normally the aggressor. Her willingness to put herself out there, when it went against everything in her nature, sent another massive heat wave to his chest and heightened his alarm.

He liked Callie. He wasn't just attracted to her physically; he liked her as a person. She was fun and thoughtful, and—oh hell, he'd admit it—she was sweet.

Which made him all kinds of wrong for her.

But with her big brown eyes pleading her case and her hand poised, ready to grip him again, he couldn't tell her no. He was just a man and, apparently, not a very strong-willed one. He didn't see any way possible, but he found himself holding out hope there might, just maybe, be a chance this could actually go somewhere for them.

With a silent prayer he wasn't making a huge mistake, which could easily end up being the second biggest mistake of his life, he lifted his hips and slid his jeans down to his thighs, fully aware of not just exposing his cock and balls, but his soul as well.

Her bright, beautiful smile eased the cold sweats that had begun to build with the realization this wasn't just sex for him any more than it was for her. This was different than every other relationship—if they could be called that—that he'd experienced over the past year. This was a body *and* mind experience. And it was terrifying.

"Thank you."

He half laughed, half choked as she resettled onto his knees. "I'm the one who should be giving thanks."

Capturing the silky strand of hair that had fallen over her face, he re-tucked it behind her ear, then cupped her face in his palms. Tilting his head to the side, he notched his chin in a come-here motion and said, "Kiss me, Callie. Kiss me like you mean it."

# Chapter Ten

*K*iss me like you mean it.

Wade's tilted head along with the pressure he applied to her cheeks as he tried to draw her close made his intention clear. However, rather than closing the gap between them and granting his wish, Callie's gaze slid from his full, tempting lips to his thick erection.

*Kiss me like you mean it.*

For the first time in her life, she wanted to kiss a man... there... and she meant it with every fiber of her being.

In all of her previous relationships, she'd maintained a strict no-oral-sex policy—give or take—but as she stared at Wade, her body and brain forgot the usual rules of engagement. Water pooled in her mouth, her breasts grew heavy, and her sex ached, making it impossible to sit still without squirming and fidgeting.

She wanted to experience him in every way—hands, mouth, and body, locked together as close as two humans could get. She wanted more from him than she'd ever cared about receiving from her previous partners, and the sensations rocketing through her body were as foreign as the strange glow lighting up her heart.

This was more than a spark of attraction. This all-consuming need surpassed her wildest dreams of what true passion would be like, and for the first time in her life, reality surpassed her fantasies. She was torn between taking the time to explore every inch of his incredible body and ripping off the rest of his clothes, along with hers, and letting the beast in both of them take over.

"I'm still waiting." His thick, husky voice was strained, and one of his hands slid around to the back of her neck, then tightened and relaxed. He seemed to be struggling with patience, rather than simply taking what he wanted, and she was torn between her old patterns and going through with her strong desire to try something new.

While sorting through the traps in her mind, she wrapped her hand around him and enjoyed the low, guttural moan that accompanied the forward roll of his hips as his patience gave way. He sifted his fingers through her hair, then wrapped it around his fist to hold her in place as his mouth crushed hers. His tongue was hot and demanding in a wild, plundering dance, while his free hand slid up her side and cupped her breast.

Desperate to take the edge off the raging need building within her, she scooted forward on his lap and rocked the center of her sex against her hand and his erection. God, she wanted so much more that would lead to total release, but she stopped herself before she humped him like an animal in heat, then broke the kiss and gasped for air.

"Not so fast." She tried to sound convincing as the words tumbled from her mouth, but she failed miserably. "I have a new favorite toy"— this truth was spoken with conviction—"and I want to play first."

His jaw clenched and his gaze practically burned a hole through her, but he released her hair from his tight grip and relaxed into the couch cushions, relinquishing control and giving her room to do as she pleased.

In a slow, measured stroke, she worked her hand up to the ruddy tip, where she gathered the glistening drops in her palm before sliding down the length of him again. She'd touched a man before, but she'd never had a raw, burning need to watch his face change as he neared climax or hear his breath turn choppy and ragged as she pleasured him.

She studied his reactions and paid particular attention to the things that made his chest rise and fall more rapidly and his jaw tighten as his teeth ground against each other. The surge of power that came from controlling his pleasure surprised her, and the adrenaline pumping through her system made her lightheaded and delirious with anticipation. She wanted his head thrown back, his face strained by the force of the orgasm gripping him... and then she wanted to hold him as he relaxed in the aftermath.

When she squeezed and circled over the tip again, his entire body tensed and he clamped his hand over hers. "Stop. Now." He gasped for a breath and added, "I can't take any more."

"That means you're right where I want you."

His breathing grew harsher and his eyes fluttered shut a few times as he struggled to keep them locked on her. "That would be the point of no return, baby." He spoke through clenched teeth, like it required every ounce of strength he possessed to hold on to his control and not let go.

But she was a woman on a mission, and she refused to be denied.

"Let me make you come." She used her eyes to plead her case. "Please. Give me this."

Without waiting for a response or for him to move his hand, she resumed her pace, paying special attention to his most sensitive spots. Having his hand over hers so they stroked him together was the most erotic moment of her life—a snapshot for her mental memory book that would never be forgotten. When she continued to caress him, he squeezed his eyes shut and kicked his head back, causing the muscles in his neck to jump and strain.

The thrill of victory coursed through her as he released her hand, and she increased the speed of her stroke and the pressure of her grip.

His hands latched onto the sides of her waist and dug into her flesh as he drilled the back of his head into the sofa and pistoned his hips up and down in rapid-fire motion.

And then there was a brief second of nothingness—the calm before the storm.

He ground his teeth so hard she feared they'd crack and growled as jets of hot fluid landed on her hand and all over his stomach and chest.

He was even more magnificent than she'd imagined, and she couldn't break the magical spell wrapping her up, keeping her gaze locked on his face. "You're so incredibly beautiful." Her quiet words were filled with awe and wonder at the power of his virility, and in his current state, she doubted he even heard them.

Which was probably good, because a man like Wade wouldn't appreciate being called beautiful.

Wade felt like a twisted, knotted dishrag that had been wrung out and hung on a hook to dry. As Callie continued to stroke him, milking the last drops from him, he jerked at the overstimulation and blinked, trying to clear his vision and regain a few ounces of coherent thought.

Shit, the first order of business was prying his fingers off her waist where he'd probably left deep imprints in her perfect skin. He hoped like hell she wouldn't be sporting bruises tomorrow. Those would be difficult to explain to her friends.

When he thought he might be able to make his voice work and string together enough words to form a complete sentence, he said, "Hey, let me go clean up so I can return the favor."

She stiffened and her eyes turned from soft and dreamy to hard and angry. "I didn't do that because I was doing you a *favor*. It was something I wanted, and I don't expect payback."

He froze with his hand halfway to her face and tried to sort out why an innocent comment, something he'd probably said to… well, way too many women… hit Callie wrong.

He'd been nervous about coming inside for fear of things spiraling out of control—like they had—but she'd been so damned cute standing there with her lip stuck out and petulance pouring off her that his resolve had cracked. Then she turned into a sexy siren, luring him in with her bedroom eyes, and he couldn't tell her no.

He didn't have a clue where they were headed or what tomorrow or next week would bring, but he was positive of one thing: he wasn't finished with tonight. She'd had her chance to play, and now he wanted a turn.

"I didn't mean to upset you." He brushed a hair away from her face and ran his thumb over her red and swollen lip. "C'mere." He coaxed her closer with his own bedroom eyes and a slow, seductive smile. This time, his kiss was less about marking her and more about tempting her into wanting more.

He kept up the assault until the tension eased from her body and she melted against him. He still didn't understand why his comment upset her, but he obviously needed a different approach. What better way to start than by getting naked? "Do you mind if I take a shower to clean up?"

"Not at all." She jumped off his lap and reached out to help him up, then laughed and withdrew her hand. "I guess I better clean up too. C'mon, follow me. You can use the shower in my bathroom."

Callie's condo was sparsely decorated without any over-the-top amenities, except the master bath. He'd noticed it briefly when he'd been in her room earlier, but this was the first time he'd gotten a good, long look.

How in the hell did a woman who had to brown bag her lunch to save for a pair of shoes afford a place like this? The bathroom was huge, with a shower large enough to accommodate at least six people. Eight oiled brass showerheads jutted out from the dark tile walls, and it took him several minutes to figure out how to adjust the water flow to each head. "Shit, a guy needs a degree in engineering to operate this shower."

She laughed and turned on the single sink faucet. "I'd lived here about six months before I realized I could turn them on and off. I usually stick with the main one, but if I've had a hard day at work, I turn them all on and call it a massage."

The image of Callie standing in her shower, back arched, using her hands to sweep her hair off her face while water cascaded off her breasts and ass had him hardening again and even more determined to get her under the spray with him.

She seemed to enjoy his body and had admitted to watching him at work, so why not use what God gave him? He worked the flannel shirt off and tossed it to the side before slowly rolling his T-shirt up and over his head. While tossing it on top of the flannel shirt, he glanced at her from the corner of his eye.

Her bottom lip was snagged between her teeth and she worked it at the same frantic pace as she dried her hands. She seemed to be trying to keep her gaze diverted to give him privacy—which was funny considering what she just washed off her hands—but after a moment, she gave up the fight and openly stared.

If he were a peacock, his feathers would've been on full display. It was crazy how she could make him feel ten feet tall and bulletproof just by the way she looked at him or with a simple, whispered word.

He toed off his boots and slid them out of the way before bending over to remove his socks. He'd never survive as a male dancer, but he didn't have to be good enough for tips; he just needed to be enticing enough to capture Callie's attention and make her want a little more of what she'd already had. He hooked his thumbs into the waistband of his barely-hanging-onto-his-hips jeans and worked them over his growing erection, then down his thighs and calves and off his feet.

Allowing his eyes to fill with heat and all the desire he felt for Callie, he looked at her over his shoulder and stepped into the open shower. "I'd love to have you join me." The smoky door was more aesthetics than function, so he left it open to give her a full view as he stepped under the spray, then grabbed the bar of soap and worked it into a lather.

The sexy siren who invited him in had turned into a shy kitten, but she didn't leave the room. She kept a firm grip on her lip while her gaze captured every move he made. He ran a soapy hand over his shoulder blade, across his chest, and down to his stomach. Ensuring he kept her visually captive, he palmed his erection and stroked himself, slowly and deliberately, to remind her of the intimacy they'd just shared.

Her red, slick lip slipped free of her teeth as she parted her mouth, and she drew in a shuddering breath. He struggled to keep his heavy lids open and his gaze locked on hers as he used his free hand to cup his balls and continued to stroke himself, imagining her hands on him again. She shuffled her feet and played with the hem of his sweatshirt, but something kept her from stripping off the clothes and joining him.

And then it hit him. He was comfortable with his nudity, but Callie probably wasn't. As long as he watched her, she'd never get the courage to strip and join him. Reiterating his desire to have her join him, he said, "I need someone to wash my back," then let go of himself and turned to face the wall.

He pretended to lose himself to the relaxing spray pounding against his chest and sides, but as the soapsuds slid off his body and puddled at his feet, he concentrated on the sounds in the room. He listened as she moved around and tried to figure out if she would join him or leave him standing there alone.

The room went dark and he looked at the ceiling—like a dumbass who needed confirmation the lights had been cut off—but he didn't turn around. God knows he wanted to, but he forced himself to stare at the decorative mosaic strip circling the shower wall, counting first the brown and then the white tiles, even after the scent of vanilla reached his nose and the first flickers of candlelight bounced off the wall.

The sound of a sliding zipper slipped a few extra beats into his heart's normal rhythm, and the steam building around his head might have come from his hot and heavy breathing. The second zipper had him clamping down on his jaw while he pressed a palm against the shower wall, locking himself in place while praying she wasn't getting rid of her boots just to get more comfortable. The sound of rustling clothes cranked him a little tighter and the blessed sound of a third zipper, which had to be her jeans, had him palming himself again, and not solely for the purpose of keeping himself occupied so he wouldn't turn around and ruin his plan.

A moment later, the sound of splashing water filled the air as she stepped in behind him and her hands brushed his back from shoulder to shoulder. "You're so big."

The softly spoken words didn't have a sexual lilt to them, so rather than take them the way he wanted, he tried to hear them as she'd intended. He was taller than most men and he had good muscle mass to go with it. The high school football coach tried to convince him to play ball for the team, but Wade wasn't interested. He enjoyed hunting and fishing and hanging out with his friends, and he didn't want to be stuck at school every afternoon, practicing. He'd always considered his size a good thing, especially in his younger, rowdier days when fighting was fun and a way to pass the time when bored. But Callie's soft-spoken comment had him rethinking things.

He swiveled his neck to see her, but he didn't turn around. "Do I scare you, Callie?"

Her eyes played hopscotch, something he'd figured out she did when she didn't want to give a completely honest answer. As she gnawed on a non-existent hangnail and thought over her answer, he was hyper-aware they were standing in the shower with nothing but steam and a few water droplets between them, but he refused to let his eyes to dip lower than her face.

After a moment, she said, "You used to. When you gave me evil glares and snarled at me." She smiled shyly. "But not now, since I've gotten to know you."

Taking advantage of the built-in tile bench that ran along the far end of the shower, he sat down to put distance between them and also reduce his size. He hadn't planned on getting into this with her anytime soon—if ever—and certainly not when he had her butt naked, but he supposed they needed to address this at some point, so it might as well be here and now.

He let his head fall back against the wall and said, "I'm sorry for the way I treated you. As Kevin pointed out, I've been ass, and I am sorry. But"—he leaned forward and braced his forearms on his thighs—"my actions were in response to the way you treated me when we worked together last year on the Vanguard project."

Her head slumped forward and her gaze fell to the floor.

"It seems both of us might be different than the other originally thought. You're not at all the hard-ass bitch you came off as back then, so what's the story?"

Her shoulder and one foot angled toward the door, but before she could bolt, he leaned forward and grabbed her hand and pulled her down onto his lap. "Talk to me, baby. I want to get this behind us…" *So we can move forward,* was on the tip of his tongue, but he bit down and cut off the words.

She crossed her arms over her chest, shielding herself from him, and said, "You were hurting, and Kevin told me to keep you busy."

"What?" Only Kevin would come up with some fucked-up logic like, *He's hurting so treat him like shit and maybe he'll forget.* "That doesn't make sense to me."

She lifted her eyes a few times, but never quite made eye contact. "Apparently, you'd just gone through a bad breakup."

A bad breakup. He supposed that was one way of putting it. Having his heart ripped from his chest and stomped on while also being humiliated was a little more accurate, but… You say po-tay-to; I say po-tah-to.

"So you decided to kick me while I was down and out?"

She gasped and horror filled her eyes as she grasped his face between her palms. "God, no!" She shook her head while vehemently denying the accusation. Mumbling mostly to herself, she said, "I knew I should've handled things my way rather than Kevin's." To him, she said, "Kevin wanted me to keep you busy, working you non-stop so you didn't have time to think about anything. That's a direct quote. The approach didn't feel right to me, and several times I considered trying to talk to you, to ask you if you were all right and if there was anything I could do. But I didn't know you, and Kevin did, so I deferred to his orders." She shrugged. "I kept you hustling so you wouldn't have time to think." She smiled softly. "I know the problems were still there, waiting for you each night when you got off work. But you didn't have time to dwell on them on my watch."

He was completely flabbergasted. All this time he'd held a nasty grudge against Callie—which was easy since she reminded him so much of Miranda—and she'd only been following Kevin's orders, who was trying to help him by working him like a damned dog.

He laughed at the absurdity. "I can't decide if I should thank or throttle Kevin." He dropped his gaze to hers and flashed his teeth while lacing his smile with wicked intent. "But I know exactly what to do to you."

# Chapter Eleven

*A*s Wade's gaze swept over her body in an intimate caress, nervous excitement had Callie trembling, while dread settled like a lead weight in the pit of her stomach. She was cradled in his arms, sitting sideways across his lap, her middle section directly below his mouth. The deep-seated hunger filling his eyes as his tongue swept across his lower lip made his intentions clear. He didn't have any long-held beliefs about oral sex being dirty or nasty. And he wouldn't stop until his mouth claimed her.

Desperate for distance that would spare them both the awkward embarrassment of her persnickety, silly, stupid prudish attitude toward something that every other couple in the world probably enjoyed, she slid off his lap and bolted to the other end of the shower.

"Hey, where're you going?" He grabbed for her arm, but her skin was slick from the water raining over them and she slipped free of his grasp.

She crossed her arms, trying to create a physical and emotional barrier, and paced the small space. She had a man in her shower—not a first, but not an everyday occurrence, either—and she needed to get grip before he lost patience and decided she wasn't worth the time or effort.

"I'm sorry for scaring you again."

His quiet apology halted her, and she spun to face him. His knuckles were pressed into the tile bench on either side of his hips, his legs bent as he prepared to stand.

"No, wait." She threw her hand out to stop him. "You didn't scare me. I scared me."

Even in the dim, flickering light, she read his confusion. His eyebrows rose and he twisted his head so his ear was closer to her, like he needed a repeat.

God, this was embarrassing, but he deserved an explanation so he didn't continue to think he'd done something wrong. Motioning for him to scoot over, she sat next to him and stared at the water spraying over their heads, landing just beyond their feet. Trying to muster as much dignity as the circumstances would allow, she said, "You looked like you were going to gobble me up."

"So my big, bad wolf impression scared you."

When she turned to him, prepared to once again reassure him he'd done nothing wrong, he grinned and winked. "Take a deep breath, sweetheart, and tell me what's going on."

Even though this was the most awkward, humiliating discussion she'd ever had, his tender smile and compassionate eyes made her feel safe and secure enough to open up. "I… ummm… I don't do oral sex."

Ugh. Putting it out there was even more embarrassing than she'd expected, and she cut her gaze to the floor, wishing she could crawl into the drain and disappear with the water. From the corner of her eye, she saw his chest expand, then slowly relax as he exhaled.

His mouth twisted and he chewed on the inside of his cheek, then leaned forward and fiddled with the body spray nozzle off to his right. As if needing to keep himself busy or distracted, he moved it up and down his legs, across his lap, across his chest, then finally settled with the water landing on his feet.

Easing back against the wall, he said, "You don't *do* oral… as in you've *never* done it, or you have, but you don't like it?"

She wrapped her arms a little tighter around her waist and slapped at the water puddled around her feet. "It's always freaked me out because it seems so dirty. I've never given it a try. Giving or receiving." As he continued to chew on the inside of his cheek and went back to playing with the nozzle, she quietly added, "But you make me want to try new things. I don't want to be Callie the Prude anymore."

She risked another sidelong glance, and the heat of his searing gaze melted her to the core. Oh yeah, he also wanted to pull her out of her comfort zone, maybe even more than she wanted to be removed. Heat built around her neck and licked at her cheeks, and she knew if a man were ever going to get his mouth on her, it would be Wade.

"We're in the shower," he said in a slow, easygoing drawl. "The cleanest place on Earth."

She laughed and ducked her head. "True." She ran her toe through the puddle and bit down on her lip. "But what about the craziness in my head. How do I deal with that?"

He brushed her hair away from her face and licked the shell of her ear before nibbling on the lobe. "You let me worry about that part."

A fevered chill shot down her spine as his mouth slowly crawled from her ear to the side of her neck and down to her shoulder. "Will you trust me to take care of you?"

*Oh, God.* "Yes." She wasn't sure she'd spoken loud enough for him to hear so she bobbed her head a couple of times, then let it fall limply to the side, giving him uninhibited access to her neck and shoulder.

Her arms were still crossed, which prevented him from going farther than the top of her shoulder, and without conscious thought, she let her hands fall to the sides, opening herself to him completely.

Without taking his mouth off her, he snaked one arm around her waist and used the other to cup her breast as he slid his tongue over the sharp ridge of her shoulder, then left a trail of hot kisses down to her breast.

She gasped and drew in a sharp breath as he worked his mouth over and around her nipple, and she nearly came undone from the mastery of his tongue. After several moments, she was so relaxed and putty-like, she feared slip-sliding right off the bench and into a heap on the floor.

"Slide around here, baby, and put your feet on the seat." She cracked her eyes open and found him crouching next to the bench, encouraging her to lie back. "Do I need to lay down a towel so it's softer for you?"

"No, I'm fine." That was actually an understatement. How about freaking fantastic? Despite the nervousness trying to creep in, he had her so loose and relaxed she thought her skin and muscles might fall off her bones.

His grin was cocky, his eyes hot, and he was quite pleased with himself for turning her into a sacrificial virgin on his altar. She had the ridiculous urge to cross her wrists and hold them out to him, letting him know she was his for the taking—in whatever way he wanted.

Instead, feeling more wanton than she'd ever been in her life, she took a deep breath and exhaled as she raised her arms above her head and rested them on the bench. The position thrust her breasts upward, and based on his flaring nostrils and dilated pupils, he'd noticed. But her bent legs were still tightly clenched, and try as she might, she couldn't pry them apart.

After running a full body scan and taking particular notice of her locked legs, he readjusted his favorite showerhead to land on her calves, then stood and unhooked the removable showerhead from its attachment.

When Kevin remodeled the bathroom, he'd insisted on several additions: the built-in bench, removable showerheads at both ends, and two additional nozzles down low. Of course, Callie, wearing her suit of naiveté, hadn't understood why he'd been so adamant that he even brought Sam in as reinforcements. *Trust me, Callie, someday you'll be glad Kevin made these additions.*

The moment of truth had finally arrived, and she couldn't believe she'd been so clueless as to their importance. Thank God Kevin had the forethought to build a shower she could use for more than getting clean. Too bad she'd never be able to thank him for it.

Wade seemed twelve feet tall and five feet wide standing beside her. He was semi-erect and the heavy mass hanging between his legs had her licking her lips and water pooling in her mouth as she, again, considered tasting him. His pull was like that of a super magnet and her palms vibrated with the need to reach out and latch onto his thick legs covered in coarse, dirty-blond hair, using them as supports while she took him into her mouth.

As he continued to adjust the nozzle, getting it the way he wanted, she felt her upper body lifting, propelling her mouth closer to him. His chest rose and fell in a sharp rhythm, and right before her mouth made landfall, he twisted his hand and directed the spray at the center of her chest, driving her backward.

"No." His tone was sharp, but his eyes danced with laughter from having used the shower spray as a weapon against her. "It's my turn to play. You lie back and be patient."

The shock of his actions left her speechless, but his playfulness had her laughing and doing as he directed. He finally found a setting he was happy with and she sighed as he directed the steady, hypnotic pattern on her feet and calves, then slowly made his way up her legs and along her side.

She closed her eyes and tilted her head away so the spray didn't land on her face, and her sigh turned to a heavy moan as the pulsing spray massaged first one breast and then the other. He brought his hand closer, then moved it farther away, constantly changing the intensity and point of contact.

*Good... so freaking good.* She'd had no idea a shower could be so tantalizing. She would never set foot under the spray again and not think about Wade, or crave more of his attention.

"Is it safe to assume you have a tankless hot water heater?" His thick, rich voice dripped in her ear, and she lifted her heavy eyelids enough to see him kneeling next to her.

"Yeah. That's something else Kevin said I'd be glad he did." She moaned again when he hit a particularly sensitive spot on her thigh. "He was right."

Wade's chuckle reverberated deep in her chest. "I figured Kevin was responsible for this setup. Kinky bastard." He moved the spray across her stomach, over her thighs, and down to her calves and feet. "You've never taken advantage of all this shower has to offer, though, have you?"

Normally, she would've turned ten shades of red over her lack of sexual sophistication, but unlike Jen, Wade's tone didn't carry judgment or censure, nor did he seem disappointed by her lack of prowess. He not only accepted her as-is, but seemed to enjoy helping her explore her newly formed sexual curiosity. Smiling, she shook her head. "No, but thanks for the introduction. My showers will be a lot more interesting from now on."

His eyes narrowed and his nostrils flared. She didn't know his thoughts but hoped they ran along the lines of him wanting to continue being an active participant. After a moment of singeing her with his hot stare, he dipped his head to her breast and redirected the water to her lower abdomen.

He lavishly licked and laved her nipple, then clamped down with his teeth and tugged. The zing shot from her breast, down through her abdomen, and straight to her sex, nearly launching her off the bench. She'd never felt anything like the sensations coiling around her midsection, and when he repeated the move with her other nipple, she whimpered with greedy need.

He skimmed his free hand across her stomach, then slipped his fingers between her thighs and spread them apart, encouraging her to open for him. The water falling over her skin was effectively washing away her inhibitions, so she relaxed one knee against the shower wall and rolled the other to the side, resting it on the bench.

Not wanting to chance slipping back into her old ways and getting caught up on the voices in her head, she kept her eyes closed and lost herself in the sensations spiraling through her, the feel of his hand stroking the sensitive flesh of her inner thigh, and—she gasped—the spray of water stimulating her sex.

"Oh, God." It was too much yet not enough. The spray stung, in a good way, and she writhed on the bench, trying to get away while also trying to get it in just the right spot to send her soaring into space.

She'd never been so turned on in her life, and she blindly grasped for Wade, needing something to ground her. She gripped his shoulder and thrust her hips, too far gone to stop.

Except then it did.

The spray moved from her swollen, throbbing sex down to her feet, and she settled back down onto the tile beneath her. Taking a risk on breaking the spell, she opened her eyes and sought his gaze.

"Why'd you stop?"

His lopsided grin and smoky eyes hit her full force in the chest, quickening her breath and making it difficult to swallow. "Things are just getting good."

"Exactly." She hadn't meant to shriek, but she finally grasped the concept of complete and utter desperation. "So why'd you stop? I didn't do that to you."

He chuckled and leaned over to kiss her lower stomach while keeping his gaze locked onto hers. After a few soft kisses and measured strokes of his tongue along her hipbone, he said, "No, you didn't, and I appreciate that." His breath was hot and whisper soft against the sensitive skin of her lower abdomen. "But I'm not ready for this to be over yet… and neither are you. We're just taking a little break."

Her bottom lip jumped out in a pout. "How do you know I'm not ready? I seemed ready to me."

His eyes smiled, then grew hot and heavy as he dipped his head again, going a little lower on her hip this time. "You said you trusted me. Well… trust me. We haven't gotten to the best part yet."

She gulped and a spike of heat rolled through her. He was going to do it. He was going to put his mouth on her, and he would make her come.

And she was going to let him.

Her breathing accelerated and she wanted to tell him to get on with it before she changed her mind. But she also wanted to trust him to take her to heights she'd never dreamed of, so she bit her lip, relaxed as much as possible, and pressed her shoulders harder into the bench, forcing herself to stay put.

"Thank you, baby." His lips crawled from her stomach up to her breasts, where he kissed each nipple before moving on up to her mouth. With his lips against hers, he said, "I promise, you have nothing to worry about. All you need to do is close your eyes and let me make you feel good."

She swallowed the last thread of fear, closed her eyes as his mouth took hers, and drifted away in the kiss. She didn't look at him when he broke the kiss and began licking and nibbling his way back down her torso. Nor did she look when he moved the spray back to her clit and slipped his hand under her butt, positioning her so the water hit more directly.

Her heart raced with fear and excitement, and she kept her eyes squeezed tightly shut as his mouth replaced the shower. And when his tongue ran through the center of her sex and circled over her clit, she cried out and nearly fainted from the overwhelming sensations rushing through her system.

The only thing keeping her conscious was her determination to not pass out and miss a thing, because he'd been right—this was the best part.

The way he handled her, respecting her fear while also easing her into the situation, made the act more intimate than sex and not at all dirty. She felt herself opening and blossoming for him, and she arched her back and cried out again as his tongue pushed inside her.

Heavy panting became her natural breathing rhythm, and even though she believed she should be self-conscious and trying to somehow contain herself, she refused to revert to her old patterns. Instead of trying to crawl back into her old emotional shell, she gave herself to him completely and fell into lust's clutches.

His fingers sank into her butt cheeks, and she thrust her hips to meet his tongue. He hummed his approval, and the vibration skittered along her nerve endings and scrambled her brain. She thrashed and panted and... God, heard herself begging him to make her come. The spray hit her clit, his tongue raked her vaginal walls, her stomach tightened and coiled, and then she erupted.

He dropped the showerhead and wrapped his other hand over her hip, holding her in place as he continued to love her with his mouth and tongue, drawing the orgasm out until she couldn't take any more.

She gasped and scratched at the intricate scrollwork tattoo that stretched across his back, over his shoulder, and down his arm. "Please stop. No more. No more."

He tilted his head enough and looked at her, allowing her to see the satisfied smile lighting his features. "Just a little more."

"No. No, I can't take it." She swallowed and half laughed, half cried. "At least… not right now."

His grin glowed in the dimly lit shower, and he eased back on his haunches as he ran his hand up the center of her stomach, to gently cup her breast. After a soft, tender kiss that had her considering the possibility of a repeat performance, he drew back and said, "Let me get a towel and get you out of here."

# Chapter Twelve

Callie was as relaxed and limp as a half-cooked noodle, so Wade adjusted the spray to fall on and around her to keep her warm, then went in search of a towel. He didn't need to go far since she'd had the forethought to hang two on the heated towel bar next to the shower door. He used one to give himself a few quick swipes to knock off most of the water, then wrapped it around his waist, killed the water, and carried the second in to Callie.

Normally at this point in the game, he'd be trying to decide if he should get her settled into bed and make a quick exit or consider this halftime with an amazing second half ahead of them. But this wasn't a game. Callie wasn't one of his usual playmates who understood the rules of what to and *not* to expect. And when she rolled her head to the side and smiled dreamily, his heart brought him to a screeching halt. Apparently, the chilled chunk in his chest liked her and wanted to make sure he handled her with care so she didn't get hurt.

But dammit… what about him getting hurt?

After drying her off to the best of his ability, he scooped her up and carried her to the bedroom. "Thanks for trusting me to take care of you."

Her dimple winked at him as she gave him a quick smile, then wrapped her arms around his neck and rested her head on his shoulder. He would be happy standing here, just like this, with her in his arms for the rest of the night. But when she yawned for the second time, he scratched that plan in favor of something more comfortable for her.

He flipped back the pale-green cover and paisley-patterned top sheet, then gently laid her down. "Crawl under the covers so you stay warm and hand me your towel."

Her brow wrinkled with confusion. "Aren't you joining me?"

*God help me.*

She didn't play games or try to be coy, but her guilelessness was the most potent aphrodisiac he'd ever encountered. She was sweet seduction wrapped in a firecracker package, and she didn't even realize her power.

He used his thumb and middle finger to rub his eyes while the mental haranguing erupted. He'd known if he set foot inside her apartment and closed the door behind him, things would get out of hand. They hadn't gotten so carried away Callie would have regrets come morning—at least he didn't think she would since they hadn't gone any further than high school kids did in the back of a truck on Friday and Saturday night. But if he crawled into bed with her, he wouldn't get out again until he'd taken her half a dozen times in a dozen different ways—some of which she probably didn't even know were possible. If he had his way, they'd both be calling off work tomorrow, too sore and exhausted to report.

But that was a terrible idea for several reasons. He believed, in order for Callie to enjoy sex to the fullest, she needed to be emotionally engaged, and they hadn't reached that point yet. Also, in all fairness, she had a right to know the kind of man she was getting involved with.

He'd managed to gloss over his recent past fairly well, and he'd never had unprotected sex, but in the past year, he'd given Gene Simmons a run for his money in body count. Even though in most instances he hadn't bothered to learn details about the women—like names or phone numbers—he thought most were locals. And Myrtle Beach wasn't that big. He didn't want to take a chance on any skeletons falling out of his closets, especially when they might land on an unsuspecting Callie.

He couldn't think of anyone who would intentionally try to hurt him or someone involved with him, but the women of his past would probably believe Callie meant as much to him as them—nothing. Out of ignorance, things might be said to turn Callie into an innocent victim of his whorish past.

When he dropped his hand from his eyes to tell her he couldn't stay, he found her sitting on her bed, knees drawn to her chest, the blanket tucked securely under her chin, the towel on top of the covers at the foot of the bed.

*Shit on a stick.* He couldn't walk away and leave her with this confusion and uncertainty wrapped around her like a sticky, inescapable spider web. He wouldn't allow his problems to become her insecurities, so he said, "I'll be right back," then snatched her towel from the foot of the bed and hustled to the relative safety of her bathroom.

Curling up with her while they were both naked was an absolute no-go. He scooped his jeans off the floor, crammed his feet into the legs, and carefully drew up the zipper, making sure not to damage anything in the process.

Callie hadn't moved a muscle and didn't even appear to be breathing when he returned to the bedroom. "Which side do you normally sleep on?"

The question confused her even more, but after a moment, she patted the bed next to her hip and said, "This side." She giggled and tucked her hair behind her ear. "At least I start out on this side. I normally end up all over the place."

He walked around the end of the bed and mentally prepared himself for the physical onslaught of crawling between the warm covers with a soft Callie. "Duly noted. Thanks for the warning."

"Wh—what are you doing? I thought you were leaving me."

He scooted to the center of the bed and shifted her around so she was tucked up next to his side. "I want to snuggle, but"—he brushed a piece of hair away from the corner of her mouth and outlined her bottom lip with his finger—"I can't lie in bed with you and not take things too far."

She scraped her teeth over her bottom lip, like he'd tickled her, then asked, "What would be too far?"

"You pinned to the mattress, me on top of you, buried balls deep." Her mouth parted and she drew in a long, shuddering breath as a deep flush reddened her face, proving he'd made the right decision to not push things any further. "You're a good girl, Callie. You don't know what you're getting into with me."

"Tell me, then, so I can make my own decision about whether or not to continue, rather than you deciding for me."

The way she shrank back and chewed her lip, like she feared an explosion, might stem from her previous fear of him, but he didn't think so. She wasn't used to speaking her mind in such a forthright way, and pride at her willingness to stand up to him punched at his chest.

It also gave him one hell of a hard-on.

When he continued to admire her but didn't answer, she grabbed his upper arm just below the edge of his tattoo and shook him. "I've shared my ugly past with you, but other than how you ended up in Myrtle Beach, you've told me nothing."

He sighed. "Your ugly past isn't your doing. Your dad did some lousy things and you got caught in the fallout, but you didn't make the bad choices."

Through the filtered light from the bathroom, he could tell the sleepy, starry-eyed expression she wore in the shower had been replaced with sharp, focused determination. She wasn't letting the subject drop until she'd gathered more intel.

He sighed and settled in, trying to get more comfortable. "Thanks to Kevin's cockamamie plan, you know I went through an ugly breakup. Did he give you the gruesome details?"

Her eyes softened and her lips turned down. "No. He just told me to work you so you didn't have time to think. But you had the look of someone who'd recently experienced a devastating loss."

He'd rather suffer through another apple pie moonshine hangover than discuss his past, but he'd already decided if he was going to move forward with her—despite the risks involved and all the people it might piss off—she had a right to know.

He rolled onto his back and slung his arm over his eyes, hiding his lingering hurt and humiliation. "A week before our wedding, I started noticing things about my fiancé that didn't add up. She quit answering my calls and texts. It would take her hours to call me back, even when I knew she wasn't supposed to be in any appointments or meetings. Sometimes she'd tell me she was going one place, but when I talked to her, she'd say she was somewhere else."

His chest tightened and sweat broke out on the back of his neck. Christ, he didn't want Callie to know what a fool he'd been, but she was right. She'd shared her story with him, and she had the right to hear his.

"I'd tried and tried to reach her one night, without any luck, and spent the whole night up worrying about her. When I finally got in touch with her the next morning, she told me she was fine and then broke off the engagement. I was completely blindsided and thought she'd just gotten cold feet and needed some reassurances everything would be okay. I drove to Riverside that night, and that's when I found out she'd been cheating on me for months."

Callie wrapped her arm over his waist and squeezed while shifting closer to him, like she instinctively knew how cold he'd gotten and she was trying to warm him. Still unwilling to look at her but grateful for her touch, he flexed the arm tucked under her and drew her as close as they could get without him crawling inside her.

"In addition to our disastrous first encounter, thanks to Kevin's infinite wisdom"—*gee, no bitterness there*—"I also avoided you because you reminded me of her. Every time I saw you, I was reminded of what an idiot I'd been."

Callie stiffened and sucked in a sharp breath. *Shit.* Now she probably thought he was using her as a surrogate for his long-lost ex. Cutting off the thought before it rolled downhill and gathered speed, he quickly added, "You *used* to remind me of her, but not anymore."

"In what ways am I like her?"

Lowering his arm, he dipped his head and cut his eyes to the side so he could look at her without directly facing her. Smiling for added reassurance, he said, "Now that I've gotten to know you, I hardly notice the resemblance anymore."

She licked her lips and swallowed roughly while holding his gaze steadfast. "In what way *did* I resemble her?"

He barked out a laugh. "You're like a damned pit bull with a bone, aren't you?"

She giggled but still didn't let go of her tasty morsel. "Is that one of the ways I resemble her?"

"Jesus." He sighed with exasperation. "Aside from the strong physical resemblance, you both come from money. It's like it's part of your DNA or something. It comes across in your mannerisms and the way you walk and carry yourself. It's something that's obvious to those of us who don't come from money. But she's a spoiled brat who had everything handed to her. She never had to work for anything, was never told no, and is a selfish, cold-hearted snake."

Callie gnawed on the corner of her lip, then pressed them together and rubbed them back and forth across each other. "If she's so awful, why would you marry her?"

A sharp, ugly laugh burst from his tight lungs. "Because I'm an idiot. She played me, and I took the bait. Big time. I met her one weekend while in Riverside with Kevin and Lizbeth—Kevin's ex, Miranda's sister. I fell hard and fast. Six hours after meeting her, I was in love, and a year later I was engaged. I was so wrapped up in my feelings, I didn't realize I was nothing more than a diversionary plaything... Her idea of slumming it for a while."

Callie rubbed her hand back and forth across his chest in a slow, soothing motion, and he couldn't resist closing his eyes and losing himself to the soft, rhythmic sweep of her delicate fingers over his skin.

"She had to care about you too, or she wouldn't have agreed to marry you." Callie's voice was soft and tender and a little desperate, like she wanted to find a reasonable explanation to spare him the hurt and humiliation.

He tightened his grip on her as another chunk fell off his glacial heart. "I used to tell myself that too, but I don't think that's the case. She got caught up in the *idea* of getting married, mostly being the center of attention as the blushing bride and the fun of planning a big fairytale wedding. If I hadn't figured out what was going on, I'm not sure what she would've done. Gone through with the wedding and then refused to move to Myrtle Beach? Or moved here, then traveled back and forth to Riverside to see the other guy?"

He shrugged. The answers didn't matter, but it had taken him months to stop the unnecessary madness of the continual "what-ifs" running through his mind. "It pisses me off that I didn't see the cold, calculating, manipulative side of her sooner. Like from the beginning."

Callie stiffened and her hand stopped moving. Then she sighed and resumed the slow, steady sweeps. "My dad is the same way, but I didn't see it, either. It only took you a year." She laughed bitterly. "I was almost twenty-four before I saw the truth about my dad."

He wrapped his free arm over her and squeezed, pulling her into the tight embrace of his arms, trying to ward off her chill the way she had his. "I guess that's why they say 'love is blind.'"

Lost to their thoughts, they fell into a surprisingly comfortable silence. After a moment, she said, "Have you dated much since then?"

His quiet comfort turned choppy with tension and his stomach churned. She was so damned inquisitive he'd expected her line of questioning to end up here, but he still stiffened in response. "I haven't *dated* anyone since Miranda."

Her fingers stilled, and after a moment, when he didn't volunteer more information, she quietly said, "I pretty much already know, so you might as well go ahead and tell me."

His breath seized in his chest and he blinked hard a couple of times, trying to clear the thick, black cloud descending over their serenity. "What do you mean?"

"I've overheard conversations between Marianne and Sam. They don't spend all day talking about you, but I've picked up on things here and there. They care about you and are worried."

*What the fuck?* Should he be pissed that his sex life was a hot topic of conversation, or feel all warm and fuzzy because Sam and Marianne cared enough to worry?

And if Callie already knew…

*Is that why she's with me?*

She'd admitted to wanting to expand her boundaries and experience new things… Fuck, was she Miranda all over again?

Anger, hurt, and fresh humiliation burst to the surface with a thundering punch. He pushed her arm off him and scooted away like he was trying to escape a dangerous animal. "Is that why you're with me, Callie? You looking to do a little slumming with a bad boy who can show you a good time on the wrong side of the tracks before you settle down with a nice, respectable man?"

"What?" Callie gasped with shock at Wade's accusation, and she shot to a sitting position, not even caring as the sheet tumbled to her waist, leaving her exposed. "God, no. How can you think that?"

He lifted an eyebrow and continued to glare. "Are you not looking for someone to"—he dropped his gaze to her bare breasts—"expand your boundaries? Sounds like you'd heard enough from Sam and Marianne to know I could get the job done."

Anger gathered in the pit of her stomach and crawled up her throat. "That isn't fair. If anything, I found your…" the word *sordid* was on the tip of her tongue, but she refused to sink to his level and hurl insults just to be hurtful, "…recent affairs intimidating. So much so I feared you'd reject me because I'm not up to your usual standards." In an attempt to cover her exposure—and not just physically—she gathered the sheet in her fist and tucked it under her chin.

Confusion and doubt swirled with the anger clouding his hard brown eyes. His forehead creased and she could tell he wanted to believe her, but his past hurts wouldn't let him accept her explanation.

Appealing to his rational side, where logic ruled over emotion, she said, "I couldn't have seduced you in my living room or joined you in the shower if I was just out for a good time."

She fell back on the bed with a heavy *thwump*. "I don't even know how to go out with a guy just for a good time. That's why Jen's always calling me a prude."

His eyes narrowed with fresh anger, something she took as a positive sign. At least he cared enough to be offended on her behalf.

"I didn't set out to be this way. It just happened. Yes, I want to explore new things, but not just sexually and not because I see you as... a plaything." Her face curled with disgust and regret at saying the word.

She would never think of him that way, and knowing someone else had, caused a heavy ache to settle in her chest, making it difficult to breathe. "You make me want to be brave and adventurous. You bring out a side of me I didn't know existed." She smiled and dropped her gaze. "But I've enjoyed meeting her."

He closed his eyes and his jaw popped the way it did when he clenched his teeth with annoyance. After several tense moments, he scrubbed his hand over his face, as if washing away the remnants of the past few minutes—and maybe even the past year—then drew in a deep breath. He nodded once, which she hoped meant he believed her, then said, "Why would your supposed *friend* say something like that to you? And why do you remain friends with someone who treats you the way she does?"

Both questions were easy to explain, but the second was less uncomfortable, so she started there. "Jen comes across a bit harsh sometimes"—she paused and smiled at his raised eyebrows—"and entitled and selfish, but deep down she's a good person. She's been a good friend to me, especially over the past two years."

Shame over the upcoming confession caused Callie's head and shoulders to slump. "I'm glad you don't still see the resemblance between your ex and me, because that means I'm making progress." She turned her head away from him and studied the light streaming in through the partially open bathroom door. "I never cheated on a boyfriend. I never really had one to cheat on. But selfish and spoiled?" She sighed. "Yeah, that was me."

"There's no way you were like Miranda. And I find it hard to believe you were as bad as you think." His voice was soft but emphatic. "The person who offered me Dramamine and Gatorade when she needed it herself didn't appear out of nowhere. Your life might've been different than it is now, but when I look at you, I see an all-American girl, busting her ass to make her way in the world, doing the best she can, like the rest of us. Working hard to get the things she wants"—he winked—"like a sexy pair of boots that come up to here." Wicked intent filled his eyes as his gaze and finger slid across her leg, a little higher than the boots would go and dangerously close to where his mouth had been.

Guilt blew through her like a winter blizzard, freezing out the heat of his touch. She needed to tell him the truth, that she chose to work rather than live off her trust fund, but she couldn't force out the words. He saw her the way she wanted to be, as the person she'd fought hard to become, and she didn't want to lose that right now.

There would be time in the future, after they'd established a deeper connection and stronger bond, to tell him. Hopefully by then, he'd understand why she hadn't been completely honest and upfront with him about her financial situation. And he would continue to look at her with eyes filled with lust and affection, not cold, dark, and hardened like they'd been while questioning her motives for being with him.

Anxious for a quick redirect, she switched to the other, more humiliating question. "As far as me being a prude..." She shrugged helplessly. "I fell in love with my dad's protégé at fourteen. He was Prince Charming, and until two years ago, I was still waiting for him to ride in on a white horse and sweep me off my feet." Heat crawled up her neck and cheeks as she confessed her silly fantasy. "I've had a few boyfriends, but..." She sighed and played with the top edge of the sheet. "The sex was never all that, so I didn't spend much time or energy thinking about it. Or in relentless pursuit, like Jen."

*Until you came along.*

He rolled to the side and and took her down to the mattress. Hovering over her, he said, "Has anyone ever made love to you?"

With him lying on top of her, heat pouring off him and deep affection emanating from his eyes, images of Wade making love to her rushed her mind. Her heart raced and she gulped at the erotic images coming to mind. "I've had sex."

"I didn't ask if you've had sex. I asked if anyone has ever made love to you. Did they hold you close and drive into you so deeply you weren't sure where you ended and they began?"

Her breath and heart collided in her throat as she stared into his eyes and imagined the picture he painted. She had no words, but that was okay because the man who didn't normally say a lot wasn't finished.

"Have you ever stared into their eyes while they danced inside you, certain you could see straight into their soul... because they bared it to you while giving you everything they had?"

She'd never experienced anything close to what he described, and as she stared into the bottomless depths of his suede eyes, she realized she was closer to him in this moment than she'd ever been with any of her previous lovers. Her breathing was choppy and her heart sat in her throat, making it impossible to speak, so she shook her head in jerky movements, confirming what he already knew to be true.

"You're not a prude, baby. You're a tempting seductress who oozes sex appeal. You've never gotten close enough to anyone to really let go, and no one ever had a chance because your heart wasn't available." He wrapped his hand around the back of her head and rested his thumb on the pounding pulse in her neck. He swallowed hard and locked his gaze onto hers. In a soft voice filled with trepidation, he asked, "Is it available now?"

All signs of the Beast were gone as he stared into her eyes and held his breath, waiting for her answer. Staring into the eyes and soul of this deeply compassionate, tender man, she realized he could easily steal her heart if she wasn't careful.

But she didn't want to be careful anymore. She wanted Wade.

With tears pushing at her eyelids and her breath coming in ragged puffs, she nodded like a bobble-head and hoped he understood.

"Then let's take things slowly and see what happens. I'm concerned about being the man you ultimately need, but I'm willing to give it a go if you are. And when the time is right..."

The sentence faded away as he lowered his lips to hers, slipped his tongue into her mouth, and gave her a scorching preview of things to come.

# Chapter Thirteen

*D*etermined to act like a mature adult involved in a real adult relationship, Callie didn't lose her head over not seeing Wade for a full thirty-six hours, even though she desperately wanted to spend every waking moment wrapped up in his arms, exploring her newfound sexuality.

But real-life relationships included work and friends, so rather than spending all of his time cuddled with her, Wade spent Thursday in Anticue, preparing for the renovations on Gavin and Sunny's bed and breakfast, and she worked at The Chesapeake, measuring rooms and windows and ordering furniture and drapes. After work, he went to the campground, and she took advantage of a rare evening alone to finish the dressing table.

Even though they hadn't seen each other, they talked and texted several times, and every communication left her warm and bubbly with an infatuated schoolgirl smile plastered on her face. The conversations were more intimate than before their shower and discussion; the texts grew increasingly flirty and naughty.

The only surprise of the day came when Kevin dropped by The Chesapeake to tell her she'd be spending the next few weeks working in Anticue with Wade. The thought of working so closely with him excited her, especially given the hour-long drive to and from Anticue each day, but she was also a nervous wreck, wondering how Sunny would feel about working so closely with Callie.

Even though Callie had nothing to do with her father's resort development business and had done everything in her power to stop him from strong-arming Sunny into selling her property, Callie still couldn't look her in the eye without drowning in guilt and shame.

Her father's determination to move forward with his plans to develop a resort on Anticue had driven him to use *whatever means* necessary to gain control of Sunny's bar. Callie had tried to stop him but fell short in her efforts.

She'd called Gavin the second she suspected foul play. She'd snooped in her father's office to gather information, and she'd teamed up with Gavin in an underhanded transaction that gave him control of the fishing pier. The move stripped her father of the largest and most crucial piece of property necessary to follow through with the development.

But that transaction also pushed her father over the edge with a nothing-to-lose attitude that almost cost Gavin and Sunny their lives.

A shudder ripped through her with the memory of the horrifying events of that night, catching Wade's attention. "Why didn't you tell me you were cold?" Even though the heat was already so high sweat had formed on his forehead, he cranked the fan up another notch, sending a burst of heat through the cab of the truck. He glanced at her from the corner of his eye, then did a double take. "Are you okay? You're awfully pale."

"I'm fine." In an effort to keep Wade from melting, she cut off the heater fan completely and pulled the edges of her coat tighter around her waist. "I'm just tired and have a lot on my mind."

Truth was Wade could crank the heat up until the cab became a sweltering sauna and she'd still be cold. Her chill radiated from deep within and until she moved past her discomfort of working with Sunny, she'd likely stay chilled to the bone.

Another concern was Gavin catching onto her personal relationship with Wade.

A stranger would pick up on the simmering attraction between her and Wade, and since Gavin had known her since she was fourteen… yeah, there'd be no keeping secrets there. What would Gavin think about it? Did he like Wade? Even though Wade was a construction worker and didn't have a large trust fund, would Gavin think Wade was good enough for her?

*Do I care what Gavin thinks?*

The unexpected thought startled her, but the answer shocked her more. No, she didn't care if Gavin gave his blessing or not. She carried a complex mix of feelings for Gavin and he would always hold a special place in her heart, but she was finished letting other people influence her decisions. In the past, she might've stopped seeing Wade if her parents or friends didn't approve because she wasn't strong enough to stand up to the criticism and possible rejection that would accompany their disapproval. But not anymore.

Wade didn't have money and his background drastically differed from hers, but none of that mattered. He was kind and caring, always considerate, and a perfect gentleman. She liked how she felt when with him and who he inspired her to be even when not together. If the other people in her life didn't approve, tough cookies.

"I'm sorry you have so much on your mind." The way his brow furrowed and eyes crinkled at the corners, she had the feeling he was concerned her unease stemmed from their talk and the new direction their relationship had taken. Little did he know he was her "Wheaties" and her life had never been better than now. "Anything I can help with?"

As they took the exit and closed in on Anticue, she clasped his hand

and drew it up to her cheek. "You can hold my hand. My overactive imagination often conjures problems where none exist, but when I'm with you, I feel like I can conquer the world."

Wade sat at his desk, a stack of purchase orders in front of him, his stomach reminding him every few minutes they were well past their normal lunchtime. Since their arrival in Anticue, Callie, Sunny, and Gavin had been hard at work inside the Victorian, while he spent the majority of the day in his office, focused on paperwork and ordering materials. He normally wouldn't have put lunch off until so late, but he wanted to eat with Callie and didn't want to interrupt her until she'd finished hammering out details with Gavin and Sunny. He also hoped if they worked extra hard and skipped lunch, they might finish up early enough that he could have a little one-on-one time with Callie before meeting up with the guys.

Movement through the window caught his attention and gave his stomach a touch of hope that the trio had wrapped things up and lunch would be in their near future after all. He glanced outside and found Gavin and Sunny standing next to her piece-of-shit Honda that had to be on its ninth life.

Wade laughed and ran his hands over his face, unable to believe she still drove the same car she'd had… well… obviously forever. When he first met Sunny, she and Gavin hadn't been together all that long and Sunny was saving to send her younger brother to college. But now? They'd been married for well over a year and had a beautiful partnership, personally and professionally. Gavin had recently traded in his Lexus SUV for a pickup truck, but Sunny refused to upgrade. She said she'd drive it until the wheels fell off, and based on the looks of things, that day couldn't be too far off in the future.

As Gavin leaned over and spoke to Sunny's belly and then kissed it, Wade muttered to the papers on his desk, "Well, I'll be damned."

Now he understood why Sunny seemed so tired and rundown the past few days. Normally as effervescent as a glass of sparkling wine, she'd been dragging herself from room to room, and the day before, he found her propped up against a wall, sipping on a ginger ale.

He cut his gaze back to the car and shook his head. Damned if Callie would drive a rusted-out piece of shit while pregnant, and sure as shit she wouldn't strap his child into the back of something that would fall apart with a large enough pothole. He might not always be able to keep her in a new Mercedes, but she would drive something safe.

Wait...

*What?*

He'd barely started getting comfortable with the idea of trusting someone enough to get serious, and now he was thinking about kids?

The problem was he kept finding himself wandering down these mental pathways despite the roadblocks and barriers he threw up to prevent the mental musings. He never meant to take the conversation as far as he had the other night, but the part of him that had been dormant for so long decided to take over everything: his body, his mind, and his mouth.

He'd fallen for everything about her and couldn't help himself. The way she rambled when nervous made him smile, and he loved her sense of adventure and the wide-eyed wonder with which she approached new things. He admired her incredible inner strength and tenacity and respected her intense loyalty to her friends, even though he felt Jen was mostly undeserving. She had a huge heart and capacity for caring and was sexy as hell in her own unique, unassuming way.

*Shit.*

He shook off the distressing thoughts as Sunny drove away and Gavin headed back inside, then piled the purchase orders in a stack. From the sound of things, his stomach was concocting a mutiny and wouldn't be denied much longer, so he locked up the office and went in search of a lunch partner.

The house had a wide, expansive porch that wrapped around all four sides, and the round columns anchoring the porch at the corners were so large Wade couldn't get his arms around them.

He pushed open the heavy wooden and glass front door and stepped into the foyer, then listened for the sounds of footsteps or voices. It could take a long time to find someone in a house this size without vocal cues, and after a moment, he pinpointed Callie's and Gavin's voices as coming from the kitchen.

He turned to the left, cut through the front sitting room, and entered the dining room as Callie said, "Gavin, I need your opinion on something."

The sound of her voice tossed his stomach and warmed his heart. His body tensed and his ears perked up, going on high alert so he didn't miss a thing she said or did.

He skidded to a stop in the middle of the dining room and shook his head. It might be too early to think about marriage and baby carriages, but there was no denying he was deeply infatuated with everything about her.

A thud, as if Gavin dropped a heavy box, rattled the floor and echoed through the house. "Sure. What's up?"

Callie's slow response had Wade smiling as he imagined her chewing on her finger, debating the best way to approach Gavin about granite countertops or pine flooring. "For the past six months, Tiffany's been taking cooking classes."

*Tiffany?*

Wade cranked his head to the side and pulled at his ear, like he needed to clear things out because his hearing had gone wonky. Did Gavin know Tiffany?

"She's started talking about opening a catering business." The words spilled out in a rush, like she feared Gavin would interrupt her before she finished if she didn't talk at supersonic speed. "Everything she cooks is amazing and she'd be really good at it. She's got the contacts, especially if you add Jen's family's contacts and my mother's. Believe it or not, she has a great work ethic." She giggled. "I mean, who would've thought I'd be working my little fingers to the bone, right? Anyway, she loves cooking, and she's developed and mastered some unique, interesting dishes. She's excited about opening this new business, and I'd like to encourage her to go for it."

When she stopped to suck in a breath, Wade found himself grinning like a fool. He adored her nervous ramblings, and pride at her concern and desire to help her friend puffed up his chest.

However, he was also confused.

Why have this conversation with Gavin? How well did they know one another?

When he and Callie arrived, Gavin greeted Callie with more enthusiasm than he'd ever greeted other Mazze Builders' employees. Thank God he'd never cuddled Wade in a giant hug or nuzzled his face in the crook of his shoulder; Wade would hate to get fired for punching a client in the face. At the time, Wade assumed Gavin and Callie met while working on the fishing pier and restaurant renovations, but now he wondered if they had another connection.

"I think encouraging her is fantastic." Another thud as Gavin dropped another box, then water running in the sink. "I assume you have something other than verbal encouragement in mind, though."

Callie's indrawn breath was so deep Wade heard it from the dining room. "I want to invest in her business to show her how serious I am and that I believe she can be a huge success."

Wade shook his head once, then blinked a couple of times and shook it again. The woman who ate brownbag lunches wanted to invest in a friend's business? Just to give her a shot of confidence? Where would she get the money? Surely she didn't plan on taking out a second mortgage.

As the silence expanded in the kitchen, Wade eased closer to the door. He felt like an ass eavesdropping, but it was past time for him to join the conversation, and he sure as hell wasn't leaving until he'd gained some insight into this baffling conversation.

"Callie"—Gavin chuckled—"how much do you think she'll need to get started? Just a ball park?"

"I don't have any idea. I don't know if she has any money saved up or if her parents will help. She's not going to open a full restaurant, just a catering business, so she won't need as much start-up capital as she would for an entire restaurant." She paused and took another deep breath. "I haven't said anything to her yet because I wanted to talk to you first."

Wade ran his thumb and finger back and forth over his forehead, like massaging his brain might help him understand better.

"The first thing you need to do is have a long conversation with Tiffany where the two of you lay out everything. I'll help you put together a list of questions and topic points. If you both agree, then you need to put everything in writing before you proceed. I mean every-thing." His voice took on a hard, bitter edge. "You and I both know how quickly a business arrangement can turn deadly. There's a need to be wise with your investments, but really... You have a thirty million-dollar trust fund, so investing in Tiffany's business isn't a big deal. But

I'd hate to see you ruin a good friendship. If it were Jen, I'd tell you to go for it and not worry about fucking up a friendship. But Tiffany is different. You need to be careful."

Wade's boots were anchored to the floor, his limbs numb, lungs frozen, mind cramped, heart cracking and separating from his chest cavity with every passing second.

*Did Gavin just say Callie had a trust fund?*

*A thirty million-dollar trust fund?*

*As in a three with seven zeroes after it?*

*Thirty... million...*

*Thirty... fucking... million...*

No matter how many ways he tried to reframe it, he couldn't get a good reference point for just how much money that was. Or what having that much money even meant. Aside from having the clear understanding Callie sure as shit didn't need to save for a pair of boots, or anything for that matter.

A disembodied image of Miranda's head, split wide with laughter, danced around in his mind's eye. Callie *was* Miranda all over again, and since she obviously wasn't broke, he wondered what else she had lied about.

Was her father really in prison? She obviously hadn't been as desperate for a job as she made it sound, so had she made up that entire story?

As feeling slowly returned to his arms, he circled his hand over his chest, trying to ease the ache that expanded with each intake of air that failed to get past the hard lump in his throat.

How could he have been so stupid? Again.

But how could he have known? How would he have suspected anything was off when she ate ramen noodles—why on God's Earth would someone who didn't have to eat those—and aside from her luxurious shower, her apartment didn't have the appearance he would expect from someone sitting on thirty. Million. Dollars.

"I have something to share with you too." Gavin's voice was serious and subdued, and while Wade really wanted to turn tail and haul ass back to his trailer, he couldn't make his legs move. "Sunny's pregnant."

Since seeing Gavin and Sunny together moments before, this wasn't news to Wade, but apparently it was to Callie. This should've been the point where she gasped with excitement and said something along the lines of *Oh my God!* or *That's awesome!*

But all he heard was a whole lot of silence, followed by a quiet, "Oh," that sounded like it had been ripped from her chest.

And that's when the last remaining light bulb burst to life to spotlight the missing puzzle piece: Gavin was Prince Charming.

Wade remembered hearing an off-the-cuff comment about Gavin's boss trying to kill him, but Wade didn't realize he meant literally. He thought his boss had worked him too many hours or too many weekends or hadn't given him a decent vacation. But Callie said she'd been in love with her dad's protégé, the same man her dad tried to kill. That would explain Gavin's warm greeting, why Callie seemed so uncomfortable around Sunny, and why Callie went to Gavin for advice.

And why the news of Sunny's pregnancy left Callie speechless.

Shit, he needed to get out of here. The rage and hurt bubbling in his gut was going to have him exploding all over the place or ripping every fucking wall out of the house on his way to the door. He needed fresh air and perspective and some super glue. Because that was the only thing that could possibly save his fragile, freshly repaired heart from completely disintegrating.

# Chapter Fourteen

*C*allie stared at the tense set of Gavin's jaw and his wary eyes and tried to get a bead on his emotional mindset. He seemed so serious she wasn't sure if he was concerned about her reaction or if he still hadn't completely digested the news himself. "How do you feel about a baby?"

"Me?" he asked with a hearty laugh. "I'm thrilled. We weren't trying to get pregnant, but we weren't doing anything to prevent it either. There's so much going on right now we don't feel we're missing out on anything by not having children. But we're definitely okay with another project." Although he'd been reserved when first sharing his news, now he bubbled with barely contained excitement. "I wasn't sure Sunny would ever want kids after spending her entire life raising Robby, but she said having one of her own would be different, so..." He rocked back on his heels and grinned. "Sunny will finally be getting a new car and one of those *baby on board* window things."

His happiness was infectious and his joy overflowed into Callie. She wrapped her arms around his neck in a giant squeeze-the-breath-out-of-him hug and said, "You'll make a great dad."

"If"—he gasped for air—"I live that long."

She giggled and let go, then took a step back. "The baby will surely have blue eyes, but I wonder if it'll have Sunny's blond hair or your black." She clapped her hands together and bounced on her toes. "Is it a boy or a girl? When is she due?" She gasped with awareness. "That's why she looks so tired. What does Robby think? Oh my God! We need to turn one of the bedrooms into a nursery! You're going to go ahead and move in here, right?"

Gavin laughed and shook his head at her rapid-fire questions. "We don't know the sex yet and probably won't find out until it's born. Yes, that's why she's so tired. She's due the end of July." He rolled his eyes to the ceiling and thought for a minute. "What else did you ask me? Oh, yeah, Robby... he's excited. He said he's going to buy the kid all the noisiest toys he can find since Sunny always hid his noisemakers. And yes, we are moving in here, so yes, we'll need to make a nursery." He threw up a hand to cut her off before she started on a new tangent. "But not yet. There's plenty of time for that. First we need to finish the downstairs common areas and guest rooms. Then we'll start on private rooms."

He glanced at his watch. "Before anything else happens, though, we need to get lunch. Your boy's gotta be getting hungry."

Even though she expected him to pick up on her attraction to Wade, the comment still caught her by surprise and she reacted with a sharp intake of breath and bulging eyes before she could stop herself.

"Come on, Callie," Gavin said with a laugh. "It's nearly impossible not to get singed by the heat radiating off you two. Why didn't you tell me you're dating Wade?"

She tucked her hair behind her ear and straightened the fabric samples she'd brought for Sunny and Gavin to choose from. "I'm not really sure we are dating. I mean, I guess we are. We've never gone out to dinner and a movie or anything like that, but..." She stopped the rambling and took a deep breath. "We've had lunch and he took me to the state park the other night to hang out with his friends. There was a campfire and moonshine."

This time Gavin was the one who failed to hide his surprise.

"I know, right? He's so different than everyone else I've dated, but that's one of the things I like most. I especially like who I am when I'm with him." She chewed on her lip and studied the floor. "He's a good guy. I hope he sticks around for a while."

Gavin brushed her hair over her shoulder and drew her in close for a hug. "He's a fool if he doesn't. I wouldn't have said that a few years ago." He laughed when she drew back and glared. "What? You know it's true. You used to be a brat. But you've matured and grown into a damned fine woman, Callie Holden. I like Wade and agree he'd be good for you. But he's lucky to find you too."

It wasn't easy to hear how Gavin used to think about her, but he was right and only spoke the truth. She wasn't proud of the entitled brat she used to be, but she'd worked hard to be a better person, and hearing Gavin acknowledge the change caused tears to burn the backs of her eyes. "That means a lot. Thank you."

He winked and wrapped his arm around her shoulder. "Let's get some lunch?"

"What's open in the middle of January around here?"

Gavin scooped up his keys from the kitchen counter and flipped off the overhead lights. "I have chicken salad made up at the fishing pier restaurant. That okay?"

"Yum. I love your chicken salad."

"Everyone loves my chicken salad." His self-deprecating laugh indicated he was joking, but everyone *did* love his chicken salad. He'd even been featured in a well-known coastal magazine because of it.

"Hey," Callie called out to Wade as she pushed open the trailer door and stepped inside. "You ready for—"

Wade lifted his head from the paperwork and greeted her with a glare so dark and chilling she shivered. His gaze shifted beyond her to Gavin, who was standing in the doorway behind her. Other than the pulsing of his jaw, a clear indicator of how tightly he was clenching his teeth, his face held no expression.

"What's wrong?" Her voice was little more than a whisper and filled with dread. She had no idea what had happened, but something devastating had obviously occurred while she was working with Gavin and Sunny. Her mind immediately jumped to his friend and his upcoming dive. "Is Tyler okay?"

Wade jerked back, startled and confused. "What?"

She sank into the chair in front of Wade's desk and reached for his hand, but he snatched it out of reach. His gaze wasn't nearly as cold and dead as seconds before, but also didn't hold the warmth he normally looked at her with. "Something's obviously wrong. Did Tyler go diving today?"

He blinked a few times and rubbed his hand over his eyes as he tried to catch up with her train of thought. "Yes. No." He shook his head hard, then started again. "No, he didn't go diving today. I just talked to him and he's fine."

Behind her, Gavin cleared his throat and said, "I'll wait in the car."

When Gavin stepped out of the trailer and let the door slam shut behind him, Wade pushed back in his chair and a string of vehement curses poured from lips.

Callie's head spun with confusion, but talking wasn't garnering her any new information so she tried to reach him again, this time using the age-old trick of getting to a man through his stomach. "Are you ready for lunch?"

"Naw, I'm good." He picked up the hours-old sweet tea he'd gotten on the way to Anticue and took a long drink. He looked like he had more to say, but rather than speaking, he pushed his tongue over the front of his teeth and returned his attention to his desk.

"Are you sure? I'd love for you to come with us."

He didn't look up from his paperwork, but his hand stopped moving across the page long enough for him to say, "Would you now?"

His drawl dripped with sarcasm, and she flinched at the harsh response. "Yes, I would." She had no idea what had him so riled up, but she didn't appreciate being the target of his ill mood, and her own temper flared. "What's going on? Why are you acting like this?"

He cleared his throat and shook his head, glancing to the door again. "Go have lunch with Gavin." The cold, nasty grin cutting across his face reminded her of an evil villain in a horror movie. "Or should I say Prince Charming? I'm going to finish up this paperwork so we can get back to Myrtle Beach." His evil grin dissolved into sad resignation. "I have plans for tonight, and with any luck, I can get an early start."

What could've possibly happened between the time she and Wade arrived this morning—when he held her hand and asked if he could help her—and now, when he looked like he would happily chew off her head? In a last-ditch effort to appeal to the man she arrived with, she said, "Please talk to me. You're obviously angry with me about something, but I have no idea what. Until you tell me, I can't fix the problem."

A sharp bark of laughter escaped him. "Some things can't be fixed, and we've got nothing to talk about, princess."

The cold winter wind slashing across her cheeks couldn't compare to the deep freeze in Callie's chest as she stumbled to Gavin's truck. While he gave her and Wade privacy, he moved his vehicle so he had a direct view of the office and had obviously been keeping a close eye on things. With a defeated sigh, she opened the door and flopped into the passenger seat.

"Lunch for two today?"

Fighting off the tears still clinging to the backs of her eyes, she nodded and reached for her seatbelt. "Yeah, I guess so."

Gavin put the shifter into drive and circled around the driveway, then turned right onto the paved two-lane road that led to the end of the island where Sunny's bar, The Blackout Bar and Grill, and the Anticue Fishing Pier were. "He didn't tell you why he's so irritated?"

"Irritated?" She laughed incredulously. "He was practically foaming at the mouth."

Gavin grinned. "Okay, I'll give you the anger, but I didn't see any foam. And I'll bet you a hundred bucks he can get a lot angrier. And meaner."

"You know I don't have a hundred—" The rest of the words dried up in her throat and her eyes popped wide as understanding dawned. Twisting in her seat to face Gavin, she said, "That's it. He must've overhead us talking about Tiffany's catering business."

Gavin lifted a shoulder in a careless shrug. "I didn't hear him come in, but that doesn't mean he didn't. But why would that set him off?"

Callie's mind took off at a sprint, recreating the conversation while trying to remember if she heard any unusual sounds coming from other parts of the house. She hadn't heard the front door open, and he definitely hadn't come in through the side door leading into the kitchen, but him overhearing their conversation was the only thing that made sense.

She'd been so busy trying to figure out what was wrong it didn't even register with her until just now that he'd referred to Gavin as Prince Charming. Something had cued him in to that information, and as far as she knew, no one else had been at the house today. And the venom he spewed while calling her princess? Definitely not a term of endearment this time.

Since she hadn't answered Gavin's question, he asked in a more direct way as he turned into the fishing pier gravel parking lot. "Let me guess. He doesn't know about your trust fund?"

He *didn't*, but she was certain he knew now.

She shook her head, but realized Gavin hadn't noticed because he'd been focusing on parking the truck. "No." She climbed from the vehicle and followed him up the plank sidewalk and ramp that led to the second-story restaurant. "You, Jen, Tiffany, Jason, Kevin, and I assume Sunny are the only ones who know."

He slipped the lock free, pushed the door open, and threw on the interior lights. The building was cool and quiet on this January day, but during the summer, it was nearly impossible to cut through the crowd standing in line or seated at the tables.

She followed him down the center isle of tables and chairs and took a seat at the back counter, overlooking the open kitchen. Gavin said he wanted his customers to be able to see their food being prepared, but she personally believed he'd left the area open so he could visit with his customers rather than be enclosed in the kitchen by himself.

He opened the refrigerator and started gathering items: a bowl of chicken salad, mayonnaise, lettuce, bottles of water. After setting them on the counter, he grabbed plates, bread, and chips from the cabinet and a couple knives from the drawer. "Why haven't you told him?"

"It's complicated."

He laughed and tossed slices of bread onto a plate, then handed her the mayo and a knife. "We have time."

As they tag-teamed the sandwiches, she explained there had only been one good opportunity to tell Wade about her trust fund—really, how did one causally slide that into conversation—but she hadn't told him because she didn't want to risk changing the way he looked at her.

But by not telling him, she'd done exactly that.

"So what are you going to do?" Gavin asked while squishing his palm down on his sandwich to flatten it into a manageable thickness.

No longer hungry, she played with the crust of her bread and picked at a piece of chicken on the plate. "I don't know. He kind of had the impression I'm broke, so now he probably thinks I've lied to him about everything."

Gavin chewed on his sandwich and took a drink of water. "I'm afraid to ask, but how did he get the impression you were broke?"

She told him the story of taking her lunch to save money and how Wade saved her from a horrible fate by taking her to Five Guys. "Only today, he finds out I'm not broke—although I am, because I don't use any of that money."

Gavin finished off the last of his sandwich and started making another. "So explain to him why you choose to live off your salary rather than the trust fund or the money you got from selling me this fishing pier. And that you really do have to save up for anything you want to buy."

"What if he won't listen?"

Gavin swished water around in his mouth, then swallowed. "If he won't listen, he's not the guy for you."

She laughed without humor. "You make it sound so simple."

He shrugged. "It is that simple. If you can't talk to him and he won't listen, you don't have anything to build on in the first place."

One of the things she liked most about Wade was his willingness to listen. Not just hear the words, but to really listen to what she said. She got the feeling he didn't necessarily agree with her decision, but he'd listened and understood her reasoning for remaining friends with Jen and Tiffany, despite Jen's tendencies to be rude and overbearing. And when she explained her aversion to oral sex, he not only listened, but he figured out a way to get her comfortable with it and make it work.

Heat infused her face as she remembered his unique approach. Lord, had he ever made it work.

She didn't want to discuss finances, but she'd already discussed so many other difficult subjects with him, how could this be any worse? And Gavin was right. If Wade wasn't willing to listen, then what did they have to work with anyway?

Unwilling to waste one of Gavin's famous chicken salad sandwiches, and figuring it wouldn't hurt to take Wade a peace offering, she said, "Can I have a piece of foil or something to wrap this in to take to Wade?"

Gavin laughed and slid the bowl of chicken salad and the package of bread over to her. "Of course, but one sandwich won't do anything but piss him off. You better take two or three."

# Chapter Fifteen

*F*or the second time in as many years, Callie was forced to endure a heart-wrenching trip from Anticue back to Myrtle Beach. The first time had been the night she got the brilliant idea to ride to Anticue to spy on Gavin and Sunny.

She'd gotten more than she bargained for—albeit what she deserved—and had been forced to face the cold, hard truth: Gavin wasn't, nor would he ever be, hers. The hour-long drive home would've been horrendous if not for Jason's reassuring grip on her hand. Or Jen and Tiffany's nonstop verbal assault, trying to keep her distracted so the image of Sunny on her knees in front of Gavin didn't burn a hole in her head.

This time the piercing ache in her chest was similar, but there wasn't anyone holding her hand for comfort and the incessant talking filling the air wasn't directed at her. The man who normally used his words sparingly had managed to spend almost an hour on his cell phone, and the conversation didn't show any signs of letting up.

It was so out of character she'd considered snatching the phone from his hand to check if he really was talking to someone or if he was just pretending to be in conversation so he didn't have to talk to her. The only thing that made her believe he wasn't just chatting up empty air was the phone ringing just as they got in the truck—almost as if the call had been staged—and how animated he'd been since.

Based on his easy laugh and teasing tone, the mystery caller was a woman, and she had a way of bringing out the best in him. The tendrils of jealousy snaking through Callie had her crossing her arms and focusing all of her attention on the passing scenery in an attempt to keep the green-eyed monster from squeezing the life out of her.

Callie wanted to be angry that his caller knew him so well and had the ability to make him laugh, when all she'd managed to do was hurt him. But she couldn't be angry with anyone but herself for not having been honest with him when she'd had the chance. Her selfishness brought her to this place, and she had no one to blame but herself.

"All right, Mercy. I appreciate it. The boys will owe me for this." He laughed. "Which means I owe *you*. Again."

As he disconnected the call and tossed his phone onto the seat beside him, Callie's mouth opened and words she couldn't stop flew out. "What kind of name is Mercy?" Shoot, she hadn't meant to speak the thought out loud. She hadn't intended to say anything at all about the call, but the question was out there and all she could do was hold her breath and wait to see if he would acknowledge her.

Wade glanced at her from the corner of his eye and bit the inside of his lower lip, like he was trying hard not to smile. "A stage name."

Myrtle Beach was filled with interactive dinner theaters, most of which Callie had attended at one time or another, but the name seemed unusual, even as a stage name. "She's an actress?"

Wade tossed back his head and laughed. "Not exactly." His laughter faded into an affectionate smile. "Although she does put on one hell of a show."

Understanding hit with a thundering force, lodging Callie's breath in her throat and momentarily stopping her heart. Heat infused her face and neck, and all she managed to squeak out was, "Oh."

Callie had never felt more prudish than in this moment, and mortification at her lack of sexual experience and finesse had nausea rising through her chest and into her throat. He was used to hanging out with strippers, who were obviously comfortable with their sexuality, and she couldn't even give him oral sex without a shower.

Hell, she hadn't even gone that far. After confessing her stupid hang-up to him, he'd worked hard to make her comfortable and had given her pleasure, but he'd received nothing for his efforts.

The interior of the cab closed in on her from all sides, forcing her to crack the window and gasp as cold air whipped across her face. When her lungs no longer burned from lack of oxygen, she rested her clammy forehead against the cool glass and shut her eyes to block out the world for the remaining fifteen minutes it would take to get to the office. The sound of gravel crunching under their tires as they turned into the office parking lot was sweet music to her ears, and the truck had barely stopped when she opened the door and jumped from the cab.

She wanted to get in her car and drive straight home where she could cry into a pitcher of margaritas, but she needed to talk to Kevin about a few renovation details first. Without looking at Wade or waiting to see if he intended to go inside or directly to his truck, she grabbed her bags from the backseat, slammed the door, and headed for Mazze Builders' employee entrance.

Wade's footsteps pounded on the concrete sidewalk behind her, indicating he intended to go inside, but she didn't turn to look at him. When she entered the building and turned to the right, he turned left and went down the hallway toward the office he shared with the other foremen.

She slowed her pace as she neared Kevin's office and took a few deep breaths to collect herself. However, rather than finding Kevin at his desk, she found his wife, Sam. Kevin was a big man so his large oak desk was perfect for him. On the opposite end of the scale was Sam.

Short and petite, the desk dwarfed her, and a giggle pushed at the back of Callie's throat at the sight of Sam tucked behind the monster desk. She had a site plan spread out in front of her, a pen in her hand, and was jotting down notes on a yellow notepad. Callie checked behind the door to see if Kevin was at the drafting table in the back corner, but he was nowhere to be found.

"Hi, Sam. Is Kevin around?"

"No, he had some errands to run." After finishing a notation, Sam looked up from the site plan and frowned at Callie. "Are you okay?"

*Not even close to okay.*

Callie didn't intend to share today's events with anyone, not even her best friends, and definitely not with one of her bosses. Slapping a smile on her face, she said, "Yeah, I'm fine."

She was as bad at lying as she was at sex, and Sam didn't hesitate to call her out on it. "I've seen that kind of *fine* a few times in my own mirror." She rounded the desk and closed the office door. "What did Wade do?"

The question startled Callie and she flinched and took a step back before she could stop the reaction. "What?"

How did Sam know about their relationship? Did Kevin know too? Were office romances frowned upon? Not that it mattered anymore, but having everyone know she and Wade had been an item didn't settle well with her. Not because she was embarrassed of being with him, but she was ashamed of the way things ended. She didn't want anyone to think she'd intentionally set out to hurt Wade.

"How do you know about Wade?" The question was quiet and broken as she fought off a fresh wave of regret and tears.

"You've been in Anticue with him all day. Who else would have you this upset?"

"Oh!" Callie drew in a sharp breath, then released it on a nervous laugh as she shuffled her feet and stared at the floor. "Right. Yes. Anticue."

"I assumed he'd done something stupid on the job to upset you." Sam took her elbow and led her to the chair in front of the desk she shared with Kevin. "But now I'm wondering what else is going on."

She cocked an eyebrow as she waited for Callie to explain, and Callie imagined this was the same look Sam gave her daughter, Michy, when she was waiting for Michy to confess to some wrongdoing.

Heat infused her cheeks. "Apparently I'm not very good at being sneaky or secretive."

Sam laughed and crossed her arms and ankles, a gesture so much like Kevin, Callie marveled—not for the first time—at how much alike they were. "That's a good thing, Callie. Sneaky people usually aren't good people. Now what's going on?"

Callie swallowed and chewed on her lip and tried to decide if she should continue lying, even though she doubted she'd be any more successful at her next attempt than she'd been at the previous. Sam's expression was kind and open and held no judgment, so Callie took a deep breath and spilled her guts. She started with lunch, when she told Wade about saving up for a pair of boots, and ended with the conversation he'd overheard today.

Sam listened thoughtfully while Callie told her story, then smiled and nodded sympathetically. "You've probably already figured this out, but Wade can be a real hard ass if he thinks he's been double-crossed. But that's because if he trusts someone enough to give them a little piece of himself, then he trusts them completely."

She looked at Callie pointedly. "When it comes to loyalty and commitment, he's a lot like you. When you're working, you're fully committed to the job and your task. I've seen you with your friends, and given your current circumstances, it can't be easy to be around them all the time. Yet if one of them calls you for anything, you never hesitate to run to their aid. Wade's the same way. He's an all-or-nothing kind of guy, and given his strong reaction today, where you're concerned, I'd say he's already all in."

"But when he's crossed, I bet he's all out." Callie hated the pathetic whiny despair in her voice, but she couldn't keep it in check.

"I don't think it can be turned off that quickly or easily. He's also reasonable and fair, and while it might take some coaxing,"—Sam gave her a conspiratorial smile—"I'm sure he'll eventually listen to your explanation."

"How do I get that to happen? He's made it clear he's not interested in listening and his schedule seems to be pretty booked up through the weekend. Based on the phone conversation he maintained all the way back from Anticue, he has plans for tonight." She swallowed the uncomfortable lump in her throat at the unbidden images of Wade with a stripper. "Tomorrow he's going diving with his friends—"

"There ya go." Sam straightened and made the announcement like it made all the sense in the world.

Callie, however, didn't understand anything. "Where's what go?"

"If you go with him tomorrow, you'll have plenty of time to talk while his buddies are diving. You can't get a more captive audience than on a boat in the middle of the ocean."

Callie sucked in a breath and fought off the shudder threatening to rip through her spine. She'd never been on a boat in the ocean before, and she wasn't sure she could bring herself to do it, even for the opportunity to talk to Wade. Plus, she had another problem. "I don't know what time or where they're leaving from. And even if I just show up, there's no guarantee he'll let me get on the boat with them."

Sam smiled and shoved off the desk. "That's easy enough to take care of." She rounded the desk, stripped a sticky note off the top of the pad, scribbled a note, and stuck it to Kevin's computer. "When Kevin comes back, I'll have him take care of everything."

Fear jerked Callie from her slump. "I don't want to involve Kevin. I shouldn't have gotten you involved."

Sam waved off her concern and leaned back in her chair. "Don't worry, sweetie. We girls have to stick together when it comes to these hardheaded men. Either Wade or Kevin will call you with the details. You get ready to present your case."

Saturday night was usually the boys' night to howl at the Sunset Strip, but after his shitty day, Wade needed the stress relief tonight. He'd called Tyler to make sure the guys didn't mind moving their play date up a night—the general consensus was spending two nights at the gentleman's club wouldn't hurt anyone—and then he called Mercy.

Callie had connections at her kind of club; he had connections at his.

Mercy's timing in returning his call couldn't have been better. Or worse. It had saved him from conversation with Callie, but he'd felt awkward and uncomfortable talking to a fuck-buddy in front of her. Then he remembered why he needed Mercy in the first place. His guilt evaporated on the wind, and he couldn't have cared less if Callie overheard.

He pulled into a parking space in the Strip's side parking lot, put the truck in park, and scrubbed his hand over his face. Okay, saying he couldn't have cared less wasn't exactly true.

Conversations with Mercy were always humorous, as well as excep-tionally hot and tinged with innuendo. Normally, it became a game to see who could make the other squirm the most with provocative comments and implied promises. But with Callie riding shotgun, he'd tried his damnedest to keep the conversation as close to PG as possible, so yeah… Fuck him, he supposed he did care.

His stretch for the keys was interrupted by his ringing cell phone. His heart pitter-pattered out of rhythm and he held his breath, wondering if Callie was giving another go at talking. Gratitude warred with disappointment as Kevin's name popped up on caller ID. Wade was leery about talking to Kevin because he didn't want to hear shit about any phone calls he received from Gavin, but Kevin was better than Callie.

She'd tried talking to him when she brought him lunch, but he'd thrown up his hand and cut her off with a grumbled, *Not now.* Realizing he'd moved up the scale from saying they had *nothing to talk about* to *not now* and that *never* hadn't been a part of his vocabulary, some part of him must be considering hearing her out.

But not tonight. The wounds were too fresh.

Before his phone tossed Kevin into voicemail, he answered with a casual, all-is-cool, "Yo."

"Hey, how'd things go in Anticue today?" After eight years of friendship, subtle nuances in one's voice often gave away undercurrents of irritation, even when the speaker tried to sound casual and normal. Kevin's words were benign enough, but irritation bled through, giving Wade warning that the shit was about to hit the fan.

Kevin told him Gavin would pick up on any tension arcing between Wade and Callie, and at the time, Wade assumed Gavin was just that damned intuitive. Now he understood Gavin wasn't super sensitive to everyone, only Callie.

He slapped his forehead as another dimly lit bulb sparked to life. "Is Gavin the client who recommended Callie to you?"

"Yep."

*Fuck.* He was screwed.

"I have a feeling you already know how things went." Which meant he probably also knew today's meltdown had nothing to do with the job. Throwing in a quick defensive jab to cover his hurt, he added, "You're the one who told me to be nice, and I always follow orders."

"I told you to be nice, not date her."

"Yeah, well, you know me. You tell me to be nice to a lady and I'm going to give it"—he paused for effect—"and her all I have." Heavy sarcasm was his natural tendency when threatened or backed into an uncomfortable position, but comparing Callie to his "usual" left a bitter taste in his mouth, despite the pain she'd inflicted.

"Seems you're back to your normal assoholic self."

Wade blew out a breath and let his head fall against the seat. "Is there a purpose for this call?"

"Just checking in. I hear you're diving tomorrow."

Wade shook his head to force his brain to catch up with the sudden change of subject. "How did you know that?"

"I have my ways."

*Callie.*

"Yeah, well, your *informant* is partially right. Tyler and Alex are diving. I'm manning the boat."

"What time are you heading out?"

"Six." His hesitant response was as much a question as an answer. "Why?"

"Where're you leaving from?"

The hair on the back of his neck stood at attention as suspicion crept in and grew heavy in his chest. "No more answers until you answer my question. Why?"

"Callie needs to know where to be and what time so she can go with you."

"What?" Wade's screech sounded like a pre-pubescent boy with his nuts caught the wrong way in his jockstrap. Taking a deep breath to settle his choppy breathing and racing pulse, he clamped down on his phone and ground out between clenched teeth. "Did you know she has a huge trust fund?"

"Yes."

"And you didn't tell me?" His voice was a little lower, like he'd matured ten years since the last time he spoke, but no less incredulous.

"Not my place to tell, and it's not important."

Wade shook his head and fought off the urge to beat his steering wheel. "Not important? Are you serious? She's just like Miranda, yet you forced me to work with her. And be nice."

"Again, I'll reiterate, I told you to be nice. I didn't tell you to date her. And despite your attempts to sound unconcerned and unaffected, I see through your facade, dickhead. If you went the extra step to start seeing her, you already know she's nothing like Miranda."

Wade really, *really* hated it when Kevin was right.

"So tomorrow... which marina?"

"This is an abuse of power."

Kevin laughed.

"Seriously, who's being an ass now?"

Once again, his argument was only met with laughter, so he tried a different approach. "The weather is supposed to be bad, which is why I'm still trying to talk Tyler out of going." Even though it was a waste of breath. Once Tyler had his mind made up, there wasn't any stopping him.

"If it gets so bad you need to cancel, I expect you to notify Callie ahead of time."

"You suck. You know that? Really, really suck."

"Sam never complains."

Wade wanted to slap his hands over his ears, but instead, he slapped his forehead, then rubbed back and forth a couple of times. "Why is this so important to you?"

"It's important to my wife." Kevin's voice held that soft, *I'm such a sap* tone it always carried whenever he spoke of Sam, and Wade had to fight the urge to roll his eyes. Although, in truth, he was glad Kevin found Sam, and he could imagine himself getting the same gooey-eyes and syrupy-sweet tone when talking about Callie.

If things hadn't gone down the shitter.

"Why does Sam care?"

"Don't know, but she's become a regular old Cupidette lately." There was a pause before Kevin finished. "Give Callie a chance to explain. I don't care what happens after that, and if you decide you can't live with the truth, so be it. But do yourself a favor and let her explain why she didn't tell you about the trust fund and why she doesn't use it."

*She doesn't use it?*

Kevin's final words bounced around in Wade's head long after Kevin disconnected the call. Why didn't she use it? And if she didn't… *Shit.* If she only lived off her Mazze Builders' salary, then it would stand to reason she might have to save up for a pair of boots.

*Shit, shit, shit.*

Hope flickered to life in his chest. Maybe she hadn't intentionally deceived him. Maybe this was all a big misunderstanding. He still wasn't ready to talk because he feared this newfound hope would make it impossible to be objective, so he took the chicken-shit way out and sent her a text.

*Byron's Marina 5:45 a.m.*

He'd leave it up to her to figure out where the marina was. If she made the effort to find them, that would tell him a lot. And if she got out of bed in the middle of the night to go out in the ocean, something she'd told them the other night she'd never do, it would be the equivalent of hogtying him with his ears wide open.

# Chapter Sixteen

*W*ade spent so much time at the Sunset Strip, finding his way through the crowded room in total darkness wouldn't be a problem. But getting to Mercy's dressing room or an exit was different than locating a specific table with a certain group of guys. After several moments of absorbing the thumping bass and giving his eyes time to adjust to the club's dim lighting, he spotted the guys in the VIP section of the club, front and center for the action.

"'Bout time you got here," Tyler yelled over the hip-grinding, down-and-dirty music pumping through the club's top-of-the-line sound system. He saluted Wade with a double shot glass, tossed it back, then licked his lips and held up his hand to catch their server's attention.

Sheila, a longtime Sunset server and friend to Wade, wove through the red and black club chairs on the main floor. As she approached their table, Tyler circled his finger around the group, indicating another round for everyone. She tossed him a thumbs-up and caught Wade's eye. Her smile was bright and she seemed glad to see him as she notched her chin and raised her eyebrows. Over the past year, they'd gotten damn good at playing charades, so he understood the unasked question and nodded yes, he did want his usual beer.

He flopped down in the empty chair next to Tyler and scrubbed his hands over his face. He really wanted something stronger than beer.

Hell, even Tyler's moonshine sounded good right now. But getting hammered tonight and spending tomorrow hung-over wouldn't solve his problems.

The music pumping through the speakers was loud, but not nearly loud enough to drown out the words that kept echoing in his head. *She doesn't use it.* Proving there was no end to his idiocy, he found himself clinging to those words like a frigging life raft and hoping against all hope they actually meant something. Like she hadn't so much straight up lied to him as deceived him by omission.

Right... because there was totally a difference between the two.

"Hey, stranger," Shelia said, interrupting his thoughts by dropping his beer into his field of vision and planting a kiss on his cheek. "Where the hell have you been?"

He smiled and shrugged helplessly. "Work's been kicking my ass." The excuse was lame, and based on the way she rolled her eyes hard enough to tug her head sideways, she didn't buy the story any more than Mercy had. But being honest and saying he needed a change of pace and scenery seemed insulting, so he stuck with the lame train, riding it all the way to the end of the tracks.

"Next time," Tyler said as she set out the rest of the drinks, "save yourself a trip and bring us two rounds."

Based on the last time he talked to Tyler, Wade figured the boys had already been at the Strip about forty-five minutes. Considering Tyler was about to polish off his second shot in five minutes, he'd be down for the count in another thirty minutes. Not good when he planned on diving tomorrow.

Wade flashed his hand as he brought it to his neck, catching Sheila's attention, then shook his head *no*. To Tyler, he said, "That's not a good idea."

"Nope," Tyler said, tossing back the new shot. "But I don't care."

"Well, guess what, asshole…" He punched Tyler in the arm to make sure he had his full attention. "I do care. And if you're diving tomorrow, this'll be the last round you have."

Tyler's jaw popped and his eyes narrowed, as if giving Wade a warning they were about to throw down in the upscale gentleman's club if Wade didn't back off. He held his stare and flashed a few strong warning signs of his own. Diving would be iffy enough without adding complications. Drinking within twelve hours of a dive was a no-go for most divers, but Wade was especially cautious about those types of thing. If Tyler wanted his help, he'd play by Wade's rules.

After another tense moment, Tyler muttered, "Fine."

"I'm serious, Ty. You're a fucking choirboy from here on out. You got it?"

"Yeah, Mom, I got it." He turned his chair, putting his back to Wade like a sulking teenager, and focused on the stage.

Wade exhaled sharply, trying to release the irritation building up in him like a time bomb, and glanced at Alex.

Alex held up his glass of water and mouthed, "Thanks," leading Wade to believe he'd already had a similar, unsuccessful discussion with Tyler.

A strobe light flashed and a disco ball threw colored orbs around the room as a siren blared, letting patrons know something spectacular was about to happen. The club's main lights dimmed even more and a spotlight hit the center stage where Ginger—a stacked redhead whose body moved in ways that weren't natural—hung upside down from a pole.

Ginger's signature song, "Pour Some Sugar on Me," filled the air and added extra zing to an already electrified atmosphere. After Ginger finished, three more bodacious ladies took the stage, and then came Mercy's turn. Her long blond hair was covered by a thick black wig and an Egyptian headdress. Gold bangles shimmered at her wrists and ankles, and a sparkly white skirt and top barely covered the goods. As she started performing her famous Cleopatra dance, all eyes at the table turned to him.

He froze with his beer halfway to his lips and glanced around at his friends. "What?"

"Are we allowed to watch her?" Matt asked. The lack of smile and his ultra-serious expression added to the grave tone. No shit, he wasn't kidding. They were seriously asking Wade's permission to watch Mercy strip down to her birthday suit.

"What the fuck? Of course. We were never serious. And even if we had been… you think I come in here busting the heads of any guy who looks?"

Tyler and Alex exchanged a look, while Garrett massaged the back of his neck. "No," Alex said in the same diplomatic tone he'd always used when mediating between Wade and Tyler. "But we're not other guys and it's just weird to… you know… watch what's yours."

"She's not mine. Watch away. And tip well. She hooked us up with the table, and she's saving for her next tuition payment. She can use the extra cash."

If he was right in his calculations, and she'd passed all her classes like she said, she should only have three more semesters left. Once she graduated, she could give up this life once and for all, finally feel good enough about herself to find a nice guy, and quit messing with losers she met at the club.

Guys like him.

Ten minutes after finishing her performance, she exited the hallway leading to the dressing rooms and made her way to their table. She'd replaced her Cleopatra wig with another black one, this one long enough to cover her ass. She'd gained a lot of attention recently as one of the most sought-after girls in the business, and she rarely let anyone in or around the club catch a glimpse of her without a wig and makeup. The disguises only provided a small amount of protection, but any layer of anonymity was better than none.

She smiled and waved to the guys as she sat sideways across Wade's lap and wrapped her arms around his neck and nuzzled his cheek. "It's been a long time, sugar. It's good to see you."

He and Mercy had been friends for almost a year, and most of that time they'd been sleeping together. She was the only woman, since Miranda, he'd spent the entire night with and the woman he saw the most of. And not just because she was a stripper. Every inch of her body was imprinted on his mind, and the familiarity of having her tucked in close should've been a trigger for his body to wake up and play. But after his shower time with Callie, his body and mind had learned what he shared with Mercy couldn't compare to the intimacy of being with Callie. And even though their relationship had hit the rocks and he intellectually knew the odds of them working it out were slim, his body, nor his heart, cared.

They weren't in a settling mood and both failed to respond to Mercy's close proximity.

"You did good with the table, M. Thanks."

Mercy was a stage name, but her real name was Mercedes. Wade refused to call her by her stripper name when they were alone, but she vehemently protested to him using her real name. She insisted using her given name would add a layer of emotion neither was prepared for, so after much debate, they settled on M.

She laughed and flipped her long, fake black hair off her shoulder. "You call and I answer. You know that. Besides, the girls like it when your buddies are in town. They're fun without being lewd, and they tip well."

"I'm glad to hear they're good for something." He offered her a sip of his beer before taking a drink himself. "How you been?"

Shadows crossed her eyes and she glanced away. "I'm good." When she returned her gaze to his, her mask was securely back in place. Running a silky hand down the center of his chest, she said, "I'd be doing better if I saw more of you."

There was no mistaking the invitation in her voice or the wicked gleam in her eye that promised a night of raw-and-raunchy, sweaty sex. Normally, it would've been an invitation he couldn't refuse. But not tonight. Even though he wasn't clear on his current relationship status, he wouldn't spend the night with M, then meet up with Callie in the morning. He'd done some shitty things in his life, but he drew the line with this.

Taking her hand in his, he kissed her fingers and smiled. "I'm sort of not available at the moment."

Something besides disappointment flashed behind the mask… something that looked like envy. Not envy for the woman in his life, but for him finding something more solid than a revolving door of lovers. A lifestyle she shared. A lifestyle she might finally be willing to leave behind.

"I've been waiting for this day," she said while giving him a bitter-sweet smile. "You're too good of a catch to stay on the market for long."

"I'm not so sure about that, but I appreciate your kindness in saying so."

With a heavy sigh, she dropped her arm from his shoulder and prepared to stand. "I should get dressed for my next performance."

As she readied to push to her feet, he grabbed her hand and held her in place on his lap. "Just because I'm not free for a booty call doesn't mean I'm not here for you. You hear me? You need anything, you call."

"You're a sweet man, Wade Neumann." She cupped his face in her hands and pressed a light kiss to his lips. "Your girl's lucky to have you."

"Mercedes," he said, low enough to not be overheard by anyone, not even his friends, but harsh enough that, combined with the use of her real name, he got her attention. "The spare bedroom is still yours, anytime."

"What would your girl say about you shacking up with a stripper?"

He laughed, remembering Callie's expression and reaction earlier in the day when she realized what kind of stage Mercy performed on. "She'd be scandalized. But she'd get over it."

"No one wants their man living with a stripper, honey. That's asking a bit much."

"If you're living with me, you'll be going to school full time and not stripping. Right?" He gave her a little shake when she only stared at him as if he'd spoken in tongues. "The offer is always on the table, regardless of what's going on in my life."

After a moment, she said, "I've got your number. I'll give you a call."

After another good-bye kiss, she waved to the guys, thanked them for their generous donations to the girls working tonight, and told them to get ready for the next round. As soon as she disappeared from sight, the guys started in.

Yes, he silently agreed to being an idiot, but not for the reasons they thought.

Yes, he did know how smokin' hot Mercy was—and that was an understatement, thank you very much—but again, he kept the thoughts to himself.

No, he wasn't pussy-whipped... especially since he and Callie hadn't technically had sex...

The more they harassed, the more difficult it became to keep his thoughts to himself and the more pissed off he got. He wasn't angry with them, necessarily, but at life in general. He was still furious with Callie for deceiving him, whatever the method or reasoning. He was angry with Kevin for forcing him to take Callie diving—although, truth be told, had he flat-out refused, Kevin wouldn't have pushed the issue.

And that pissed him off too because Kevin was smart enough to know that as well. Which meant he also realized Wade felt something for Callie—something serious—or he wouldn't be giving her any chance at reconciliation.

The biggest issue Wade had at the moment, however, didn't have anything to do with Callie or Kevin. The whole situation, and his reaction, made him realize he was still so tied up in knots over his past, he couldn't break free enough to move on with his life. And until he pried those chains off, he'd never have a future with Callie or anyone else.

*Fuck.* Rather than sit here and let the guys provoke an explosion, he needed to get the hell out, go home, sit by the fire, and get his shit together. He tossed a couple bills on the table, stood, and said, "Guys, I've got some shit to take care of. I'll see you in the morning."

On the way home from the Strip, Wade ran a mental loop of his day, from beginning to end and back again, trying to make enough sense of the *holy-shits* to figure out what each of them truly meant. Finding out Callie had a thirty million-dollar trust fund was simply out of his realm of comprehension. No matter how many times or different ways he worked the numbers, he couldn't grasp the true effect of that particular *what-the-fuck*. He didn't even know of any businesses, not personally anyway, that were worth thirty million, and to find out

Callie was sitting on that much… Nope, his brain cramped up and shut down every time he touched the subject.

Figuring out Gavin was Callie's Prince Charming stung at first because it seemed further proof of how far out of his league Callie really was. But the more he thought about that particular *damn,* the less it seemed to matter. Gavin made a fortune at his previous job, which Wade now understood was working for Callie's father, but at heart, he and Wade weren't that different.

While working on the fishing pier/restaurant renovation, Wade stayed after work a couple evenings and sat on the pier with Gavin, tossing hooks, drinking beers, and talking about life. Gavin grew up on a farm, like Wade. They both missed the simple, country life but also agreed having a little slice of the beach was a nice substitute. Granted, Gavin's slice was three times the size of Wade's, but Wade loved his Pawley's Island bungalow. Sitting on the patio, watching the sun rise and stars set as the waves rolled onshore brought him tremendous pleasure, and there wasn't much he would trade it for.

Last on his list of craptastic awesomeness to chew over was Callie's reaction to Sunny's pregnancy. Her response led him to believe she wasn't as over Gavin as she thought, but the more he thought about it, the more he wondered if he wasn't projecting some of his own hang-ups onto Callie.

He'd watched her closely throughout the afternoon, and there weren't any indications that Gavin meant more to her than a good friend. But then again, she hadn't acted like someone with thirty million dollars, either.

*She doesn't use it.*

And Miranda sure as hell hadn't acted like someone who'd been cheating for months. *Fuck.* He drilled his fist into the dashboard of his truck and growled with frustration.

That right there was the crux of all his problems. Every fucking time, no matter the subject, he always ended up on this same damned road.

He was well beyond his romantic feelings for Miranda, and if she showed up on the beach in front of his house and begged him for another chance, he'd run inside as fast his legs would carry him and deadbolt the door behind him. But he still carried so much other garbage, he didn't stand a chance of making a relationship work until he'd unloaded the unresolved resentments and constant distrust.

He parked in his gravel driveway, walked around to the front of his tiny one-story, two-bedroom house, and lit up the patio fire pit. The sky was clear and glittered with a million stars. The wind was light, so he didn't have to worry about the fire or blowing embers, and the soft, easy-rolling waves created a soothing cadence. It was a perfect night to purge the past.

Once he was sure the fire would continue to burn, he went inside to gather the trash. He took a shoebox off the top shelf of the hall closet, set it on top of the large box sitting on the floor beneath it, and carried both through the living room, out the front door, across the screen porch, and onto the patio where the fire had grown good and hot.

He was tempted to go back in the house for a beer, but he wanted a clear head for this. No drowning any of it out tonight. It was past time to fully feel… to deal… and hopefully to finally heal.

As soon as he cracked open the top of the large box, a wave of Miranda's perfume slapped him in the face. The smell caused a rush of memories to assault him, leaving an uncomfortable ache in his stomach and a familiar pang in his chest. But after sneezing a couple times, he realized he never really liked her perfume. He'd always found it oddly comforting because its bold and spicy scent was perfect for Miranda and the smell always made him think of her when she wasn't around. But by itself... *blech.*

After sneezing a couple more times, he began sorting through the remaining bits and pieces of their life together... sticky notes... scraps of paper pulled off the edges of larger sheets... origami animals... photos. Since they hadn't lived in the same town, they spent a lot of time traveling back and forth between Riverside and Myrtle Beach. She didn't work, so most of the time she came to him. He usually left for work before she woke and always before she left, and when he came home, he'd often find love notes stuck to the mirror, on the beer in the fridge, tucked into the blankets, or under his pillow.

And like a fucking pussy, he'd kept them all.

Everything in the box was supposed to be a symbol of her love for him, and she almost always told him how much she looked forward to spending her life with him. Since the breakup, he'd often wondered if she photocopied the shit and left the same note at all her boyfriends' houses.

A sad smile touched his lips as he took out the pictures from their visit to Tyler's the summer before the wedding. She stood beside him, arms wrapped around his neck, kissing him on the cheek while looking at the camera. The smile fell from his face as he stared into her eyes, once again searching for something... anything that should've clued him in to her unfaithfulness.

He'd gone over that trip too many times to count, trying to recall a missed red flag... something in her voice... odd expressions on her face... secretive phone calls. It sure as shit hadn't been evident when she curled up with him at night and screwed his brains out. Even Tyler had a hard time believing the truth because Miranda had been the perfect fiancée, saying and doing all the right things to make everyone believe she was as crazy in love as Wade.

So how could he have known? How did a man protect himself

when there weren't any outward signs of deceit?

That's what scared him the most. Callie was sitting on thirty million dollars, yet he naively thought she was as poor as him. Hell, he thought she was worse off than him because she was eating ramen noodles, for fuck's sake.

How could a man trust anyone to be as they seemed?

*How can a woman?* A small gentle voice echoed in his head.

He thought back to Kevin and Sam's rocky start. Jesus, talk about reasons not to trust. Kevin had been involved with someone else when he met Sam—and there weren't any misunderstandings or claiming things weren't as they seemed.

They were *exactly* as they seemed. He was involved with Lizbeth and before ending the relationship, he started seeing Sam. Yet Sam somehow found a way to forgive Kevin and to trust him, despite the evidence against him.

Wade knew, beyond a shadow of a doubt, Kevin would never, ever cheat on Sam. She was his world, and he'd never do anything to break her trust. So obviously, sometimes the risk was worth the reward, but...

*Shit. How?*

He dropped his elbows to his knees and buried his face in his hands. Sam was obviously stronger than him, because he just didn't know how to get to that place she'd found with Kevin.

With a heavy sigh, he scooped up the scattered contents, put the pile back in the box, and dropped the whole thing into the middle of the fire. Ash and flames flashed and scattered, displaced by the weight of the box. He flopped down into his old and worn Adirondack chair and watched his past slowly ignite, then burn and lift off into the night sky as either smoke or flickering flecks. When very little remained, he leaned over and picked up the small shoebox from beside his chair and set it on his lap.

It weighed less than a pound, but the contents held him down like a thousand-pound tether. He flicked off the lid and stared at the cream invitation with its engraved lettering and black bow, then shifted his gaze to the small gray jewelry box.

The day she broke the engagement had been a nightmare and, until recently, he hadn't even realized he was still sleepwalking through it. He took a deep breath, closed his eyes, and went back to that day.

He'd spent hours the night before trying to reach her by phone, text, and social media. Her phone kept going straight to voicemail, and she wouldn't reply to any of his texts or messages. He'd barely slept for worrying himself sick, and when he finally reached her the next morning, his relief had been extreme. And short-lived. Her response was short, simple, to the point, and devastating. *I'm fine, Wade. Look… I'm sorry, but I can't marry you.*

She disconnected the call without another word, leaving him confused, numb, and frozen to his office chair. When he finally regained some of his sense, he tried calling her back, but she refused his calls. Shortly after, Lizbeth called to ask what was going on because Miranda had just announced to the family that the wedding was off.

He'd been in such a state of shock and disbelief, and firmly entrenched in denial, he hadn't said a word to Kevin or any of the guys on his crew. He put his phone in his pocket, got up from his desk, and went back to work as if nothing had happened. That evening, he drove to Riverside.

An hour later, he was back on the road with an unwanted engagement ring—he didn't want it back; she didn't want to keep it—and an eviscerated heart.

He swallowed the lump of emotion that accompanied the memories and took the ring from the box. Moving it around so it caught the light, the facets sparkled and glittered in the darkness of night. A full carat wasn't a tiny stone, but probably wouldn't compare to the one she'd eventually end up with.

How many carats would thirty million buy?

He laughed and shook his head. Nope… couldn't make sense of it by going that route either.

His practical side wouldn't allow him to toss the ring into the fire, so until he figured out a good use for it, he tucked it back into the velvet case and slipped the box into his shirt pocket.

He didn't know why he'd kept the invitation, but there certainly wasn't a need to torture himself any longer. What could've, should've, would've been with Miranda was over. He didn't even want to go back, but he'd been stuck in the same damned rut for so long, he hadn't even realized he'd given up hope of ever getting out.

Until Callie came along and showed him things could be good again.

He circled his hand over his aching chest and squeezed his eyes shut. He only possessed the emotional capacity to handle one problem at a time, and tonight his focus was letting go of everything from the past… and that needed to include the past week with Callie. Tomorrow, depending on what she said and how he felt about it, they might be able to start again. Tonight, he was wiping the slate of his life clean.

He took the invitation out of the box, folded the crisp, linen paper into an airplane, and launched it into the flames with perfect precision. The fancy paper curled at the edges, like it was trying to escape the heat of the flames, then burst into a brilliant tiny fireball. He didn't know how long he sat there, watching the waves roll onshore and the remnants of his life with Miranda turn to ash, but by the time the flames settled to simmering embers, he felt better. The weight of the world had been lifted off his shoulders, and he took the first deep breath he'd had in a year.

How to get past the trust issue with Callie remained a mystery, but he'd agreed to hear her out—something he would've done even without Kevin's interference—so he'd start there and see where it led.

As he laid his head back and looked down his body at the flames, the box in his pocket caught his attention. It might've been bad luck for him, but there had to be someone who could use the thing for good…

As his eyes closed and he drifted off to sleep, an image of Mercy floated through his mind. His eyes popped wide and he bolted upright in his chair. She could sell the ring and use the money to finish school. If she took him up on his offer to stay in his spare bedroom, she wouldn't have to pay rent or utilities. She could work less, a lot less, and double up on her classes to finish sooner. Then she could quit beating herself up for doing what she'd needed to do to survive and move on with her life.

Getting her to agree wouldn't be easy, but he'd always believed a strong will and determination could move mountains. She was stubborn, but not as bad as him.

He smiled as he thought about the call from Kevin. He'd shut Callie down all day, yet she'd still managed to find a way around him to get what she wanted.

Mercy had met her match with Wade, but he might've met his match with Callie.

# Chapter Seventeen

Callie double-checked her GPS to confirm her location and make sure she was headed in the direction of Byron's Marina, then tightened her grip on the wheel and squinted, trying to get a clearer look at the road through the thick marine fog. It wasn't lost on her that Wade only gave her the name of the marina and a time, not an address or directions, but when someone extended an olive branch, you didn't demand they hand over the whole tree.

She'd been so relieved and grateful he was open to seeing her, she'd immediately searched the location and plugged the information into her GPS, then spent the entire night on her couch, staring at the ceiling, rehearsing the upcoming conversation. No matter how many times she practiced, though, when it came time to actually get it right, she'd probably end up rambling and babbling and nothing would come out as planned.

After another half mile, she sighed with relief as a yellow-and-red sign reading BYRON'S MARINA appeared through the mist. Now that she'd found the right location and no longer needed to focus on her driving, nervous anxiety about the rest of the day burst from her stomach and escaped through her fingertips.

Not only was she nervous about seeing Wade and the way the conversation would go, but she'd never been on a small boat—large yachts cruising around the bay didn't count—nor had she been out in the open waters of the ocean. As her overactive imagination conjured images of giant sea creatures and capsized ships, panic enveloped her, forcing her to slam on the brakes at the entrance to the parking lot and draw in several deep breaths so she didn't pass out. Or throw up.

*I can do this. I can do this. Everything will be fine. Tyler does this sort of thing all the time. If it were too dangerous, Wade wouldn't go. I can do this. Take one more deep breath, ease into the parking lot, put on a happy face, thank Wade for allowing you the opportunity to go with them, and get your butt on the boat without collapsing.*

Following her own directives, she drew in a deep breath, then another for good measure, took her foot off the brake, and coasted into the parking lot. Wade was standing next to his truck, gathering things from the backseat. When she pulled into the space next to him, he glanced over his shoulder, revealing mild curiosity about who'd parked four feet from his butt, but other than that, he gave away nothing.

In a brief flash of sensible clarity, she imagined restarting her car, driving home, and crawling back into her nice, warm bed to get the sleep she'd missed out on last night. But she'd come this far, and she wasn't turning back now. He might not be thrilled to see her, but he was going to listen to what she had to say. Then, as Gavin pointed out, if he wouldn't accept her apology, they didn't have a future anyway.

She cursed the nerves choking her as she grabbed her raincoat and a blanket from the backseat. The temperature was supposed to climb closer to normal today, putting them in the mid-sixties, but the forecast also called for rain in the afternoon. She didn't know how long they'd be out, but she wanted to be prepared in case the weather turned bad. With a deep breath, she shoved open the door, pasted on a confident smile, and exited her car.

"You found it." Wade's tone was ultra-cool, ultra-conservative, and he still showed no signs of being glad to see her as he slung a large duffel bag over his shoulder and reached into the truck for another bag.

Her confidence slipped a little, and she kicked a rock with the toe of her shoe. "Is that a good thing or not?"

He sighed and cocked his head while studying her with unreadable eyes. "I don't know yet. I guess we'll have to wait and see."

His response wasn't exactly what she'd hoped for, but at least he was willing to talk—which was more than he offered yesterday. "Fair enough. Thanks for letting me go with you guys." She hung her purse and coat over her shoulder and wrapped the blanket over the same arm, freeing up a hand. "Can I help you carry anything?"

"Naw," he said, grabbing another bag from the truck. "I've got it. But thanks."

While he was at least speaking to her, the normal warmth of his eyes was missing, as was the easygoing, flirtatious banter she'd grown so used to. She shivered against his chilly reception and the cold wind blowing off the water and hunkered down deeper into her coat. This was either the bravest or dumbest thing she'd ever done and ranked right up there with telling her father she and Gavin had screwed him over. That night hadn't gone well at all and had almost gotten Gavin and Sunny killed.

*Please, God, let this day go better.*

She followed Wade across the gravel parking lot and down the wooden pier to the boat at the end of the dock, where Tyler and Alex stood waiting. The boat had a flat bottom and open deck. The front half, where the captain sat, was covered; the back half was open. A row of air tanks lined the left side; a couple of benches ran along the right. Several duffel bags, similar to Wade's, lay in the center of the boat, and one of them was open, revealing a wetsuit and a pair of flippers.

She cut her gaze to Wade's bags and used her nonexistent X-ray vision, trying to see inside. She hadn't gotten the impression he was diving, but maybe he'd changed his mind. Or maybe he brought his equipment with him so if he became desperate for an escape, he could go overboard.

*Stop it.*

She shook her head and drove back the negative thoughts. He'd given her the right time and place. Now it was up to her to make sure he didn't regret his decision.

"Hey, Callie," Tyler said, reaching out a hand to help her board. "How's it going?"

She had no way of knowing how much Wade shared with his friends, but she'd made it clear the other night she didn't do boats. Ignoring their personal drama, she spoke to her individual fears. "I haven't thrown up yet, so I'd say we're off to a great start."

Tyler laughed and pulled her into a quick hug, and she found herself ducking, half expecting him to rub his knuckles over her head in a noogie. "I'm glad you decided to come with us and give it a try. You'll have a great time."

"What?" she shrieked and shook her head emphatically while backing away from him. "I'm not—"

She realized Wade's scowl had given way to a grin, and Alex was also laughing. Her muddled brain finally caught on to Tyler's teasing tone, and she collapsed onto the bench at the back of the boat with relief. She might not be one of the guys, but they'd certainly accepted her into the fold and were treating her like one.

"You have a dry suit?" Alex asked Wade as he took one of his bags off his shoulder and added it to the pile.

"Hell no. I don't dive enough for that fancy shit. I have a regular old wetsuit, and I don't intend to use it." He gave Tyler a pointed look. "I'm just here to ride and keep you out of trouble. I figured if I was tagging along, though, it made sense to bring my gear."

Tyler shook his head and sipped on his coffee. "Dude, you really need to relax and stop worrying so much. Everything's gonna be great. We've got the magnetometer." He pointed to a white-and-yellow device that looked like an arrow on steroids. "The weather is looking good for this morning. We're gonna find that fucking boat, and then I'm going to be able to tell you, 'Told ya so!'" He slapped Wade on the shoulder and turned to Alex. "We ready to roll?"

"We're ready." To Callie, Alex said, "Sit up here next to me. We're enclosed so you shouldn't get wet, but..." He cocked his head to the side and studied her from the corner of his eye. "Do you really get seasick?"

"I have no idea. I've never been on a boat or in the sea."

*But I'm getting nerve-sick... Does that count?*

He laughed and amended his question. "Do you get sick riding in a car or flying?"

"No."

"Good. Going out will be rough, but if you keep looking straight ahead, you should be okay."

*Rough?* Should *be okay?*

Callie swallowed the ball of nerves blocking her throat and glanced to Wade. She really wanted to sit next to him and hold his hand, but that would be pushing too far, so she put on her brave face and nodded to Alex. "Okay, thanks." Looking around the edges of her seat, she said, "I don't suppose there's a seatbelt on here anywhere."

She'd said it laughing, as a joke, and fortunately, Alex took the comment as intended. "My driving isn't nearly as bad as Wade's. You'll be fine."

Despite her efforts to appear relaxed, or at least not overly concerned, she sighed with relief when Wade stepped up behind her and latched his hands over her shoulders. Leaning in close to speak directly in her ear, he said, "I might be pissed as hell, but I'd never let anything happen to you."

The heat of his body wrapping around her, as well as his words of assurance, sent a strong signal to her heart, but the pain—not anger—filtering through his voice caused a rising tide of tears in her eyes. She bit down on her lip to stop the quivering and blinked back the excessive moisture blurring her vision. "Thanks. I'm sure I'll be fine once we get underway."

As they motored out of the marina and into Intercoastal waterway, Callie grew slightly more comfortable with the gentle rocking of the boat. She couldn't say she was relaxed, but she'd just started to believe the trip wouldn't be as bad as she'd expected when they rounded the end of the island and all hell broke loose.

Small, choppy waves rolled at them from all sides, tossing the boat to and fro, here and there. From the sky, she imagined they looked like the little silver ball bouncing around on a roulette wheel. An appropriate image, because making it back to shore alive seemed like a real gamble.

Panic quickly settled into her chest and stole her breath, then gave it back in short, jerky snatches. If the entire trip was like this, she'd never survive. She needed to get off. Now. Under the influence of a panic attack, one's thoughts weren't always logical, and this was one of those times. She grabbed the railing and, desperate for an escape from the washing machine, considered jumping overboard.

Either sensing her panic or reading her thoughts, Wade pressed down hard on one shoulder, then used his other hand to grab the hair at the nape of her neck, locking her in place. Bending over so he filled her field of vision, he said, "Breathe, Callie." His tone was firm and commanding. "This'll only last a minute. Once we get out of the inlet and into the open water, it'll be much smoother."

She latched onto Wade's voice and gaze and used them as grounding devices. She also grabbed the hand still holding her shoulder and squeezed until her fingers were white. She didn't calm completely, but he said he'd never let anything happen to her, and she believed him.

Sure enough, as soon as they left the inlet, the water changed into big, slow-rolling waves. It didn't take long to lose sight of land, and a quick check of her cell phone confirmed her suspicions… They were in the middle of nowhere. Her anxiety battled the peaceful sway of the boat to keep her in a slightly agitated state, but she forced herself to appear relaxed and at ease.

After an hour of cruising, Tyler tossed the mini torpedo into the water and gave Alex directions on which way to go. Wade explained to her that the magnetometer would pick up large pieces of debris on the ocean floor. While Alex drove the boat back and forth in a crisscross pattern, Wade and Tyler marked large red Xs on a laminated map. Once satisfied they had enough locations to work with—a total of five—Tyler pulled in the magnetometer, and he and Alex got to work exploring.

Four times, using GPS to locate the positions they'd previously marked on the map, Alex steered them to each spot, Wade dropped anchor, and Alex and Tyler suited up. They dropped into the water, spent approximately ten minutes exploring the ocean floor, then returned to the surface without having found Tyler's missing ship. Tyler's irritation grew with each unsuccessful dive, and while there wasn't enough money in the world to get her into the water, she found herself desperately hoping the fifth and final dive allowed Tyler to find what he'd so desperately been searching for.

Alex stopped the boat on the last red X, Wade dropped the anchor, and Tyler suited up. Rather than grabbing the single tank he'd been using, Tyler grabbed a double tank off the rack and slung it over his shoulders. "Get your double, Alex. I've got a good feeling about this one, and we're going prepared to explore."

Alex rolled his eyes but didn't argue against Tyler's optimism. Without saying a word, he pulled his dry suit on over his clothes, slipped on his tanks, then followed Tyler to the back of the boat.

Callie watched them disappear into the dark water, then turned to Wade. "I've figured out if they don't find anything, they'll be back in ten minutes. If they do find something, how long will they be?"

Wade shrugged. "About thirty minutes."

"That's it?" They'd spent four hours looking for a boat he'd only explore for twenty minutes?

"Yeah, this time." He glanced to the sky and frowned. "We're running out of time with this approaching storm. But if it's here, he'll have the exact GPS coordinates so he can come back whenever he wants."

Wow, so much work for such a small payoff. She shook off the thought and refocused on her purpose for being here. Regardless of whether or not they found the boat, this was her last opportunity to talk to Wade without an audience, and she'd be damned if she'd gone through all of this for nothing. With a deep breath, she swiped her sweaty palms on her jeans and started.

"All right. I guess I better talk fast."

# Chapter Eighteen

*W*ade propped himself against the boat railing and patiently waited while Callie chewed on her fingernail and composed her thoughts. Part of him wanted to tell her to get on with it, but another, larger part of him feared this might be the last meaningful conversation he had with Callie, and he didn't mind waiting a few more minutes.

She'd been a trooper all morning and he couldn't have been more proud of the way she'd handled her fears. He'd known it would take tremendous courage for her to get on the boat, and for a brief, heart-stopping moment, he'd thought she might back out. His stomach plummeted when she slammed on the brakes at the entrance, and it took everything in him to stay at his truck and let her work through her fears on her own, without his intervention or reassurances.

He couldn't hand over his man card by letting her see how glad he was that she'd come, but his heart expanded and thumped a little harder when she finally pulled into the lot, parked, and actually got out. At that point, he knew, unless she admitted to something heinous, he'd be taking her home as soon as they got back on shore, and he probably wouldn't let her leave again until Monday morning.

"Okay," she said, dropping her hands to her sides and shaking them out like a boxer preparing to go a few rounds. "I have money from two difference sources."

He wanted to say *only two,* but kept his sarcasm under wraps.

"The first came from the sale of the Anticue Fishing Pier."

A cough and laugh caught in his throat, choking him. "I'm sorry. You owned...?" *No way.* Callie owning a fishing pier was wrong on so many levels. He couldn't even finish the sentence.

She smiled, but her expression lacked humor and her eyes were dull and tired. "Yes." When he didn't reply, because he had no idea how to respond to something so ludicrous, she continued. "My father wanted to build a resort on Anticue, but there are ordinances in place to prevent large developments. From what I understand, it took him several years and several rounds of elections to find the right people"— she made air quotes with her fingers—"who would be willing to change the ordinances in his favor."

*Let's just break it down, shall we?* "You mean people he could bribe."

"Right. He also needed to acquire enough property on which to build the resort. So, while getting the political components in place, he started buying property at the end of the island where the fishing pier and the Blackout Bar and Grill are. He acted on his own, without the blessing of Holden's board of directors, so rather than deed the property to Holden Enterprises, which would throw up flags, he put some of the parcels in my name and some in my mother's name."

"If he owned the company, why did he need the blessing of the board?"

"It's a long, complicated story, but *he* didn't really own"—more of the air quotes—"the company. My mother's father started Holden Enterprises, but back then it was called Pelletier Resorts. None of my uncles wanted to follow in my grandfather's footsteps. They mostly just wanted to spend the money."

She cast her eyes to the ground and shifted from foot to foot. She'd mentioned several times that she used to be like Miranda, and he wondered if this was a moment of introspection for her, where she saw herself in the comment.

She took a deep breath and continued. "After my parents married, my grandfather made my father the CEO. The board eventually agreed to change the name to Holden Enterprises, since my father was the face of the company, but my mother retained controlling interest and Daddy still had to report to the board. At the end of the day, my mother had the ability to fire my father. Something she did swiftly when everything came to light."

Again, he had no idea how to respond to that information, so he settled on a generic, "Damn."

She smiled weakly. "Yeah. So anyway, as Gavin started unraveling the mess, he discovered the fishing pier was in my name. In a power play of our own, I sold the fishing pier to Gavin, which gave him possession of the largest piece of property on the island. Sunny refused to sell, and since the Blackout adjoins the fishing pier parcel, there wasn't any way Holden could build a resort. Which stopped my father in his tracks." Her throat jumped as she swallowed roughly. "And sent him on a rampage."

All of this had taken place several years ago, so she was no longer in danger, but as the big picture started coming into focus, his knees weakened and he slumped against the railing. "Sooo you sold the fishing pier to Gavin without your father's knowledge?" Considering he tried to kill Gavin and Sunny, Wade couldn't imagine things had gone well for Callie, either, and cold dread over what she'd say next grabbed him by the throat.

She nodded and took a deep breath and even managed to flash a little dimple. "Yeah. To say he was furious is an understatement. Things with him and Gavin had gotten rough—at that point Gavin was involved with Sunny and his allegiance was no longer with my father— so I took Daddy to dinner and broke the news. My father is a big man."

She glanced at Wade. "Much like you. I'd never seen the monster I often heard other people whisper about." She swallowed a few times as if she were having difficulty getting her throat to work. "That night, I saw it all. I thought he would have a heart attack or a stroke when I told him what Gavin and I had done. He swept everything off the table, threw his chair across a restaurant filled with people, and swore to everyone within a three-block radius that he'd kill Gavin and disown me if we didn't cancel the sale."

*Holy shit.*

He couldn't imagine how terrifying that must've been for Callie, and thinking about her in danger—especially from her father—infuriated him. Unable to maintain his distance any longer, he reached for her hand.

Rather than accepting his hand, she launched herself into his arms and trembled against him. His protective instincts kicked in and he tightened his grip, reassuring her she was safe.

After the trembling stopped, she pulled away and began to pace. "Gavin warned me Daddy would threaten to disown me if I didn't recant the sale, but I didn't care. I didn't agree with what my father had done, and owning the fishing pier meant the world to Gavin." Her smile was sweet and sheepish. "At the time, his wishes were extremely important to me. I wanted to help Gavin, who was as desperate to shake free of my father's control as I was. The sale also gave me the money I needed to get out of my parents' house, so it was a win all the way around." She rolled her head to the side. "Well, for everyone but my father. And I had no idea he'd follow through on his threats against Gavin and Sunny."

She stopped pacing and looked Wade in the eye. "I told you Kevin saved me too, and I wasn't lying. I'd gone to college, but I had no work experience. None. Ever. I wanted to get out and make my own way in the world, but I didn't know how. I was like an exotic pet that suddenly found itself loose in the wild." A real smile brushed across her lips, and Wade found himself smiling along with her at the quirky comparison. "My chances of survival weren't good, but I was determined, and I had Gavin on my side. He introduced me to Kevin, and fortunately, he liked my suggestions. He was willing to give an inexperienced diva a chance."

The broad smile spreading across her face reminded him of a brilliant sunrise brightening a dark, night sky. "I've never been prouder of myself than the day Kevin hired me. I loved the feeling of accomplishment, and I wanted to keep experiencing those small victories."

Her excitement for the job and her achievements was evident in the way she bounced on her toes and in her growing smile.

"I used the money from the fishing pier to buy my condo and get a new car, so I wouldn't have to worry about those payments. Then I took the rest of the proceeds to my friend Jason, who helped me invest it. I haven't touched a penny since."

She grabbed the flaps of his open shirt and tugged. "When I told you I was saving up for a pair of boots, I wasn't lying. I only have the money from my paychecks in my bank account. I don't have to pay rent, but I do pay association dues and insurance and utilities and food, just like everyone else. And if I want a new pair of boots, I have to give up something in order to get them."

Her dark-brown eyes implored him to believe her, and even though he was trying to fight the tide, he felt himself being pulled under and carried away in their depths. He found it hard to believe that someone who'd lived a nice, cushy life would give it all up in favor of eating packaged noodles. But then he thought about his mother.

She didn't have to work, and his father would've preferred she didn't. But she wanted to, and when Wade started middle school, she went to work part time. When he started high school, she moved up to a full-time position.

Even though he was a breath from slip-sliding away in Callie's explanations, she'd said there were two sources of income, and he still needed to know the second, largest part of the equation. "Where does the chump change… you know, the measly thirty mil come in?"

She narrowed her eyes like she didn't appreciate his sarcasm, and he almost smiled. Almost.

"When I turned twenty-five, right after I went to work for Kevin, I gained control of my trust fund. I've never touched a penny of it. I've instructed the lawyers that unless someone's life is in danger, they're not to give me access to any of it." She bit down on her lip and rolled her eyes to the side. "I'm not sure how I'm going to convince them Tiffany's business is a matter of life or death, but I'll work that out later. Anyway, I'm still trying to figure out how best to use it. My father showed me greed can turn a person into a monster, but I view money itself as being like electricity. It can light a house and provide heat or fire an electric chair and kill someone. Electricity isn't bad; it's the way it's used. Money is the same way." She shrugged. "I'm just trying to figure out the best use for it."

She rubbed her arms and stared at the open waters surrounding them. "I considered telling you all of this the other night, but I saw the way you looked at me when you thought I was like Miranda. And I've seen the way you look at me since you decided I'm not like her." She returned her steady gaze to him. "I like the new way better, and I was afraid if I told you about the trust fund, or the remaining fishing pier money, you'd go back to looking at me with contempt, and I didn't want that. I'd hoped for a little more time, to get to know each other better before I told you the whole truth."

With a heavy sigh, he took his ball cap off his head and readjusted it a few times before pulling it down low on his forehead. She was right about money being a valuable asset if used properly, and the way she worded it made him feel like an ass for thinking less of her for having it. She was also right about the way he would've reacted.

Hell, he'd proven her right, hadn't he?

Callie was a beautiful woman, inside and out. She might've been born into money, and she might've taken advantage of her circumstances for most of her life, but at her core, she was nothing like Miranda. She was brave as hell, and he couldn't image the guts it took to stand up to her father, especially in the face of his violent tendencies. She had more balls than most men he knew, and her loyalty to her friends—who he still wasn't sure deserved it—was something he admired.

He still couldn't grasp the idea of her being worth more than the entire population of his small town, but that was a male pride thing he'd have to work through. Only one question remained.

"What about Gavin?"

She blinked a couple times, then frowned. "What about him?"

"When he told you Sunny was pregnant, your response was less than enthusiastic. Are you sure your heart is as available as you think?"

She frowned and rubbed her forehead, as if trying to jar the memory loose.

Helping her out, he said, "You weren't as excited for your *friend* as I would've expected."

Her eyes widened and brightened and she shook her head as if to say, *Silly boy.* "He was so serious when he gave me the news... not nearly as excited as I would've expected *him* to be, so I was worried about what he thought of the news." She drew back and her eyes narrowed. "You didn't hear all of the conversation, did you?"

He scratched behind his ear and shook his head. "No, I left after hearing your response."

She crossed her arms and gave him a look that reminded him of his third grade teacher, Mrs. Music. Bitch could pop a knuckle with a ruler before he even realized she'd come up behind him. Callie had the stance and attitude; the only thing she lacked was the bun, those ugly knee-high stockings that drooped down around her ankles, and the mother-fucking ruler. He shuddered and rubbed his eyes to clear the image.

"I'm thrilled for them. Yes, Gavin used to be my Prince Charming, but"—she dipped her gaze, then rolled her eyes back up to him—"I sort of have a new picture of what my prince might look like, and he doesn't ride a white horse." She took a tentative step closer and smiled. "I think he might drive a black truck… a really big, loud, and totally obnoxious truck."

He laughed and wrapped his arms around her waist, drawing her close. He didn't have any further questions, and while he still had plenty of doubts about his ability to be her Prince Charming, there were no lingering doubts about Callie.

"I think he's adventurous." She continued. "And he makes me want to be adventurous, too. I've been a lot of places in my life, but I've never truly lived. I want him to keep encouraging me to try new things, like going out on a boat in the middle of nowhere."

She stopped and looked around, seemingly realizing for the first time they were still alone, and Alex and Tyler's ten minutes had expired ten minutes ago. "They're not back." Her eyes widened and she bounced with excitement. "Does that mean they found it?"

About halfway through their conversation, a little ping sounded in his brain, making him aware that Tyler and Alex had yet to return. But he hadn't wanted his focus on Callie to be diluted. Still didn't.

Dropping his forehead to hers, he said, "I guess it means they found something, which means we have a few more minutes until they resurface."

She grinned as her gaze locked onto his. "Does this mean we're good? Do you understand why I didn't tell you about the money?"

He sighed and nodded. "Yeah." He paused and thought for a moment. "My ego is still trying to grasp the concept of thirty million and knowing you can buy whatever you want, whenever you want, wherever you want, and I'll never be able to compete. But I guess I'll figure that out in time."

"Please don't let that come between us. We'll figure it out together. How about that?" Her smile grew mischievous. "I hear make-up sex is really phenomenal… Can we find out tonight?"

He laughed and slid his palm up the length of her spine to the nape of the neck. "That was my plan. And not just tonight, but tomorrow morning… tomorrow afternoon… tomorrow night. And probably even Monday morning before work."

The more he talked, the softer her eyes became, and his mind started running through the possible scenarios for getting a jump on the plan right now. Giving her a preview of what to expect, he pressed his lips to hers and slipped his hand between her jacket and her sweater.

A loud splash and flailing from the side of the boat pierced his thoughts, and he pulled away from Callie to peer over the side rail, expecting to find a sea turtle or a porpoise.

Instead, he found Alex, panicked, out of breath, and in dire straits.

Wade's own panic began to stir as he scanned the area near Alex. "Where the fuck is Tyler?"

"Trapped." Alex gasped as he removed his mask and tossed it into the boat. "We found the ship"—he gasped for air, then coughed and gagged—"and had just started to explore when something happened." He coughed and gagged again. "I don't know if it was an errant fin kick or if a shark bumped into the side, but rust and debris fell all around us and we got silted out."

He'd been slowly making his way to the ladder as he spoke, but as he tried to climb up, fatigue had him stumbling and slipping back into the water.

Wade threw out his hand to catch Alex, then hauled him onto the boat.

"When the dive shop filled my tank, they didn't open the isolation valve, so I only had one tank of air. I didn't realize what was happening with my air until a moment before everything went dark." He collapsed onto a bench and ran his hand over his face. Grief and despair filled his voice and eyes. "I barely had enough to get to the surface to get you." Wild desperation flashed at Wade. "You've gotta go down and find him."

"Son of a bitch." Rage mixed with dread and panic pumping through Wade's system and had him so lightheaded he had to take a second to catch his breath and let his vision clear.

Callie's voice finally pierced the red-and-black veil blinding him. "What can I do to help?"

He shook off the emotional blinders that weren't doing Tyler a damned bit of good and said, "Grab my bags from the hatch."

He briefly glanced at Alex's dry suit, but his additional three inches and thirty pounds made getting into Alex's dry suit an impossibility. He fought off the chill rising up inside him as he stripped off his clothes, and the cold air causing goose bumps to rise on his skin reminded him of the approaching storms and cold front. The clouds were getting thicker, which meant the visibility underwater was getting worse, which would make it even more difficult to find Tyler. Not like a little surface light helped anyway if they had zero visibility, but... *Fuck.* He was going to kill Tyler.

If he wasn't already dead.

While he pulled on his flimsy wetsuit, which wouldn't be nearly enough protection for this time of year, he mentally worked out a plan. He glanced at Alex, who was lying flat on his back on the floor of the boat, still in his dry suit, looking like hell warmed over. This scenario was going from bad to worse, and Wade feared none of them would get out of this alive.

He looked at Callie and gnashed his teeth. Fuck that, they were all getting out of this. Maybe a little banged up. And definitely bent. But he'd promised Callie he wouldn't let anything happen to her, and dammit, if it was the last thing he did, he'd make sure she was okay.

To Alex, he said, "Give me a layout of the ship."

"The ship's on its side. Rooms go off the center hallway on both sides. You go down into the rooms on the right, up into the ones on the left. We were about halfway down the hallway. The last time I saw Tyler, he'd gone into a room on the port side."

Finished suiting up, Wade grabbed his reel, a line he would run from the anchor into the ship along with him. When he found Tyler, they could follow the line out to the anchor, then resurface directly at the boat.

"How quickly did you surface?"

"Entirely too fast."

Not the answer he'd been looking for, but also not a surprise.

Callie hadn't said a word since handing him his bag, but her widening eyes and shallow breathing told him she'd been closely following the conversation. "What does that mean?" She turned to Alex. "What do you mean you came up too fast?"

"If you resurface too quickly, you get what's called *the bends*." When she continued to stare at him, obviously waiting more information, he added, "The nitrogen in your blood bubbles up—"

"I barely passed science," she snapped. "Dumb this down for me, please."

Alex coughed. "It's kind of like the difference between opening a soda slowly or fast. Too fast, and you get big bubbles that fizz and make a mess."

Wade could tell hysteria was threatening to overtake her, but tapping into the courage that allowed her to stand up to her father—the same courage that got her onto this goddamned boat and into fucking mess in the first place—she took a deep breath and kept herself under control.

"Callie," he said, walking to the VHF radio as he slipped his air tank over his shoulders. "This is the radio." He turned the dial to channel sixteen so all she had to do was key the mic and talk. "If I'm not back in fifteen minutes, use the radio to call the coast guard."

Her breathing was coming fast and shallow and he feared she'd start to hyperventilate if she didn't get it under control. Putting his hands on her shoulders, he dipped his knees so they were eye to eye and made her look directly at him. Shit was critical, and she was smart enough to figure that out. But her life, and probably Alex's, depended on her keeping it together for a little while longer.

"Do you understand what I'm saying? Fifteen minutes, then call the coast guard. Tell them you have two overdue divers who are still down, and you have another on board with the bends." He pointed to the instrument panel. "They'll help you figure out the coordinates so they can find you." He turned to Alex. "If you need them sooner, have her call."

Alex nodded, then promptly closed his eyes and took a few slow, deep breaths.

Jesus, this was a no-fucking-win situation, but he couldn't waste any more time. Tyler was an experienced diver and a pro at conserving air, but if he started to panic, he'd burn through his tanks faster... if he had two full tanks and not one, like Alex.

Wade scrubbed a hand over his face and forced himself to take a few deep breaths of his own. He couldn't chance not getting to Tyler in time, so he needed to put his faith in Callie and trust her to do what was necessary to save herself and Alex.

And if he didn't make it back to the surface...

He knelt next to Alex and shook his shoulder to get his attention. When his eyes cracked open and Wade was sure he had his attention, he leaned in close and said, "Take care of her for me." Alex shut his eyes and shook his head, probably not denying Wade's request, but simply stating he didn't want to have this conversation. So Wade shook him again. Hard. "Dammit, Alex. She means the fucking world to me. Promise me you'll take take. Care. Of. Her."

"Won't be necessary, but yeah, I promise."

Wade stood and gave Callie a quick kiss, because if he kissed her any longer than a brief peck on the lips, he'd never let her go and he'd never get overboard. He pulled on his mask, put the respirator in his mouth, and rolled into the freezing water, all the while praying that wasn't the last time he saw Callie's beautiful face. Because God help him, if it came down to abandoning Tyler or continuing to search until he'd sucked in his last breath...

He could never live with himself if he didn't give everything he had.

# Chapter Nineteen

*T*error gripped Callie and she leaned over the rail, grabbing for Wade as he disappeared beneath the inky surface of the water. She tried to scream his name, begging him to return to the boat, but the sound was lodged in her throat and wouldn't break loose. Her limbs were numb with shock, and she felt frozen in a state of suspended animation, waiting for someone to press a button to get the reel of her life moving again. Better yet, she wanted to wake up and find she'd been having a terrible nightmare when she was actually home in bed with Wade, his strong arms wrapped around her, both of them safe.

A groan from behind her pierced the veil of illusion and forced her to acknowledge that while she was trapped in a nightmare, she was very much awake. Staring into the dark abyss of the Atlantic wasn't going to bring Wade back faster, nor would it free Tyler, and she certainly wasn't doing Alex any good.

It felt like she was giving up on Wade or somehow abandoning him, but she knew he'd want her to take care of Alex, so with stiff, jerky movements, she pushed off the rail and shuffled across the deck to the other side of the boat. Alex had pulled himself up onto a bench and was sitting motionless with his elbows on his knees, his head in his hands, staring at the floor.

She knelt next to him and rested her hand on his knee. "What can I do to help you?" When he didn't respond, she said, "Maybe we should try shedding your skin." She laughed a little, letting him know she was working hard to lighten the mood and his cooperation would be appreciated.

He didn't laugh, but his lips twitched and he nodded in agreement. Given the situation, that was the best she could hope for, and she was grateful he was willing to play along. He'd taken off his tanks as soon as he got onboard, but still wore the weights as well as his fins and the suit itself. She still didn't understand how the dry suit worked, but his clothes were, indeed, just as dry as they'd been before he left the boat. His skin, however, was cold and clammy.

"I brought a blanket with me. Let me grab it for you."

He didn't seem to notice her speaking to him as he rubbed his short hair, then fell sideways to lie on the bench. Getting him out of his gear seemed to exhaust him, and along with extreme fatigue, regret and fear poured out of him in waves. She also wondered if he might be going into shock.

Callie had never felt so helpless in her life, so she focused on what she could do. She kicked Alex's suit to the back corner of the boat, where they'd been keeping their wet gear, and made her way to the hatch at the front.

"Wade has a wetsuit, not a dry suit, right? Which means he will get wet?"

In slow motion, Alex lifted his eyes to her and slowly nodded. "Yeah, which won't do shit for him. The water is fucking *cold*."

Another wave of fear sucker-punched her in the gut, knocking the breath out of her, but she refused to succumb. Crying wouldn't help, and she needed to keep her wits about her. She felt helpless, but she wasn't. Wade had given her specific instructions, and she needed to be prepared to follow through in the event he didn't return within the fifteen-minute window. She also needed more information on what, exactly, was going on with Alex so she knew best how to help him.

In the hatch with her blanket, she found the guys' heavy wool blanket—the same one she and Wade used the night they were at the campfire—a stack of towels, her spare coat, and a handful of old rags. Anything that looked useful for either mopping up water or keeping someone warm was brought into play.

After draping their wool blanket over Alex and tucking it tightly around him, she gathered Wade's clothes from the floor. They'd gotten damp from the water on the floor of the boat, so she slung them over the chairs at the front so they could dry, at least a little, before he returned.

And dammit, he would come back.

Bile rose in her throat and tears burned her eyes as she remembered the look in his eyes as he went overboard. As he locked gazes with her, she knew exactly what he was telling her.

If Jen or Tiffany were down there, would she come back to the surface and save herself, knowing they would die if she left them?

No. She wouldn't. She wasn't brave like Wade, but she could never leave her friends alone to die. She would do everything in her power to free them, and she wouldn't stop until she'd either gotten them loose or run out of air. One of the things she loved and admired most about Wade was his loyalty to his friends, and she knew with every fiber of her being he'd either come back with Tyler or neither of them would come back.

She shook off the morose, debilitating thoughts and made her way back to Alex, who was curled into the fetal position, quietly moaning. Needing the life-affirming touch of another human being, as well as hoping to give him some measure of comfort, she took hold of his hand and squeezed.

"Alex, I need you to help me understand what's going on down there. Okay?" He nodded, so she continued. "Is Tyler trapped, like, caught in something? Or is he lost?"

"He's lost." He paused and licked his lips, like he was searching for moisture, so she grabbed a bottle of water and helped him take a drink. "The boat's on its side, so the rooms are up and down, not left or right. There are a lot of sharks in the area, so either one of us accidentally kicked the wall of the hallway, or one of the sharks bumped into the side of the wreckage."

Callie shuddered at the thought of Wade and Tyler swimming with sharks and focused on Alex's words.

"All the rust and algae that's been building up for decades broke loose and fell into the water around us. Visibility dropped to zero, and I lost sight of Tyler. A few minutes before that happened, I realized I had a problem with my tank." His lip curled with anger as his gaze cut to the tanks in the rack. "See the valve between the two tanks?" When she nodded, he said, "That's an isolation valve. It separates the air between the two tanks. When the dive shop filled my tanks, they didn't open that valve, so I only had one tank of air."

"Oh crap."

He tried to grin, but it looked more like a grimace.

"But that means Tyler has twice as much air as you. Right? So he has more time to get out."

Alex lifted a shoulder in a helpless shrug. "Hopefully. I don't dive that much, so I'm not accustomed to double-checking everything like I should have. He dives all the time, so hopefully he checked his gear before we even left the shore."

Callie released a deep breath, feeling a little better about the situation down below. "What's going on with you?" The term they used was strange and she hadn't the foggiest idea what the Pepsi metaphor had to do with anything.

"The bends. If you come up too fast, the nitrogen in your blood expands. It hits the joints and the spine and is not a pleasant experience."

She rethought the soda metaphor and the difference between opening it slowly—no bubbles—or opening it quickly—a messy explosion. And sometimes, if she drank too quickly, the gas bubbles would come back up through her chest and into her throat, seemingly expanding as they rose.

Oh, God. That pain was terrible, and if Alex had something similar going on all over his body…

She rubbed her hand across her forehead and reconsidered her options. "Wade said to wait fifteen minutes before calling the coast guard. Do you agree?"

"Yeah—" He started to nod but froze and then curled into the tightest ball she'd ever seen.

The pain or cramp that hit was severe, and she made an executive decision to ignore Wade's advice, and Alex's second, and figure out how to reach the coast guard on her own. If they agreed to wait until Wade and Tyler returned and reassured her Alex would be okay, then she'd be fine with their decision. But for her own peace of mind, she needed another opinion on this matter, and it was time to reach out and touch someone.

*Please, God, let me figure out how to work the radio. And let there be someone on the other end.*

Emulating what she'd seen on television and in the movies, she pressed the button on the side of the microphone and yelled, "Mayday, mayday, mayday." She released the button, waited ten seconds, and when nothing happened, tried again. "Mayday, mayday, mayday. Can anyone hear me?"

Panic crept in and began feeding her worst fears.

*What if they were out too far out to be heard?*

*What if no one ever heard them?*

*What if Wade didn't come back up?*

A broken, crackly voice came through the radio. "This is… Coast… Guard…"

Overwhelming relief buckled her knees and she collapsed into the chair. Trying to recall what Wade told her, she said, "I have an overdue diver, a diver down searching for him, and a diver on board with… the bends."

It was such an odd term she half-expected them to laugh at her for being so gullible. But that was okay. They could laugh all they wanted, just as long as they offered assistance.

"Are… on board… ma'am?"

She only got bits and pieces of their communication, but she thought he'd asked if she was the only other person on board. "Yes. Which means we're all in trouble. The diver who went down to search told me to wait fifteen minutes before calling, and it's only been about ten. But the diver on board is in a lot of pain and… well, sometimes I don't follow orders well."

"Yes, ma'am… your location… Do you know… GPS coordinates?"

She'd watched over Alex's shoulder all morning while they dragged the mini-torpedo back and forth, so she felt confident in her ability to not only give them GPS coordinates, but accurate coordinates.

"How long… overdue diver… missing?"

She wanted to scream that he wasn't missing, only temporarily misplaced, but rather than squabble about semantics, she looked at the clock on her phone and did some quick calculations. "About forty-five minutes. He was with another diver and they got silted out?" Again, the terminology was like speaking Greek, but she was pretty sure she had it right. "His dive partner only had one tank of air and had to resurface.

The rescue diver has been down… thirteen minutes."

As tears stung her eyes again, she squeezed them shut and dug deep in her gut for an iron will that would keep her from breaking under the pressure and becoming paralyzed with fear. There'd be time for falling apart later. For now, she *would* pull it together, *keep* it together, and do whatever was necessary to get them out of this.

While swimming to the bottom of the ocean, Wade refused to think about the penetrating cold chilling him to the bone or the heavy cloud cover making it impossible to see, even without a thick silt field, or Callie's wide brown eyes, screaming with fear. None of those were productive thoughts, and rather than allow himself to be distracted, he needed to keep his focus on the task at hand.

He needed to find the same entry point Tyler and Alex used so he'd be in the right area. He needed to figure out a way of judging the halfway point of the hallway. And he needed to sweep the rooms as quickly and efficiently as possible, finding Tyler with enough time left to haul their asses outta there.

*Gee… should be easy enough.*

When he reached the anchor lying on the ocean floor, he tied the end of his line to it and attached his reel to his belt. They'd dropped anchor so close to the ship they were practically on top of the thing. The hatch directly in front of him was open, and the silt cloud filtering through the opening, being swept away in the ocean currents, let him know he was in the right spot to enter.

He squeezed through the rusted-out opening, pressed his hand to the side of the hallway, and made his way along the narrow passage.

The farther he went, the thicker the silt cloud became, and visibility dropped to zero. Going on nothing but a gut feeling, he bypassed the few rooms at the edge of the thickening cloud, figuring Tyler could've made his way out of them easy enough, then began a steady in and out of the rooms in the thickest part of the silt.

Down to the right… up to the left… down the hallway until he found the next one… down to the right… up to the left…

He entered the fifth doorway, ran his hand along the edge of the wall, and began his circle. He'd been working on the theory that Tyler would make his way to a wall or the hallway to try and find his way out, and he hoped like hell he hadn't missed him in one of the other rooms by only sweeping the outer edges of the room.

As he made the turn from wall two to wall three, he bumped into a solid object. He felt around to determine if it was a man or a part of the ship and nearly shit himself when the mass moved and grabbed his shoulder. Thank God, the bastard was alive!

Emotion threatened to overwhelm Wade, but he still needed to get Tyler out of here and back on deck, and he didn't have any way of knowing how much air Tyler had left because he still couldn't see anything. Right now, they needed to get the hell out of here. There'd be plenty of time for celebrating later.

Finding Tyler's hand, he guided it to the line attached to Wade's belt and tugged, letting Tyler know it was tied off and all he had to do was follow it out to safety. It only took a few minutes to swim out into the open water, but even there, visibility was poor.

Wade couldn't see much, but Tyler's wide, wild eyes and terrified expression gave Wade a boost of encouragement and hope for the future. Tyler had thought this might be the end for him, and he'd definitely not been at peace with the idea. Wade wished like hell they could've skipped this little part of the adventure, but if this was what it took to wake Tyler the fuck up and realize life was worth living, then so be it.

Wade didn't know how long he'd been gone, but he was certain he was beyond his fifteen-minute time limit. Hopefully Callie had already called the coast guard, because a quick check of Tyler's gauge indicated things were still critical and there was no time to do decompression stops along the way.

Alex's bends wouldn't be any fun. Tyler's were going to be severe. They'd gotten this far, but unless Tyler got into a decompression chamber, he still wasn't out of the woods.

Wade pointed to Tyler's gauge, made a slashing motion across his throat, and pointed to the surface, letting Tyler know there wasn't time to pass *Go* or stop on *Boardwalk*. He needed to scoot to the top as quick as possible.

Taking a moment to pull his shit together, Wade untied the reel from the anchor line, then followed along in Tyler's wake. As he neared the surface, the vibrating hum of a large boat motor filled his ears, and if he wasn't mistaken, he also caught the steady *whump-whump-whump* of helicopter blades.

He chuckled, as much as was possible with a regulator in his mouth, and shook his head as disbelief, pride, and admiration filled him, making him feel light enough to float right on through the surface of the water and into the sky.

The woman who was terrified of going on a boat, who'd slammed on the brakes at the entrance and almost turned back for the safety of home, had saved the day. And possibly two lives.

God, he loved that woman. She never failed to surprise or amaze him with her courage and tenacity. He might be a fool for making the leap so quickly, but life-and-death situations had a way of highlighting the important stuff—a big heart, caring soul, and generous spirit— while sweeping all the other, non-important bullshit under the rug.

# Chapter Twenty

*A*fter establishing radio contact with the coast guard, everything sped up while at the same time slowing down for Callie. She felt as if she'd left the boat, left her life, and slipped into an alternate universe that was a crazy funhouse—minus the fun. It was like looking at the world through a series of distortions and mirrors while trying to find her way through a maze of ever-changing floors.

The coast guard put out a distress call to any other vessels in the area, and moments later a large fishing vessel with a crew of five approached. Normally, she would've been terrified of her rescuers—a rugged group of men who didn't appear to have showered or shaved in weeks—but under the circumstances, she forgot to judge them based on appearances and long held stereotypes.

Two men from the trawler boarded the boat with Alex and her. One took over communications with the coast guard, while the other explained Alex's condition to her—in useful terms, without metaphoric comparisons to soft drinks. *The bends,* slang for decompression sickness, got the name because it causes the person to bend over in terrible pain. Unfortunately for Alex, the only way to help him was by getting him into a hyperbaric chamber, aka decompression chamber.

He also told her Tyler would most likely suffer as well, only worse because of the length of time he'd been at the bottom of the ocean. He would need long decompression stops while resurfacing but probably wouldn't have enough air to do them.

Taking all of that into consideration, the coast guard diverted one of their helicopters from a training mission to pluck Alex and Tyler off the boat and get them to Charleston and into decompression chambers as quickly as possible.

The entire plan, however, hinged on Tyler and Wade resurfacing.

Alex remained curled on the bench, so she sat in the floor next to him, took hold of his hand, then rested her head on her crossed arm and silently repeated her new mantra.

*They're going to be fine. They're going to be fine. Dammit, they are going. To be. Fine.*

After five minutes of constant repetition, she began to believe it but was still shocked and stunned and completely overcome with joy and relief when she heard a fisherman on the other boat start yelling, "There! Look! One of the divers is up."

Alex's eyelids fluttered open and he locked gazes with her as he drew in a deep, shuddering breath. Neither of them could see which diver surfaced, and the fisherman said one, not two, but based on Alex's sigh of relief and the tremor working through his body, he knew the same truth she did.

Wade wouldn't have surfaced without Tyler.

It was within the realm of possibility that Tyler managed to get out of the wreckage on his own and back to the surface without passing Wade, but based on the information Alex had shared, that scenario didn't seem likely.

Giving Alex's hand a reassuring squeeze, she said, "I'm going to check on them. I'll be right back."

She stood and watched as the fisherman who'd been helping Alex fished Tyler out of the water, then searched for Wade. Flutters of anxiety and tendrils of fear blossomed in her gut as her visual search elicited nothing but rough, choppy water.

Maybe she'd been wrong in her assumption that Wade was with him. Maybe Tyler had gotten by Wade without being seen. She gripped the railing and leaned over, as if getting closer to the water would somehow help her see better.

Just as panic began to squeeze her throat, making breathing nearly impossible, she heard splashing and saw Wade shoot through the choppy waves. Her knees weakened and she sagged with relief, and when he climbed onto the platform and made eye contact, her emotional house of cards crashed.

All the fear she'd kept bottled up erupted in a flood of big, fat, ugly tears, and her shaking became so uncontrollable she collapsed onto her knees. She tried to gather herself together, but she was too far lost in the maelstrom of the emotional storm to regain her grip and control.

"Hey, baby. Shhh… Come here." Her heart thudded wildly and she cried even harder as Wade knelt before her and pulled her against his bare chest. "Everyone is okay now, sweetheart. Shh… I'm here. Tyler's here. You have the freaking coast guard here. You did good, baby." He continued to hold and rock her while stroking her hair as the fragmented pieces of her mind slowly came back together.

He'd taken off his tanks and rolled the top part of his wetsuit down to his waist. The sharp sting of his ice-cold skin pressed against her cheek finally penetrated her awareness enough to shock her out of meltdown, while at the same time bringing on a fresh wave of fear.

"Oh, my God. You're freezing." She slapped her palms against his chest, then moved them up to his neck and onto his cheeks, checking to see if he was cold all over. Alex said the wet suit wouldn't keep Wade warm, and based on his frigid skin temperature, he'd been right.

She swiped her hands across her cheeks, sweeping away the tears, then shot to her feet and back into action. She'd been vaguely aware of the activity around her—it was hard to miss a helicopter circling overhead, creating a mini-hurricane—but the coast guard had taken over the care of Tyler and Alex, leaving Wade as her only concern.

She grabbed the wool blanket Alex left lying on the bench as the coast guard crewman prepared him for liftoff, and draped it around Wade's shoulders. "Get out of that suit, and I'll get your clothes. They're a little damp, but they have to be better than the cold, wet suit."

"Callie, I'm fine." He tried to grab her arm to bring her back to him, but she shook him off and charged toward the front of the boat and his clothes.

"I know you're fine." Reciting her mantra in the face of this new concern grounded her, so she kept it going. "You're all going to be fine. Perfectly fine. But you need to get into dry clothes." A tinge of hysteria crept into her voice, but she couldn't keep it out. She was barely keeping herself together, and any thoughts of something else going awry would topple her into never-never land.

"Callie, please…"

She saw Wade studying her from the corner of her eye, but conversation wasn't getting him warm, and she refused to answer. When it became obvious she wasn't going to respond to his plea, he began stripping off the rest of his gear. Alex had already been hoisted into the helicopter, and while one of the crewmen readied Tyler, the other evaluated Wade.

Even though everyone agreed he had mild hypothermia, he refused to be transported to the hospital. He assured the coast guard he would stay wrapped up in blankets, use Callie's body heat to supplement his own, and go easy on the return trip to keep jarring to a minimum.

She had no idea how he planned to get through the inlet without being beaten to pieces, but she kept her mouth shut and didn't argue.

As soon as the helicopter lifted away and the fishermen who'd boarded the dive boat made their way back to their own vessel, Wade grabbed Callie and wrapped her in a desperate, nearly suffocating hug.

"I'm so fucking glad to see you." The words were broken and filled with emotion as he buried his face in her hair.

Returning the hug with equal intensity, she allowed a shiver to run through her as she considered how badly things could've ended, but she refused to break down again. "I've never been so scared in my life. God, I knew you wouldn't come back up without him—" Her voice broke on the crest of a sob, so she cut off the words and focused on the tight, strong arms wrapped around her and the solid mass of his body pressed against hers.

They clung to each for what seemed like forever, afraid of letting go for fear the other would slip away—for good this time. After a while, when his trembling subsided and her nervous jitters waned, he leaned back and brushed her hair away from her eyes.

Pressing his forehead to hers, he said, "I could stand here and hold you like this forever. But we need to get going before the weather gets us and we have to deal with that too."

Wade planned to meet up with the boat owner at the dock, turn over the keys and gear, then get in his truck and drive to Charleston. She, however, had different plans, and as soon as her phone picked up a cellular tower, she sent Jen a text.

*Emergency. Need Raul to drive us to Roper Hospital in Charleston. K?*

Thirty seconds later, she received a text back:

*OMG! Of course! R u ok? Where do u need him 2 b?*

Through a series of texts, she gave Jen the location of the marina, briefly explained the situation, and asked Jen not to tell anyone else so

Wade wouldn't have additional drama to deal with. For all of her faults, Jen was fantastic at discretion and keeping secrets… probably because she had so many of her own.

When they pulled into the marina, Wade glanced at the shiny black car, then did a double take as Jen started waving. He didn't say anything about the unexpected welcoming committee, but the muscle in his jaw jumped a few times, indicating he had some pretty strong thoughts on the subject—none of them good. While he met with the boat owner, she grabbed their blankets, towels, and coats, then made her way to the parking lot.

Raul was serious, as usual, and silently nodded in greeting from his post by the driver's door. Jen was even more serious, definitely not the usual, as she gave Callie an appraising look, then charged and threw her hands around Callie's neck, nearly knocking her off her feet.

"Thank God you're okay." She stepped back and checked Callie again from head to toe, then pulled her into another quick hug. "Do you want me to go with you to Charleston?"

Callie's brain had a difficult time processing Jen's question, since she was normally bossy and overbearing and never asked Callie what she wanted, but instead usually took control of every situation and told Callie how things would go.

After a moment, Callie said, "I don't know how long we'll be, and we'll be bringing Alex and Tyler back with us." Plus, if Wade felt up to it, she had some life-affirming activities planned for the back of the car, and privacy was a must. "I'd rather go alone, if you don't mind."

She held her breath and waited for Jen's reaction to the rejection, but rather than getting ugly, she smiled and grabbed Callie's hand, then gave her another hug. "I've never seen you like this over anyone." She glanced to Wade, who was walking to his truck with his gear. "Not even Gavin. I don't get it, but you obviously care a lot about him, so I'm glad he's okay." She returned her attention to Callie and grinned. "I can't believe you called the coast guard and saved the freaking day."

Callie opened her mouth to clarify she'd just made the call; the coast guard and fishermen had saved the day, but Jen stopped the flow of words by adding, "My little girl is growing up."

Speechless and unable to respond, Callie stood with her mouth open, staring at her friend. She never realized Jen saw her as being little or small and incapable of handling herself, but that certainly explained a lot. Like why Jen always felt the need to direct Callie, even when Callie didn't want or need Jen's overbearing mothering.

Maybe something good had come from the day's horrible events and they'd finally be able to find some kind of equal footing. It would be nice to leave the constant tension between them in the past.

Wade stepped up behind Callie and pressed a hand to the small of her back. "I need to get going. Are you staying here?"

"Hell no." She took a deep breath and made eye contact with Jen, warning her to stay out of the impending discussion, then turned to Wade with a smile. "And you're not driving. Raul is."

His eyebrow rose a notch and he blinked a few times, but other than that, his face remained a blank mask. Realizing he didn't know Raul and might even think the car and driver were hers, she quickly added, "Raul is Jen's driver, and he's here to take us to Charleston. You've been through a lot today, and you have to be tired. I would imagine you're going to have an adrenaline crash, and the hypothermia will leave you tired as well."

As his eyebrow notched a little higher, she held up her phone and smiled.

"Google. As soon as we got back into cell range, I checked the symptoms and researched what to do to help you. Let Raul drive us so you can rest. Depending on how long we have to wait for Tyler and

Alex, we might even need the car for naps. When they're ready to come home, we can bring them back with us in this, which will be a much smoother ride than your bouncy truck."

He still didn't look convinced, so she gave him a sassy smile, stood on tiptoes to whisper in his ear, and pulled out the big guns of persuasion. "I've never had limo sex. Have you?"

His eyes narrowed and his shoulders stiffened as a little choking cough escaped his throat. "You don't fight fair."

She shrugged apologetically. "Did it work?"

He looked intrigued, but not entirely convinced, so this time she appealed to his emotional side. Framing his face with her hands, she held his head and his gaze. "Please let him drive so you can ride in the back with me. I want to hold you all the way there to reassure myself you're really okay."

The muscle in his jaw tensed, then he pressed his lips together and shifted his gaze to the car. It wasn't a full capitulation, but the tide was turning, so before he flat-out refused again, she tossed her keys to Jen and said, "Take my car home. I'll get it from you when I get back to town. I'll keep you posted on what's happening and when we'll be back. Thanks for letting Raul help us."

"Of course. What's mine is yours. You know that." Another quick hug and then a hurried, "I love you," left Callie speechless for the second time in five minutes.

As Jen rushed off to Callie's car, Raul came around to the passenger side and opened the door. Speaking to Wade, he said, "I've contacted DAN for an update on your friends. They're in chambers and doing well. I have directions to the hospital and will take you directly to them."

Everything about Wade's demeanor softened and relaxed. He seemed surprised and a little overcome as he extended his hand to Raul for a shake. "Thank you." Emotion cracked the words, so he cleared his throat and nodded once, then motioned for Callie to get into the car ahead of him.

The car was neither super-stretch nor over-the-top fancy, but it worked well for Jen and her friends and would be great for today's needs. A single seat ran along the left side, then wrapped around the front, backing up to the driver. A short seat ran along the ride side, and a bar was sandwiched between the end of the seat and the door.

The privacy glass was already raised, which was incredibly convenient because Callie probably would've been too nervous and backed out—or fumbled around and made a mess of things trying to raise it herself. Not to mention never being able to make eye contact with Raul again.

Callie set her bag and the stack of blankets and jackets on the floor, then sat on the long seat and waited for Wade to join her. "Do you know Raul?" she asked once the door was shut and they were closed in together.

Wade glanced at her, then continued his perusal of the interior of the car. "Do I look like the kind of guy who knows limo drivers?"

Ignoring his cranky tone, she said, "Then how does he know your friend, Dan?"

He stretched his long legs out in front of him, rested his arm across the back of the seat, and laid his head back, showing for the first time his exhaustion and the toll the day had taken. "DAN stands for Divers Alert Network. They coordinate with the coast guard when there are diving accidents. He must dive himself or has friends who do."

Callie tried to imagine Raul diving but had a hard time envisioning him doing anything but driving a car. He'd worked for Jen's father for years, but like so many people in her life, Callie realized she didn't know anything about him personally.

Taking Wade's outstretched arm as an invitation to curl up against his side, she grabbed the heavy wool blanket and sidled up next to him. A wave of contentment rushed through her and escaped on a sigh when he wrapped his arm around her and pulled her tight.

Resting her head on his chest, she stretched her arm around his side and squeezed. "They're going to be okay, right?"

"Yeah, they'll be fine now that they're in the decompression chamber. Alex would've been fine eventually. Although his life would've been hell for a while. But Tyler was down there a long time." He scrubbed his hand over his face and stared at the ceiling. Speaking quietly, and more to himself than her, he said, "He was so close to being out of air. There wasn't any way to do safety stops, so the bends would've hit quickly. He'd have been in deep shit without the chamber."

She shivered against the chill of his words as well as the cooler-than-normal temperature radiating from his body. She'd stayed wrapped around him all the way back into shore, like she was riding on the back of a motorcycle, and thought she'd helped warm him a little. His body temperature, however, still seemed well below normal.

Snuggling closer, she asked, "What about you? Do you need the chamber?"

"No, I'm fine. I wasn't down long enough to get into trouble."

"What about the hypothermia? Are you warming up at all?"

He tipped his head to the side and looked at her through the fringe of his lashes while flexing his arm to tighten his grip on her. "Oh, yeah. You always heat me up." Her pulse fluttered as his eyes softened and he swallowed deeply. "You're incredible, you know that?"

Warmth spread through her at the pride radiating from him... and with the pride she had in herself for handling the situation so much better than anyone—including herself—would've expected. She didn't ever want to go through anything like that again, but she'd proved she could handle stressful, life-threatening situations if necessary, and she was damned proud.

"Hey." Wade tipped up her chin and swiped his thumb across her cheek, gathering a stream of tears she didn't even realize were falling. "Don't cry, baby. It's all over now, and everyone, including you, is fine."

She bit her lip to fight off the tremble as her mind broke loose and she lost control of her emotions again. "I wasn't worried about me. You could've died down there. You *would* have if you hadn't found him."

She didn't pose it as a question. She didn't need to. She knew the deal as well as him, and the tic in his jaw, along with the raw intensity radiating from his eyes, was further confirmation.

"But I did find him. And thanks to you, the coast guard was waiting and now they're getting the treatment they need."

"I was scared."

He closed his eyes and wrapped his other arm around her to pull her onto his lap. "So was I, baby. But it's over now, and I'm damn glad that's not the way the story... our story... ended."

They sat in silence, curled together, each lost to their own thoughts. After a moment, she said, "Wade?"

"Hmmm?"

"I'm ready."

He cracked his eyes open and caught her gaze. "Ready for what, baby?"

"For you to make love to me."

# Chapter Twenty-One

$\mathcal{W}$ade's body tensed and the arm wrapped around her tightened as a choking sound escaped the back of his throat. "Now?"

He sounded incredulous, and despite her increasingly sexed-up state, she laughed. "Yes, now." She shifted around on his lap and straddled his knees, facing him. The position worked well the other night on her couch. Hopefully it would work even better now.

"I need to touch you. To feel you moving inside me so I know you're really okay. I want to look into your eyes, and this time, I want to see life and promises of a tomorrow." She tugged on her lip with her teeth and battled the nerves tightening her throat. "And when you look into my eyes, you'll see the same thing. I'm ready to give you everything, Wade. Please."

His chest rose and fell rapidly and his eyelids grew heavy while the pupils dilated, making his irises a dark, rich brown. "What about a soft bed and a pillow?" He glanced toward the front of the car. "And privacy?"

"Raul can't see or hear anything. Trust me, he's had lots of practice with Jen. He probably thinks we're already naked."

Wade's upper lip curled as he glanced at the seat, probably imaging Jen's naked butt in the exact spot he sat. "Another reason to wait until we're home."

"I don't want to wait." The intensity of the day, knowing she'd come close to losing him just as she'd found him, made Callie crazy with desperation and bordering on out-of-control reckless. Ignoring his reservations, she reached for the fly of his jeans and fumbled with the buttons. "Please don't deny me this."

His hands tightened on her waist, and she could tell from his choppy breathing and pounding pulse he wanted this as much as her. But he still held himself back. "My wallet is in my bag in the truck. I don't have a condom."

She'd never experienced such a desperate driving need and the urgency to have Wade inside her shocked even her. She twisted to the side and reached behind her to open the bottom drawer of the bar, revealing the super-sized box Jen always kept on hand. "Problem solved."

Heat and desire flashed in his eyes as he glanced to the box, and a second later, she was flat on her back on the seat. He wedged one knee between her legs and settled the other on the floor. One elbow rested above her head and his other hand pressed to the floor for balance.

"This isn't how I imagined our first time." His soft, tender voice still seemed hesitant, and she had the impression he was giving her another chance to change her mind.

That was so not happening.

"Me neither. But I also never considered the possibility of you dying before we had a first time." She tugged at the hem of his partially tucked-in shirt. "I'm not willing to wait another minute." She paused. "We'll have a second and a third and a fourth time, right? We can do the bed thing later."

His grin was slow and sexy as he lowered his mouth to hers. "Absolutely."

At first, it was a soft brushing of lips against lips, but then the kiss grew hard and hot, and his tongue branded her as it swept over her bottom lip, then demanded entry into her mouth. She didn't know how his internal body temperature was doing, but if he was like her, he'd be in danger of going from hypothermia to overheating any minute.

"You wanna be on top?" he asked, breaking the kiss, giving them both the opportunity to gasp for much needed air. "I can't imagine the seat is real comfortable for you?"

"No." She slid her palms under the hem of his shirt and pushed them upward across his abs and chest, dragging the shirt to his neck in the process. There was no time for slow exploration right now, and after stripping off the shirt, she went to work on his pants. "I'm comfortable right here. I'll be even better when you're naked. On top of me. In me."

A smile curled his lips and his eyebrow rose. "What happened to you out there? Where's my shy little kitten?"

She stopped trying to strip off his jeans long enough to look him in the eye, making sure he couldn't miss the seriousness of her answer. "What happened is I now know how fragile and fleeting life can be. I'm not wasting another minute. This is too important. *You're* too important. You're the best thing that's ever happened to me, and I'm not waiting another second to be with you."

He made another of those strangled sounds and clenched his eyes tight, then drew in a ragged breath as he pushed himself up and looked out the window. "We only have forty-five minutes. At the most."

The regret filling his voice had her laughing. *Sweet, sweet man.* If he only knew her sad history...

"I can live with forty-five minutes. But if you don't get busy, we're not going to have that long."

God, she loved it when his eyes turned dark brown and gooey and filled with heat and promise. "Yes, ma'am."

He swept her hair off her face and fanned it around her head on the seat. His touch was so incredibly soft and gentle. She found it hard to believe these were the same hands that had been fisted in anger, ready to pummel the guy at The Blue Lagoon.

"You're beautiful." He kissed her temple, her cheek, and the corner of her mouth. "And smart." He dipped lower and kissed the side of her neck before moving up to her ear. "And resourceful. And strong."

She struggled to concentrate on his words while his tongue swept the shell of her ear and his teeth nibbled her neck, but she eventually managed to whisper, "I've never seen any of those qualities in myself."

"I'll remind you every day until you believe it."

He kissed his way back down the side of her neck until he ran into the top of her turtleneck and sweater. She'd always worn high-collared clothing, not only to stay warm, but because she was so conservative, but she suddenly understood why Jen wore low-cut, easy-to-slip-off tops.

It was time to go shopping and make serious wardrobe changes.

Equally frustrated with her clothing, Wade sat back on the seat and pulled her with him. He yanked the sweater and turtleneck over her head and, no longer hesitant or holding himself back, he wasted no time in flicking open the front closure of her bra. After tossing it onto the floor with her sweater, he grabbed the blanket from the seat behind him.

"Let's spread this out under you so you're more comfortable."

After he had her stretched out on the seat the way he wanted, he undid her belt, unfastened her jeans, and tugged them down until they bumped into her shoes. He might've been leery of limo sex in the beginning, but he was fully involved and ready to go now, and the growl escaping his throat had her giggling and reaching out to help.

"How about this...?" she said, easing his hand away from the hem of her jeans as he continued to tug. "I'll undress me; you undress you?"

She fought off a grin as he narrowed his eyes in warning. "You think I can't handle a pair of shoes and jeans?"

Giving up the fight, she giggled again. "I'm sure you can, but I'd rather them not end up in shreds. I'd like to go into the hospital with you, and I don't want to have to explain why I'm wrapped in a blanket and nothing else."

He glanced out the window again and his eyes widened. "Jesus. Raul's hauling ass." He scooted away from her and reached for his buttons. "Okay, deal." He paused and raked a scorching gaze over her. "This time. Next time, it's a bed and all night."

Heat blossomed in her belly and spread over her skin in a thin sheen of sweat. Oh yeah, she would look forward to the next time, the bed, and all night. But for now, their new arrangement worked for her, and less than a minute later, they were both naked, she was once again lying on the blanket on the seat, and he was sheathed in a condom, hovering over her.

He dipped his head and circled her nipple with his tongue, then clamped down with his teeth and pulled. *Holy hell!* Everything between her nipple and toes blazed from the force of the tug. She arched her back, cried out, and grabbed the back of his head, holding him in place, hoping he'd do it again.

He didn't disappoint, and she arched her back even higher as he switched to her other breast and lavished it with kisses and strokes and, oh God, another of those magnificent tugs that caused a splattering of sparks and fire to race through her stomach and into her sex.

"God, so good, but I need more." She sounded even more desperate than she'd been before, and she wiggled beneath him, trying to maneuver him into place.

The car swayed as Raul changed lanes and Wade lurched to the side, barely catching himself from falling by grabbing the back of the seat. "Limo sex is overrated. You know that, right?"

She wrapped her legs around his waist, locking him into place while at the same time trying to pull him closer so he'd be perfectly aligned with her. "I told you I'd never done it before. And if you were down here with me, your center of gravity would be lower and you'd be much safer."

A grin crawled across his face as he ran his finger down the center of her stomach. "You can be quite persuasive when you want something." He continued lower with his finger and when he ran it through the center of her sex, his head fell back on his shoulders with a groan. "God, you're so wet."

"And ready. And waiting."

He repositioned her legs so one was over his shoulder and the other lay along the back of the seat, giving him ample room to slip between them. Even though she was on her back with him on top of her, this was miles from the typical missionary position she'd experienced in the past, and she'd never been more needy or ready.

And based on the burning intensity in his eyes and the set of his jaw, she'd also never been more wanted.

He closed the gap between them and nudged at her entrance. He was larger than anyone she'd been with, and for a brief moment her eyes widened and she caught his eye while holding her breath, uncertain she could take him.

She should've known she had nothing to worry about, though, because as he rocked forward, then drew back and rocked forward again, he kept his gaze locked on hers, making sure she was okay, never going too far or too fast. He was so gentle with her, so concerned about her and her comfort; she released her fears and hesitation and relaxed, opening to him.

As he continued the slow, steady process of easing in and back out, she lifted her hips to meet him, silently urging him on, begging him to fill her. She half-expected him to ram into her, but he never did.

Instead, he continued the slow in and out, easing in a little farther each time, all the while never taking his eyes off hers.

The moment was perfect, better than anything she could've ever imagined, and tears stung the backs of her eyes at the sweet, tender, gentle, and loving way he handled her. She was certain, at some point, there would be an opportunity for fast and wild mind-blowing sex. But for now, he was giving her exactly what she wanted. He was allowing her to see into his soul and the love and affection pouring not only from his eyes, but also being conveyed in every stroke and touch reassured her there would be a tomorrow. And then another. And another.

When he'd finally pushed all the way in, he slipped his hand under her butt and lifted, changing the angle, filling her even more. She'd never experienced anything so intense while at the same time so tender, and in a matter of seconds, she was riding the crest of an orgasm, ready to break over the edge.

She jerked her hips, encouraging him to take her faster, but he maintained the same frustratingly slow pace. He dipped his head and latched onto her breast, rolled his eyes up to her and flashed a sexy grin, then clamped down on her nipple with his teeth.

The orgasm hit with the force of a rocket and she would've screamed, but Wade was there covering her mouth with his, absorbing the sound. As the waves began to subside, he picked up speed, rocked into her with more force than he'd previously used, and moved his hand around to her clit.

She'd always been a one-and-done girl in the past, but everything with Wade was different, and before she knew what was happening, she'd started the climb to the top of the peak again.

"That's it, baby, give me another one."

"I... don't... think..."

The sentence died off when he pinched her clit and rocked into her hard, hitting someplace deep inside that had never been touched before. She disintegrated into another ball of orgasmic bliss, and this time she wasn't alone.

He rocked his hips harder and faster, clenched his jaw, and let go with a powerful orgasm that shook her inside and out. He collapsed and she relished the feel of his weight pressing down on her, forcing her deeper into the seat. After several deep breaths, he pressed his hand to the floor, preparing to lift off her, but she wasn't ready to let him go yet.

She grabbed his shoulders, keeping him in place. "Wait." She didn't know how to express her feelings without scaring him off, but she wanted... needed him to understand how much she cared. "I've never been this over the moon about anyone." She hesitated, then smiled and added, "Not even Prince Charming. What I thought was love was nothing more than a crush, infatuation. I didn't have a clue what real, mature love was all about. But I think I'm beginning to understand."

Wade slowly lowered his lips to hers, then slicked his tongue along her lower lip before slipping it inside. When he'd kissed her thoroughly, he pulled back and stared into her eyes. "You were the reason I made it back to the surface. I wouldn't give up on finding Tyler, but I was determined to make it back to you."

He took a deep breath and continued. "I'm not real good with words, but... I want to make this work. I still have my doubts about being who you need me to be." His gaze roamed around the interior of the car. "I'll never be able to give you this." He laughed. "Hell, I guess if you want one, you can buy it yourself." He sobered and chewed on the inside of his cheek. "I'm not sure how I feel about that either, but..."

He gathered her up in his arms and pulled her onto his lap as he sat back on the seat. "I'm absolutely certain how I feel about you. If it's all right with you, we'll figure the rest out together."

# Chapter Twenty-Two

$\mathcal{W}$ade pulled into the parking lot of The Chesapeake, put his truck into park, and stared at the clubhouse in front of him. He found it hard to believe how much his life had changed, again, in just a few short weeks. This time, rather than the abrupt change leading to a broken heart and leaving him lost to a world of misery, the change had filled his heart with more love than he thought possible and made him happier than he'd ever dreamed.

He and Callie hadn't talked about the diving incident since the day it happened. However, the reality of their fragile existence stuck with them both and permeated every part of their lives. They weren't morose, and neither planned on future traumatic events, but they'd gotten a crash course in the importance of living life to the fullest, and that's exactly what they were doing. Together.

He spent most nights at Callie's, since she was still adapting to his rustic home and beach life—which meant having sand on the floor, no matter how often they swept, and dealing with rogue grains in the bed. Several times he'd gotten her out on the patio to enjoy a fire in the pit, but he had yet to introduce her to the joys of sex on the beach. He could tell from the way she bit her lip and cast dreamy eyes to the water's edge whenever he broached the subject that she was slowly warming to the idea, and it was just a matter of time until she gave in.

The Anticue renovations were going well, and he and Callie had the first guest reservations on the books. Sunny still hadn't gotten a new car, but she'd agreed to start looking as soon as the lethargy and all-day sickness passed.

Wade was still trying to convince Mercy to take the ring, but she was taking longer to come around than he'd hoped. He'd even used Callie's example of electricity to explain this was a chance for the ring to bring good into somebody's life, but she was too proud to accept "charity." There wasn't anything he could do but continue to remind her the ring was hers whenever she was ready to accept the gift.

Tyler and Alex had fully recovered and things were back to business as usual, with one exception. Tyler was still miserable without Laney, but he finally saw his life held value, even without her, and he vowed to cut back on the crazy stunts. He would always push the envelope, but now at least he measured the risks.

Wade grabbed the wrapped present from the seat beside him, climbed down from his truck, and made his way to the front door of the clubhouse. He hadn't been back since the day he moved on to work in Anticue, and he was curious to see all the changes Callie had made.

There was a car in the lot with North Carolina tags, so rather than call out and interrupt her meeting, he followed the sound of voices coming from the back conference room. He stepped up to the open doorway and peeked inside, hoping to catch her attention to let her know he was there, and had the air knocked from his lungs like a giant fist sucker-punched him and his brain was as scrambled as his morning eggs.

Miranda's older sister, Lizbeth, sat across the table from Callie, and they were laughing and conversing like they'd known each other forever. Catching sight of him from the corner of her eye, Callie's laugh morphed into the wide, love-filled smile she reserved strictly for him, and as always, his stomach fluttered and his heart swelled in his chest.

"Hey," she said, extending her hand toward him, inviting him to join them. "What a great surprise. Come on in."

Lizbeth, who'd allowed her mouth to drop open in a most unlady-like fashion, quickly snapped it closed and nervously licked her lips. Picking up on the weird vibe passing between him and Lizbeth, Callie said, "Do you two know each other?"

He ran his hand over his head, unable to believe how small the world was sometimes. "Believe it or not, yeah, we do." To Lizbeth, he said, "Good to see you, Lizbeth."

Despite their extreme differences in backgrounds and tastes and, well, pretty much everything, he'd always gotten along well with Lizbeth, and he didn't hold any of her sister's actions against her. She must've been concerned about his reaction, because she seemed to be holding her breath, waiting for an explosion. When he showed her none of the animosity he carried toward her sister, she smiled and rose from her chair. "It's good to see you too. How have you been?"

If she'd asked him that question six months ago, he'd have smiled and lied and said *great.* Now, however, as Callie rose from her chair and came to him, his smile was genuine and there wasn't a need to lie about anything. He always stood a little taller and prouder with her next to him, and the words, "I've never been better," were the absolute truth.

He wrapped his arm around Callie and pulled her against him, then kissed her temple. Now that the shock of seeing Lizbeth had worn off, he offered Callie more of an explanation. "Lizbeth is Miranda's sister."

Her eyes widened and her mouth dropped open in a silent, "Oh." She studied him for a minute, probably trying to decide for herself how he really felt about being confronted by his past. Hoping to reassure her, he tipped his head and caught her gaze, then gave her a small, private smile and a wink.

Returning his attention to Lizbeth, he said, "How about you? You doing all right?"

He hadn't seen or spoken to her since his split with Miranda, which happened to be the same day she'd split with Kevin, and he'd often wondered how she was getting along.

"Oh." She pasted on a socialite's smile and drew back her shoulders, putting on a good front. Exactly as he would've done before Callie. "I'm great." She held out her hand and motioned back and forth between him and Callie. "Obviously, you two are an item."

Callie beamed and gazed at him as if he were the sun and the moon while wrapping her arms tight around his waist. "Yep," he said with a laugh as he set the wrapped box on the table, then took a seat and pulled Callie down onto his lap. "We're the most unlikely pair in the world, but our differences make us better and stronger. We're both learning to enjoy diverse things, mostly those things that are important to the other. Although, I have to admit, Callie's learned to like the beach more than I've learned to enjoy a tux." He shuddered as he thought of the fundraising event he'd promised to attend with her and her mother the following weekend.

Lizbeth laughed and tossed her head back, sending her long auburn hair sliding over her shoulder and down her back. She grinned at Callie. "I can imagine. Promise me you'll take pictures when that happens again."

"I definitely will." Callie clasped his hand and squeezed. "Kevin hired Lizbeth to help with the grand opening in a few weeks, so she's going to be here quite a bit between now and then." She bit her lip and sucked in her breath while awaiting his reaction to the news.

He smiled at her, hoping to once again reassure her, then turned to his attention to Lizbeth. "That's great. I look forward to catching up with you."

As he looked at Lizbeth, who favored her sister in so many ways, he marveled at the mysteries of the universe. He'd been devastated by his loss of Miranda and wasn't sure he'd ever recover. He turned to look at Callie. And now he wondered how he'd gotten so lucky to have things work out the way they did.

As he and Callie continued to stare at each other like a couple of starry-eyed lovebirds, Lizbeth cleared her throat and began gathering her things. "I have everything I need for now, so I'm going to take off." She shoved her papers and calculator into her bag and slung it over her shoulder. "I'll get with you later in the week to finalize the details."

Callie broke eye contact with him and giggled as a blush crawled up her neck. "Sorry, I tend to get distracted when he's around."

Lizbeth laughed and tossed her hand in the air. "Sweetie, that's completely understandable." Her smile faltered briefly before she caught the slip and re-pinned it in place. "I'm glad you've found someone who makes you happy, Wade. You deserve nothing but the best."

"Let me walk you to the door," Callie said, pushing to her feet.

"No, no." Lizbeth waved her off. "I can show myself out."

"I'll walk with you," Wade said, then startled Callie by lifting her and setting her on the conference room table in front of him. "You stay right there." He started out of the room, then turned and pointed to the box on the table. "Don't touch that until I've come back."

He laughed as her shoulders dropped and a pout puckered her pretty pink lips. She'd cut her gaze to the gift a couple times, and he knew the second he walked out of the room, she'd be all over it. Hopefully, she wouldn't recognize the wrapping paper and she wouldn't shake it hard enough to figure out the contents on her own.

Since it was dark, he walked Lizbeth all the way to her car and waited until she'd driven out of sight. Going back inside, he locked up and flipped off all the lights—the equivalent of hanging a CLOSED sign on the door. There was a chance Kevin would stop by to check out things on his way home from work, but locked doors and darkened windows would be a good indicator he wasn't welcome. Even if he did own the place.

When he returned to the conference room, Callie had the box on her lap, looking guilty as sin.

"You've been shaking it, haven't you?"

She shrugged and flashed him a dimple. "If you really didn't want me touching it, you wouldn't have left it lying right there."

Laughter bubbled from his chest as his heart expanded even more. It was so hard to believe this woman, who brought him so much joy, was the same woman he'd spent a year avoiding. He'd had a lot of healing to do, and things wouldn't have worked out between them then, but it still seemed a shame they'd lost a year together. However, crying over wasted time accomplished nothing, and he'd much rather focus on their bright future.

"Can I open it now?"

He stuffed his hands in his pockets and rocked back on his heels. "I should make you wait another day for breaking the rules."

She dipped her head and batted her eyes. "But you won't."

He laughed and shook his head. "No, I won't. Go for it."

It was the first time he'd seen her open a gift, and there wasn't any careful untying of the bow or slipping the ribbon off and unwrapping the paper so it could be reused. This was balls to the wall ripping and tossing, and ten seconds later she had the top off, staring at the boots she'd had on layaway, her mouth and eyes wide open.

"Oh, my God." She pulled one of the boots from the box and held it to her chest while looking at him with eyes full of wonder. "How did you know where they were?"

"Jen can be useful," he grudgingly admitted.

Since the day of the diving accident, he and Jen had reached a truce of sorts. She still didn't think he was good enough for her friend, but she accepted him.

And he… Well, he felt the same about her.

Callie pulled the other boot from the box and drew in a long, deep breath, sniffing the leather like it was the most exotic fragrance she'd ever encountered. "Thank you." Tears filled her eyes as she glanced at him again. "You shouldn't have."

"Why not?"

He moved the chair out of his way and took hold of her ankle, then slipped the tiny ankle boot off before taking the long, thigh-high boot from her hand. He'd intended the act of redressing her in the new boots to be a hell of a lot sexier than it ended up being, but putting on a pair of boots as long as a leg wasn't easy. After slipping on the second, he stood back and admired the sexy boots and the even sexier woman.

"They're even hotter than I expected." He ran his palms along the inside of her thighs and spread her legs apart. "I may not be able to give you a yacht or a mansion, Callie, but I can give you a pair of boots." He stepped in between her legs and settled his hands on her waist. "I'll always do everything in my power to make you happy."

She wrapped her arms around his neck and pressed her forehead to his. "Being with you makes me happy."

"Yeah?" he asked in a playful, teasing tone as he tugged the hem of her skirt a little higher. "I like the sound of that."

Her breath hitched and she glanced at the door. "What if Kevin stops by?"

He wrapped his arm around her waist and lifted her so he could slide the back of her skirt out from under her while also taking down her panties. "The door's locked. The lights are off. He'll understand that means *do not disturb.*"

She swallowed roughly and let her head fall back as he ran his tongue up the side of her neck to her ear. "Okay, I'm convinced." Her words were breathy and her eyelids fluttered shut. "Wade?"

"Yeah?" He slid her panties over the boots and down her legs, then let them fall to the floor.

"I think you could make me a little happier tonight."

"Is that right?"

She nodded and licked her lips. "Yes. Please."

Callie was growing more adventurous and bold with their sexual games, and he was thoroughly enjoying the benefits of her newfound sexuality. His cock twitched and his heart beat erratically as he unbuckled his belt and slipped it free, then unsnapped and unzipped his jeans.

When his cock sprang free, she wrapped her hand around him and pulled an upward stroke that had him groaning deep in his throat. He stepped up to the table and pulled her to the edge, then slid into her in one long thrust.

Callie wrapped her ankles around the backs of his legs and used the heels of her boots to spur him on, urging him to take her hard and fast. Happy to oblige, he drove into her in long, pounding strokes, and within minutes, both of them were crashing over the edge into orgasmic bliss.

She collapsed against his chest and gasped for air while he wrapped his hands around the back of her head and held her close. When her breathing returned to normal, she said, "Thank you. I love my boots."

He kissed her forehead, her temple, and the corner of her mouth. With his lips against hers, he said, "I like them too. But I love you."

You've just finished reading *Going All In (Heat Wave Novel #4)*. If you enjoyed this book, please help others discover it by leaving a review.

**If you'd like to stay abreast of contests and new releases, please join my newsletter: www.alannahlynne.com/contact/**
**or follow me on**
**Facebook: facebook.com/AuthorAlannahLynne**
**Twitter: @alannahlynne**
**Tsu: www.tsu.co/AlannahLynne**

Other books in the *Heat Wave* series are:

Saving Me (Heat Wave Novel #1)
Last Call (Heat Wave Novel #2)
Crossing Lines (Heat Wave Novel #3)
A Matter of Time (Heat Wave Novel #5)

Each book in the *Heat Wave* series stands alone and can be read out of order.

Keep reading for a sneak peak of
*MATTER OF TIME* (Heat Wave Novel #5),
followed by the complete novella,
*A CHRISTMAS HEAT WAVE.*

# Prologue

---

*Sixteen Years Ago…*

"$\mathcal{L}$izbeth Sanders, stop for one minute and look at me. I don't understand why you're in such a rush to get back to college. You've never hurried off like this before."

Ignoring her mother's command, Lizbeth continued to the large walk-in closet and slipped another dress off its hanger. A silly image of a Disney princess twirling around her room, humming and singing with the joy of being madly in love with Prince Charming, flitted through her mind. The only thing she needed to make the scene complete were forest animals lining the windowsills and bluebirds fluttering around her head.

"Classes don't start for another three days." Her mother tried again when Lizbeth failed to acquiesce to her demand to stop throwing clothes in the suitcase. "Why don't you stay through the weekend?" When Lizbeth returned to the closet for another dress and a pair of pants, her mother modified her approach. "At least stay for dinner."

"Mother," Lizbeth said while trying to summon a well of patience to keep her blissful bubble intact. "I've been here two weeks. It's not like I breezed in this afternoon only to turn around and leave a few hours later."

"I know," her mother said with a sigh as she settled onto the end of the bed. "But we won't see you again until Thanksgiving, and we miss you. What's so important you need to rush back today anyway?"

*Logan Steele.*

Just thinking his name had Lizbeth's heart swelling with love and her head swimming with excitement and anticipation for the weekend ahead. Since her roommate wasn't returning until Sunday, Lizbeth and Logan would still have the apartment to themselves. And after being separated for two long weeks, they had a lot of catching up to do.

But her mother didn't need to know any of that, so Lizbeth smiled and said, "I'm just excited to get back and see all my friends. Not many stayed in Raleigh for the summer."

At least that part was true. And because most of their friends, including her roommate Stephanie, left for the summer, Lizbeth and Logan had spent months playing house, living together in Lizbeth and Stephanie's apartment, getting a glimpse of the future. They now had a clear picture of what life would be like once they finished school and were married, and they were anxious to get started on their life together.

Breaking into her thoughts, her mother said, "Why do I think there's more you're not telling me?"

Lizbeth laughed as she stuffed a cashmere sweater into her suitcase, then turned and hugged her mother. "I'm in college. I don't tell you lots of things. And trust me. You don't really want to hear them."

"There must be a boy involved," her mother mused. "There's always a boy."

*Not like this one,* Lizbeth thought. *There'll never be another one like Logan.*

Even his identical twin Lucas didn't compare to the man Lizbeth had fallen in love with. They might be identical in their physical appearance, with the exception of Logan's scar that resulted from a nearly fatal motorcycle accident, but their inner essence couldn't be more different. Both were good, honest men who possessed an exorbitant amount of confidence and swagger. But Logan made Lizbeth feel alive and safe and protected in a way she'd never felt with anyone.

On the surface, Lucas should've been the twin she fell for. He was polished and refined and would've fit in nicely with her family and the upper crust her parents associated with. But Logan, in his jeans, T-shirts, and motorcycle boots, was the one she burned for, the one she never wanted to live without.

She'd never experienced the kind of love she felt for Logan, and from the moment her eyes settled on him her freshman year at NC State, she knew he was the one. He'd been a sophomore and still trying to sort through his feelings for his on-again, off-again high school sweetheart, Bobbi Jo. Through Lizbeth's freshman and sophomore year, they kept their relationship platonic, but when he came back to school last fall as a free agent, everything changed.

They'd been nearly inseparable since that first night, which was part of the reason they decided to take summer classes. They didn't want to be apart for three months, and by going straight through the summer, he could graduate in December and start racing Supercross full time in January.

At twenty-two, he was several years older than most competitors just joining the full-time circuit, but he chose to see that as an advantage. He'd continued to race on a part-time basis to stay competitive, and he was religious about his workouts, which kept him healthy and race-ready. His body hadn't sustained the abuse and injuries a lot of competitors dealt with, and mentally, his intense focus and determination backed by the additional years of maturity made him a force to be reckoned with.

His travel schedule would be rough, but by keeping Raleigh as his home base, they hoped to have a couple days together each week.

If there were any questions about how difficult the separation would be, the past two weeks of hell had answered them. When he called her last evening to tell her he would be back in Raleigh by lunchtime today, she'd started a mental countdown until they were together again. And now that it was past noon, she couldn't wait another minute to get on the road.

Three hours later, she drove past her apartment and headed straight to the condo Logan shared with Lucas. They'd agreed to meet at her place at seven, but when they last talked, he sounded like something was wrong, and she was concerned. He tried to play it off as being tired and stressed because his last race hadn't gone well, but she needed to see for herself that he was in one piece and hadn't suffered any serious injuries.

His truck was backed up to his building, his motorcycle still loaded in the bed. Since he normally kept the bike locked in a friend's garage, her concern escalated. She jumped from her car and took the stairs two at a time, then pounded on the door. When no one immediately answered, she knocked again, more forcefully.

She was about to beat again when Lucas jerked the door open and yelled, "What?" His irritation shifted to shock upon seeing her, and he whipped his head around to glance over his shoulder into the living room. Turning back to her, he said, "Lizbeth… what are you doing here?"

His alarm at her appearance, something that was as common as the sun rising, caused panic to dance across her skin. It wasn't her imagination. Something was wrong—seriously wrong—and the sheen of moisture coating her skin from the August heat and humidity turned into a cold sweat as she struggled to catch her breath.

Crossing her arms over her stomach to squelch the rising nausea as well as hide her trembling, she said, "What's going on, Lucas? Where's Logan?"

As if on cue, Logan swung around the corner of his bedroom and headed down the hall, carrying a large cardboard box. He wasn't wearing a cast... no limp... but he appeared tired and worn down and seemed barely able to carry the box in his arms. In general, he looked like hell. And that was before he glanced up and saw her standing in the doorway.

He froze in place, eyes wide, eyebrows raised. His surprise quickly switched to anguish as his brows drew down over his moss-green eyes and his mouth pinched at the corners. He crumpled forward, as if punched in the gut, and her name whispered out on a sharp exhale.

Panic and despair filled his expression as he cut his eyes to Lucas, seemingly searching for help.

Returning his gaze to her, he said, "I thought we were meeting at your place." His voice always sounded like he'd swallowed broken glass—a result of the accident that severely damaged his vocal chords—but today it was completely broken. His shoulders slumped forward even more, and he muttered, "Come on in," before continuing toward the living room.

Lucas stepped to the side and let her pass, then quickly shut the door. Stopping in front of Logan, he pressed his hand to his shoulder, as if trying to give his brother a booster shot of strength, and said, "I'll be in my room if you need me."

She scanned the living room and realized nearly all the contents of Logan's room were either boxed up or piled in the corner. Her mind scrambled to understand as the mood in the room plummeted from sad to morose, like a member of the family had died.

The stupid forest animals evaporated and the bluebirds twittering around her head crashed to the ground.

Her earlier elation was choked out by twisted fingers of fear squeezing her throat. "What's going on, Logan?" She rotated in a circle and let her gaze settle on the items scattered about. His clothes, his racing gear, his shaving kit… everything he owned was ready to be carried out to his truck. Panic numbed her lips. Her tongue was so thick, her mouth so dry she could barely speak. "Where…?" She swallowed and licked her lips and tried again. "Where are you going?"

He dropped the box onto a pile, ran his hands over his short black hair, then dropped onto the sofa as if his legs wouldn't hold him up any longer. Lifting glassy, tear-filled eyes to her, he said, "Sit down, Lizbeth. We need to talk."

# A Christmas Heat Wave

## A Heat Wave Novella

## Alannah Lynne

# Chapter One
## Sam

Sam Mazze jerked her head back, dodging the burst of steam shooting up from the pan of boiling potatoes. The cubes bubbled and rolled in the frothy water, evading capture as she attempted to stab a piece to test its tenderness. Eventually, she managed to nick the corner of one with the tine of the fork enough to confirm her constant checking wasn't getting the job done. She replaced the lid and vowed to leave them alone for at least ten minutes, then moved on to the top oven—what she'd come to think of as the guest of honor's tanning bed.

Watching her husband, Kevin, truss up the turkey had gotten her a little hot and bothered, not to mention envious. The bird, however, either wasn't kinky or he'd tried to escape, because when she removed the foil blanket to check his tan, she found the string popped loose and him lying there, spread eagle, flashing her.

She shook her head and sighed. "You're a freak, Sam. You've been completely corrupted." She wasn't complaining. She loved the sexual adventure and excitement Kevin brought into her life. But it was a little embarrassing to always be thinking kinky, especially when looking at the Christmas turkey.

Setting aside her naughty thoughts, she switched her attention to the second oven. Her seven-year-old daughter Michy's favorite, homemade macaroni and cheese, bubbled around the edges of the ceramic bake ware, while Sam's personal favorite, fresh baked garlic knots, filled the air with downhome comfort. She'd fallen in love with Kevin for hundreds of reasons, but gaining possession of his mother's garlic knot recipe had been the final gotcha.

She sniffed the air like a bloodhound on a scent and followed her nose across the kitchen to the creamy garlic-butter dipping sauce. The minced garlic had settled to the bottom of the bowl, while the colorful parsley and shredded Romano floated on top of the melted butter. Her saliva glands joined the party and made temptation impossible to resist.

She cut her eyes to the kitchen door and cocked her head to the side, listening for the sound of running shower water. Kevin hadn't asked her to sample the sauce, but as the hostess, she had a responsibility to her guests to make sure everything was perfect. How would she know if she didn't do a taste test?

Using the spoon Kevin conveniently left in the bowl, she vigorously stirred the contents, then ran her finger around the inside of the rim to gather the remnants. Her eyes rolled back in her head as the flavors burst to life on her tongue. "God, that's good."

The sample left her greedy and needy for seconds, so before she dove in with both hands, she fled from that side of the kitchen and found herself in front of the bar. Again. Kevin had the bar so well stocked, even Sunny, a professional bartender, would be impressed. One of the bottles of beer shifted and wiggled as a piece of ice melted beneath it. Any other day, she would take that as a sign from the universe she should grab the bottle up, pop the top, and say, "Ahhhh."

But this wasn't any other day. It was Christmas Eve. Her and Kevin's first Christmas together as a married couple. Her first attempt at entertaining as Mrs. Mazze.

She took a deep breath, trying to get a grip on her tangled nerves. It was ridiculous to be so anxious when all of their guests were their closest friends, but she wanted this Christmas Eve to be perfect.

Kevin and Sam lived in Myrtle Beach on a full-time basis, but Kevin had maintained his residence in Riverside, North Carolina, on the Pamlico River. He and Sam used it as a vacation retreat as often as possible, and Kevin's best friend, Erik Monteague, and his wife, Kat, lived next door.

Since Kat was nine months pregnant, traveling wasn't recommended. It was also easier for Sam and Kevin to travel with a seven-year-old than for Erik and Kat to lug around a one-year-old and all of her *stuff*.

Sam shuddered as she thought of Kat chasing a toddler around while trying to keep herself from toppling over. Contrary to popular belief, the pill wasn't an effective means of birth control. At least not for them. Two babies falling into the magical one percent sounded more like one hundred percent to Sam, and she hoped like hell they figured out a more effective plan. She didn't think either of them would survive having a third child anytime soon.

Kat's beloved grandfather, who had moved from Charlotte to Riverside to be near his granddaughter, would also be joining them, as would Steve Vex, Kevin and Erik's close friend who was in town, visiting his mother for the holidays. Sam and Kevin's clients-turned-friends, Gavin and Sunny McLeod, and Sunny's younger brother Robbie were coming for dinner but needed to leave early to get back to New Bern, a quant town about an hour to the south of Riverside, to be with Gavin's grandfather.

Lizbeth Sanders, Kevin's ex, might also stop by. She needed to drop something off for Kat before she left the country, and Sam still wasn't sure how she felt about sharing her home—and therefore Kevin—with Lizbeth. Not only did Lizbeth have history with Kevin, from what she understood, Lizbeth and Erik also shared a past. Hell, the way it sounded, Lizbeth had shared a lot of things with a lot of men in

Riverside.

Somehow, though, Kat had managed to put Erik and Lizbeth's past aside in favor of developing a good working relationship with Lizbeth to benefit the women's shelter. Sam's shoulders slumped and she sighed as she acknowledged her need to follow Kat's example.

Lizbeth hadn't done anything offensive or wrong—that distinction belonged to Kevin when he started seeing Sam before ending his relationship with Lizbeth—and she'd gone out of her way to help straighten things out between Kevin and Sam.

Sam twisted her mouth and fiddled with the top of the ice bucket as she thought the situation over. She supposed there wasn't a better time than Christmas to let bygones by bygones, so if Lizbeth showed up, Sam would put aside her personal insecurities and give her a warm welcome.

As if in agreement, the chorus of "Have a Holly, Jolly Christmas" burst from the built-in overhead speakers, startling her from her thoughts. Before she could move a safe distance away from the bar, Kevin slipped up behind her and whispered in her ear, "Don't even think about having another beer. You're not getting wasted before the evening starts."

She considered lying, but since she sucked at being deceptive, she turned to face him and smiled sheepishly. "How do you know I've already had one?"

He dropped his chin and gave her a blank look. "One? You've had two. I know how many we started with,"—he tipped his head to side, nodding to the beer—"and I can see the empty spaces in the ice."

"Oh." She giggled and wrapped her arms around his waist. "I guess I'm not as sneaky as I thought."

"You're not sneaky *at all*." His eyes softened and a gentle smile curved his lips. "*Piccola*," he said, using his favorite Italian term of endearment for her, "you need to relax." He rested his hands on her hips and dipped his knees so they were eye level. "You and Michy did an amazing job of decorating. It's like a winter wonderland in here. The two of us whipped up a meal everyone will enjoy. But most importantly, we're together, and we're sharing the evening with great friends."

"I know. It's just..." She pressed her forehead to his shoulder and sighed. "I want everything to be perfect and for everyone to have a great time."

"I have a suggestion for getting things started." His smile was slow, sexy. "I promise you'll have a great time."

"Oh, no you don't." His fresh-showered scent along with the heat of his body pressing into hers was turning her brain mushy and had her logical thinking capabilities tiptoeing out the door. She needed space before she turned into a hormonal blob and forgot about everything, including the garlic knots. She pressed her palms against the hard planes of his chest and stepped back. "What you have in mind isn't *relaxing*."

He laughed and stepped in front of her, cutting off her escape as she rounded the end of the large center island. His eyes crinkled at the corners and his lips twitched as his gaze dropped to the obnoxious felt Christmas tree sewn to the front of her bright-red sweater. He batted at the fuzzy Christmas balls hanging from the tree like a cat would a skein of yarn. "This sweater makes you look hot."

She planted her hands onto her hips and glared. "You promised to never lie to me."

"I'm not lying. You always look hot."

She scrunched up her face and flicked the jingle bell sewn to the top of the tree. "It's hideous." She'd spent what seemed like hours looking for an alternative to satisfy Michy. But her daughter's heart and mind were set on wearing matching sweaters, and Sam couldn't say no to those big, blue eyes, especially at Christmas. "I would've preferred my

Grinch sweatshirt."

"The Grinch wanted to ruin Christmas, *piccola*, not make it spectacular for everyone he loved." He scooted the pecan and pumpkin pies over, then wrapped his hands around her waist and lifted her to the counter in front of him. With a tender touch that contrasted with the intensity of his gaze, he trailed his fingertip down her cheek, then brushed her hair over her shoulder. "If I'd known this would be so stressful for you," he said, nuzzling her neck, "I wouldn't have suggested we invite everyone over for dinner."

If she lived to be a hundred, she'd never tire or become immune to the melodic timbre of his voice. It was like smooth, rich chocolate, and whether he was being sexy and cajoling or negotiating a business deal for his family's construction company, listening to his easy drawl never failed to ease her soul.

He knew the effect he had on her, too, because illicit promise shimmered in his eyes and a cocky grin curved the corner of his mouth as he ran his hand down her arm. He linked their fingers together and drew her hand to his lips. Soft kisses along her inner wrist had her heart thumping erratically and challenged her will to keep things cool. But when he nibbled her finger and lifted his eyebrows in playful admonishment, she broke into laughter.

Speaking around her finger, he said, "You've been into the garlic butter."

"Of course I have. You should've known better than to leave it unguarded." When she tried to pull away, he clamped down harder, holding her in place and sending a sizzle of awareness through her entire body. Playful moment over, her head fell back and she groaned with desire. "You're a wicked man, Mazze." Maybe, if she was really lucky, she'd get an extra special present and he'd spank her for being a bad girl.

"You love wicked."

God, did she ever. And when he kissed her neck, she turned to putty in his hand. She rolled her head to the side, giving him better access, and wished she had on a skimpy summer top, rather than a bulky sweater that covered up way too much skin. He nibbled her neck, making her squirm as shivers raced down her spine. The goose bumps dotting her skin were deceiving because on the inside, she was melting down.

"Okay, that's enough," she whispered, trying to sound convincing. When he didn't stop, she tried again, with a little more force this time. "Okay, okay. We need to stop. Michy might catch us."

"She's upstairs watching TV." He drew back and grinned. "And if she does decide to come downstairs, the damned jingle bells on that sweater will give us plenty of warning."

"I knew it!" She laughed and swatted his shoulder. "I knew you couldn't possibly love her sweater as much as you let on."

Her laugh faded into a God-I-love-this-man smile as she stared into his eyes. In moments like this, she wondered how she and Michy had gotten so lucky. Michy rarely asked about her biological father anymore, and in the past several months, she'd started calling Kevin *Daddy*. Fortunately, the love affair went both ways. Kevin adored Michy and Sam knew, no matter what, he would always treat her like his own. "I love you."

He shuffled closer to the counter and eased between her legs so their bodies were pressed together. Wrapping his hand around the back of her head, he held her in place and gave her a slow, sultry kiss. He broke away long enough to whisper, "I love you, too," then moved back in. This time the kiss wasn't sweet and tender, but hot and possessive. His tongue swept the inside of her mouth, branding her as his, while his hand snaked under the bottom of her sweater and up to her breast.

"We need to stop," she said, gasping for breath. "Our guests will arrive at any minute." She'd said the words, but only a small, quickly evaporating part of her meant it. The larger part of her hoped he had all the angles covered, because now that he'd lit the match, a kitchen quickie would be the only way to extinguish the fire.

He cupped her breast in his palm and stroked her nipple through her bra. "They'll ring the doorbell."

From the mudroom entryway, a throat cleared. "Not everyone rings the doorbell. Some of us walk right in."

Startled by the unexpected intrusion, Sam threw her arms around Kevin's neck and launched herself into him. As her brain processed the voice as belonging to Erik, her heart rate slowed and she dropped her forehead onto Kevin's shoulder with a deep exhale.

Kevin ground his teeth and snarled, "One of these days, asshole, one of these days." He eased his hand out from under her sweater, smoothed it down, then wrapped his arms protectively around her. Stroking her back, he said, "You okay, sugar?"

"Yeah, I'm fine." Her body, no longer prepared for flight, had settled to the point she was perfectly capable of climbing off the island and properly greeting their guests. But she was content and wanted to stay cradled in his arms for another few minutes. She rested her cheek on his chest and smiled at Kat and Erik.

Kevin, however, must've continued to glare because Erik said, "What?" He looked at the sweet baby girl in his arms with wide-eyed innocence, then to Kat. "Don't we always walk in without knocking? Just like they do at our house."

Kat shot him a chastising look. "We could've stepped back out and rung the bell."

With his blue eyes sparkling, like they always did when he was up to mischief, Erik kissed Caroline on the cheek, and in a singsongy voice reserved especially for her, said, "Yeah, but aggravating Uncle Kevin is so much more fun."

As the playful interaction between Erik and his daughter continued, Sam was grateful she wasn't facing Kevin so she didn't have to see the painful longing in his eyes. He wanted a house full of kids, and every time the subject came up, she saw on his face and heard in his voice how badly he wanted a biological child of his own. A desire she understood. He loved Michy, but she wasn't his flesh and blood.

However, the thought of getting pregnant terrified Sam. Almost as much as the terror she felt when she wondered how they would work through this issue without being torn apart.

Ready for a mental subject change, she said, "Santa isn't going to bring either of you guys new toys if you don't behave."

It'd taken her a while to get used to Kevin and Erik's antics, especially when she or Kat got caught in the crossfire. But over time, she'd grown comfortable with the playful jabs and realized it was a natural part of their relationship. They were more like brothers than friends, but unlike her relationship with her brothers, Kevin and Erik genuinely liked each other. No, correction, they loved each other. They talked every day and despite the verbal punches, they had each other's back no matter what.

It was painful to admit, but she also loved Kat and Erik, and more than most of her biological family. The holidays would've been empty without them, and she was grateful they had an entire week to spend together.

Leaning into Kevin, she kissed him on the cheek and said, "You're right. I don't have a thing to worry about. This is going to be the best Christmas ever."

# Chapter Two
## Kat

---

*K*at Monteague couldn't believe the transformation in Kevin and Sam's house over the past several days. Sam and Michy had turned their river retreat into a winter paradise even an elf would appreciate. Every doorway, window, and banister was dressed in fragrant garland, twinkling lights, shiny ornaments, and silver, burgundy, and green satin bows.

It was nothing like the sterile silver-and-white decorations the paid decorator always used to trim the tree and add a little holiday glitter—sans cheer—to Kat's childhood home. This house had been decorated with love, and everyone entering felt that love wrap around them like a warm, welcoming hug, inviting them to come inside, make themselves at home, and rejoice in the holidays.

Kat waddled over to the island, set the red velvet cake she made that morning next to the pies, then wrapped her hands under her enormous belly... Like using her arms as a giant sling would somehow keep the baby strapped in for a couple more days.

Braxton Hicks contractions had been the norm over the past several weeks, but the ones that cranked up after lunch weren't playing. There hadn't been a *significant* increase in intensity or frequency, but she was pretty sure the baby didn't plan on waiting around for its due date, which wasn't for another three weeks.

If *Bambino Due*, as Kevin liked to call it, was anything like Erik, once its mind was made up, there'd be no stopping it. She could only hope the contractions slowed down or stalled out long enough for her to still be at home with Caroline and Erik on Christmas morning.

One thing she was sure about, worrying and stressing wasn't going to help or change anything, so she distracted herself by drawing in a deep breath and bathing her lungs in the comforting scents of the season. Turkey, stuffing, garlic, and cinnamon filled her nostrils and overrode the discomfort in her belly.

"Gawd, it smells amazing in here. You guys have outdone your-selves."

Sam smiled proudly as she pushed against Kevin's shoulders to back him up, giving her room to jump off the counter. "Kevin outdid himself. I just stood around and watched." She threw a sheepish glance at him over her shoulder. "And taste-tested. A little."

She leaned to the side and looked around Kat. "Where's your granddad?"

When Kat's grandfather moved to Riverside to care for her after her near-fatal accident, he could never have imagined the extended family he would gain. He and Erik had forged a tight bond while sitting vigil over her hospital bed after her accident. During that same time, Kevin and Steve had kept a close eye on both Erik and Granddad, which earned them a ton of respect and gratitude from her grandfather and also cemented a lifelong bond between all the men.

When Sam and Michaela came into the picture, they adopted Granddad as their own since Michy didn't have a grandfather in her life. Granddad adored Michy and loved spending time with her on the pier, fishing and watching the world float by. Kat knew her grandfather must miss being near her mother, his only daughter, but he was never lonely.

"He'll be here in a minute. He's on the phone with my mother," Kat said, helping Erik take off Caroline's coat. "Since she'll be on the slopes tomorrow, he figured he'd better try and catch her tonight."

As Caroline kicked her feet back and forth, desperate for escape from her daddy's arms, Kat dodged the black patent leather Mary Janes and straightened the flipped-up hem of her red-and-green plaid skirt.

"Sheww, I need faster hands." As another mild contraction got its groove on, she relocked her hands under her belly and thought, *And stronger arms.*

When Sam gave Kat a small, sympathetic smile, her heart jumped to her throat. For a moment, she thought Sam recognized the signs of labor and was empathizing with Kat's plight, but then she realized Sam was simply being sympathetic to the whole absent-mother thing.

Something the other woman understood as well as Kat.

Over the past year, the two of them had done a lot of bonding where family was concerned. Even though they wished for better relationships with their true, biological families, mostly for their children's sake, they wholeheartedly agreed their adopted families—the ones they'd married into—were infinitely better than the biological ones they'd distanced themselves from. It was sad to admit, but if forced to choose, both Sam and Kat would pick their adopted families every time.

"Is she coming when the baby's born?" Sam asked in a light, nonchalant tone, trying to make conversation without putting a damper on the day. She took Erik's and Caroline's coats, then waited for Kat to remove hers. Not an easy feat, since it was nearly impossible to move, or even breathe, without giving away her closely guarded secret.

*Not likely,* Kat thought wryly as she considered how quickly that day seemed to be approaching. Her parents were in Vail with her brother and his family for Christmas, and they would never alter their plans for Kat, regardless of the reason. They'd dropped everything and rushed to her "aid" once before, when she'd been in the hospital, clinging to life. It wasn't an experience any of them wanted to repeat.

"I doubt it," she said, matching Sam's conversational tone. She handed over her coat and, without being obvious, slowly exhaled as the contraction relaxed. "It took them six weeks to find time to visit when Caroline was born, because, you know, the end of the year is soooooo"—she drug out the word in a smug, nasally whine, mimicking her mother—"busy for them."

"That's okay," Kevin said, scooping Caroline up into his arms and snuggling her close. "Leaves more hugs and cuddles for us. Right, *piccolina*?"

Caroline giggled as Kevin tickled her belly, then stopped abruptly and turned her wide blue eyes toward the ceiling. A thousand horses—actually, one little girl—clattered above them. There was a moment of silence, and Kat pictured Michy sliding around the corner at the end of the hallway. Then the jangling of jingle bells accompanied Michaela's pounding footsteps as she bounded down the stairs.

Kevin knelt and set Caroline on her feet as Michy bolted into the kitchen, then skidded to a stop on her knees in front of them.

"Kay-Kay!" She grabbed Caroline's hands and did a funny little dance, which Caroline tried to mimic.

A big smile curved Kevin's mouth as he watched the girls play, but rather than enjoy the scene playing out before them, Sam's face fell and she turned away from everyone. Kat didn't know what was going through Sam's mind, but it was impossible to miss the tension radiating from her.

Everyone knew Kevin was ready to add to their family—shoot, he'd been ready the moment he and Sam said I do. But for some reason, Sam was holding out. Judging from the pained expression crumpling her forehead and creasing her eyes, it was more complicated than the excuse she'd been using: waiting until they finished building their new house and had room for another child.

Erik turned to Kat and frowned, confirming he'd also picked up on the strange vibe. His frown deepened with concern when she casually lifted her shoulder and used her eyes to say, *I don't have a clue what's going on.*

"C'mon, girls," Erik said, taking the coats Sam still held in her arms. "Let's clear out of the kitchen so Uncle Kevin can do his thing."

Sam dropped her chin and planted her hand onto her hip, which was cocked out to the side with a ton of attitude. "What makes you think Kevin is cooking?"

His previous concern forgotten, Erik laughed and leaned over to kiss her cheek. "Because you love us and wouldn't subject us to your cooking." He paused and sniffed the air. "Is something burning?"

"Oh shit!" Sam grabbed a potholder and ran for the oven. "I forgot the garlic knots."

Amusement and humor glinted in Erik's eyes. "I rest my case," he said, chuckling as he herded Michaela and Caroline around the end of the island and toward the living room.

The ringing chimes of the doorbell caught everyone's attention, especially Caroline's. When she jerked her gaze up to the ceiling, trying to find the source of the noise, she stumbled and bumped her head on the doorframe, then collapsed into a pile of tears in the middle of the doorway.

"You're all right, Kay-Kay," Michy said, dropping to her knees on the floor next to Caroline.

Since the two girls and Erik blocked the exit, Kevin backtracked through kitchen and disappeared into the dining room, which had access to the living room. "I hope that's the cavalry," he said, laughing.

"I'm more than ready to turn over the kitchen to Gavin."

As Erik scooped up the still bawling Caroline and disappeared around the corner, Sam yelled after him, "There's two packages in the middle of Caroline's blanket. Let her open them so she has something new to play with."

"I thought we weren't exchanging gifts until tomorr—" The confusion of the past several moments had offered a diversion from her stomach, but as the most intense contraction yet clamped down on her uterus, Kat couldn't ignore it any longer. She grabbed hold of the edge of the counter, bent at the waist, and breathed through the pain.

"Oh my God." Sam set the baking sheet with the well-done garlic knots onto the cooling rack and spun around to face Kat. "You're in labor."

Kat vehemently shook her head no. "It's just a little... hitch." She blew out a deep breath and straightened as the contraction relaxed.

"Bullshit." Sam pulled off the potholder and rounded the island to stand beside her. "How far apart are they?"

"I don't know. I haven't timed them." Truth be told, she was afraid to time them for fear of making the situation more real. She wanted to keep pretending the baby wasn't in a race with Santa, so she could continue believing she would be home on Christmas morning with her little girl and Erik. "I'm fine, really. I've been having Braxton Hicks contractions for weeks. That's all this is."

Sam huffed. "I've had a baby. I know the difference." She bounced on her toes, practically vibrating with energy. "This is so exciting."

The more animated Sam got, the harder Kat's heart pumped. She glanced to the living room to make sure Erik hadn't overheard and wasn't rushing in to whisk her away. Putting a finger to her mouth, she whispered, "Shhh... Erik might hear you."

Sam's mouth dropped open. "He doesn't know?"

"No." Even as she said it and once again shook her head for emphasis, she wondered how he'd missed the labored breathing and stuttered steps that accompanied some of the earlier contractions. "I don't think so."

Sam rolled her eyes. "Erik isn't blind or stupid." She took a step back and studied Kat from head to toe. "I give you another thirty minutes, tops, before *everyone* figures it out."

Kat swallowed, forcing the lump in her throat to retreat, and fought back the tears burning the backs of her eyes.

Seeing her distress, Sam's face softened and she grabbed Kat's hands. "Why don't you want anyone to know?"

It was ridiculous to feel guilty for something she couldn't control, but her emotions were all over the map, and another wave of regret pushed through her. "You guys have worked so hard putting all of this together. I've seen you and Michy over here working well past not only her bedtime, but yours, as well. You've been baking for days." She grinned. "You want to talk about a big deal? You in the kitchen... doing anything is a *big* deal."

Sam laughed. "We'll see if it's edible." She looked beyond Kat into the living room. "I still don't understand what that has to do with"— she waved her hand over Kat's belly—"this."

Kat pressed her lips together and shrugged. "I don't want to be the center of attention. This is your big day." She paused and bit her lip to stop the quivering. "I'm also trying to stay firmly entrenched in the land of denial. I don't want to be in the hospital on Christmas. I want to be home with my family and you guys."

Sam grabbed Kat and wrapped her in a big hug. "If necessary, we'll bring Christmas to you." She took a step back and clapped like Michy did when super excited. "I better get Gavin in here to finish this up. We need to hurry and eat."

"Sam, please…" Kat sighed and leaned against the counter. "Don't say anything to anyone. If they get closer together or more intense, I'll tell Erik. With luck, they'll ease up or even stop."

Sam's lips twitched as she fought back a grin and patted Kat on the arm. "If your water breaks, and it better not break while sitting on my new couch, are you going to tell everyone you peed on yourself?"

Kat covered her face with her hand. "You're a mess. No, I won't go that far, but my water isn't going to break."

*Dammit, my water better not break.*

# Chapter Three

## Gavin

---

$M$ost people wouldn't enjoy being elbow deep in flour on Christmas Eve, but as Gavin McLeod moved around the gourmet kitchen, making the gravy and laughing at Sam trying to salvage the garlic knots, he was in heaven. Kevin's expression had been one of tremendous relief when he opened the door and found Gavin, along with his wife Sunny and his brother-in-law Robby, standing on his stoop. Brief conversation confirmed he needed a little help in the kitchen, and Gavin was happy to take over.

Gavin wasn't a professional chef, but he loved to cook and had always wanted to open a restaurant. His dreams recently came true when he bought and remodeled the Anticue Fishing Pier, which now included a restaurant where beach-goers could grab a quick bite to eat while giving the fish a break.

He didn't understand the rush, but Sam expressed urgency in getting tonight's meal served, pronto, so he rolled up his sleeves and got to work. Kevin and Erik were in the game room, visiting with their friend Steve Vex, who arrived moments ago. Kat's grandfather had also recently slipped in through the kitchen door and joined Kat, who was in the living room watching *The Grinch* with Caroline and Michaela. Sunny was filling the glasses with ice water, and Robby stood off to the side, ready to help wherever needed.

"I need a beer and a baster," Gavin said with a laugh and wink at Sam. "Do you know what a baster is?"

She lifted her eyes and glared at him, but the twitching in her lips gave away her barely restrained laughter. "Man, much more of the bash-Sam's-culinary-skills and I'm going to develop a complex. I think I can handle the baster."

"I'll get the beer," said Robby, a typical college student with half of his brain engaged and alert to any indication of a party, while the the other half was always scanning for females. "Can I get anyone else anything?"

"I'd love one," Sam said, her eyes wide with delight as her head shot up from the drawer. But in the next breath, she seemed to think better of it and her shoulders sagged as she sighed. "I guess I should wait—"

The chime of the doorbell cut her off and had her cocking her head sideways. "I wonder who that is." Her brows dipped into a sharp V and her mouth twisted. "Oh, yeah, never mind. It's probably Lizbeth." Resuming her search for the baster, she muttered, "I'm busy getting dinner on the table, so it's okay that I'm not stopping to chat it up. Right? Right."

Amused, Gavin wanted to weigh in on her self-debate, but before he could think of a smart-ass remark, Kevin stepped into the doorway and said, "Hey, Sam. I have a surprise for you."

She froze and cut her eyes to him. "Okay." Hesitation slowed her movements as she stood and handed the baster to Gavin, then shoved everything back into the drawer and bumped it closed with her hip. "I hope it's a good surprise."

Before she got across the kitchen to where Kevin stood, a tall man with shoulder-length dark hair stepped into view.

"Lucas!" She squealed with delight, then stopped for a moment, as if she couldn't believe her eyes, before rushing forward to tackle him in a massive hug. "This is a *great* surprise! What are you doing here?"

The man laughed at her exuberance, then returned the hug and buried his face in her hair at the crook of her neck. When he held on a little tighter and longer than Gavin would've expected from someone who wasn't her husband, he shifted closer to Sunny as she returned from the dining room, making it clear to Mr. Touchy-Feely that Sunny was off-limits.

After a moment, the guy leaned back and kissed Sam on the forehead, then wrapped his arm around her neck. "I was supposed to have Daria tonight, but"—his jaw clenched and his eyes turned cold—"Loralei decided at the last minute to visit her parents in Florida, so..." He shrugged. "Spending Christmas with you is the next best thing to being with my little girl."

Sam's joy evaporated and sadness darkened her eyes. "I'm so sorry. I keep telling you, all you have to do is give the order and I'll open up a can of whoopass on that selfish ex of yours."

Humor and deep affection filled his eyes. "You're so thoughtful, but that won't be necessary." He leaned in close and in a low voice, said, "I'll save the orders for more pleasant tasks."

Sam flushed and dipped her head and eyes. *Interesting.* With an uncharacteristic giggle, she said, "Just let me know if you change your mind." Looping her arm in the crook of Lucas's elbow, she turned him to face the inquisitive crowd. She started the introductions with Robby since he was closest, then led him to Sunny and Gavin, who was desperately trying to concentrate on pouring the gravy into the boat and not on the peculiar interaction between Sam and the surprise guest.

"Lucas, this is Gavin and Sunny McLeod." Gavin's hands were full, so he nodded in acknowledgment while Sunny extended her hand for a shake. As he watched his wife's hand disappear into Lucas's, Gavin's grip tightened on the ladle and he wondered when he'd gotten so damned jealous and possessive about something as benign as a hand-shake.

"Sunny and Gavin own a bar and a fishing pier/restaurant in Anti-cue," Sam explained. "And once we get through the holidays, we're going to begin construction on a bed and breakfast for them. They started off as clients but have turned into great friends. Guys, this is Lucas Steele. He also started off as a client of Kevin's and, well..." She pressed her lips together and gave a nervous little laugh as her face reddened. "He's also become a dear friend."

Interest crowded out concentration as Sam and Lucas shared an intimate smile, and Gavin cursed as he spilled gravy over the side of the gravy boat. He hadn't ever gotten the impression Kevin and Sam were swingers, but something was going on with Lucas, and he couldn't stop his mind from making a left turn into a dark alley, searching for a possible answer.

"Have you ever heard of Pandora's Playground in Myrtle Beach?" Kevin asked.

"Yeah," Gavin answered as he set the skillet in the sink and moved on to the mashed potatoes. "Downtown Myrtle Beach in the old theater, right?"

"That's the one." Pride radiated from Lucas as he tucked his hands into his pockets and rocked back on his heels.

Before moving to Anticue, Gavin lived in Myrtle Beach and spent a fair amount of time on the strip where Pandora's was located. He'd never figured out exactly what Pandora's was because the signage was vague, but he'd watched the renovations with great curiosity. They'd done a phenomenal job of maintaining the original integrity of the building, so he understood Lucas's pride.

Sunny had been gone from Myrtle Beach for several years by the time the restoration took place, so she glanced from Gavin to Lucas, confused. "What's Pandora's?"

"Only the most awesome kink club in the world," Sam blurted out, then threw her hands over her face in embarrassment.

"Oh, really?" Gavin grinned and glanced at Sunny.

Her eyes were wide and she'd rocked forward on the balls of her feet. They'd snagged her attention, and even though she probably wasn't aware of her actions, she was trying to get closer to them and the conversation so she could gather more details.

"Sunny has a kinky side," he said, pushing her into the conversation, because he doubted she'd jump on her own. "We should check it out sometime."

She gasped and her mouth fell open as her cheeks reddened to a shade that would make Rudolph envious. Shocked into silence, she held his gaze for the longest time, then flicked a quick glance to Sam.

Sunny's expressions were normally like neon signs, clearly broadcasting everything she thought. But as she gnawed on her lip and looked at everything in the room but him, he didn't have the foggiest notion what she was thinking. After a moment of deliberation, she shrugged and gave him a small, shy smile. "Sure. That sounds... interesting."

"You'd have a great time there, but we need to coordinate our schedules," Sam said. "I don't want to see either of you naked. And you sure as hell can't be there with us. I'm never completely naked, but I could never look you in the eye again if you witnessed some of the things Kevin does to me."

Kevin and Lucas threw their heads back, laughing, which intensified when they realized Erik had walked into the kitchen during Sam's confession and tossed peanuts all over his face and neck, rather than into his mouth.

"I've always wondered about you guys. Especially after that time

Kevin stole my cologne and shirt." He turned to Sam accusingly. "Do you know anything about that little incident?"

Sam bit her lip and dropped her head into her hands. Based on the way her shoulders shook, she was laughing... or maybe crying hysterically.

Kevin seemed less amused as his eyes narrowed and he wrapped his arm possessively around Sam. "Just because she likes the cologne doesn't mean shit," Kevin grumbled, seemingly more to himself than anyone else.

"You know what?" Erik said, throwing up a hand. "I don't want to know. I just hope like hell you enjoyed it because that happened to be one of my favorite shirts."

"Oh, she enjoyed it immensely," Lucas said with a laugh that had Sam laughing even harder and blushing so badly even the tips of her ears were red.

Erik's mouth dropped open as he looked from Kevin and Sam to Lucas incredulously. "Yeah, I definitely don't need to know." Turning on his heel, he said, "I'm going to check on Kat and Caroline. Give a shout if I can do anything to help."

"I want to know," Sunny said, snatching a beer out of the ice. She popped the top with practiced ease and handed the bottle over to Sam. "Drink up, honey, and do tell."

# Chapter Four

## Sunny

---

$\mathcal{S}$unny had never seen Sam so flustered. Her face flamed bright red while her eyes bounced off every available surface in the kitchen but failed to stick to the people. With the way she was scraping her upper teeth over her bottom lip... if she didn't lighten up soon, she would end up with a big-ass, ugly hole in the middle. Sheer force of will kept Sunny from grabbing her by the arm, dragging her out of the room away from everyone, and grilling her for details about this mysterious club.

But Sam was the hostess, and Sunny couldn't monopolize her attention. She also didn't know how long she'd be able to attend a club like that without feeling awkward and out of place.

"Grab yourself one so I'm not drinking alone," Sam said after a solid gulp that knocked out half the bottle.

Sunny had spent most of the day trying to figure out the best way to deal with this situation. She'd run a thousand scenarios through her mind, mentally practicing ways to decline a drink—something she didn't normally do—so her response would be comfortable and natural and not throw up any flags. However, as she glanced at Sam and tried to keep her attention off Gavin, her heart raced and her palms grew sticky. Being dodgy wasn't her strongest personality trait. "I'm good for now. Robby and Gavin each have one, so you're safe."

"We have Pepsi in the refrigerator in the laundry room," Sam said, referring to Sunny's second favorite drink. "And coffee for after dinner."

Damn, Sam had Sunny covered all the way around. Everyone knew she didn't start her day until she'd had her coffee, and nothing sent her into a tizzy like waking up to find the cupboard bare. Both Pepsi and coffee were loaded with caffeine—which was Sunny's preferred food group—but she'd started cutting back over the past few weeks.

The decrease hadn't been enough for anyone to notice, but rather than drinking a full pot in the morning, she'd cut down to half, and she'd stuck to one soda during her shifts at the Blackout, instead of the three or four she normally drank.

Sam's thoughtfulness filled Sunny's chest with warm fuzzies. However, that kindness would complicate things. She really wanted to keep her secret under wraps until morning, as a Christmas surprise for Gavin, but didn't see any way to play this off for the entire evening.

She and Gavin hadn't been trying to get pregnant—she hadn't tracked her cycles or checked her temperature or any of the other things women did to make sure they had sex at just the right moment—but they hadn't been *not* trying either.

They'd been so busy over the past few months—opening the restaurant and buying the new house to convert into a bed and breakfast—they were lucky to bump into each other in the hallway, let alone bump into each other naked. She couldn't imagine trying to coordinate schedules to get it on during a specific time of the day—or even on a specific day—so for the time being, they'd left things to nature.

Over the last few weeks, she started noticing tenderness in her breasts and her fatigue had been greater than normal. She chalked it up to stress but started cutting back on caffeine and alcohol, just in case. This morning, the little pink plus sign confirmed one of their bumps-in-the-night created life, and while she could probably drink wine or soda at this early stage and not harm the baby, she wasn't willing to take the chance.

Acting as nonchalant as possible, she picked up the water pitcher and, even though all of the glasses had already been filled, escaped to the dining room. "You're sweet, thanks. I'll grab something in a little while. I'm good with water for now."

Her younger brother, Robby, who was on the other side of the kitchen, pivoted on his heel and stormed after her. "Did you say you were okay with water?"

She couldn't pretend to fill glasses that were already overflowing, so she turned to face him. With wide eyes and a stern set to her mouth, projecting a *leave it the hell alone* message, she said, "Yeah, I'm fine for now."

Intimidating gestures had *never* worked on Robby, and she didn't know why she thought this time would be any different.

His silver eyes—identical to hers—scrutinized her warily as he pressed a hand to her forehead. "You aren't feverish." He leaned back so he could peer around the doorway of the dining room at Gavin. "Has she been like this for a while? Do we need to take her to the emergency room?"

Sunny smacked away Robby's hand and moved around him, back into the kitchen. She set the water pitcher on the island and, making a last ditch effort to maintain her cover, said, "Gavin has been fussing at me for drinking too much caffeine." She shrugged. "I'm trying to do better."

Her gaze wandered around the kitchen, desperately searching for a diversion to the attention focused on her, but her mind was a whirling dervish and she couldn't come up with anything plausible. From the corner of her eye, she saw Gavin pick up his beer and saunter her way. She stood, frozen in place, searching for a subject change but helplessly coming up empty.

"I worry about you drinking so much soda because it's not good for your kidneys," he said evenly. "But beer is good for you in that regard. Here"—he held his bottle out to her—"drink this and flush them out. Then you can drink a soda and be good to go." His tone remained even, but his eyes held an unmistakable challenge.

She glanced at Sam and found her friend standing there, eyes wide, mouth hanging open. Sam's expression wasn't one of bewilderment or curiosity, but strangely enough, she seemed shocked and somewhat terrified at the realization her friend might be pregnant. Her reaction confused Sunny, but she couldn't worry about Sam or what she was thinking with Gavin wiggling the beer bottle in her face.

The jig was up. She didn't have anyone fooled, not even her clueless-to-this-type-of-thing baby brother. His eyes were wide and bouncing between Gavin, the bottle, and Sam, like he was watching a ping-pong match. Lucas appeared amused and interested in seeing how this would play out. Kevin seemed a little conflicted, like Sam, and even though he was smiling, the joy didn't reach his watery eyes.

"Well?" Gavin said, jerking her attention back to him.

Buying herself a few more minutes, she wiped her hand on her slacks so the bottle didn't slip from her grip and lifted it to her lips. Gavin's breathing was shallow and his swallowing harsh as he watched with laser-like focus as the amber liquid rose into the neck. As it seeped through the opening and touched her lips, she stopped and lowered the bottle.

Sam exclaimed, "You too?" as Gavin wrapped his arms around her in a crushing grip and swung her around once.

Robby, never one to accept things at face value, interrupted the moment to seek further confirmation. "Sis, are you telling us you're pregnant?"

After a sweet, tender kiss from Gavin, she turned in his arms and pressed her back to his chest while he rested his hands protectively over her stomach. "The test this morning says I am."

Robby's face fell, and he shook his head sadly. "After all those conversations we had about using protection and wrapping it up..." He tried to keep up the ruse of being disappointed in her, but he couldn't hold back his grin. He gave Sunny and Gavin a big group hug, then turned to Sam. "This is so freakin' cool. I'm gonna be an uncle."

"I heard. That's awesome." Sam was working hard to play along and be excited. She wore a smile and said the expected words, and even went so far as to tip her bottle in salute before giving Robby a hug. But something else... something less celebratory and more agonizing was going on behind the scenes. Her mouth said, "Congratulations, guys," as she moved in and gave Sunny and Gavin hugs, but her crumpled eyes and thinned lips indicated she felt something else entirely.

She cut her gaze to Kevin, but rather than make eye contact, her stare landed on his chest and never moved higher. She took a deep breath and swallowed hard, as if gulping down shards of glass, then lifted the bottle and didn't stop until she'd drained the last of the beer.

Kevin didn't allow his gaze to linger on Sam either, but he did seem genuinely excited for them as he stepped up to shake hands with Gavin and enveloped Sunny in a warm, affectionate hug.

Lucas offered his congratulations before moving off to the bar and grabbing two beers. He popped the tops, took a drink from one, then held up the other and looked pointedly at Kevin over his shoulder.

Kevin nodded once, then turned to Gavin. "Anything I can do to help you in here?"

"Nope," Gavin said. "I've got it covered."

Kevin dropped a kiss on the top of Sunny's head and slapped Gavin on the back. "Merry Christmas, man." Without saying anything else to anyone, he met Lucas at the edge of the living room, took the beer from him, then disappeared around the corner.

Over the past couple of months, Sam and Sunny had had several conversations about kids. Kevin loved Michaela, but he'd made no secret of wanting another child, or even a couple of children. But whenever the topic came up, Sam always found a way to change the subject.

Sunny didn't know if Sam didn't *ever* want more children or if she wasn't ready now. But it was painfully obvious the subject of children would be an issue for Kevin and Sam in the future if they didn't talk things out and come to some sort of resolution soon.

Knowing this was a sensitive issue for Sam, Sunny felt the need to apologize for making her announcement during their Christmas dinner. "I'd planned on telling him tomorrow morning, but I should've known he'd figure it out when I didn't drink. I'm sorry for hijacking your party."

Sam laughed and gave her another hug. "Don't be silly." She cocked her head toward the living room and leaned in close. "Kat's going to be the real hijacker." This time her laugh was genuine and her eyes sparkled with excitement. "She's in labor."

When Sunny gasped, Sam put her finger to her lips and said, "Shhh… She doesn't want anyone to know yet." She snorted out a little laugh. "She thinks she's going to be able to hide it from everyone, including Erik, until we get through dinner."

Sunny put her hands over her mouth to suppress her laugh. "This should be interesting."

"No shit." Sam lifted her bottle to her lips for anther drink, then frowned when she realized it was empty. With a sigh, she set the bottle on the counter and said, "We better get this show on the road before she misses dinner completely."

# Chapter Five
## Erik

"So how much longer do you think she'll hold out?" Steve Vex, Erik's best friend since kindergarten, asked as he stepped up beside Erik and followed his line of sight into the dining room, where Kat was leaned over a table, picking up unused silverware.

Despite her insistence at being capable of helping with cleanup, time was running out.

She knew it. Erik knew it, even though she was still trying to pretend he wasn't only blind, but stupid. And based on the fact that Steve—who was completely clueless to this type thing—had dialed into it, *everyone* knew it. Hell, even Michaela had clued in when Kat stopped midstride and doubled over to catch her breath, then clenched her teeth to the point of cracking while chewing a piece of turkey.

Erik sighed and shrugged before taking a big gulp of sweet tea in an effort to wash down his irritation. "I'm afraid we're going to find out how stubborn she can be. She's been having contractions all afternoon but tried to hide them from me." He huffed, unable to completely hide his annoyance. "Like I wouldn't notice. Sure, I'm a man and we're not particularly prone to picking up on details, but… Jesus."

He prided himself on being tuned into Kat and aware of her needs, especially when pregnant or sick, so it hurt that she believed he remained oblivious to the fact she was in labor… and in pain. Deep in his gut, he recognized this wasn't about him, but rather her desire to be home with their little girl on Christmas morning. But it still chapped his ass that she'd tried so hard to keep him in the dark—and thought she'd succeeded.

Steve took a drink of his beer and scratched the back of his head. "I don't understand. Why not just go to the hospital and have the baby?"

Erik chuckled and pinched the bridge of his nose. "It's not quite that easy. You don't roll up and say, 'Okay, we're here to have a baby' and then boom, be done. Her labor with Caroline lasted almost eighteen hours. Based on what I've seen so far, this one will come faster, but there's no guarantees."

"You guys betting on how long until she caves?" Kevin asked, wandering over to join them with Caroline in his arms, her head on his shoulder, sound asleep. Kevin loved his little girl almost as much as Erik, and he and Kat were incredibly grateful to have such good friends who would always be there for them and their children, no matter what.

"Hell no," Erik said with a hard shake of his head. Discussing the situation was one thing. Betting on his wife was an ugly beast he didn't want to tangle with. He liked being happily married, thank you very much.

Through an evil grin, Kevin *bwacked* like a chicken, then said, "Sam started one in the kitchen. I think the pot is up to sixty dollars."

"Oh, shit." Erik jerked around to look for Kat. "Does Kat know?"

As Caroline started to stir, Kevin rocked back and forth and quietly said, "I don't think so. At least she hasn't let on like she does."

"Thank God." Erik ran a hand over his face. "If it were the latter, she'd squat in your kitchen floor and push the kid out, just so no one wins."

Steve paled and cut his eyes to Erik. "Is that even possible?"

Erik laughed and shook his head at his clueless friend. "How do you think women had babies before hospitals?"

Steve's face crinkled and his throat worked a couple of times, like he'd swallowed something his stomach was preparing to reject. "It's probably best if I never get married and have kids. I'd be the dad passed out on the floor, completely useless to my wife."

Erik laughed at the image but disagreed with the statement. Steve was rock solid when he needed to be, and he'd make an outstanding husband and father. Erik wondered, however, if Steve would ever find a woman who made him want to settle down. The whole notion of staying in one place for more than a few weeks was a scary proposition to Steve, and he'd fought like hell over the past couple of years against anything remotely smelling of domestication. It would take a dramatic life change—or miracle—for Steve to stay put long enough to establish a home for a wife and child.

Switching his attention back to Kat, Erik studied her over the rim of his glass as he took another drink of tea. "I called the doctor a while ago, so she's prepared. I also let Annie know, so she's on standby to come out and stay with Caroline."

Annie had been Erik's mother's housekeeper and Erik's nanny, but when Caroline was born, he swiped Annie right out from under his mother. And he didn't regret the move for a second.

"Annie doesn't need to drive all the way out here." Kevin's tone was sharp and his brows dipped low. "Caroline will stay with us."

"Your morning will be crazy with Michaela opening her presents and your family driving in from Raleigh. You have enough going on. You don't need to worry about Caroline too."

Kevin's eyes narrowed. "I'm not worried. It's not a bother. She'll stay here."

"Um..." Steve hesitated, probably deciding whether or not he should step in between Kevin and Erik–again—like he'd had to do many times over the past twelve years. "I can stay at your house with her." He gave a little shrug. "If Sam and Kevin get her ready for bed, all I have to do is get her up in the morning. Right?"

Kevin and Erik glanced at each other, then burst into laughter.

When Caroline roused and looked around, Kevin shushed her by wrapping his hand around her head and rocking back and forth.

"Well, I guess technically that's right," Erik said. "Do you know how to change a diaper?"

A little of Steve's confidence waned. "I've watched you. I can figure it out."

"What about feeding her?" Kevin asked.

Steve threw up his hands in frustration. "I get her out of bed, put on her coat, and haul her across the yard to you."

Erik laughed, enjoying the moment of being with his two best friends and the chaos that always ensued when they got together. He'd been worried their relationship would change as they married and settled down. But he and Kevin spoke every day, even if for just a minute while driving to work or between appointments. And they both stayed in touch with Steve as much as possible, given his crazy travel schedule. As a professional BMX rider, they'd long given up on trying to figure out where Steve would be and when. Fortunately, Kat and Sam got along as well as Erik and Kevin—better, actually, since they'd never had a knock-down, drag-out fight.

*That might change if Kat finds out about the pool Sam started,* Erik thought wryly.

Kevin chuckled and leaned in toward Steve so he could talk softer and not risk waking Caroline again. "Wouldn't it be easier to leave her here?"

Steve sighed. "I want to do something to help. I'm gone so much I miss out on everything going on in y'all's lives."

Erik clapped his hand over Steve's shoulder. "How about this? Caroline can stay here, but you stay at our house with Granddad. He'll be in the guesthouse out back, but Kat will feel better knowing someone's on property with him. These guys are close, but you'd be right there if he needed anything."

Steve's face brightened. "Deal."

With the logistics of Caroline and Granddad worked out, Erik switched his focus to Kat. His gaze dropped to her ankles as she gathered the last of the silverware and disappeared into the kitchen. It was past time to get her swollen feet out of those chunky wedged shoes, and baggy sweats and a T-shirt would be way more comfortable than the festive maternity dress she'd been in all evening.

"Wish me luck. I'm going in—"

His words were cut off by Kat's squeal, followed by Gavin saying, "Whoa, I've got you."

By the time Sam shouted Erik's name, he was already on the move, with Kevin and Steve right behind him.

He found Kat doubled over, clutching the edge of the counter, a puddle of water at her feet. The time for denial was over; if this was anything like Caroline's delivery, things were about to get serious.

Kat had been determined to have Caroline naturally... right up until her water broke. When the next contraction had started, she'd grabbed Erik's arm, pulled him down so they were face to face, and spoken loud and clear. "Get me drugs. Now!"

Now, he crouched down, so he was in her line of sight, and smiled up at her as she breathed through the contraction.

Through short puffs of breaths, she said, "I'm... in... labor."

His laugh was sharp and lacked any real humor. "Really?" When she was able to stand comfortably, he took her hand and helped her upright. "Baby, I've been timing the damned contractions for the past two hours." He shook his head and sighed. "I talked to Amanda about an hour ago. She said as long as your water didn't break, you could wait until they were five minutes apart." He dropped his gaze to the puddle on the floor. "I think it's time to get you changed and head on in."

Her jaw went slack. "You already called the doctor?"

"Yeah, you obviously weren't going to. I already made arrangements for Caroline and your granddad too." He nodded at her grandfather, who'd been dozing on the couch but came wide awake with the commotion. "Granddad said you were the one having the baby, not him, so he's staying here. There's no sense in takin' up a chair in the waitin' room when he can get a good night's sleep in his own bed."

She pressed her hand to her mouth and giggled at his impression of her grandfather, just as he'd hoped. If history repeated itself, the next few hours would be intense with little room for laughter, so any humor he could inject at this point was a bonus.

"Steve's going to stay at our house, so he'll be near Granddad. Caroline will stay here." He glanced at Sam. "I hope that's okay."

"Of course it's okay. We wouldn't have it any other way."

He chuckled and headed toward the coat closet. "Yeah, so I gathered."

Kat burst into tears, stopping Erik in his tracks. "I want to be home with you and Caroline on Christmas morning. Not in the hospital."

Oh, hell. Her emotions had been all over the map for the past few weeks, but now that full-blown labor had set in, he needed to tighten the belts and prepare for a wild rollercoaster ride. "Baby, as fast as this labor is progressing, you'll have the baby tonight and be home by tomorrow evening."

As Caroline scrunched up her face and prepared to launch her own arsenal of tears, Erik took her from Kevin and bounced her up and down. "Hey, baby girl. Mamma's gonna give you the best Christmas present in the world. A real, live baby doll!" He was animated and excited, hoping she'd follow suit, but it was well past her bedtime and the grumpies had set in for the night.

Over the top of Caroline's head, he made eye contact with Sam. Afraid another contraction would hit soon, he wanted both arms free so he could focus on Kat and not have to worry about Caroline becoming more distressed.

Understanding the screaming plea in his eyes, Sam straddled the puddle of water and reached for Caroline. "Hey, sweetie. Blow your mamma and daddy a kiss goodnight, and let's get you ready for bed. Uncle Kevin will get your portable crib while Michy and I give you a bath."

"Can Kay-Kay take a bath with me?" Michy asked, appearing in the doorway. She'd been totally engrossed in a television show, but hearing her name propelled her onto the scene. Kevin grabbed her by the shoulders and pulled her back a second before she splashed into the puddle surrounding Kat. "Can she sleep in my room?"

"We'll see," Sam said, stepping out of the way as Gavin appeared with a mop and a bucket.

"I found these in the mudroom." Gavin set to work and good-naturedly said, "I can already tell I have so much to look forward to."

Sunny laughed, but Kat sniffled, then drew in a shuddering breath. "I'm sorry I made a mess on the floor."

"Stop it," Sam said, waving off the apology. "At least it wasn't on my new couch."

Kat looked at Sam and managed to laugh at what seemed to be a private joke between the women.

Wrapping her arm around Kat's neck, Sam said, "Go home, change, and get to the hospital so we can find out if we have another little Kat or a little Erik."

Everyone, including Erik, wholeheartedly agreed the world would be a much better place if they had another little Kat.

Struggling to hold back more tears, Kat said, "I'm sorry for ruining your Christmas Eve dinner."

"Are you kidding?" Sam said, wearing a huge grin. "This party will be legendary. We'll be talking about this when we're eighty, laughing about how you tried to hide the fact that you were in labor, and all along, everyone was betting on when you'd finally give up and go to the hospital." She glanced at the clock. "Lucas, you win."

# Chapter Six

## Lizbeth

---

*L*izbeth Sampson took her foot off the gas and eased into Kat and Erik's long, circular driveway. Lights shined inside the guesthouse where Kat's grandfather lived, but aside from the sidewalk lights—which Kat and Erik left on when gone—their house was dark. When she spoke to Kat earlier in the day, she said they were having dinner next door at Kevin and Sam's and asked Lizbeth if she would mind stopping by there to drop off the gifts she'd gotten for the kids at the women's shelter.

"No problem," Lizbeth said. And she hadn't thought it would be. However, as she sat in her car, staring across the yard at the side of Kevin's house—correction, Kevin *and Sam's* house—the little knot in her stomach ballooned and rose to her throat.

She'd stayed at her parents' house as late as possible, hoping Kat would be home by the time she left. But if she was going to make it home in time to pack for her early morning flight, she couldn't delay any longer. With a slow exhale of defeat, she let her foot off the brake and steered her car toward the house next door.

It was strange pulling into the driveway she'd parked in a thousand times before. Only then, *her* clothes hung in Kevin's closet, *her* toothbrush stood next to his in the holder, and someone else's ring hadn't been on his finger.

She parked behind a BMW with South Carolina plates and drew the collar of her coat up around her neck as she walked to the door. The only good thing about running away from home for the holidays was enjoying a week of lying in the sun, soaking up tropical heat.

As she stepped up to the door, images from the past rushed her. *Slipping her key into the lock... Making herself at home in the kitchen... Kevin greeting her at the door with a smile and a glass of wine.*

Her relationship with Kevin had lasted longer than she'd expected going into it, and she'd never thought it would last forever, but she still missed his easygoing nature and smiles that lit up the world. With a deep breath for fortification, she lifted her finger to the button and rang the bell.

"I'll get it," a man—not Kevin—called out from inside the house. As heavy footsteps crossed the foyer and neared the door, she stood as tall and composed as possible, pasted on a smile, and projected an air of confidence she didn't possess.

The door swung open and...

Her confidence and smile crumpled and everything inside her shifted and tilted as her past slammed into her, hitting her full force in the heart and gut, knocking the breath from her lungs.

She grabbed the doorframe to keep from collapsing and stared into the same green eyes that had haunted her every night for the past fifteen years. Her brain sizzled and popped, but she had enough faculties about her to search his face and neck for the telltale scars, allowing her to discern with which twin she'd suddenly found herself face to face. At finding his bottom lip perfectly curved and the skin around his neck unmarred, the invisible fist wrapped around her throat eased its grip.

"Lizbeth?" Shock, equaling hers, filled his voice—a voice that was smooth and even, not raspy and jagged from shredded vocal chords, further confirming she stood before Lucas, not his brother Logan.

"What in the world are you doing here?"

"Lucas." The word, forced from her clenched throat, was barely a whisper.

"Hey, Lizbeth," Kevin said, appearing at Lucas's back. He frowned as he got a better look at her and reached for her hand. "Are you okay? You're white as snow." It took a little effort to pry her fingers off the doorjamb, but once he had her free, he tugged her into the house. "Come into the living room where you can sit down."

She shook her head no, but he didn't see her. He'd picked up on the strange flow of energy zinging between her and Lucas, and his eyes narrowed as he slowed his pace, then came to a halt.

"She's a little shocked at seeing me," Lucas said, taking a step back to give her breathing room. "Lizbeth and I go way back, but we haven't seen each other in years."

"Seriously?" Kevin switched his attention to her. "What a small world."

From the corner of her eye, she saw Lucas nod in agreement, but she kept her gaze locked on Kevin, clinging to his familiarity while allowing the feel of his hand holding hers to ground her. After a moment, when she thought she had enough control to speak, she withdrew her hand from his grasp and turned her attention to Lucas.

She opened her mouth, but full sentences escaped her. "I'm sorry… I just—I can't believe—" She shook her head and tried again. "It's good to see you, Lucas."

"You too, Lizbeth. You're as beautiful as ever." The way his eyebrows rose over his green eyes as they jumped back and forth between her and Kevin indicated he was as curious about her relationship to Kevin as Kevin was about her relationship to Lucas. Thankfully, both men were kind enough not to ask, at least not in front of her. Lucas's posture relaxed as he slipped a hand into his pocket and leaned against a column near the entryway. "I hope you're doing well."

She smiled and cleared her throat and forced the lie from her lips. "Yes, yes, I am. I'm doing very well. Thanks." After a long moment of awkward silence, she remembered what brought her to the door in the first place. "I'm looking for Kat," she said to Kevin. "I have gifts for the shelter. Since I'm leaving early in the morning, she offered to deliver them for me."

Kevin broke into the wide grin that always caused her heart to race like a wild stallion. "She's not here. She's at the hospital."

Even though he was beaming, alarm shot through her. "Hospital? Is everything okay with the baby?"

"Yep." He rocked back on his heels. "Her water broke right after dinner, so they're getting an extra-special Christmas gift."

"Oh… wow…" She was happy for Kat and Erik, but standing here talking to an ex about another of her exes in front of Lucas Steele—a carbon copy of the man who'd stolen her heart years ago and never returned it—was incredibly depressing, and she couldn't find the right words or any amount of enthusiasm.

More anxious than ever to finish her business so she could get home, pack her bags, and run away from everyone and everything, she looked over her shoulder at her SUV.

Reading her thoughts, Kevin said, "She told us to expect you, so leave the gifts here. I'll make sure they get to the shelter tomorrow. Do they need to be delivered at any particular time?"

"No, just sometime tomorrow." She searched his face. "Are you sure? I hate to impose." Kat volunteered at the shelter and was always up for a visit, but it seemed wrong to ask Kevin to take care of this for her.

"It's no problem," said Sam, who was so petite Lizbeth hadn't seen her standing behind Kevin.

Lizbeth wondered how long she'd been there witnessing her discomfort, which, from where she stood, bordered on humiliation.

Stepping forward, Sam offered her a warm, inviting smile. "I apologize for the baboons leaving you here at the door like this. You're welcome to come in."

Lizbeth hadn't seen Sam since the day she showed up on Sam's doorstep and encouraged her to give Kevin another chance. While Kevin had made a mistake, it wasn't one Lizbeth felt warranted losing Sam over, and as she stood in front of Sam now, a kind, caring person who obviously adored Kevin, Lizbeth found herself smiling back at the woman she would love to hate. "Thank you, but I need to get home and pack."

"Pack?" Sam frowned with confusion. "Isn't your family all local?"

"Yeah." Self-conscious, Lizbeth dropped her gaze. "I'm flying out tomorrow morning to spend a week in the Bahamas." As shock mixed with confusion on Sam's face, Lizbeth shrugged and laughed nervously. "What can I say? I'm a chicken. Rather than stay home and face the holidays alone, I'm going on vacation."

Her parents and sister joined her last year, but Miranda had a new man in her life and she didn't want to leave. Her parents also decided to stay home, so this year, Lizbeth was on her own.

"Oh." Sam studied Kevin's face, her thoughts obvious.

She was contemplating inviting Lizbeth to spend Christmas with them.

Sam was perfect for Kevin and much better suited to him than Lizbeth had ever been, but while she was happy they'd found each other, being around them was painful. Throw Lucas Steele into the mix and Lizbeth would be eating razor blades before the day was over.

Searching for a quick diversion before Sam could follow through with her impulsive idea, Lizbeth asked, "How's Wade?"

Wade Neumann was Kevin's foreman and had been engaged to Miranda, Lizbeth's sister. Miranda broke his heart by backing out a week before the wedding, and Lizbeth had spent the past several months worried about how Wade was doing but afraid to reach out to him for fear of making his distress worse.

The subject change seemed to catch both Kevin and Sam by surprise, but Kevin switched tracks quickly enough and answered. "He's all right. He's in Georgia with his family for the week. Do you want me to tell him you asked about him?"

"No, he'd probably rather not hear from any of us. He's such a nice guy. I hate what Miranda did to him. I hope he's been able to move on."

Kevin shrugged and rocked his head side to side. "I think he's getting there." He studied her face with warm, brown eyes and she knew he was wondering the same thing about her. Had she been able to move on?

They hadn't spoken since the day she came by to gather her belongings, and while things ended amicably between Kevin and her, a failed relationship was always painful. Based on her recurring dreams and how often he popped into her thoughts, she still wasn't completely over him. But he hadn't actually voiced the question, and since his wife was standing by his side—along with Lucas Steele, whose eyes didn't miss a damned thing—she simply smiled and carried on with the pretense that all was right with the world.

Turning for the door, she said, "Do you mind helping me with the gifts? Some of them are big and bulky... like a bike." She laughed self-consciously and gave a little shrug. "I can't stand for any of the kids' wish lists to go unfulfilled, so... I have quite a few things."

# Kevin

Kevin's head was reeling. Not from the number of gifts they'd unloaded from Lizbeth's SUV into his garage, but from knowing she'd dated Lucas. He'd always known she got around but... hell's bells. Lucas had been married for ten years, so it had to have been when they were much younger. But just knowing she'd once been involved with Lucas cleared up so many things—especially the sex.

"Something on your mind?"

Kevin jerked his head around and made eye contact with Lucas. He was happily married to Sam and loved her with his whole heart, but there were so many things about his relationship with Lizbeth that haunted him. He would love some answers so he could find peace about the way things between them had gone down.

"How long ago did you and Lizbeth date?"

"Not me," Lucas said, shaking his head as he walked toward the front door. "She dated my evil twin, Logan."

Kevin's steps faltered. "You have a twin?" How could he and Lucas have been friends for all these years and him not know this?

"Yep." Lucas looked over his shoulder and flashed a grin. "Scary to know there's two of me, huh?"

"Yeah, shit, I had no idea." Kevin ran a hand over his face, trying to fit this new information into the theory he'd been developing. "Is he... like you?"

Lucas stopped and turned around to face Kevin with a blank expression. "We're identical."

Kevin nodded thoughtfully. "So he's an asshole too."

The corner of Lucas's mouth lifted. "Get to the point. What do you really want to know?"

When Kevin stayed planted in the middle of the driveway, Lucas came back to meet him. He was uncomfortable continuing this conversion—digging into his past relationship with Lizbeth felt like he was somehow betraying Sam—but he needed answers and resolution. "Is he a Dom?"

Lucas shoved his hands into his pockets and stared off into the moonless sky while chewing the inside of his cheek. "Yes and no. He's displayed Dominant tendencies, but he and his wife married young. I doubt she's ever been willing to let him express that side of himself. They don't get much more conservative or vanilla than her." He studied Kevin's face. "Why?"

"I've never seen Lizbeth so flustered. She's normally self-assured and on top of her game. She must've cared a lot for your brother."

"Yeah, and he felt the same for her." He sighed and cocked his head to the side, deep in thought. "Honestly, I think he still does. Had life not thrown him one hell of a curve ball, I'm sure he and Lizbeth would've stayed together for a long time. Probably forever."

Kevin chewed on his upper lip, thinking this information through. Hell, he was knee deep at this point. He might as well go all the way into his ass and see if Lucas agreed. "Lizbeth always liked rough sex. But it got to the point that rough wasn't even enough for her. I never figured out what she needed, but it was obvious she needed... more. Knowing she has a history with your brother, who is probably a Dominant, I'm wondering if she needed to be controlled, but she thought rough sex was what she wanted." He paused to give Lucas time to comment. When the asshole only continued to stare at Kevin with a *go on* expression, Kevin prompted. "Is that possible?"

"Yeah." Lucas nodded thoughtfully. After a moment, he said, "Can you get her to Myrtle Beach?"

Kevin's mouth dropped open. "Have you lost your damned mind?"

"Why are you guys standing out here in the cold?" Sam asked from the open front door.

Lucas locked gazes with Kevin and smiled like the son of a bitch he was. *Shit.* The bastard was going to throw Kevin under the bus, and he had no idea how to explain to Sam why he and Lucas had been discussing his previous sex life.

"I'm trying to convince Kevin to invite Lizbeth to Myrtle Beach."

Sam crossed her arms over her chest and dipped her chin. "And why would he do that?"

"Yeah," Kevin said, matching Sam's pose. "Why would I do that?"

"Because Logan is separated from his wife. If you can get Lizbeth to Myrtle Beach, I'll invite Logan to come for a visit at the same time. We can test that theory of yours, and they can have a second chance at love."

Kevin stared in disbelief, but Sam, a sucker for romance, jumped at the chance to play cupid. "We can do that. Can't we, Kev?"

He rolled his eyes to the sky and sighed with exasperation. There were so many ways for this to go wrong and backfire on all of them, but despite his reservations, he heard himself say, "Yeah, we can do that."

# Chapter Seven
## Erik

---

*A*s Kat's teeth clamped down on her lip and she squeezed his hand until his fingers were white, Erik bit back the screams echoing in his head and concentrated on keeping Kat as calm and relaxed as possible. He'd once told Sam there was no savin' him, but she'd proved him wrong by bringing love, light, and laughter into his otherwise dark world, and Caroline had magnified all of life's pleasures a hundredfold.

He loved his girls more than life itself and knew this new baby would only add to their joy. But getting a baby into the world was torture, and he would move heaven and hell and everything in between to spare Kat the grievous pain of childbirth.

He'd suspected this little one would come faster than Caroline, but he'd never imagined things would progress so quickly Kat wouldn't be able to have an epidural. Not only had they been too late for the epidural, but the nurse hadn't even had time to give her the meds to "take the edge off" before the baby started making an appearance. Au naturel it was, and seeing her in so much pain tore him from his frame.

"You're doing great, Kat. Keep bearing down just like that." Amanda Hunt, Kat's ob-gyn, said from her seated position between Kat's legs. From where he stood, leaning over Kat's shoulder with his head next to hers, Amanda looked like a quarterback, hands up, ready to catch the football. All she needed was the snap. Three nurses in Mickey Mouse,

Scooby Doo, and Barney scrubs flanked her like linebackers, ready and awaiting instructions for the next play. "Another couple of good pushes and this baby will be out."

As the contraction relaxed, Kat flopped back against the bed and drew in a couple of breaths. The sweat coating her forehead trickled down her temples, and she blew air up and over her face, trying to cool herself down. "I need that cold washcloth again."

"You got it, baby." He grabbed the cloth they'd used earlier from the bedside table and pressed it to her forehead.

She jerked her head back and forth, trying to dislodge it. "It's not cold. I need cold."

"Yes, ma'am." He wadded the cloth up in a ball for easy flight across the room, looked at Mickey, who stood closest to the sink, and rocked his arm back and forth so she understood he intended to toss the cloth to her. "Will you run this under cold water for her?"

Mickey glanced up at him from her offensive stance and put out a hand. "Wait a couple of minutes. The baby's almost here."

*Wait?*

Rage rushed through him as he stared at her, dumbstruck. *What the fuck?* He heard Amanda; he wasn't an idiot. However, the baby almost being here was the reason Kat needed the cold compress. She wouldn't need the damned thing afterward. She needed relief now, and by God, she would get it. *Now.*

Rearing back, he launched the cloth and caught Mickey square in the chest. "She wants a cold cloth. Get her a fucking cold cloth."

Shock registered first on the woman's face, followed immediately by guilt. "Yes, sir." With water running over it, she wrung the washcloth out several times to make sure the warm water had been replaced with cold, then gently placed the compress on Kat's forehead.

Kat smiled weakly at the nurse and rolled her gaze to him. She mouthed, "Thank—" but before she got *you* out, the next contraction rolled up on her.

Like a champion fighter in a heavyweight match, she didn't whine or complain or try to back off. She leaned forward, gripped the sheet with one hand, clamped down on his hand with the other, and growled like a tiger as she put everything she had into the job of having a baby. She had one mission in mind: get this baby delivered as fast as possible so she could get home to Caroline early on Christmas day.

"Good, Kat... keep going, keep going." Deep concentration filled Amanda's eyes as she narrowed her gaze and clenched her jaw.

Even though he couldn't see what was happening—which was fine with him—he figured she was looking at the baby, maybe even touching the head. Kat must've been watching Amanda's expression also because even when the contraction relaxed, she kept pushing.

Barney exclaimed, "Oh my goodness, look at that head full of black hair."

"That's good... keep going." Amanda's arms worked furiously, but the deep frown lines in her face melted into a smile. "One more..." Another moment passed before she drew in a deep breath, then exhaled with sharp relief.

A second later, Kat did the same, then eased back onto the mattress as the linebackers jumped into action.

So damned proud of Kat and her hard work, emotion filled his throat and eyes, preventing him from saying anything. He blinked back tears of joy and love and flipped the washcloth over to the cool side to wipe the sweat from her eyes. After pressing a kiss to her forehead and brushing a tendril of hair away from her eye, he tried to say, "I love you," but all that came out was a garbled, emotional mess.

As the blessed sounds of infant cries filled the room, Amanda lifted the baby for them to see and said, "Congratulations, you two. He's absolutely beautiful."

## Sam

As far as Christmas Eve celebrations went, this would go down in Sam's personal history book as the most eventful, definitely the most memorable, and more than likely the best ever. Nothing went as planned—burned garlic knots and having Kat's water break on the floor never would've made her top ten things to do on Christmas Eve—but the day had been spectacular, and she wouldn't change a thing.

"Okay," Kevin said, shrugging out of his coat as he shuffled into the bedroom. He flopped down into the chair beside the window and laid the coat over the chair's arm before leaning over to unlace his shoes and toe them off. "I've shared the good news with Steve and Granddad and Lucas. I cracked Michy's bedroom door open and peeked inside, but she and Caroline are sound asleep, so I didn't wake her."

Sam released the deep breath she'd been holding since he said he'd opened Michy's bedroom door. "Thank God. If she wakes up now, she'll never go back to sleep." She turned back the comforter and fluffed the pillow. "We'll be having Christmas morning in the middle of the night."

He scrubbed a hand over his face and dropped his head back against the chair. "Thanks for everything you've done over the past week, *piccola*. You and Michy did an amazing job with the decorations." A bright smile, offset by his five-o'clock shadow, lit his face as he lifted his head. "I've never seen a tree so big." He seemed too tired to maintain the smile as it slipped away, but his eyes retained their warmth, melting her heart and drawing her across the room to him as he patted his leg.

"Thanks for making this house a home."

She draped herself across his lap and wrapped her arms around his neck. "Maybe next year you can get a couple of extra days off work and help with the decorating. We'll teach you how to make the garland to hang around the doorways."

He chuckled as he tightened his arms around her waist and pulled her close. Nuzzling her neck, he said, "Sounds as exciting as making those mud pies Michy loves so much."

Content being wrapped up in one another's arms, they sat quietly together for a long while, him drawing lazy circles on her leg while she played with the curls at the nape of his neck. She reflected on the day and how different life with Kevin was compared to when she'd been married to Michael. She thought back to the beginning of their relationship and how her fear and insecurity had almost torn them apart once.

And how they might yet if she didn't wrangle them under control.

"Did you know Sunny and Gavin were trying to get pregnant?"

The hand making slow circles on her leg stopped, and his muscles tensed beneath her. "Nope. You?"

"No." As an awkward silence replaced the comfortable quiet, his body hardened like curing concrete, making it uncomfortable— physically and emotionally—to sit so close. Needing space, which basically meant she wanted to run away, she climbed off his lap and went to the closet to start undressing before finishing the conversation. "Sunny and I haven't talked much about it, but I thought she wanted to wait until they'd gotten the bed and breakfast opened. Sort of like I want to get settled into my new job and the new house and stuff before…"

*Before what?*

The subject of kids came up a lot, but they'd never actually sat down and figured out a plan for expanding their family. Kevin would've started on their honeymoon, but she kept using the job and house they were building as reasons to put off any committed discussions. They'd only been married three months but had been together over a year, and neither of them was getting any younger. Plus, it would be nice to have kids at the same time as their friends.

But every time the subject came up, like now, she panicked and could never finish—or even properly start—a conversation taking them any closer to resolution.

Finished changing, she went to the bathroom, brushed and flossed her teeth, brushed her hair, and straightened the counter. The only other thing she could do to waste more time was clean the toilet, and she refused to use the nasty chore as a procrastination tool. When she went back into the bedroom, Kevin still sat in the chair, fatigue and weariness having nothing to do with the excitement of the day dulling his features.

The conversation had been started and the door was still open, so she'd never have a better opportunity to explain her fears than now. She took a deep breath and let the words fly. "Sex is a big part of our relationship. A *huge* part of our relationship. I'm just now learning all kinds of new things about myself. You're learning things about yourself. We have a great time experimenting at the club. We can't do that if I'm pregnant. After the baby is born and I have all that baby fat hanging off me..." Realizing she was dangerously close to the real, underlying issue, she started to tremble and stumble over her words.

He must've sensed they were finally getting to the naked truth as well because his eyes narrowed slightly with increased focus, taking in every detail, from the way her hands shook to the rapid rise and fall of her chest to the tear that leaked from her eye. He didn't tap his foot impatiently or grind his teeth with irritation but quietly sat and waited, giving her time to gather her thoughts and regroup.

She held his gaze and used her eyes, imploring him to understand. "I'm afraid when I'm big and pregnant and not interested in sex..." *Shit*. She swallowed hard, terrified of continuing but also knowing she couldn't turn back. "I'll get fat during pregnancy, and if it takes a while to lose the baby fat... I'll be tired and emotional from the hormone swings and stressed, trying to take care of the baby and Michy and dealing with my job and not paying as much attention to you." She took a deep breath and, on the exhale, got to the point. "I'm afraid you'll lose interest in me and"—she gulped—"find someone else." *Like my ex-husband did.*

He didn't say anything for the longest time, just worked his mouth around as he gnawed on the inside of his cheek. After a while, he said, "So when I get old and need a little blue pill to get it up, I should worry about you finding someone else."

"What?" She gasped, shocked and confused, not to mention offended. "That's ridiculous! There's so much more to you than"—she ran her hand up and down his body—"a hot body. You're... you're my everything."

He nodded once and screwed his mouth up again. His intense stare made her uncomfortable and self-conscious of standing before him in a nightshirt while he was fully dressed. Talk about feeling exposed.

"I see. But I'm a shallow asshole who's only sticking around because of your hot body and the soft spot between your legs." He spoke so quietly and calmly, for a second she thought she'd misunderstood.

"That's not what I meant, and you know it."

"No, that's pretty much what you said."

She dropped to the edge of the bed, dejected and confused, knowing she'd made a mess of things and unsure of the best way to stop the train wreck already in progress. "I get scared. Everything was going fine for Michael and me until I got pregnant." She chewed on her lip and thought back to the way things had been before Michy was born—and how quickly they changed afterward. "I think he and Sheila started their affair while I was pregnant."

She looked at him, trying to gauge his reaction, desperately hoping to find he understood what she meant. He pushed his tongue against his front teeth, something he often did when angry, trying to get his thoughts together before speaking. He stood and paced the room a few times, then stopped with his hands on his hips.

"I'm getting tired of being cast from the same mold as your ex. The way I handled things with Lizbeth was wrong, but I thought we'd moved past all that. Hell, she's forgiven me, but apparently you still haven't."

He threw his hands up in the air and went back to the chair. "You stand there and tell me I'm so much more than a convenient dick for you to fall onto, but you turn around and act like that's all I am." He slipped his feet into his shoes, retied the laces, and stood with his coat in hand. "I don't know what else I can do to make you understand I'm not Michael."

She stood in protest as he put his coat on and started toward the door. "It's one in the morning. Where are you going?" She hadn't meant to sound critical, but she heard the accusation in her tone, the same as he did.

Hurt and anger warred in his dark-brown eyes as he stared her down. "I'm going to the hospital, Sam. I'm not going out to find some Christmas ass. I'm just going to the hospital."

# Chapter Eight

## Kevin

---

*I*t took a little finagling and a lot of sweet-talking, but Kevin finally got his all-access pass to Kat's room. He'd like to think his winning personality and charm did the heavy lifting, but the pecan pie he swiped from the kitchen for the nurses had probably been his golden ticket.

"Hey," Kat said, with a contented smile on her face and a baby in her arms, as he eased the door open and stuck his head in. "I didn't expect to see you tonight." Her smiled faltered and her motions stilled as her eyes searched his face, obviously catching the emotional pain he felt oozing from every pore of his body. Nodding for him to come in, she said, "But we're glad you're here."

Erik unfolded himself from the chair in the corner, where he'd been slumped like a bag of dirty laundry, and rounded the end of the bed. Narrowed, assessing eyes met Kevin's. "You okay?"

"Yeah, I'm fine," Kevin said, even though the lie didn't fool anyone, not even the nurse in the corner who cocked her head to the side and gave him an eye roll. "I just needed to come and count fingers and toes for myself."

Erik clapped him on the shoulder and nodded to the chair he'd vacated. "Take my seat. I need to walk around a bit anyway."

Kevin slipped around the end of the bed but remained standing next to Kat. Holding his arms out, he asked, "Do you mind, mamma?"

"Of course not." Kat's lips twitched and although her eyes didn't sparkle nearly like Erik's, amusement glistened in them. "I'm glad to know you don't mind middle of the night visits. Remember this when we call you at two in the morning to come over and feed him or clean up barf."

He appreciated her keeping the moment light and not making a big deal out of his unconventional visit. Following her lead, while at the same time taking advantage of the opportunity to throw a jab at Erik, he winked and threw a little sexy vibe into his body language. "You can call me anytime... Especially in the middle of the night."

Erik shook his head and chuckled, but Kat laughed outright as she handed her precious bundle over to him. The weight of the baby in his arms, the unmistakable smell of a newborn, the cooing and sniffles, and those sweet blue eyes cracked open to check him out, nearly brought him to his knees.

He'd always loved kids and, even as a die-hard bachelor, had hoped for a couple of his own one day. He hadn't spent much time thinking about it, but even while enjoying the hell out of his bachelor lifestyle, in the back of his mind, he'd recognized he was getting older and each passing year signified another lost opportunity to start a family of his own. But until Sam, he hadn't found the right woman, and he was eternally grateful he hadn't settled for someone else.

She was his whole heart—except for the piece Michy owned. If they never had a child together, he'd learn to live with that—unless it was because Sam feared he'd run out on her when she gained weight, like her piece of shit ex had done. That excuse was unacceptable to him, and he'd be damned if he'd continue to let her make him over in Michael's likeness.

As his arms tensed around the little one, he forced himself to relax and enjoy the moment with *Bambino Due*. Playing with one of the tiny hands, he said, "I guess I need to start calling you Alden now, rather than *Bambino Due,* huh?" Shocked by the little guy's strong grip on his finger, he laughed and said, "You're ready to grip a ski rope already, aren't you?" He tore his gaze away from the tiny fingers and tiny nose and glanced at Kat. "Alden is obviously after Granddad. Where does Bruno come from?"

She nodded to Erik, whose walk hadn't lasted but about thirty seconds before he stopped and leaned against the wall. "My grandfather, on my dad's side. I never met him, but from what I understand, he was a great man."

"So you're named after two great men." Kevin played with the little finger with the big grip. "You grow up to be like your grandfathers and not like your daddy, okay?"

"Or your Uncle Kevin," Erik said, matching Kevin's light and teasing tone.

"Amen to that," Kat said with a laugh. A moment later, she turned serious. "Kevin?" She waited for him to look up before continuing. "You and Erik are two of the finest men I know. I don't know what's going on at home, but Sam and I are damned lucky to have you two. Don't you forget it."

The sweet comment warmed his heart as emotion filled his throat. "Thanks, sugar." He was surprised at the croak in his voice and cleared his throat before starting again. "But I think we can all agree that Erik and I are the lucky ones."

The nurse in Mickey Mouse scrubs crossed the room to leave, but Erik stepped in front of the door, blocking her path. "Sorry about the washcloth thing."

Kevin quirked a questioning eyebrow at Kat, who giggled and said, "It was just a *little* thing."

"Honey," the nurse said, patting Erik's arm, "you were taking care of your wife, just like you should've been. There's no need to apologize for that. It would be nice if all the women who came in here had someone who cared as much as you." She smiled warmly and squeezed his arm. "You have a very Merry Christmas." She turned to Kat and Kevin. "All of you."

After the nurse left the room, Kevin glanced at the clock on the wall. "I'm sure Michy and Caroline will be up at the crack of dawn, so I better head home for some sleep. Hopefully you guys will get some too."

Erik pointed to the foldout chair in the other corner. "Have you ever slept on one of those?"

"Nope, can't say I have."

"No one ever has," Erik said emphatically. "You might lie down on it, but unless you're drunk enough to pass out on a gravel road, you're not sleeping on that thing."

Kevin glanced at Kat out of the corner of his eye. Her head was tilted to the side with her eyes closed and mouth open as she drew in deep, even breaths. He handed Alden over and in a low voice, so as not to wake her, said, "At least one of you is going to sleep." He wrapped his arm around Erik and Alden and said, "Merry Christmas, bro. Congratulations."

## Sam

"Samantha, why are you tearing the kitchen apart?"

Sam jumped at the sound of Lucas's voice, banging her head on the top shelf of the refrigerator in the process. "I could've sworn we had a whole pecan pie left over, but I can't find it anywhere."

Lucas snagged an apple from the bowl on the counter, buffed the skin on the sleeve of his sweatshirt to remove the wax, and took a big bite. After chewing and swallowing, he said, "Kevin probably took it with him to the hospital."

She stopped her search and turned to look at him over her shoulder. "How did you know where he went? Did you talk to him on his way out?"

He shook his head and took another bite. "The guest room is over the garage. I heard the door open, but I didn't talk to him." He picked at a piece of apple caught between his teeth and studied her. "Why do you seem so surprised? Where else would he have gone at this hour?"

A lot of empty space hung in the air between his question and her answer as she tried to think of a reasonable response, one that didn't make her sound like a paranoid wife who suspected her husband of cheating on her. Because the truth was she never suspected him of cheating. He'd never given her any reason to doubt his faithfulness, but fear it would happen—especially as she gained weight—always clung to the back of her mind.

"What's going on in that head of yours?"

She sighed and flopped down on the barstool at the end of the island and gave him a non-committal shrug. Resting her chin in her upraised hand, she said, "Why would he take the pie? I can't imagine pie is high on Kat and Erik's priority list right now."

He took another healthy bite of the apple and shook his head. "Not for them. To bribe the nurses so they'd let him into Kat's room." He shrugged. "At least that's what I'd do. I'm sure they frown on middle of the night visitors."

"Ooohhh..." She slumped farther onto the stool. His logic made perfect sense, but never in a million years would she have thought to take something to bribe the nurses. Just one of the many differences between women and men.

"What's going on? Why are you on a desperate search for pie at this time of night?"

"I couldn't sleep." As if only now realizing she had company in the kitchen at two-thirty in the morning, she said, "Why are *you* down here?" Damn. She sounded way more defensive than she'd intended, and there wasn't a chance he wouldn't pick up on her edginess, because he logged everything. Sometimes, because of his uncanny ability to read people and situations, she swore he was psychic.

"I couldn't sleep either." After another couple of bites, he finished the apple, dropped the core in the trash, then went to the kitchen sink and washed his hands. She thought he might not delve further into her reasons for being a kitchen mouse, but then he said, "My reason for not sleeping is an eight-year-old girl and how much I'm going to miss being with her tomorrow morning."

He sat down on the barstool diagonal from her, locked his cast-iron gaze on her, and said, "Your turn." When she didn't respond, he pushed the issue. "Kevin didn't mention going to the hospital, so this must've been an impromptu visit. You look like you've truly lost your best friend, so I'm assuming you had a disagreement."

"Sort of. I said something I shouldn't have." Guilt, even though she hadn't intended to be accusatory, washed through her again. It would be a long time before she forgot the hurt in Kevin's eyes as he'd been forced to explain he was going to the hospital, not *out to find some Christmas ass.*

"Go on."

His gaze was direct and had her squirming on her seat, despite her attempts to stay still and unaffected. Thinking he'd get tired of waiting for an answer and go back to bed was like waiting for a cat to lay an egg. Part of her hoped he'd let the subject drop, but the bigger, smarter part of her recognized this as an opportunity to work through some of this. Maybe if she opened up to him, he could help her gain some perspective and get a handle on her runaway, not to mention unreasonable, fears.

"You're a lot like Kevin." She ignored his eye roll and huff of disgust and played with the fraying edge of her old T-shirt while searching for the right words. "When you were married... you played with other women. From what I understand, you also let other men... like Kevin... play with Loralei." She learned of that little tidbit through a conversation she'd overheard between Kevin and Lucas. She'd been shocked and appalled but mostly confused. Lucas seemed to love his wife and was devastated by their separation. How could he let other men touch her? What made him seek out other women?

She hadn't asked questions then, but as she thought things through now, she wondered if that conversation had watered her seedlings of fear, allowing them to take root and grow.

"My wife got off on watching me with other women." His tone was direct and matter-of-fact without any hint of defensiveness. "I did it to enhance her pleasure—not because she wasn't enough for me—and I only played with women she approved."

Sam rested her forehead in her hand and stared at Lucas, trying to comprehend this new information. She was more confused now than ever before. "What woman wants to see her husband with another woman?"

He shrugged. "Some do. Just like some husbands like to watch other men fuck their wives. I don't judge others' kink." He smiled gently and winked. "I sure as hell don't want them judging mine, so... glass houses and all."

She rubbed her hands over her tired, itchy eyes. "I could never watch Kevin with someone else. Ever. It would be the end of our marriage." *It would probably be the end of me.*

"Kevin doesn't have any interest in being with anyone else, so you're good." His eyes were sharp and serious, punctuating the truth of his words. At least to the best of his knowledge.

"How can you be so sure?"

"When the two of you are at the club and you're watching a scene, he's watching you. He's constantly trying to figure out what you want, what he thinks you'd like to try or are interested in. He only has eyes for you and is solely focused on your pleasure." He chuckled. "I find it funny that he's so opposed to titles, like Master or Dom, because a very good Dom lives inside him. However, he's right. They're only labels and don't define the person." He glanced at her from the corner of his eye and his mouth lifted. "You ever tell him I said he was right about anything, I'll deny every word."

Deep in her gut, she knew Lucas spoke the truth. He wasn't supplying her with new information, but having it laid out so simply was a novelty. She was an idiot to doubt Kevin's devotion or faithfulness, but she didn't know how to stop.

"I don't make a conscious decision to not trust him, but I can't seem to get out of my own way."

"Have you ever made the conscious decision *to* trust him?" When she stared at him, confused, he continued. "I see this with subs at the club all the time. If they don't make a deliberate effort to work through their fear or whatever hang-up they have, they automatically revert back to their old, familiar scripts. Not until they intentionally decide to do things differently, and work on changing, do things get better."

Easy enough in theory, but… "How do I do that?"

"The first thing is deciding to trust him. Let him know when you're insecure or scared so you can work through it together. He can take steps to reassure you and, if necessary, make changes in his behavior.

The biggest thing is to talk to Kevin." He smiled. "Communication is the key to everything."

The smile dissolved and his eyes darkened, and she wondered if he was thinking of his own marriage. Had a lack of communication been part of their problem? She considered offering a set of ears if he wanted to talk, but held back. She hadn't known Lucas long, and she guessed he had other friends with whom he'd feel more comfortable discussing the intricacies of his marriage.

"Thank you for talking this out with me. I feel better." She thought about Kevin's face. "And worse. But I'm going to start making changes tonight." She stood up and folded her arms around his neck. "Would you mind wrapping me up for Kevin?"

His green eyes lightened and his smile returned. "I'd be happy to."

# Chapter Nine

## Sam

$\mathcal{S}$am should've known better than to enlist Lucas's help. All she wanted was a simple bow tied around her wrists and ankles to prevent her from running away when the conversation with Kevin became difficult. But that was too simplified for Lucas—a stickler for details, who prided himself on a job well done and excelled at everything he did. She suspected the project also gave him an opportunity to focus on something other than Daria and how much he missed her, so she'd sat back against the headboard, held her wrists and ankles still, and let him do his thing.

"There," he said, taking a step back to evaluate his work and make minor adjustments where needed. "That's much better than a single bow." He smiled smugly and met her gaze. "Something you could've easily escaped from."

She'd tried to play the situation off as wanting to be one of Santa's sexy helpers, but of course, he'd seen through her—as usual—to the true reason she wanted to tie herself up. Sometimes—okay, most of the time—the man's Superman-like X-ray vision frightened her. Trying to joke her way out of the moment, she lifted her wrists and admired the intricately wound pieces of ribbon. "I definitely won't be escaping from these. Ever."

A slow, easy smile softened his features as he leaned over to brush a piece of hair away from the corner of her eye. "*You're* not supposed to be able to get away. I'll be here to watch over you and make sure you're safe until Kevin gets home. After that"—he shrugged—"he'll decide when you've had enough, not you."

She dropped her chin and sniffled. "You really are the bastard Kevin claims."

Pleasure rippled through her as he tossed his head back with roaring laughter. He'd been congenial and pleasant to everyone at dinner, and only someone who knew him well would've caught the shadows in his eyes as he put on a solid front. But being away from Daria, especially on Christmas, weighed him down, and she was happy she'd given him a brief respite from his sadness.

The bedroom door opened and Kevin stepped inside, a curious expression on his face. He cocked his head to the side and his eyebrows arched as he took in the scene before him—her in a new, red-and-black negligee, matching ribbons binding her wrists and ankles, Lucas leaning over her, laughing. During the course of their relationship, Lucas had helped Kevin with scenes, but he'd never interacted with Sam alone. Now, finding the other man in his bedroom with his wife bound on the bed, Kevin didn't appear concerned or angry, simply curious.

In the back of her mind, she realized, in this moment, he was a poster child for what real trust in a relationship was all about. But before she could delve deeper into the thought, Lucas turned to look at Kevin over his shoulder and sighed with relief.

Standing and turning, he threw his hands in the air in exasperation. "Can you believe your unruly wife called me a bastard?"

The corner of Kevin's mouth lifted and his eyes crinkled. "She's a wise woman."

"You two deserve each other," Lucas grumbled before turning to peek at Sam over his shoulder. He winked and mouthed good luck before strolling toward the door. Slapping Kevin on the edge of the shoulder as he walked past, he said, "Now that she's bound and… well, I'm sure you have a gag around here somewhere… I'll leave her in your capable hands."

The energy in their bedroom was very different than when Kevin left, but the change had been because of Lucas. His departure was like a vacuum, sucking out all the laughter and leaving her and Kevin in a state of unrest similar to before. Nerves jangled in her stomach and she swallowed hard to push down the nausea rising into her throat. "Hey."

"Hey." He stood for a moment, his head tilting from one side to the other as he took in the intricate rope work binding her ankles and wrists, the way the negligee rode high on her thighs, the low, scooping neckline revealing a lot of cleavage. Questions about the why behind her current state filled his eyes, but a healthy dose of appreciation also filtered through.

After a moment, he slipped off his coat, then draped it over the back of the chair before sitting down to unlace his shoes. "It's not going to work."

Her breath lodged in her throat as terrifying numbness rocketed through her. He no longer seemed angry or upset, but his firm, unbending tone caused a mixture of dread and excitement to mix with the paralyzing fear gripping her. Was he getting into a role…? Or was he saying *they* weren't going to work? "What—" She struggled against the bindings, trying to free herself so she could better grasp the situation. "What's not going to work?"

If he heard the panic in her voice, he didn't respond to it. He simply pulled off his socks and dropped them on top of his shoes, then stalked to bed, like a lion moving in on his prey. He stopped at the edge of the bed, rested his hands on his hips, and chewed on his upper lip. "You provoking me and Lucas to get a Christmas spanking."

His tone was still harsh and broached no argument, but his eyes had softened and held no hint of anger or bitter resentment. An ocean of relief escaped on her exhale, as she realized he'd slipped into the role he thought she wanted him to take on, considering he found Lucas—a Dominant—in his bedroom, tying her up. "In fact, from now on, I'm only going to spank you when you're a good girl."

She bit down on the inside of her lip to suppress a grin, rolled her eyes up to him, and batted her lashes.

Sitting on the bed next to her, he traced the knots in the ribbon with one finger, then ran his hand up the inside of her leg, over her knee to the apex of her thigh. "Maybe I should let Lucas spank, since you also offended him."

"Nu-uh, no way." Her eyes went wide with horror and she shook her head emphatically. She thought he was kidding, but she wasn't taking any chances. "He doesn't play when he spanks."

"Maybe I should stop playing, too." He flattened his hand and pushed it under the hem of her nightie, up the center of her stomach, until his fingers wedged against the elastic of the built-in bra.

"I like your spankings." She laughed. "But you already know that. I love the way your eyes burn for me when you have me bent over your knee or over the back of the chair." Her breath hitched as she imagined being in position now. "I love knowing you're as hot as me. I especially love what comes next."

He didn't respond with words, but she caught the flaring of his nostrils, the narrowing of his eyes, and the sharp swallow as he imagined the scene as well. She'd started this whole thing with a plan: talk to Kevin about what had happened… communicate, as Lucas suggested. But the trail of fire that following his touch as he slipped his fingers under the elastic of the bra and massaged her nipple with his thumb had her rethinking the overrated plan. His forefinger joined his thumb to pinch and roll her nipple, causing her to arch her back and press herself harder against his hand.

He worked her for a moment, making her delirious and hot and desperate. His touch gentled and rather than torment her nipple further, his hand slipped lower and cupped the underside of her breast. The knuckles of his other hand brushed her jaw in a tender caress before slipping around to the back of her neck.

"Open your eyes and look at me, Sam. Take a good, long look. What do you see in my eyes now?"

She had difficulty switching tracks to focus on something that seemed important and serious, but she managed to wipe away the lustful haze coloring everything and tune her full attention to him. His dark eyes were intense and focused—on her. She felt as if he really did see into her soul, and the intensity of his gaze ripped through every fiber of her being. His thumb moved back up to stroke her nipple in a slow, leisurely fashion, but his gaze never left hers. The depth of love shining through his eyes was overwhelming for someone who wasn't used to being so openly loved and cherished, and she found it difficult to maintain eye contact.

As she glanced away, he gave her nipple a solid pinch and said, "I'm waiting. What do you see?"

"Love." She swallowed down her emotions and drew in a ragged breath. "More love than I ever imagined a heart could hold, and all of it's directed at me."

He nodded and the corner of his mouth lifted, but his eyes maintained their intensity. "I love you more than I can ever tell you. I try to let you see it in my eyes when we're making love. I do little things on a daily basis to show you how much you mean to me." He shrugged helplessly. "I don't know how else to prove to you I'll never want anyone other than you. You're *my* everything."

She'd tried to keep her emotions in check, but when he echoed the words she'd spoken earlier, she couldn't hold back the trail of tears any longer. "I'm sorry. I'm so sorry I hurt you." She lifted her hands and spread her fingers as much as the bindings would allow. Cupping his chin, she said, "I don't want you doing more than you already do. From now on, I'm doing the heavy lifting in this department. Making sure you know how much you're loved. Proving I'm secure in your love and... I'll trust you completely. Deep in my heart, I do. It's just that... well... sometimes I let the old scripts run, and they get me into trouble."

The hand working her nipple stopped. "Let the old scripts run?"

She grinned and swiped at a tear. "I've been talking to Lucas."

"I figured." His hand slipped down to her ribcage and circled around to the small of her back. Holding her in place, he placed a soft, gentle kiss on her lips and used his other hand to wipe away the remaining tears. "He's right, though, about those old scripts taking over." As an afterthought, he added, "Don't you dare tell him I said that."

She laughed, recalling Lucas saying essentially the same thing. An outsider might believe Kevin and Lucas didn't like each other, but in reality, their relationship was a lot like Kevin and Erik's. They loved to harass each other but also had a ton of respect for each other's opinion and beliefs and valued their friendship.

She nipped at his lip. "Your secret is safe with me."

"Whose idea was this?" he asked, moving her hands around as he studied the weave of the ribbon.

"Well, I asked him to tie me up so I couldn't run away from you until we'd worked through this. But, Lucas being Lucas... he took it to the extreme."

"Of course he did." He rested her hands on her lap and dug into his front pocket. Dragging out his pocketknife, he said, "Then you won't be upset if I get rid of them?"

The intricate rope work was beautiful, and she hated for Lucas's hard work to be destroyed. But whether untied by fingers or sliced by a blade, there wasn't any way to preserve the knots—and she needed to wrap her arms around Kevin and hold him close—so she held up her hands and said, "This will be our secret too."

He winked and carefully slipped the blade between her hands, then sliced through the strands in a single upward stroke. "Agreed."

Before she had a chance to grab him around the neck and pull him to her, he stood and stripped off his shirt. He wasn't wasting time getting undressed, but she wanted to do this for him.

She stilled his hand as he reached for the buckle of his belt. "Let me." Her ankles were still bound, so it took a little finagling and a lot of grace—which she didn't entirely manage—to roll onto her knees and scoot to the edge of the bed for an easier reach.

Her heart raced as she unlatched the belt from the catch and slid the leather free. She lifted her eyes to his, letting him follow her thoughts, still holding out hope for a Christmas spanking.

He chuckled and shook his head. "You're incorrigible."

"I can't help the way you make me think or the things you make me want to do." She licked her lips as she unbuttoned and unzipped his khakis and slid them, along with his boxers, down his thighs.

Heat infused his eyes as he watched her through the fringe of his dark lashes. He pushed his fingers through her hair, then grabbed hold and held her off as she leaned over, prepared to slide her mouth over him. "Is this a guilt job?"

With lips hovering above his erection, she rolled her neck and eyes up to look at him. "What?"

"There's hand jobs and blow jobs. I guess this is a guilt job because of what happened earlier?"

Her stomach roiled at the tinge of hurt infused in his words. She pressed her hands to his abs, ran them along the ridges of his ribs up to his pecs, and wrapped them around his neck. She nipped playfully at his bottom lip before running her tongue across the seam of his lips, encouraging him to open for her. He allowed her to control the kiss... for a moment.

He fisted her hair tighter in his grip, angled his mouth over hers, and deepened the kiss so he completely dominated her mouth. She loved the way he kissed her as if his life depended on it. The way his tongue swept inside her mouth, claiming every part of her. And the way he ended every kiss with so much heat she thought she might spontaneously combust.

As soon as she caught her breath, she shook her head back and forth in jerky twists. "No, this is about greed."

He quirked his eyebrow and waited for further explanation.

"Millions of women out there who would love to have a piece of you."

He snorted as humor sparked in his eyes. "Millions?"

She shrugged. "Okay, that might be a slight exaggeration. How about thousands?"

He chuckled and stroked her cheek with his free hand while maintaining his grip on her hair with the other. "I didn't know you were so dramatic."

"Oh, c'mon. What about Angela in Planning and Zoning. We both know she has all kinds of"—her eyes roamed over his glorious body—"plans for your zones."

He threw his head back as laughter poured out of him. This was how she wanted his life with her to be. She wanted to make him laugh and feel good and didn't ever want to put hurt in his eyes again.

Kevin turned heads everywhere they went. He was more than good-looking; he was gorgeous in a masculine way. He had a Greek god's body and a charming personality that drew people to him. She'd heard the stories of how life used to be for the "Wildman." Erik swore all Kevin had to do was crook his finger at a woman and she'd glide across the room to him as if in a trance.

But in all the time they'd been together, she'd never seen him flirt with another woman. Even when Angela at P&Z was pouring it on thick, he'd smile and tease back, but never in a way that would be misconstrued as flirting or misleading. He was his usual charming self but always remained professional. Angela's husband was a badass who owned the local gun shop and rifle range and would shoot the balls off any man who messed with his wife. But in her heart, Sam knew that wasn't what held Kevin back.

At a restaurant or the club, if a woman came onto him or flirted in an overly aggressive way, he'd dial back the wattage on the smile, drop the temperature of his eyes, and if Sam was nearby, pull her to his side, making it abundantly clear he was taken. He was hers. All hers.

Logically, she knew this. Somehow, she needed to figure out how to get out of her own way and not let the past control her. She refused to let the past jeopardize her future with the best thing that ever happened to her.

"It's also a love thing." She ran her hands down his back to his spectacular ass, dug in her short fingernails, and raked them around his hips. "I love the way my lips have to stretch to accommodate you. The taste of you on my tongue. The way your head drops back and your thighs tighten as you fight to hold on to your control."

The heat in his eyes intensified and his nostrils flared as she cupped his balls in one hand and wrapped the other around his thick erection. She smiled as he groaned deep in his throat and his shoulders relaxed.

"I love the sounds you make." She stroked him, applying more pressure with her thumb along the underside. "I love the way the muscles in your neck and shoulders strain as you pump in and out of my mouth, trying not come as I work harder to push you over the edge."

His chest rose and fell with harsh breaths and his voice was rough as he said, "Show me."

# Chapter Ten

## Kevin

---

*E*very muscle in Kevin's body tensed as Sam leaned over him again and licked her lips, preparing to take him. He was so highly charged, the second her mouth touched him, he jumped like he'd been shocked in the ass with a cattle prod. Then again, Sam's lips wrapping around his cock always had that effect on him. He'd slept with a lot of women in his lifetime—not something he was necessarily proud of, but he had a solid record for comparison—and none of them had ever unraveled him, thread by thread, like Sam.

Her mouth was wrapped around him, but she was in him.

As she flattened her tongue and ran it along the sensitive underside, he gripped her hair tighter, directing her movements and slowing the pace. In his highly cranked state, it wouldn't take much to steal his control. And true to her word, she worked her mouth with finely tuned precision, driving him closer to the edge of the precipice while he fought to hang on.

He didn't want to come in her mouth tonight. When he careened off that cliff, he wanted to be locked together, face to face, eye to eye, making damned sure she saw—again—how much she meant to him.

After another couple of wicked strokes with her tongue, he was off balance and barely hanging on, so he tugged on her hair and said, "Stop."

At his sharp tone, she froze and rolled her head to the side to look up at him. "Did I hurt you?"

"No, sugar, not in the slightest. I have other things in mind for you."

Anticipation mixed with the lust glistening in her eyes. He loved that she took so much pleasure from sucking him off, and he would enjoy returning the favor. "Lie on your back, put your hands at your sides, and don't move."

She shivered at his commanding tone and quickly complied. Her ankles were still tied together with Lucas's fancy rope work, so Kevin gripped her ankles and lifted them toward the ceiling, putting her body at a ninety-degree angle. She wore a matching barely-there red satin thong, which was good because Lucas had never seen her completely naked and bad because Kevin couldn't get where he most wanted to be.

He slipped his fingers under the strip of fabric and moved it to the side. He liked her in this position, her pussy and ass exposed to any fun and games he might want to play, and made a mental note to add hooks to the bedroom ceiling in their new house. He would enjoy having her legs suspended like this without having to use one of his hands to hold her in position.

Teasing her the way she had him, he ran his tongue over his lips and eased down for a slow, leisurely lick. Her fists tightened onto the sheets and she released a low, guttural moan as he swiped his tongue through her center, gathering the accumulated moisture before dipping into her slick channel for more. He ignored the first little wiggle, but when she outright squirmed beneath him, he slapped the curve of her ass. "I told you not to move."

A battled raged within her eyes as she considered her options. Would he spank her again if she kept moving or would he stop altogether?

Answering her unasked question, he said, "I'll stop, so I suggest you lie still and let me do my thing."

"I can't," she said through clenched teeth as she wiggled again. "It feels too good. And no, I'm not trying to provoke you." She added a little laugh. "Although that was a nice bonus."

Everything about his little sex kitten delighted him, from her open-minded approach to anything he wanted to try to the way she loved to crank him up and propel him to the edges of ecstasy. But tonight was more about the emotional than the physical, so he shook his head and muttered, "Like I said before… incorrigible."

She pressed her back into the mattress and lifted her hips to meet him as he ran two fingers through her thick cream, then thrust them inside. When he stilled and quirked an eyebrow, she glanced around her raised legs, trying to figure out why. She wasn't used to him demanding she stay still during sex, like Lucas demanded of his subs, so it took her a moment to catch up.

A whine of complaint, as well as a heavy sigh, escaped her clenched teeth when she realized the infraction. "Okay, okay… I'll work harder." After a moment, she relaxed her muscles, sank into the mattress, and allowed him to take over again.

"Much better." He resumed a slow in-and-out rhythm, fucking her with his fingers as he sucked her clit into his mouth. In a matter of minutes she was whimpering, panting with her efforts to stay still, and begging him to make her come. She'd worked so hard at following his order, he rewarded her by slipping his ring finger into her ass as he clamped down on her clit with his teeth and stroked upward and out with his fingers.

He was rewarded in exchange, because watching Sam come was one of his greatest pleasures in life. The way she threw back her head, screamed out his name, and gripped the closest part of his anatomy—

which right now was his arm—filled his heart with awe and wonder, knowing in this moment, she was giving him absolutely everything.

As the waves receded, he withdrew his fingers, then kicked his slacks and boxers free of his legs. He grabbed the knife from the nightstand and ruined the last of Lucas's handiwork, then slipped his hands under her waist and moved her to the center of the bed so he had room to lie on top of her without breaking off his legs at the knees.

With one solid thrust, he slid in to the hilt, pinning her to the bed. "Open your eyes and look at me, *piccola*."

It took a moment to comply, but when she finally managed to crack them open, he found her beautiful blue eyes glassy and unfocused. The haze would clear soon enough, at least enough for her to grasp what he needed to show her. "Keep your eyes on mine." When they drifted closed, he rocked into her again and in a sharp, commanding tone, said, "Keep. Your eyes. On mine."

His sharp tone grabbed her attention, but she still struggled to keep them open, let alone focused.

He eased into her in a slow glide but stopped when she lifted her hips to rock against him. "Do you want me to make you feel good?"

"You already did." His heart, and a little of his resolve, melted as she wrapped her arms around his neck and kissed him sweetly. "You always make me feel good."

"Good. There's more where that came from, but..." He held her tightly to him, waiting for the drug-like effects of her previous orgasm to wear off. "This is important to me, *piccola*."

She must've picked up on the quiet plea in his voice because she blinked a couple of times and even shook her head once, shedding her delirium and grounding herself in the present.

With his elbows planted on either side of her head, he stroked her temples with his thumbs and whispered words of encouragement as he began a slow and steady in and out. "It's hard to maintain eye contact for an extended period of time, especially when things get intense or uncomfortable."

"I'm not uncomfortable." She gave a vixen's smile and scored his back with her nails before gripping his ass and urging him to stroke deeper and harder.

She might be content to stay locked on him in this moment because the pleasure thrumming through her was a slow and steady beat. But when her emotions spiked to a crescendo with her orgasm, she would close her eyes and turn her head away from it. Like she always did.

He slipped his left hand under her ass and lifted, changing the angle of his thrust, making sure he hit the right spot to send her spiraling out of control. Her eyes fluttered as she raced toward another release, forcing him to stop and issue another reminder. "Sam, keep your eyes on mine."

Her head thrashed back and forth as her hips rose and fell beneath him, urging him on and cracking his determination to see this through on his terms. "I can't. It feels too good." She gripped his face in her hands and ran her thumbs over his lips. "It would be a pleasure to look at you all night long if you want, but not right now."

He shook his head. "It won't matter then."

Confusion wrinkled her brow as she searched his expression for clues as to why this was so important. He'd never had a hang-up about her looking at him during sex before, but whatever she found during her search must've convinced her. She renewed her efforts, and even though her lashes flickered, she kept her gaze locked onto his and smiled.

After a bone-melting kiss, coupled with the intense driving force of his body into hers, they stood together at the precipice, ready to jump. Matching his thrusts to his words, he said, "You'll always be enough for me, no matter your size, no matter your age."

Tears filled her eyes as her hands slipped around the back of his neck and latched onto the hair at the nape. "I love you." She swallowed once, and again, and a third time. "I'll go off the pill at the end of this cycle. I'm ready to trust you... completely."

Her unexpected words caught him off guard and he lost all rhythm. She was sexually ramped up, but she was lucid and he had no reason to doubt she meant what she'd said. The thought of having children with her caused his chest to expand to the point he thought he might explode. Knowing she was ready to trust him—really trust him—took his breath away.

He watched as she fought her inclination to turn away from him to protect herself as he increased his strokes and drove into her, sending them both spiraling out of control—eyes locked together, souls fusing into one.

He was sure she'd need reminders in the future, but he was content for now, knowing she'd gotten his message loud and clear. "I love you, Sam Mazze. Now and forever."

She didn't answer him with words but used her internal muscles to clamp down on him, holding him tight within the walls of her silky flesh, milking the last drops from him.

He ran his thumb down her cheek and across her lip before cupping her jaw in his hand. "That's right, *piccola*, you hold onto me just like that because I'm never going anywhere."

# Epilogue

## Kat

$\mathcal{A}$ knock on the door brought Kat's head up, her gaze away from the precious baby in her arms. Erik, who'd been attempting to nap in the foldout chair, scrubbed a hand over his face and looked over his shoulder.

"Is everyone decent?" Sam asked, peeking her head inside.

"As decent as ever," Kat said wryly before glancing at the clock on the wall.

*Six thirty in the morning? Does no one in the Mazze household ever sleep?*

"Good, because it's Christmas morning," Sam said, pushing the door wide open. "We have business to take care of."

Kevin stepped in behind Sam, an energetic Caroline wiggling in his arms and an equally excited and energetic Michy bouncing on her toes beside him. Her grandfather was the next to file into the room, followed by Steve, who pulled a cart carrying a Christmas tree. Lucas trailed, steadying the tree to make sure it didn't topple over.

"Oh, my God!" The exclamation came out as a whisper because, although it had never happened before, Kat was speechless.

Erik rolled himself into a seated position and put out his arms to catch Caroline as Kevin set her on her feet and she made a wobbly beeline for her daddy. "Good morning, sweetheart." He gave her a kiss on the cheek, brushed the baby-fine hair out of her eyes, then wrapped his arm under her and lifted her with him as he stood. He seemed as dazed and confused as Kat. "What are you guys doing here?"

"I promised Kat we'd bring Christmas to her, so…" Sam turned and held out her hands in a silent *ta-da*. "Here we are."

"Can we open presents now?" Michy asked, about to bounce out of her shoes.

Moisture filled Kat's eyes as she smiled at Erik, who appeared as emotional and overwhelmed as her. Swiping away a renegade tear, she said, "Yes, Michy, absolutely. You've obviously been very patient… I can't believe you guys did all of this." She glanced at the tree. "Where did you get the tree?"

Sam burst into laughter as Kevin and Lucas exchanged a glance. "They cut the top out of the tree in the playroom, and we redecorated it."

"What?" Laughter rolled through the room as Michy's face fell and she turned wide, disbelieving eyes to Kevin. "You cut up our tree?"

"Just the one in the playroom, *piccolina*, not the big one in the living room."

She scrunched her face and thought on it for a minute. After brief deliberation, she gave Kat a sweet, innocent child's smile and said, "Mamma and Daddy said the most important thing was for all of us to be together, so"—she shrugged—"that's okay."

Whatever issue Kevin and Sam had been having the night before had apparently been resolved because he wrapped his arm around her waist and pulled her to him before leaning over to whisper in her ear. Lucas got down on the floor and started sorting gifts, and Steve jumped in to distribute them.

"I wanta hold my newest grandbaby," Granddad said, taking the seat next to Kat's bed.

Erik was next to him a second later, setting Caroline on the bed and taking Alden from her for Granddad. As Caroline crawled up the bed to give Kat a hug, Erik leaned over and kissed them both on the top of the head.

Kat's heart had never been filled with so much love and happiness. She had Erik, her baby girl, a new baby boy, her grandfather, and the best friends in the world. She was so overcome with emotion she couldn't speak, so she smiled and squeezed Erik's hand and let the happy tears streak down her face as she watched Michy rip into her first gift.

Every important thing in her life was in this room right now, and she'd never felt more blessed. She cleared her throat and after a couple of tries, she finally got the words past her quivering lips. "Merry Christmas, friends. Merry Christmas!"

www.ingramcontent.com/pod-product-compliance
Lightning Source LLC
Chambersburg PA
CBHW031429240626

47154CB00001B/264